The Magic in Your Touch

The Magic in Your Touch

Sara Bell

P.D. Publishing, Inc.
Clayton, North Carolina

ISBN-13: 978-0-9754366-3-9
ISBN-10: 0-9754366-3-5

First Printing 2005

9 8 7 6 5 4 3 2 1

Cover art and design by Stephanie Solomon-Lopez
Edited by Day Petersen/Lisa Keeter

Published by:

P.D. Publishing, Inc.
P.O. Box 70
Clayton, NC 27528

http://www.pdpublishing.com

Acknowledgements:

They say it takes a village to raise a baby and the same holds true for the writing and development of a novel. It is with heartfelt thanks I tip my hat to Barb and Linda, the nicest, easiest to work for publishers in the biz; to my editors Day and Lisa for making even me sound good; to Steph, whose insightful cover design brought *Magic* to life; to my yahoo group, for all the feedback and support you've given me over the years; to my mom, Ruth Ann, the proudest most enthusiastic book salesman I could ever ask for; to my Grandpa Burt, car consultant and resident sweatheart; and last but not least, to my husband David and our two beautiful daughters who ate a slew of frozen pizzas and T.V. dinners while *Magic* was being born.

To Steven Matthew K, Bret Kidder, and Michael Philips, without whose love, guidance, and support I would be lost. You are truly the three best friends a girl could have.

And to David, for being even sexier now than the day I married him.

Chapter One

Nathan Morris stretched in an effort to loosen his knotted back muscles. Hours of examining patients and filling out mountains of paperwork had taken their toll. His partner in the practice, Amy Vaughn, did more than her share, but after watching her work three fourteen hour days in a row, Nate finally insisted she take a couple of days off. He kidded her, saying her husband Mike was going to forget what she looked like. In reality, he envied her the security of home and family. *Which is what I thought I almost had with Rick.* He laughed at his own stupidity. The moment Rick's parents had threatened to withdraw their financial support, Rick had gone running home to Mommy and Daddy, and the relationship was over. *So much for eternal love and devotion.*

Nate shook himself out of the past and glanced at the clock. It was well after six and already dark. Autumn in Reed, Illinois, was going to take some getting used to. Having been raised in the South, Nate was still adjusting to the cooler temperatures and shorter days, but he found them to be welcome changes. Three years of residency in Atlanta Northern Hospital's Neonatal Intensive Care Unit had left Nate with a serious case of burnout. When the opportunity came along to open a practice in Reed, he didn't even have to stop and think about it. The fact that Amy, his best friend since the third grade, had decided to move to Illinois with him was just a bonus, as was Reed's reputation for being a "gay friendly" town. Since Nate had only been in Reed a grand total of three months, he had yet to test that theory. The only people he saw on a regular basis were his patients, and he hardly thought, "Hi, I'm Dr. Morris, and I have a preference for penises," an appropriate way to start a conversation.

He gathered up the last of the day's paperwork and headed toward the front of the converted Victorian cottage. The thought of going home to his lonely apartment was not inviting, but it was better than sleeping on one of the exam tables. He turned out all the lights and grabbed his keys. Before going out the door, Nate set the alarm and punched his code into the keypad. He fit his key into the deadbolt and was just about to turn the lock when he felt a blinding pain on the right side of his head.

"You're a dead man, faggot."

The voice was little more than a harsh whisper, but to Nate the words might as well have been screamed from the top of the Reed County Courthouse. From the corner of his eye, he saw his attacker raise whatever object he held, ready to strike again. Fighting waves of nausea and knowing he was too dazed by the blow to fight back, Nate used what strength he had left to open the unlocked door and trip the alarm. The shrill beep caused his assailant to run just as Nate fell to the ground. He was unconscious before he hit the porch.

* ~ * ~ * ~ * ~ *

Nate woke up on one of his own exam tables. He tried to move, but a pair of soft, strong hands stopped him.

"Oh no, you don't, buster. I have not spent the past twenty minutes trying to wake you up just so you can get up too soon and black out again. As it is, I'm still deciding whether or not to pack you into an ambulance and send you to Chicago for an M.R.I." The tiny spitfire pulled a light out of her pocket and peered into his eyes. "Your pupils are reacting normally. Any nausea or dizziness?"

Nate smiled in spite of himself. "I'm fine, Amy. You know my head is the hardest part of my body." He gave her an exaggerated leer. "Most of the time, anyway."

Her hazel eyes filling with relief, Amy punched him on the arm and put the light away. "If you can crack sex jokes, I know you're all right. Now tell me what in God's name happened to you." She swung her long, brown hair over her shoulders and pursed her bow lips.

Not for the first time did Nate admire her beauty. She made quite a contrast to her husband Mike's white-blond hair and clear blue eyes. "You know, I should have married you back in the fifth grade when you first proposed to me."

Amy laughed. "Sorry, but I don't think I have anything you'd be interested in."

Nate shook his head, an act he regretted the minute the pain returned. "Yeah, well, I didn't have anything Rick wanted, either, so I guess you had something in common with him after all, huh?"

"If I wasn't just sure you had a slight concussion, I'd shake you for even saying that." She leaned in closer. "Rick Landon was an idiot. Probably still is, for all I know. You were too good for him, Nate, and that's the last time I'm going to say it." She straightened. "Now tell me what happened."

Nate recalled everything he could; most of it was fuzzy. Mike

Vaughn came to stand by his wife just as Nate got to the part where his attacker threatened him and called him a fag. Nate watched as all the color drained from Amy's face and Mike shook with rage.

Mike took Amy's place at the head of the exam table. "You're sure that's what he said?"

"No doubt."

Mike turned to his wife. "How soon can you find another pair of doctors to buy out your practice?"

Though his words were cryptic, Amy got his meaning. "Shouldn't take long. This is a new practice, so most anyone could step in."

Nate sat up, grimacing as fresh waves of sickness washed over him. "We're not selling out just because some bigot took a shot at me. Even if I was scared enough to leave — and I'm not — you don't have to go, too. You've already put down roots here."

Amy started to speak, but Mike cut her off. "There's no way you're leaving without us. Likewise, if you stay, we stay. We're family. That's the reason we all moved here from Atlanta together in the first place. If you want to stay, then we'll just have to find the bastard who did this."

Amy took her husband's hand and reached out to Nate with the other one. "He's right, you know. We are a family. The sheriff is on his way, so let's wait until we talk to him before we make any decisions. In the meantime, let me check you over."

Mike went into the lobby to wait for the cops while Amy examined Nate. She tested his reflexes and checked his vitals, her hands shaking slightly as she monitored his pulse. "You have no idea how terrified I was when I got that call from the alarm company. To race over here and find you lying in a heap on the porch like that..." She shivered. "That's one experience I would gladly go a whole lifetime without repeating."

Nate could feel her fear and hated the jerk who'd hit him even more for scaring Amy. Still, he didn't exactly relish having to talk to the sheriff. He'd seen enough of police responses to gay bashing to know that he was just as likely to get some homophobic prick who could care less whether or not the world had one less fag in it. He suppressed a groan as he heard a large engine pull into the parking lot. The cavalry had arrived.

Amy insisted Nate stay put, so he was forced to wait while Mike spoke to the sheriff. Nate couldn't hear what they were saying, but Mike was clearly angry. When Amy finished her exam and opened the door to let the officer in, Nate prepared himself to see a sixty-year-old man with a beer gut and a bald spot. The six-foot-three-inch stud who walked in the door was not what he expected.

The man had the bluest eyes Nate had ever seen. His hair was mid-night black with not a hint of gray, the perfect foil for his left over summer tan. Even through his khaki uniform shirt and tight jeans, Nate could tell the man was well built.

The sheriff stuck out a calloused hand, first to Amy, then to Nate. "Sorry it took me so long to get here, folks. I was out on another call when my dispatcher told me what happened. I'm Brandon Nash." His voice was rich and smooth. Nate wanted him to keep talking just so he could hear it again. Then the sheriff opened his mouth, and his next words made Nate want to scream for the man to shut up.

"Your friend out there tells me you think you were the target of a gay bashing, Dr. Morris. I have to tell you, I find that hard to believe."

Anger coursed through Nate's blood, driving away all remnants of pain. He moved to the side so that the swelling of his face and jaw was visible under the harsh fluorescent lights of the exam room. "Does it look like I did this to myself, Sheriff Nash?"

Nash didn't flinch. "No, sir. There's no question that you were attacked. I just wonder if maybe you were mistaken about the motive. This town is pretty tolerant towards gays and lesbians."

"The man who jumped me called me a faggot and told me I was dead. Doesn't exactly sound like the Reed County Welcome Wagon, now does it?"

The sheriff's handsome face never changed expression. "No sir, it doesn't. All I'm asking is, could it be possible that someone would want this to look like a gay bashing? Do you have any enemies?"

Amy and Mike, who'd been listening from the open doorway of the exam room, rushed to defend Nate's character, but Brandon Nash's blue eyes never left Nate's face. It was almost like he was searching for something.

Nate found himself growing uncomfortable under the scrutiny. He decided to ease the tension by lashing out. "To answer your question, I don't have any enemies that I know of, other than my parents, who hate me because I'm gay. Oh, and my brother, who avoids me because he's afraid my queerness might be contagious. None of them would touch me, though. They'd be too afraid of catching something from the 'unclean homo'. I think you're overlooking the obvious. Maybe the good people of Reed don't want a faggot for a doctor? Did you consider that?"

For the first time since the interview started, Nash's eyes flashed with irritation. He put his notebook down on a nearby counter and looked Nate straight in the face. Had they both been standing, Nash would have towered over Nate, as he was at least four inches taller. Since Nate was still seated on the exam table, they were almost eye-to-eye. Nash edged closer to the table until they were nearly nose-to-nose.

Nate could feel the sheriff's breath on his face, could smell peppermint, coffee, and some kind of aftershave that made him want to nuzzle his face in the man's neck. He only hoped the sheriff didn't notice his reaction. He needn't have worried. Nash's eyes never broke contact with his own.

"No, it never occurred to me that the people of Reed might not want a 'faggot' for a doctor. After all, they elected one sheriff."

The room fell into total silence. Amy and Mike may have been speechless, but Nate was absolutely stunned. Nash was the only one who seemed to be enjoying himself.

"Now that we've established that I'm probably the last person in the world to ignore a gay bashing, let's get on with this so I can file a report."

Nate answered the sheriff's questions, all the while wondering about the man asking them. He was sexy enough to make even a straight guy look twice, but that wasn't what drew Nate to him. Brandon Nash had some unknown element that made Nate want to get to know him, to find out what he liked, what made him feel good. The sudden interest in a total stranger hit Nate as quite a shock. It was probably all just wishful thinking, anyway. A man who looked like Nash was certain to have a boyfriend, maybe even a life-partner. He was so lost in thought, Nate didn't hear Nash's last question. "I'm sorry. What did you say?"

For the first time since the interview started, Nash gave him a genuine smile. "I said, are you sure we shouldn't take you over to the hospital to have you checked out? Chicago's only about a thirty minute drive."

Nate was about to decline when Amy spoke up. "I think you should go to the hospital, Nate. I'll feel a lot better if you do. My exam was pretty thorough, but, to be safe, you should have an M.R.I."

Mike nodded. "I agree with Amy. I'll drive you."

Mike reached for his keys, but Sheriff Nash stopped him. "My shift ended about half an hour ago. I can take him and get the doctor to sign a report on his injuries all at the same time."

Nate felt himself losing control of the situation. He hated it when people talked about him like he wasn't in the room. Nate wasn't ready to spend time alone with Nash, either, especially when he was half-addled from a blow to the head. "Amy already checked me out. She can fill out your report." Nate's stomach turned over as Amy started shaking her head.

"No. I really think you should have an M.R.I. I can write the orders, and you can take them with you."

He turned around just in time to see Amy nudge Mike in the ribs. "Honey, don't you remember that proposal you have to prepare for your client?"

"Huh?" Another nudge to the ribs, this one harder, and the light dawned. "Oh, you mean the proposal I was working on when the alarm company called." He gave Nash an apologetic grin. "I've been offered a junior partnership at a firm in Chicago. Not a bad commute, and the pay is pretty good for a guy who just passed the bar a year ago. Of course, if I don't turn in my work on time..."

Nash nodded. "Wouldn't want that to happen. I'll take Dr. Morris to the hospital. Don't worry about it."

Before Nate could protest further, he found himself being hustled into a state-issue S.U.V. with the sexiest man he'd seen in a long time. Like it or not, he was in Nash's hands.

* ~ * ~ * ~ * ~ *

Brandon hated evening calls. Reed was small enough that his deputy, Sam Whit, and he could usually handle all the calls themselves without having to pull the junior deputies off their regular shifts. Unfortunately, no one told that to the eighteen-wheeler that had jackknifed off of Interstate Twelve just three miles outside of town. No one was hurt, thank God, but the truck had been carrying live poultry to the processing plant two towns over. Nothing set the tone for the night like trying to dodge speeding motorists while catching live, angry chickens. Sam managed to stop traffic and enlist a handful of volunteers to help with the round up, but the whole scene looked more like a sketch from a bad vaudeville show than a police procedure. After being pecked for the fifth time by creatures he only wanted to see fried with gravy, Brandon had been grateful to field another call. He could still see Sam's face when he told him he had to leave. After a hellish six months at the F.B.I. academy together and twenty-five years as friends, Brandon knew Sam well enough to know his buddy would get even at the earliest opportunity. He only hoped the poor guy didn't get mites from all those feathers.

Brandon stole a glance at the man slumped in the seat next to him. He'd heard tell how good looking the new doctor was, but the gossip didn't do the guy justice. Nathan Morris was shorter than Brandon, maybe five-eleven, but his body was well sculpted and muscled. His chocolate eyes were red-rimmed, but still beautiful, as was his fine-featured face. His hair was dark blond and fell in disheveled spikes; a look which suited him.

The ride to Chicago was silent, but Brandon figured his passenger was in too much pain to talk, if the grimaces and grunts he was making were any indication. He wondered what the good doctor would sound like in bed. He forced himself to stop thinking about it when the bulge in his jeans started to rise.

Brandon pulled the S.U.V. into one of the spaces marked for police vehicles and cut the engine. Coming around to the passenger side, Brandon took the doctor's elbow and helped him out.

Nathan's voice came out low and rough. "Thanks, Sheriff, but I can go in by myself."

"Call me Brandon."

"Okay, *Brandon*, I can do this by myself. I did my residency in a hospital a lot like this one. I know the drill, and most of it is hurry up and wait."

Brandon smiled and started leading him toward the emergency entrance, locking the doors of the S.U.V. with the remote on his keyring. "Normally, I would agree with you, but I just happen to know someone who works here. He actually owes me a favor. I think he'll be able to get us in and out a bit faster." While he was talking, Brandon took Nathan past the emergency wing to a row of elevators inside the hospital proper.

"Where are we going?"

"Relax, Doc. We're going up on the third floor to Neurology. The guy I told you about has an office up there."

Brandon pushed the button for the elevators. The one closest to them opened, allowing a woman and four half-grown children to get out. One of the larger boys bumped into Nathan, nearly knocking him off his feet in his already addled state. Brandon caught Nathan to his chest, trying to ignore the arcs of sensation that went through him at the contact. Both the woman and the boy apologized, but Brandon's focus was on the man he held in his arms. "Doc, are you all right?"

"Nathan."

"Huh?"

"My name is Nathan or Nate. I figure if you're going to hold me like we're about to do the tango, the least you can do is call me by my name."

Brandon pulled back to see the grin on Nate's face, the first smile he'd seen from the man since the moment he walked into the doctor's office. "You look more like a Nate to me than a Nathan, so we'll go with that. And if you're joking around, you must be okay."

"That's what Amy says. Do you want to let me go now?"

Brandon did as he was asked, immediately missing the warmth from Nate's body. As they boarded the elevator, he stayed close enough to catch him again, if necessary. Other people crowded in, making conversation difficult. The silent ride gave Brandon a chance to clear his head of the strange effect Nate was having on him.

The third floor of Chicago General wasn't as crowded as the lobby. Brandon was able to lead Nate through the hall at a fair clip. He didn't realize how fast he was going until Nate stumbled. Brandon apologized. "Sorry, Nate. I wasn't thinking."

Nate grinned, again, making Brandon's knees feel weak. "Normally I can keep up. When I'm not punch drunk, that is."

"Maybe we should have called an ambulance. Are you even supposed to be walking around?"

"Amy checked me over before we left. The M.R.I. is just a precaution. I do feel guilty that you have to spend your evening here with me, though. I feel like I'm messing up your plans."

Brandon stopped in front of a row of doors and said, "If by 'messing up my plans' you mean taking me away from the glamorous prospect of sharing a frozen pizza with my dog, then I can only invite you to mess up my plans more often."

"No family? No boyfriend?"

"I have plenty of family, but I don't live with them anymore. I figure thirty-two is a little old to be sharing a set of bunk beds with my kid brother. As for the boyfriend, I had one of those, too, but he belongs to someone else now, thank God."

"I'm sorry. I didn't mean to stir up any painful memories."

Brandon shook his head. "You didn't. Jeff and I broke up four years ago. He subscribes to the theory that gay men are incapable of fidelity; I don't. Seems he had a fondness for twinks that he forgot to mention."

He almost laughed at the shocked look on Nate's face.

"He had an affair?"

"Affairs, as in plural."

"That must have hurt."

"Maybe the first time I caught him in bed with another guy. By the third time, I was just glad to be rid of him. I think the only reason I stayed as long as I did was because I felt like I had made a commitment. I guess he didn't see it that way."

"That's harsh."

Brandon shrugged. "It was a long time ago. Come on. Let's get you checked out." He knocked on the door in front of them.

The door opened a second later, and Brandon was engulfed in a bracing bear hug almost as quickly. "Hey, squirt. What brings you to Chicago at seven-thirty on a Tuesday night?"

"Damn, Keith, put me down before you snap my spine. Are you and Maria so hard up for cash that you have to drum up business by causing the injuries yourselves?" Seeing Nate's startled expression, Brandon said, "Nate, this is my brother, Keith. He's a neurologist here.

Keith, this is Dr. Nathan Morris."

Keith put his brother down and moved closer to Nate. Using one finger, he tilted Nate's head so he could better see the right side. Keith turned back to Brandon. "I'm assuming you didn't do that to his head?"

"No. Nate thinks he was the subject of a gay bashing."

Nate gave Brandon an icy glare. "No, *he* doesn't *think* he was the subject of a gay bashing. He *knows* he was."

Keith and Brandon both fought back grins as Keith said, "Yeah, I hate it when people talk about me like I'm not around, too. You're here for an M.R.I., right?"

Nate nodded. "Yes, but I don't want to bump anyone else off the schedule."

"I'll check with one of the techs, but I don't think there'll be a problem. Tuesday nights are kind of slow, even here in Chicago. Do you have a set of orders, or do you need me to write you some?"

Nate handed him Amy's orders, and Keith led them down the hall to the radiology lab. While the techs took Nate into the other room and prepared him for the M.R.I., Keith seized the opportunity to pump Brandon for information.

"So, you gonna tell me what happened, or are you planning on letting me die of curiosity?"

Brandon bit back a sigh. "Some guy waited until Nate closed his office tonight, jumped out of the shadows screaming 'faggot', and then clocked Nate over the head. I have to tell you, Keith, it doesn't feel right. When's the last time you heard of a gay bashing in Reed?"

"Never, but who's counting?" Keith grinned, and Brandon knew what was coming. "So Dr. Morris is gay, huh?"

"Don't even think about it, Keith. Jeez, you're almost as bad as Mom." Keith did his best to look hurt, but Brandon knew his brother too well to be fooled.

"All I did was make a casual observation, Bran."

"Yeah, right. Just like you made a casual observation that one of the doctors on your surgical rotation was gay and had a thing for guys in uniform. Just like the casual observation you made about how great Pastor Oakley's son was, or how nice Mrs. Jensen's brother-in-law seemed. The answer is no. Stop trying to fix me up."

The tech came back into the room and started adjusting the settings for the machine. Keith stepped back enough so that the tech couldn't hear them. "You need to have that conversation with your hormones, bud. I saw the way you were looking at the guy."

"No reason I can't look, is there? But looking is all I'm gonna do. For all I know, Nate has a boyfriend."

Keith shook his head. "Not the way he was looking back at you. I'd

almost be willing to put money on it. Besides, if Dr. Morris has a partner, why wasn't said boyfriend the one who brought him in? No way
would I let some other guy take Maria to the hospital if she was hurt."

Knowing he'd never win, Brandon let the argument drop. Twenty
minutes later, the tech finished the scan and brought Nate back into the
control area.

"Why don't you wait in my office while I read these scans?" Keith
said. "I would offer to let you read them yourself, Dr. Morris, but you
look a little worse for wear."

"Sounds good. And, please, call me Nate."

As Nate swayed on his feet, Brandon steadied him. "Come on, let's
get you to a chair before you collapse." He led the way back to Keith's
office, wincing along with Nate as he groaned in pain. "Do you need to
lie down?"

Nate shook his head. "I'm fine. I don't think it's my injuries that
are causing me to be so shaky. I skipped lunch today and then missed
dinner. I think my blood sugar probably just dropped down to the low
side."

No sooner were the words out of Nate's mouth than Brandon was
on his way to the snack machines. He came back with two soft drinks, a
couple of sandwiches, and a pocketful of candy bars. He handed one of
the sandwiches and a drink to Nate.

"Thanks."

As Nate reached for his wallet, Brandon waved him away. "I was
glad to do it. It's not exactly four star cuisine, but it'll bring your blood
sugar up."

Nate nodded. "You and Keith look a lot alike, same hair and eyes.
So, what's the favor he owes you?"

"What?"

"On the way up here, you said you knew a guy who owed you a
favor. So, what favor does Keith owe you?"

"His life. I let him make it to adulthood without killing his sorry
ass." Nate laughed, but Brandon noticed he wasn't eating much. "If you
eat all that, I'll give you a treat."

Nate smiled. "If I had a dirty mind, my imagination could go hog
wild with an opening like that."

Brandon colored and took the chair next to Nate's. Hoping to steer
the conversation into less dangerous territory, he said, "Actually, I
meant that I have a candy bar in my pocket."

Nate's grin widened. "Oh, is that what that is?"

Brandon had just taken a sip of his drink, and he sprayed soda all
over Keith's desk just as the door opened and his brother entered the
room.

Keith took one look at the cola dripping from Brandon's chin and shook his head. "I don't know what you said to my brother, but I haven't seen his face that red since the day Megan peed all over him in church."

"Megan?"

"Our baby sister."

Nate looked at Brandon. "How many brothers and sisters do you have?"

"Mom and Dad have eight kids, counting me." Brandon pointed to Keith. "That idiot over there is the oldest."

"Where do you rank on the list?"

"Third from the top."

Keith took a seat behind his desk. "Do you have siblings, Nate?"

Brandon watched a shadow fall across Nate's face.

"Just one — my brother Seth. He's twenty-two, six years younger than me."

Keith was about to ask another question when Brandon interrupted. "What's the verdict on Nate's M.R.I.?"

Taking the hint, Keith said, "Well, the scan shows no obvious signs of injury, but I think you probably have a slight concussion, Nate. Do you have someone who can stay with you tonight? I really wouldn't advise you to stay by yourself. Of course, I'm sure you already know all that."

Nate nodded. "I can stay with my friend Amy and her husband."

Brandon watched as Keith's curiosity kicked in. "You live alone then? No partner?"

Again Nate's expression darkened. "No."

"No boyfriend?"

"No."

"Any prospects?"

Before Nate could answer, Brandon said, "Jesus Christ, Keith, I thought I was the only cop in the family. Leave the guy alone, will you?"

"Sorry." Keith looked anything but. "Anyway, as I said, I think you should stay with your friends tonight. I can write you a scrip for pain killers, if you want."

"That's all right. I can manage with aspirin, thanks. May I use your phone to call Amy and let her know what's going on?" When Keith pointed to the phone on the desk, Nate said, "Thanks," and dialed Amy's number, waiting in silence as it rang. After the sixth ring, he cut the connection and said, "I got the machine. I'll call the clinic and see if she's still there."

Another call and, again, there was no answer. "Not there, either."

"Does she have a cell?" Keith said.

"Yeah, but she only carries it when she's on call. She's off for the next three days." Nate thought for a minute. "Let me check the service we use for after hours calls and see if she left a message with them." He dialed another number and waited. "Hi, Cindy, it's Dr. Morris."

Keith and Brandon listened to his end of the conversation.

"Boy, news travels fast in Reed, huh?" ... "No, I'm fine, just a good solid bump to the head. Listen, have you heard from Amy?" ... "She did? When?"

Nate covered the mouthpiece and turned to Brandon. "Mike's aunt down in Atlanta has been taken to the hospital. Cindy thinks she fell or something. It must be pretty bad because he and Amy hopped on the first plane out."

Nate uncovered the phone and said, "Who's handling our calls?" ... "No, he's a good doctor, but be sure he knows only to accept the serious calls. The drive from Chicago to Reed is too far for a light case of the sniffles. All right, Cindy, thanks. If you hear from Amy, please tell her to call me at my apartment."

Before he could hang up, Brandon took the phone. "Hey, Cindy? It's Brandon Nash." ... Brandon rolled his eyes. "No, I didn't realize your cousin was gay. And single, too. Imagine that. Listen, Cindy, tell Amy to call my place for Nate instead." His left leg twitched while he listened to the conversation on the other end. "No, you can't ask why. Okay, Cindy, see you at church."

The minute he turned off the phone, Nate said, "What was that all about?"

Keith almost laughed out loud at the look of innocence on Brandon's face, but he wisely sat behind the desk and kept his mouth shut.

Brandon said, "Oh, that. Well, Cindy and I go to the same church. Went to the same high school, too, though I'm a couple of years ahead of her."

He hid a smile behind his hand when Nate, who looked like he was about ready to start cursing, said, "That's not what I meant, and you know it. What was all that business about Amy calling your place for me?"

Brandon leaned over to better see Nate's face. "Oh, that. Well, it's real simple, actually: Amy's out of town, and you live alone. You need someone to stay the night with, but the only people in town you really know are catching the red-eye to Atlanta, even as we speak. That leaves you with one option. Plainly stated, Nate, you're coming home with me."

Chapter Two

Nate woke to the feel of gentle but rough fingertips soothing the swollen skin of his face. He opened his eyes to see the beautiful blues of Brandon Nash staring down at him.

"Wake up, Nate. We're here."

Nate shook himself to clear away the cobwebs. "I still say I can stay by myself. I hate to put you out like this."

"We had this argument back at the hospital. You're stuck staying with me tonight, might as well make the most of it." Before Nate could argue again, Brandon got out of the S.U.V. and moved around to the passenger side to help him into the house.

Brandon had brought Nate to a sprawling farmhouse just inside the Reed city limits. They went in by the back door, through a mudroom, and into the kitchen. The kitchen looked to Nate like something from a time warp. The stove was a refurbished thirties model gas with six burners and a griddle. The cabinets were natural-stained knotty pine with black iron hinges and handles. The granite countertops were spotless, but looked as though they hadn't been used in a while. A picture window was set along the far wall to capture most of the early morning light. Nate could almost see himself cooking breakfast for half a dozen smiling kids all clustered around the central work island. The minute he realized where his thoughts were taking him, he forced his mind back to the reason why he was there: someone was out to get him.

Brandon broke into his thoughts by saying, "There are six bedrooms upstairs. I'm going to put you in the one closest to mine so that I can hear you if you need me."

Nate barely had time to nod before he heard the thunder. No, not thunder exactly, more like feet. Large feet coming toward him at a dead run. He looked up just in time to see a giant blue-gray shadow pummel him to the ground.

"Sasha! Down, girl. Dammit, I said down." Brandon pulled the Great Dane off Nate as quickly as he could, but not before she gave him a healthy kiss right on the mouth. Brandon led her over to her food bowl and filled it with dry food. Once he was satisfied that Sasha was well occupied, he returned to pick Nate up from the floor.

"I'm sorry, Nate. My mom must've come by to walk her. Sometimes she forgets to lock Sasha back in the sun porch when she leaves. Here, let me help you up."

Nate allowed Brandon to pull him to his feet. "That thing is a horse." He looked over to where Sasha sat on her haunches, chewing a mouthful of Kibble. Now that she wasn't perched on his chest trying to slobber his face off, he had to admit, she was a fine looking animal. "She's kinda cute, though." That made Brandon beam with a look Nate could only describe as fatherly pride.

"She's a beauty, isn't she? Imagine how pretty she'll be when she's full grown."

"You mean that monster is still a puppy?"

Sasha looked up from her food bowl as he said it, her big, brown eyes focusing on Nate. She stared at him for a full minute before turning away and trotting out of the room.

"Looks like you hurt her feelings."

The grin on Brandon's face was contagious. Before he knew it, Nate found himself smiling back. "If you expect me to feel sorry for her, forget it. Any dog that has free run of a house this size and an owner who worships the ground she walks on is not exactly a sympathetic creature." He looked around the kitchen. "From what I've seen of your house, it's magnificent, by the way."

"Thanks. Hey, let me give you the grand tour." Brandon led Nate through the house, pointing out favorite pieces of furniture and sentimental treasures along the way.

With each step he took, Nate was more and more impressed with Brandon's home. Finally, Brandon led him to a bedroom at the far end of the upstairs hall.

"My room is just across the hall. Let me put fresh sheets on the guest bed, and you'll be all set."

Brandon walked down the hall and came back with an armload of linens. Nate helped him strip the bed and put on the fresh sheets.

"So, what do you think of the place now that you've seen the whole thing?"

"It's great, but isn't it a lot of house for a single guy?"

Brandon nodded. "Yeah, but like I told my mother when I bought it, I don't plan to be single forever. Someday, I hope to meet a nice guy, settle down, and adopt a houseful of little Nashs."

For some reason, the thought of Brandon settling down with someone else made Nate uncomfortable, but he refused to think about the reasons why. Instead, he said, "So, how did you come to buy this place?"

Brandon finished smoothing the covers and sat down on the edge of the bed, motioning for Nate to do the same. After Nate was seated, Brandon said, "Actually, my dad was born here. My great-grandfather built this house in nineteen hundred. My granddad bought it from him when he married in nineteen-forty. Grandpa went off to war and left my grandmother to set up housekeeping. Counting my father, they raised ten kids in this house. When it came up for sale last year, I couldn't stand to see it go out of family hands, so I bought it."

"What about your grandparents? Did they pass away?"

"Not on your life. Those two are going to live forever. My grand-mother said she couldn't stand another Illinois winter, so she and Grandpa moved down to Florida. They used the money from the sale of the house to buy a condo. Grandpa wanted to go to California, where they film *Baywatch*, but Grandma wasn't going for it."

Nate chuckled. "They sound like a couple of characters."

"All four of my grandparents are. My mom's folks still live here in Reed. My Grandma Taylor is something of a hypochondriac, so I imagine you'll be seeing her soon, especially since her doctor retired. Grandpa Taylor used to be the Reed County fire marshal. Now he spends all his time trying to keep track of Grandma's ailments. I hope she won't bombard you with complaints."

Nate smiled. "I don't mind. I have several patients who just need a little attention every now and again."

"Yeah, and you don't charge them, either."

"How did you know?"

"You know the lady that does your billing?"

"Marcia? She's a real sweetheart."

Brandon grinned. "Yeah, she is. She's also my cousin. She's told everyone in the family about the gorgeous new doctor who only charges the patients who can afford it. Doesn't that hurt your practice finan-cially?"

While he was talking, Brandon had scooted closer to where Nate was sitting. Nate tried his best to ignore Brandon and the attraction he felt for him. Instead, he concentrated on the question. "Actually, no. Amy and I are both trust fund babies. We have enough to help out our patients here and there."

Brandon nodded. "You said you were on the outs with your par-ents. I take it they aren't the one's responsible for the trust fund."

Nate fought to keep his voice neutral. "No. My father's mother — Grandma Morris — set up my trust. She also set up the trust for Amy. My dad is an only child, and because he and my mother had two boys, I think Grandma thought of Amy as the granddaughter she never had. She always hoped that Amy and I would marry someday." He couldn't stop the smile that crossed his face. "When I was fifteen, I told her in no uncertain terms that marriage to Amy, or anyone else of the female persuasion, just wasn't going to happen."

"Oh, man. You came out to your grandma?"

"She's the first person I ever told. I thought sure she was gonna freak. You know what she said?"

"What?"

"She said, 'Nathan, I have something I want to tell you. If you listen to nothing else I say, remember this: choose a man with a large penis. People who say size doesn't matter are generally the folks who don't have much to brag about in the crotch department.' Then she said, 'Your grandfather, God rest his soul, had a nice eight-incher. Lord, I miss that man.'"

Brandon was shaking with laughter. "Talk about my grandparents being characters; your grandmother sounds like a hoot."

"Yeah, she was. The day after I told her I was gay, she set up my trust. She put the same amount in trust for Seth, but that was just to be fair, not because she thought he'd ever need it."

"What about Amy's trust?"

"She set that up back when we were in the third grade. Amy's dad ran out on them when she was just a baby, so her mom had to struggle to make ends meet. Grandma set up the trust so Amy could go to college, but in typical Grandma Morris fashion, she put in enough for ten kids to go to medical school, same as she did with me and Seth. Amy and I do our best to return the favor by helping out our patients. Those that can afford to pay, do. The rest we try to work with."

"I admire you for that." Brandon was silent for a minute. Finally, he said, "This probably isn't the best time to mention it, but while you were sleeping in the truck, I got a call from the deputy I sent to gather evidence back at your office."

Nate rubbed a weary hand over his face. "Let me guess. Nothing incriminating was found, and no one saw anything."

Brandon got up and walked over to the window, staring out into the darkness. "Of course not, but that doesn't mean we won't find out who did this." He walked back to where Nate sat and crouched down so he could see him better. "Think, Nate. Who do you know that might have it in for you? A family member? An old boyfriend, maybe?"

It was Nate's turn to get up. He moved so quickly, he sent Brandon sprawling. "I've already told you that I don't know. Besides my parents and my brother, Grandma Morris was the only family I had. She died right before my eighteenth birthday. When I was twenty-two, I told my parents I was gay. The next day, I got served with a restraining order informing me I was no longer allowed within a hundred yards of my parents or my brother. The day after that, I got a certified letter from my father's attorney informing me I had been cut out of my father's will, and any further contact between me and my family would be handled through the lawyers." He ran his fingers through his hair and whirled back to face Brandon as the other man rose to his feet. "Why do you think my grandmother set up that trust? She knew my father would never tolerate having a faggot for a son." He sank back onto the bed, feeling more alone than he'd felt the day his whole life had fallen apart.

In spite of his feelings, he forced himself to finish. "As for old boyfriends, there was only one, and he left about the same time as my parents disowned me. So you see, no one from the past cares enough about me to even talk to me, much less soil their hands knocking me over the head. I doubt any of them even know where I am."

Without saying a word, Brandon walked over and pulled Nate to his feet.

"What are you doing?"

"You're in need of some therapy. I'm gonna provide it for you."

Nate eyed him. "I'm not sure I like the sound of that."

Brandon smiled. "Do I look like the kind of guy who would take advantage of a man with a concussion?"

"Well..."

"Okay, don't answer that. Look, let's get you some aspirin for your head, and then I'll take you somewhere that's guaranteed to make you feel better." He gave Nate his most sincere smile. "No funny business. I promise."

Nate wasn't sure why, but for some reason, he trusted Brandon. He downed the pills Bran gave him and found himself following Brandon through the kitchen and toward the back door. When they got to the mudroom, Brandon said, "Here, wear one of my jackets. It's cold out there." He handed Nate a thickly-lined, brown leather jacket and grabbed a blanket from a deacon's bench situated by the door. Whistling for Sasha, he ushered Nate outside.

The air was cool but dry, and Nate found the bracing effect of the slight breeze strangely relaxing. Sasha walked between them, her ears cocked and her head held high. They walked for several minutes in silence until Brandon pointed to a rise in the distance.

"See that hill over there?"

"Yeah."

"That's where we're going. You able to walk that far, or do you want me to carry you?"

Nate snorted. "Like you could."

Brandon's leer was pure sex. "Oh, I could carry you if I wanted to, but once I got you into my arms, I'm sure I'd think of better things to do with your body than hauling it around."

Nate's mouth went dry. "Look, Brandon—"

"Relax, Nate. I'm not gonna jump you. Hasn't anybody ever flirted with you before?"

Nate shook his head. "It's been a while."

"Sexy guy like you? I find that hard to believe."

"Amy calls me a turtle. She says once I get hurt, I hide out in my shell so no one can touch me again."

"Maybe it's time to change that."

Without giving Nate a chance to answer, Brandon led him to the top of the rise and said, "Close your eyes."

Nate could hear him shaking out the blanket and spreading it on the ground. A warm hand closed over Nate's cold fingers and pulled him forward. The same strong hands exerted gentle pressure on Nate's shoulders until he was sitting on the ground. He felt Brandon slide down beside him.

"You can open them, now."

Nate felt the breath catch in his throat as he looked out on the scene some fifty feet below. He and Brandon were seated on a bluff overlooking an open field and a large pond. On the other side of the field was a wall of trees, all sporting their fall colors. The reds and yellows cast their reflection on the moonlit pond, giving the whole valley a magic effect.

"My God, it's unbelievable."

Brandon nodded. "I come here when I want to think, or when I have a problem and need to step away from it for a little while. I used to spend the night with my grandparents just so I could sneak out here after they went to bed." He paused for a moment, considering his next words. "I spent a lot of time out here the summer I realized I was gay."

For some reason, Nate had never considered that Brandon might have had a hard time dealing with his homosexuality. He seemed so confident; Nate just assumed he'd always been that way. "How old were you?"

"Fifteen. At least, that's how old I was when I finally admitted it to myself. I think, on some level, I always knew I was different, but fifteen was the age when I couldn't hide it anymore."

"What happened when you were fifteen?"

Brandon grinned. "Billy Watson. He got into his daddy's porn stash and brought over some girlie magazines. Billy got hard from looking at the pictures, and I got hard from watching Billy. Those naked women did nothing for me, but the bulge in Billy's jeans made my dick puff right up. I knew at that moment that I couldn't hide it anymore. At least, not from myself. Telling everybody else was a different story entirely."

Usually, Nate hated to pry, but something about Brandon's manner made him feel comfortable asking questions. "So, how did you come out to your family?"

"When I was in high school, I dated girls as a cover. Oh, I made sure I never got serious with any one girl so I couldn't be accused of leading her on, but the purpose was purely to hide who I really was. Looking back, it was stupid of me not to just tell the truth. I mean, Reed is a pretty gay friendly town. Several of the major businesses in Reed are owned by same sex couples. There were even a few guys in my graduating class who were 'out'. None of that made a difference to me. I just didn't have the balls to tell my family I was gay. I decided that when I went away to college I was going to have a real relationship, with a guy."

He laughed, that husky sound that Nate was coming to appreciate for its effect on his nervous system.

"To tell you the truth, I think I was just desperate to get laid. I wasn't the most mature eighteen-year-old in the world. Anyway, my first week at Michigan State, I went to one of the gay bars in the area — one that didn't card — and met Joel. He was a freshman, same as me, and went to the same school. He was also just as green as I was when it came to sex. We dated for a few weeks, and I was absolutely certain we were made for each other. When Christmas break came, I couldn't bear the thought of being separated from him, so I invited him to come home with me." He laughed again, the sound laced with amusement at his own foolishness. "I had it all planned out: I would introduce him as a friend from school, then sneak off with him whenever I got the chance."

"Did it work?"

"It would have, if Keith hadn't followed us the first time we snuck out. We were visiting Grandma and Grandpa Taylor and decided to make out in Grandpa's old tractor barn. Keith got there just as I was taking Joel's shirt off."

"That must have been embarrassing."

Brandon stretched out his legs and crossed his ankles. "It would have been, if Keith hadn't been so cool about it. He said, 'Well, it's about time you got you some. Dad and I were saving up to buy you a male hooker.' He looked at Joel and said, 'Friend, my ass. I hope he puts out better than my girlfriend does.' Then he went back into the house. When we got back to Mom and Dad's place, Joel's things were moved from the guest room into my room. I found out later that my whole family had suspected I was gay for years. When I asked my mother how she knew, she said a mother just knows these things. Then she gave me a thirty-minute instructional lesson on safe sex. The relationship with Joel didn't last long, but at least I never again had to hide who I really was from the people I loved. Of course, I still can't look at a condom without seeing my mother demonstrating how to put one on a banana."

Nate laughed. "At least your coming out was better than mine."

"Want to talk about it?"

Any other time, Nate would have said an automatic "no". Now though, sitting in the moonlight with Brandon, wrapped up in his jacket and bathed in his scent, Nate heard the words come spilling out.

"My dad and I have always had our share of disagreements. Ever heard of the Mor-co Pharmacy chain?"

"Sure. They're one of the largest franchises in the country."

Nate watched as recognition dawned on Brandon's face.

"Your family owns Mor-co?"

"Yep. My dad does, anyway. He inherited it from his dad, who started out as a pharmacist in a one-horse Georgia town. When my dad graduated from college with a degree in pharmacy, Grandpa set him up with his own store. Pretty soon, they bought another store, and then another. Before Grandpa knew it, he had a chain. When my dad took over, he consolidated and took the company national. Dad expected me to get a business degree, or at the very least, become a pharmacist, so I could take over the family business. Needless to say, he wasn't too thrilled when I decided to become a doctor. He said, 'Why would you want to be a doctor? Don't you know we make our money off sick people? Cure enough of them, and we'll be out of business.'"

"No offense, but your dad sounds like a prick."

"None taken. He's definitely a prick. Anyhow, Dad was unhappy enough about my choice to become a doctor, but I think he might have eventually gotten over it. Having a queer son was something else entirely."

"What happened?"

The quiet strength in Brandon's voice gave Nate the impetus to continue the story. "Not unlike you, I met a guy while I was away at school. Not my freshman year, though. I was a senior. Rick Landon was my student advisor. We got to know each other while I was trying to decide which medical school to apply for. I thought he was perfect: handsome, smart, funny — the whole package. He asked me out, and I said yes. He was the first guy I'd ever dated, and I fell for him, hard. He wanted us to move in together, but..."

"But?"

"Promise you won't laugh?"

Brandon looked over to where Sasha lay sleeping on the edge of the blanket. "I won't, but I can't speak for Sasha."

Nate smiled. "You and that dog. Anyway, the reason I didn't want us to move in together is because I wanted us to wait about having sex. I wanted it to be special."

"You mean, you never—"

"No. Oh, we fooled around a little, touching and groping, but nothing any more intimate. Rick wasn't real happy about it, but he agreed to wait. We dated for almost eight months. Then, on Rick's twenty-third birthday, I did something really stupid. I asked him to marry me."

"Wow."

"Wait. It gets worse. He said yes. Then he insisted we invite both sets of parents to dinner and tell them the good news, never mind the fact that neither of our families even knew we were gay."

"He doesn't sound all that bright."

"Yeah, well neither was I. We invited our families out to dinner and told them all of it, right in the middle of the prime rib. My dad threw one of his tantrums, to which my mother replied, 'Now see there. You've upset your father again.' My brother, who was sixteen at the time, just looked at me like I was a slug that had crawled through the door of the restaurant. Rick's parents barely said anything, just got up and left, demanding that Rick go with them. The next day, I got a restraining order from my parents and a phone call from Rick informing me that his folks were going to cut him off financially if he didn't stop 'acting gay'. He transferred to another school and that was the end of it. Three months later, I read in the society section of the paper about his engagement to the daughter of his father's business partner."

Brandon reached over and took Nate's hand. "For what it's worth, I think they're all idiots."

Nate tried to tell himself the tingling in his fingers didn't mean anything. "Thanks. And thanks for sharing this place with me. And for listening."

"My pleasure." Brandon glanced down at his watch. "It's after one. Let's head back to the house." He stood up and helped Nate to his feet.

The walk back to the house was silent, but it was a comfortable silence. Sasha walked between them, watchful as ever. When they got back to the house, Sasha went to her massive pillow-bed near the fireplace in the living room, while Brandon and Nate went upstairs.

Brandon dropped Nate off at the door to the guestroom. "If you don't want Sasha to end up in bed with you, make sure the door is closed up tight. She might have gone quietly to her pillow like a good little doggie, but that doesn't mean she'll stay there." Then, before Nate had a chance to protest, Brandon leaned forward and planted a soft kiss on Nate's check. "Good-night. Sleep well." Without another word, he went to his room, leaving Nate standing and staring behind him.

*~ * ~ * ~ * ~ *

Brandon reached over and hit the snooze button on the alarm clock, but the noise didn't stop. He hit it again, and it just kept ringing. *Ringing?* It took him a full minute to realize he was hearing the phone. He hoped the ringing would stop, but the person on the other end was persistent. The phone was still ringing when he finally woke enough to pick it up. "Yeah?"

"Bran?"

"Sam?"

"Yeah, buddy, it's me."

Brandon looked out the window and saw that it was still dark outside. "Jesus, Sam. What time is it?"

"It's around four. Consider it my revenge for leaving me on the interstate last night surrounded by future McNuggets."

"Some revenge. What are you really doing calling me at four in the morning?"

"I got a call an hour ago about a possible break-in at the McCoy Apartment complex."

"I take it you found something, or you wouldn't be calling me."

"I found something, all right, but you're not gonna like it."

"Go ahead."

"It was Dr. Morris's apartment, Bran. Dewey filled me in, so I know all about the doctor being attacked last night. This looks to me like a tie-in to the assault. The place has been ransacked, but that's not the worst part."

"Please don't tell me it's more gay-bashing."

"You got it. Whoever did this spray painted the windows and doors with words like 'fag' and 'queer'."

"Fuck. I'll be there as soon as I can."

"Gottcha. Oh, I tried to notify Dr. Morris, but I haven't been able to locate him."

"That's all right, Sam. I know where he is."

Brandon hung up the phone and got out of bed, then pulled on his jeans and crossed the hall to the guest room. He started to turn the knob, but stopped when he saw that the door was already halfway open. At first he panicked, thinking the person who trashed Nate's apartment had come after him here. His heart resumed a steady beat when he saw the reason the door was open. Nate was lying on his side with Sasha curled up to his back. Her long body took up more than her fair share of the double bed, but Nate was sleeping too soundly to care. Brandon couldn't believe it, but he was actually jealous of his dog. He shooed Sasha out the door and sat down on the side of the bed next to Nate. "Nate, wake up, buddy." Those liquid chocolate eyes that Brandon was becoming so fond of opened slowly and struggled to focus.

"Umm. What time is it?"

"A few minutes after four."

Nate huddled deeper into the covers. "Do you always get up this early?"

"No, but something's happened."

Nate sat up in an instant, wincing as the pain in his sore face returned. "What is it? Is it Amy and Mike? Are they okay?"

Brandon put his hand on Nate's shoulder. "Relax. This isn't about Amy or Mike. This is about you." *God, I hate having to tell him this.* "Nate, somebody trashed your apartment."

"What about the office? Did they hit there, too?"

"Not that I know of, but I'll send someone to check." He picked up the bedside phone and dispatched one of his deputies over there to take a look. When he was finished, he turned back to Nate. "You gonna be able to handle this?"

"I don't know. Ask me again after I've seen my apartment."

While Nate dressed, Brandon went downstairs and started a pot of coffee. He'd just gone back up to his room when Nate came out, dressed and ready to go. Knowing that the best way to keep a man's mind off his troubles was to keep him busy, Brandon said, "There are a couple of travel mugs in the cabinet above the sink. Would you see if the coffee's ready yet and fill them up?" A few minutes later, Brandon went downstairs to find Nate sitting at the kitchen table stroking Sasha's head. Nate looked so right sitting in his kitchen, petting his dog, Brandon had to force himself to make his presence known and disturb the scene.

"Hey," he said around the tightness in his throat. "I thought I told you to close your door before you went to bed." He walked over to where Nate sat and rubbed Sasha up under the chin in the way she liked. "Did you know you had company in bed last night? And I don't mean me." Nate's laugh was weak, but Brandon was willing to take what he could get.

"Actually, I did close the door, but Sasha woke me up about two-thirty scratching to get in. I guess I felt sorry for her."

Brandon gave his dog a feigned frown. "So, you found yourself a soft touch, huh?"

"She's a good dog. She certainly kept me from being lonely."

Brandon laughed. "If I'd known that was what you wanted, I'd have volunteered for the job myself."

Nate's blush was followed by a quick change in subject. "The coffee's ready. I wasn't sure how you take yours, so you'll have to fix it the way you like it."

Brandon grabbed his travel mug off the counter and headed toward the mudroom. "I used to take it with milk and sugar, but now I drink it black. I guess all those years working cases for the Bureau taught me to appreciate the merits of strong coffee."

"The Bureau?"

"Yeah. I worked for the F.B.I. for a while."

"You were an agent?"

"I was a profiler."

"Don't you have to have a degree in psychology for that?"

"'Fraid so. My field of expertise is forensics." Before Nate could ask more questions, Brandon said, "Let's get going. Sam, my deputy, will wonder where we are." He looked Nate over carefully as he stood up and grabbed his coffee. "Are you sure you're up to this? I could go by first and check it out before you have to see it."

"No. I'll have to see it sooner or later. Might as well get it over with."

"All right. Let's go."

* ~ * ~ * ~ * ~ *

The apartment was worse than he'd expected, surprising since Nate had been imagining all kinds of terrible things ever since Brandon told him about the break-in. The minute they pulled into the parking lot, Nate saw the slurs painted on the doors and windows. His apartment was the townhouse type, with its own porch and patio. The guy had broken several pieces of the porch's railing and splintered a couple of the support posts. The screens had been ripped from the windows, and some of the panes were broken. The door was hanging awkwardly on its hinges, and the chairs Nate had sitting by the front door were smashed.

Brandon left Nate standing amid the wreckage of the porch while he went inside to talk to his deputies. A few minutes later, he came back and led Nate into what was left of his apartment.

The furniture had been slashed with a knife, bits of fabric and stuffing littering the floor. Nate's television was smashed to bits, as were all the dishes and glassware in the cupboards. The pictures from the walls now lay on the floor in piles of splintered wood and broken glass. Even the glass shower doors in the downstairs bathroom had been shattered.

One of the deputies reporting in to Brandon said, "We questioned

Dr. Morris's closest neighbors, Sheriff. Nobody reported hearing anything unusual last night."

Overhearing, Nate wasn't surprised. His place was an end unit and the apartment next to his was empty. The intruder had done his homework.

While Brandon talked to one of his men, Nate made his way up the stairs. More broken pictures littered the upstairs hall. The spare bedroom, which Nate used as an office, was a mass of strewn files and wrecked furniture. Like the television, his computer was nothing more than a pile of scrambled circuitry. In every room he'd seen so far, including the bathroom, words like "pervert" and "freak" glared at him from the once pristine, white walls. The spare room was no exception, only there the vandal had gotten a little more creative and called him an "ass-fucking slut."

After finding the upstairs bath in a state similar to the one downstairs, Nate made his way to the master bedroom. All his clothes lay in piles on the floor, covered in what looked like red paint. As he got closer, he could smell the metallic scent of blood. As a doctor, Nate was used to the smell. Now, though, knowing that someone had covered his clothes in the thick mess was enough to make the coffee he'd drunk in the car come back up. He ran to the bathroom and was quietly ill. He was still leaning over the commode when he felt something wet and cool on the back of his neck. Brandon held a damp cloth to his heated skin.

"Nate? Are you okay?"

Nate managed to nod. When he was certain he wasn't going to gag again, he said, "I'm usually not such a wuss. I guess all that blood was too much for me."

Brandon helped him up but didn't let go of him. "If it makes you feel any better, Sam is pretty sure it's animal blood."

"It does." He shook himself. "I guess I should go back in there and assess the damage."

"Only if you want to. Sam and the boys have already dusted for fingerprints, but I doubt they'll find anything. My guess is the person that did this is a professional."

Nate reached up and removed Brandon's hands from his shoulders. "Come on. I want to see just how bad it is." With Brandon right behind him, Nate walked back into his bedroom. He deliberately avoided looking at the pile of bloody clothes and focused instead on the rest of the room. What was left of it.

His college awards and trophies were crunched up in a pile in the corner. The dresser mirror was shattered, as was the window that overlooked the courtyard below. His mattress had been ripped to shreds, but the worst thing was the damage done to the quilt Grandma Morris had made for him. Nate picked up the torn remnants of the log cabin quilt and cradled it to his chest.

Brandon came up behind him and put his hand on Nate's arm. "Nate?"

"My grandmother made this quilt for me. It's the only thing I took with me from the house when my parents washed their hands of me. It's the only thing I wanted."

Brandon pulled the fabric from his hands and guided him out of the room. They were almost to the bedroom door when Nate stopped him. "Wait. Brandon, did you read that message on the wall?"

"Yeah, but you don't need to look at it. My men took pictures. That's enough."

"No. It was meant for me. I want to read it. Maybe I can pick up some clue as to who might have done this."

Nate turned around and gave careful consideration to the message scrawled on the sheetrock, not in paint this time, but in blood: *God is Coming. All of Sodom Will Perish.* He turned and walked out, feeling sick all over again.

* ~ * ~ * ~ * ~ *

Rage welled inside Brandon as he settled Nate into the passenger seat of the S.U.V. The amount of hatred it took to trash a place like that was almost inconceivable. Brandon had just eased into the driver's seat and closed his door when the radio sounded.

"Sheriff, you copy?"

Brandon pushed the COM button. "Yeah, Dispatch. Go ahead."

"Dewey just reported in from the doctor's office. Looks like the office got hit, too."

Brandon hit the steering wheel hard enough to make the horn sound. "Fuck!" He took one look at Nate's white face and forced himself to calm down. He mashed the COM button again. "Dispatch? Tell Dewey I'm on my way over there, now. Sheriff, out."

By the time they had finished surveying the damage to the office, Brandon was ready to explode and Nate was dead on his feet. The office was a duplication of the damage done to the apartment: more threats and slurs, scattered files, and ripped furniture. Equipment had been smashed and medicine bottles were lying broken all over the floor. They stayed until Nate started shaking. That's when Brandon insisted they leave.

He drove them back to the farmhouse, ushering Nate inside and letting Sasha out so she could run. She surprised him by refusing to go.

Instead, she walked over to where Nate was sitting on the couch and put her head in his lap. Brandon felt his eyes getting moist as he noticed the dejected look on Nate's face. "Are you hungry? I think I've got a can of biscuits in the refrigerator."

"No, thanks. I'm still a little nauseous."

"Understandable, under the circumstances."

"Yeah. What time is it?"

"Almost eight."

"Oh. What about Amy? And my patients?"

"My office is trying to locate Amy, but so far, there's no answer at the number you gave us for Mike's aunt. None of the hospitals in Atlanta have a patient by that name, either. It's possible they're on the way back here, but we'll just have to wait and see. As for your patients, Cindy's referring them all to a doctor in Chicago until we can analyze the crime scene and get someone to come in and clean it up."

"I need to call my insurance company. I have renter's insurance on my apartment, and the office is fully covered."

"You can do all that later. First, we need to have a talk."

Nate sighed. "Why do I not like the sound of that?"

"Because I think you know what I'm about to say. Nate, don't you think it's just too much of a coincidence that on the same night you receive a blow to the head, Amy and Mike — the only friends you have in town — are called to the bedside of a sick aunt over seven hundred miles away? The very same night that your apartment is trashed and your office is vandalized?"

"You aren't suggesting that Amy and Mike had something to do with this?" Nate looked ready to do battle, even as tired as he obviously was.

"Of course not. I believe the man who hit you set it up so that Amy and Mike would get that call and leave you with no choice but to go home to your apartment, alone. I think he went there to kill you, Nate."

Chapter Three

When Brandon called his office and told them he would be at home for the rest of the day, Nate sagged with relief. In less than twenty-four hours, Brandon Nash had gone from perfect stranger to pillar of strength. Every time Nate tried to sink into himself, Brandon was there to pull him right back out.

After hours spent dealing with the insurance company and worrying about why he still hadn't heard from Mike and Amy, Nate was at the point of exhaustion. He made no protest when Brandon led him upstairs and tucked him into bed. He was asleep before Brandon could close the door behind him.

During his years at Atlanta Northern, Nate had learned how to sleep through almost anything. Sleeping in the on-call room was something every doctor did at one time or another, especially a doctor in charge of critically ill newborns whose condition could take a turn for the worse at any given moment. Despite all that conditioning, Nate came awake with a start the minute he felt cool fingertips fluttering across his forehead. He opened his eyes expecting to see Brandon, not a five-foot female with red hair and eyes the same color as the sheriff's.

"Sorry, honey, I didn't mean to wake you. I was just checking to make sure you don't have a fever. Brandon said you threw up this morning."

"Yes ma'am, I did, but—"

"I know. All that blood would have made me sick, too. I could just about throttle that son of mine for taking you into that mess in the first place. And you with a head injury, too."

"Your son?"

"Yes, of course. Brandon—" She stopped for a minute. "Good grief. I forgot to even introduce myself. I'm Gale Nash, Brandon's mother."

Gale was a beauty. To look at her, no one would guess she was pushing sixty. She was short and trim, with a pixie's face and the same dazzling smile as Brandon. Nate fell in love with her right then and there. "Nice to meet you, ma'am. I'm—"

"Nathan Morris, but Brandon calls you Nate."

"Yes, ma'am. He does."

Gale sat down in the chair next to the bed. "So, how are you holding up?"

"I'm all right."

"No offense, Nate, but I have eight children. I think I can tell when someone is just telling me what they think I want to hear. You, my boy, are definitely not all right."

And before he could answer, he was being held and rocked against a warm breast that smelled of Chanel Number Five and allspice. The comfort of the scents and the feel of being held by a mother, even if she wasn't his own, was a novel feeling for Nate. One he could get used to. He allowed himself to relax and go with the feeling. When he finally pulled away, Nate was surprised at how much better he felt. He was a little embarrassed, too, to have latched on to a total stranger like that. "Mrs. Nash, I'm so sorry. I don't know what came over me."

"First, you can call me Gale, or even Mom, but not Mrs. Nash. Mrs. Nash is my mother-in-law, a lovely woman, but not exactly how I see myself. In twenty years, maybe. Second, you don't have a thing in this world to be sorry for. I'm sure if your mother were here, she would do the same thing."

Nate shook his head. "No, ma'am, she wouldn't. My parents disowned me when they found out I was gay."

Gale reached over and squeezed Nate's hand. "In that case, I hope you'll feel free to lean on us. You already know Brandon and Keith. When you're feeling better, I'll introduce you to the whole clan. Right now, though, I want you to try and go back to sleep. Those dark circles under your eyes are just screaming for some rest. After your nap, come downstairs and eat some of the supper I brought for you and Brandon. I swear that boy doesn't know how to fix anything that doesn't come in a plastic tray."

As she was leaving, Nate said, "Gale?"

"Yes, sweetheart?"

"Thanks."

"That's what family is for, Nate."

* ~ * ~ * ~ * ~ *

Gale Nash sat down at the kitchen table, madder than Brandon had seen her since the day he and his brothers accidentally brained one of Grandpa Taylor's goats with a potato gun. Not even Sasha, who adored his mom, was brave enough to come into the kitchen with the agitated woman, wisely choosing to take a nap on her doggie bed.

"What kind of mother disowns a sweet boy like that just because he's gay? I'd like to get that witch alone for about ten minutes, just enough time to put the fear of God into her."

"Mother."

"Save it, Brandon. A woman like that doesn't deserve a son like Nathan."

"From what Nate told me, I think it was mostly his father's decision. I believe his mother and brother probably just go along with whatever he says."

Gale got up and started unpacking the food she'd brought. "Maybe so, but no man is worth abandoning your own child. Do you think for one minute I would let your father tell me I couldn't see one of my babies?"

Brandon grinned as he went up behind his mom and gave her a squeeze. He might be over a foot taller than her, but all Gale's children knew she was the boss. "Not all mothers are like you, Mom." He kissed her cheek and then went to the cupboard to get some plates. "By the way, have I told you lately how lucky I am to have a mom like you?"

"Yes, but I never get tired of hearing it." She put the last of the food on the counter and then turned to her son. "So, how come Nathan is sleeping in the guestroom instead of in your bed?"

Brandon almost dropped the glassware he was holding. "Jesus, Mom, I just met the guy yesterday."

"Don't take the Lord's name in vain. And don't give me that bull. When have you ever let not knowing someone stop you from taking him to bed?"

"I admit, I've had my share of one night stands, but, for your information, I haven't been with anybody since I ended it with Jeff. Besides, Nate isn't like that, he's—"

"Special?"

Brandon paused before answering. "Yes." His mother turned her back to him, but not before he saw her smile.

"That's all I wanted to know."

Brandon closed the cabinet and went to stand in front of his mother. "You knew?"

"That you haven't been with anyone since Jeff turned from a prince into a frog? Of course I knew. And I was pretty sure you were attracted to Nate, but I wanted to be sure."

"You are absolutely spooky, you know that? How do you know so much about my sex life?"

"I've told you before, Brandon — mothers just know these things. Why do you think you and your brothers and sisters were never able to get away with anything?"

Brandon pulled a chair away from the table and straddled it. "So, Madam Psychic, tell me what you see when you look at Nate."

Gale sat down across from her son. "I see a man who's almost at the end of his rope, Bran. I don't think he's ever really dealt with losing his family the way he did. I believe these attacks have reopened a wound that never healed in the first place." She reached over and put her hand on Brandon's arm. "You did the right thing by calling me. That boy is going to need all the love and attention he can get if he's going to make it through this."

"He'll make it."

"You sound pretty sure of yourself."

Brandon shook his head. "Mom, do you remember what I was like when I came back here from Quantico?"

Gale shuddered. "As if I could ever forget. I'd heard about post-traumatic stress disorder, but, until then, I'd never actually seen it up close. Thank goodness you got over it."

"Yes, but what I haven't told you is that I still can't sleep through the night without reliving that day all over again."

The alarm on Gale's face was the very reason Brandon hadn't told her about the dreams before now. "Honey, you aren't still sick, are you?"

"Calm down, Mom. I'm fine. The psychologist they sent me to said I'd probably always have those dreams, even though I'm psychologically sound again. After three years, I've learned to live with them. The thing is, last night, I didn't have a single nightmare." When he thought about the dreams he did have, he blushed.

Gale's children didn't call her "ole eagle eye" for nothing. "Did you, by any chance, dream about a certain eligible young doctor last night?" His silence was answer enough. "Well, it's obvious he's good for you. I hope you won't do anything stupid like letting him slip away."

"Don't worry, Mom. Letting Nate go is the last thing on my mind. And until we catch the creep who's after him, I plan to keep him here with me."

"When were you gonna tell me about these plans you've made for my life?"

Brandon and Gale looked up at the same time to see a rumpled Nate standing in the doorway. Brandon's voice was hoarse when he said, "How long have you been standing there?"

"Just long enough to know that my living arrangements have changed." Nate walked into the kitchen and Brandon got a good look at him. His hair was matted down in spots and sticking straight out in others. His clothes were wrinkled from being slept in, and his face was drawn and haggard. Even though Nate looked like a reject from a zombie movie, Brandon's body went into overdrive the minute he saw him.

Gale got up and grabbed her purse. Brandon stood as his mother did and pulled her into a hug. "Thanks for coming, Mom. Oh, and thanks for bringing dinner."

"Anytime, honey." She walked over and gave Nathan a warm hug and kiss. "You hang in there. I'll call and check on you tomorrow."

"Thanks, Gale. For everything."

She patted his cheek. "That's what moms are for." She kissed Brandon again before moving towards the door. "Call if you need me." Waving to them both, she left.

Brandon took Nate's hand and led him toward the table. "Sit down while I dish up some of this stuff Mom brought."

Nate took a seat, but said, "I'm not really hungry."

"Nate, you haven't had anything since that two-dollar ham sandwich at the hospital last night. You've got to eat something."

Nate eyed him warily. "Why are you doing this?"

"Doing what?"

"This. Being so nice to me, bringing me to your house. Why would you go out of your way to help a stranger?"

"Someone is after you. I take my responsibilities as sheriff seriously, and I plan to do whatever it takes to keep you safe. In my opinion, you'll be safer here than anywhere else. Even when Amy and Mike get back, they can't offer you the protection I can. And, for the record, we aren't strangers. Granted, we just met last night, but there's a connection between us. I feel it, and I believe you do too."

"Yes."

"Yes, what?"

Nate rubbed his hand across his face. "Yes, I feel it. I just don't know what to do about it."

Brandon took the plastic wrap off of the green bean casserole. "I vote we don't do anything about it. We should just relax and let things happen naturally."

"Before we do, there's something I need to tell you, just so you'll understand why I'm so freaked out by all this."

"Go ahead."

"Last night, when I told you that Rick and I never...well, you know..."

"Never made love?" Damned if Brandon didn't get turned on just from watching Nate blush. Thankfully, Nate didn't seem to notice.

He said, "Right. Well, after Rick broke up with me, I was too afraid of getting hurt to try again, so I didn't."

"I understand, but we're just talking about relationships here, right? I mean, you've been out on dates and had a few flings, haven't you?"

"No."

Brandon almost dropped the corn on the cob he was unwrapping. "Nate, are you telling me that you're still a virgin?"

Nate nodded, but hung his head so Brandon wouldn't see his embarrassment.

Brandon crossed the room in three long strides and pulled Nate up and into his arms. "You have nothing to be embarrassed about, baby. When you're ready to make a commitment, you'll be able to give your partner a gift that not many people — male or female — can offer. That's something to be proud of."

Nate relaxed against him. "Then why do I feel like such a freak?"

"You sure don't feel like a freak to me."

Nate gave him a playful shove. "You have a one track mind, you know that?"

Brandon kissed his cheek and went back to unwrapping the food. "So I've been told. If it makes you feel any better, I haven't exactly lived like Casanova these last few years myself. I'm not a virgin, by any means, but I've been celibate since I ended it with Jeff. And it's not like Jeff and I had much of a sex life toward the end, anyway. He didn't like the hours I worked, and I didn't like the fact that he fucked around behind my back. Not exactly a match made in heaven, was it?"

"No, but thank you for telling me about it. I don't know why, but it does make me feel better."

Brandon filled two plates with green beans, corn, and his mother's melt-in-your mouth pork roast. He set one of the plates in front of Nate and poured two glasses of milk. "So, do you feel comfortable staying here now that you know I'm not expecting you to 'put out' as part of your room and board?"

"As long as you're sure you don't mind having me here, then I'm grateful for the protection." His voice dropped a little. "And for the company."

Brandon sat down at the table and said grace. As they ate, he watched Nate from the corner of his eye. Conversation was limited, but Brandon couldn't remember ever having enjoyed a meal more.

* ~ * ~ * ~ * ~ *

When she and Mike got down to Atlanta and found his aunt not only healthy and whole but off visiting relatives in Savannah, Amy had connected the phony summons to Nate's attack. She and Mike spent the whole night at the airport trying to catch the soonest flight back to Chicago. She went first to Nate's apartment, freaking out when she saw the swarm of deputies gathering evidence from the ransacked townhouse. After going to the office and finding much the same thing, Amy was ready to file a missing person's report on Nate until Cindy tracked her down and told her he was with Brandon.

He was always with Brandon. During the last week, Brandon had accompanied Nate everywhere, including going on the many shopping trips needed to replace his ruined wardrobe and personal belongings. Nate had received no threats since the night of the attack, but Brandon was taking no chances. He'd protested Nate's going back to work, but had finally given in after making Nate promise not to leave the office by himself. That morning, Brandon had even made one of his men follow Nate to work.

Even though no incriminating evidence was found and the blood on his clothes had turned out to be pig's blood, news of Nate's near miss had produced one startling side effect: everyone in town knew he was gay. That meant he was fair game for every gay man in town. Even straight women — those who had a gay friend or relative — flocked to the re-opened office to put in their bids. So far that morning, Nate had received three offers for dinner and four phone numbers. It wasn't even lunchtime yet.

Because it was his and Amy's first day back at work in over a week, the place was swamped. In a way, he was grateful. As long as Amy was occupied with patients, she wouldn't have time to hover over him. Between Gale's calls and visits and Amy's fussing, Nate was being mothered to death.

Nate knocked on the door and entered the exam room without checking the name on the file in his hand. He found an elderly lady sitting on the exam table, her short legs dangling over the side. She was wearing a turquoise blouse and an orange skirt. Though Nate was sure he'd never seen her before, there was something familiar about her.

He crossed the room and shook her hand. "Hi. I'm Dr. Morris. So, what seems to be the problem, Mrs..." he glanced down at the chart, "Taylor?" *Uh-oh. That's why she looks so familiar. I've spent every night of the last week dreaming about eyes the exact same color as hers.*

She smiled. It should have been a comforting sight coming from a sweet little old lady like her, but for some reason, Nate felt like he was about to be grilled by the Spanish Inquisition.

"Actually, Doctor, I think I may have a touch of gout. Runs in my family, you know. Speaking of family, tell me about yours."

Nate said, "Why don't we get you checked out first? We can talk about my family later."

"Of course, dear." The patient was silent while Nate examined one of her stocking-clad legs. After a minute, she said, "I hope it's nothing serious. I have to be well enough to keep up with those great-grandchildren of mine. Speaking of grandchildren, I believe you know my grandson."

Nate almost laughed but caught himself. "Really? Who's your grandson?"

"Brandon Nash. He's the sheriff here in Reed. A fine boy, if I do say so. He's a homosexual, you know."

Nate was bent over checking her reflexes when she added the last bit of information. The matter-of-fact way she said it caused him to drop the reflex hammer on his toe.

"Are you all right, Doctor?"

"Yes, ma'am. Just a little clumsy today. Mrs. Taylor—"

"Please, call me Abigail."

"All right, Abigail. I can't find any signs of gout. Are you in a lot of pain?"

"Some. Perhaps you should check me over one more time."

Nate did as he was told, praying he would find something so he could write her a prescription and send her home. He should have known it wouldn't be that easy.

"So, Doctor, I hear you're a homosexual too."

Nate stood up so fast his stethoscope slid from around his neck to the floor with a metallic thud.

"You certainly do have a case of the dropsy's today, Dr. Morris. Are you getting enough sleep?"

"Yes, ma'am."

"Such a polite boy, too. Although you never did answer my question."

Knowing he wasn't going to get around answering, Nate picked up his stethoscope and said, "Yes, ma'am, I am a homosexual, and I do know Brandon. In fact, I'm staying with him for a few days until the person who vandalized my apartment and office is caught."

Abigail nodded sympathetically. "I heard all about that dreadful business. Imagine targeting someone just because they like men instead of women. What is this world coming to?" She watched as Nate made a notation on her chart. "Doctor?"

"Yes, ma'am?"

"I wonder if I might ask you a personal question."

Nate couldn't imagine anything any more personal than what she'd already asked, but he found himself saying yes, anyway.

"Well, I heard that anal sex is very popular lately, even among heterosexuals. I thought maybe you could tell me whether or not you enjoy it. My husband and I might like to try it sometime."

Nate pressed down so hard on the chart, the plastic casing of his ballpoint pen snapped in half. Before he could answer her, the door swung open. A furious Brandon stood on the threshold.

"Grandma, please tell me you aren't giving Nate a hard time."

"Why, Brandon, what on earth are you doing here?"

"I was on my way to ask Nate to have lunch with me. Imagine my surprise when I saw your car out front."

Abigail had the good grace to blush. "I came to have Dr. Morris look at my gout. Runs in the family, you know."

"Nobody in our family has ever had a case of gout, you included."

"There's a first time for everything. Dr. Morris has been taking excellent care of me. He's a homosexual, just like you are, dear."

Nate had to hide his grin when he saw Brandon's jaw start to twitch.

"So I've heard."

"Yes. In fact, Dr. Morris was just about to tell me whether or not he likes anal sex. Grandpa and I are thinking of branching out."

"What?"

"Anal sex, dear. It's just like regular sex except—"

Brandon was across the room in an instant. He gently but firmly lifted Abigail off the table. "Come on, Grandma. I'll walk you out to your car."

"Oh, but what about my gout?"

Nate couldn't help but love the nosy little darling. He kissed her on the cheek just as Brandon was dragging her out of the room. "I think you're going to be fine, but I'll call you in a mild anti-inflammatory just to be on the safe side."

"Thank you, Dr. Morris."

"Please, call me Nathan or Nate."

"I've never called a doctor by his first name before. Are you sure it's proper?"

"Actually, it's one of my rules."

"Really?"

"Yes, ma'am. I make it a practice never to discuss anal sex with anyone unless I'm on a first name basis with them."

Brandon wasted no time hustling her out the door. While Brandon was gone, Nate called the pharmacy, finishing just as Brandon came back.

Nate motioned him into the office. He sat down behind his desk while Brandon took one of the wingback chairs on the other side.

"On behalf of my entire family, I apologize."

Nate laughed. "Not necessary. She's a real cutie. Feisty, but cute. She reminds me a lot of my own grandmother. I imagine she's heard all about our living arrangements and was curious to know what kind of man her grandson had installed in his house. So, what's this I hear about lunch?"

"Yeah, about that...there's something you should know."

"Don't tell me you're backing out of the best offer I've had all day?"

Brandon smiled, but it didn't quite reach his eyes. "No, I'm definitely taking you to lunch, but we have to stop off somewhere first."

"You're scaring me."

"Nate, somebody called your landlord this morning claiming to be with the Atlanta P.D. The caller identified himself as Detective Wade. He claimed your grandmother passed away and he needed to locate you so arrangements could be made. Since your grandmother passed away ten years ago, I think it's safe to say this was the same guy who trashed your apartment. Atlanta P.D. has no record of a Detective Wade, and neither do the surrounding counties."

"Did the apartment manager tell him anything?"

"No. One of our deputies had briefed him about giving out information on you. The manager was able to record the call on his answering machine, but I'm afraid the recording isn't very clear. Before we go to lunch, I'd like for you to go by and listen to it anyway, just in case."

"Whatever you think is best." Nate stood and grabbed his jacket.

As they were leaving the office, Brandon said, "Before I forget, Grandma wants us to come to dinner two weeks from Sunday. The whole family is going to be there."

"Are they all like her?"

"No. Most of them are worse."

~~*~*~*

Listening to the recording proved to be a waste of time, just as Brandon suspected it would. The sound quality was poor, but it was also evident that the caller was using some kind of device to disguise his voice. Nate just shook his head and walked out of the office.

Brandon drove them to Hailey's Café for lunch. As usual, the place was packed. Hailey Johnson, the owner, was an old school friend of Brandon's. She was also one of the best cooks in the county. The four-star food was no match for the spectacle provided by the handsome sheriff and the mysterious new doctor, though. The minute Brandon and Nate walked in, all eyes were focused on them.

"Do I have something in my teeth?" Nate asked.

Brandon laughed as the waitress seated them and went to get their drinks. "Malcolm Davis over at the *Reed Dailey Courier* did a three page write up about the attack on you, complete with pictures of your apartment and office. The idea was to show that the folks here in Reed are not going to tolerate gay bashing. I think all the article really did was make everybody in town want to know more about you."

Nate glanced up from his menu. "I knew word had gotten out somehow. My office was packed this morning."

Brandon was just about to say something else when their drinks arrived. Instead of being brought out by Selena, the waitress who'd taken the order, the drinks arrived by way of Shane, a twenty-one-year-old hunk who'd been eyeing Nate since the minute he'd walked into the restaurant.

Shane flashed his perfect teeth in a brilliant smile that made his dark green eyes crinkle at the corners. His hair was a lighter shade of blond than Nate's, gelled into tousled order. From where Brandon was sitting, it was obvious Shane was on the make.

"Afternoon, Sheriff," he said in a husky voice that made Brandon grit his teeth. "Here's your coffee. I know you take yours black, but I wasn't certain about your friend, so I brought milk and sugar, just in case."

"He takes his black, too." Brandon did his best to keep the irritation out of his voice, but it was damn hard to do.

"So, what can I get for you, Sheriff?"

Brandon ordered the usual: B.L.T., fries, and glass of sweetened ice tea. Then it was Nate's turn.

"So what can I get for you... I'm sorry, what did you say your name was?"

Nathan extended his hand. "I didn't, but it's Nathan. Nathan Morris."

Shane shook Nate's hand a little bit longer than necessary to Brandon's way of thinking.

"I'm Shane Haskins. You're the new doctor everybody's talking about. I heard you were cute, but no one told me you were such a babe."

Much to Brandon's disgust, Nate actually blushed.

"Uh, thanks. I think I'll have the same thing Brandon is having."

Shane said, "Good choice," but made no move to leave the table. "So, I guess you haven't had a chance to get to know many of the folks here in Reed, what with being new in town and all."

"Not really, no."

"Well, if you aren't busy Friday night, maybe you'd like to get to—"

"Shane, do you think you could put that order in now? Nate has patients waiting, and I need to get back to the office." Brandon used the same tone with Shane that he used on unruly suspects.

"What? Oh, sure thing, Sheriff." Shane left, but not before winking at Nate.

Nate gave Brandon a look of disapproval. "Did you have to be so rude? The guy was just being friendly."

Brandon snorted into his coffee. "Friendly, my ass. He was two steps away from asking you out."

"Is that a crime here in Reed?" Nate didn't expect an answer, and he didn't get one.

The meal was eaten in silence. Brandon had never felt such jealousy before, not even when he'd caught Jeff screwing around on him the first time. He did his best to keep the seething anger he was feeling under control, but when Shane brought the check and slipped Nate his phone number, Brandon's patience reached its end. He threw his money on the table, growling when Nate reached for his wallet. "I invited you to lunch. I'll damn well pay for it."

Nate said nothing. He followed Brandon out to the S.U.V. and was about to get in when Brandon put his hand on Nate's shoulder and stopped him.

"Throw it away."

"What?"

"Shane's phone number. I want you to throw it away."

"Why? He seems like a nice guy."

Brandon took a step closer, placing Nate between the S.U.V. and himself. "I don't care how nice he is. No way are you going out with that guy." Brandon could tell that Nate was starting to get mad by the flush in his cheeks.

"Who are you to tell me what to do?"

Brandon took a deep breath, but it did nothing to cool his anger. "I'll tell you who I am. I'm the guy who's watched you go to the guest room every night when what I really wanted to do was drag you across the hall to my own bed. I'm the man who's kept his hands off you because I promised you we would let things happen naturally, the whole time fighting the urge to strip you down and run my tongue over every square inch of your body. For a solid week, I've been going out of my mind wanting you and trying to keep my distance. You want to know who I am? Here, let me show you." He pushed Nate up against the side of the truck and covered Nate's mouth with his own.

At first Nate was too stunned to react, and Brandon was too angry to notice. Pretty soon, though, anger and shock gave way to desire as Brandon devoured Nate with his mouth. When Nate wrapped his arms around Brandon's neck and parted his lips, Brandon moaned and swept his tongue inside. He ground his hips against Nate, his erection threatening to break the zipper of his jeans. Heedless of anyone who might be watching, Brandon kissed Nate until they were forced to pull apart from lack of air.

Nate groaned. "Don't stop."

Brandon rested his forehead against Nate's. "I've got to, baby. I'm about two seconds away from having to arrest myself for public indecency."

Nate reached into his pocket and pulled out a piece of paper. "Here."

Still reeling from the kiss, Brandon said, "What's that?"

"Shane's phone number. I never intended to use it, you know."

Brandon laughed as he helped Nate into the passenger seat. "I hope all our arguments will end like this one." Nate's smile was answer enough.

Brandon got behind the wheel and started the engine. As he was buckling his seat belt, Nate reached over and took his hand. "What are you doing?"

"Letting things happen naturally. Was I wrong, or did you just declare ownership back there?"

Brandon pulled the S.U.V. out onto Main Street but kept a firm hold on Nate's hand. "That all depends on whether or not you liked it, and whether or not you mind being declared 'private property'."

"Yes, I liked it, and no, I don't mind."

"In that case, consider yourself off the market."

Nate got quiet for a minute. "Bran?"

"Yes?"

"What about sex?"

"Does it scare you?"

"Maybe a little bit."

Brandon brought Nate's hand up to his lips and kissed the palm. "How about if we keep it light until you're ready? You keep sleeping in the guestroom, and we'll confine all our physical activities to the 'making out' category." Brandon could almost see the tension ease out of Nate.

"Thank you for understanding."

"That doesn't mean I'm going to be able to handle watching other guys make a play for you, Nate. I may be a jealous ass, but I'm afraid there's not much I can do about it."

"I don't want anyone else, Bran. I hope you believe that."

They'd just pulled up to the doctor's office. Brandon got out and met Nate over on the passenger's side. "I believe you, Nate." He looked down at his watch. "I should go. The driver of the eighteen-wheeler that overturned last week is coming by to sign off on the accident report." He leaned in and gave Nate another kiss, only this time his touch was gentle and unhurried. Brandon was really starting to get into it when he heard a noise behind him and turned to see Amy standing there with a big grin on her face.

"Well, it's about time. If Mike had waited a whole week to kiss me, I believe I'd have taken matters into my own hands."

"Do you tell her everything?"

Nate whispered, "Almost" in such a sexy voice that Brandon was tempted to kiss him again. When he saw the look of concern cross Nate's face, he stopped.

Nate was watching Amy. "What's wrong, girl? You look like somebody just peed in your sandbox."

Amy shook her head. "Not exactly, but close enough. While you and Brandon were at lunch, you had a visitor. He's in your office waiting for you. I came out here to give you a heads up."

"Who is it, Amy?"

"It's your brother, Nate. Seth is here to see you."

Chapter Four

When Nate thought back to that night six years earlier when he'd ceased to be a brother and a son, he always pictured someone else, a man who existed in another lifetime. The new life he'd worked so hard to carve for himself offered a certain amount of insulation against the pain of his abandonment. Walking into his office and seeing Seth again would rip away all the layers of protection he'd built up. Nate wasn't sure if he was ready to have his shell torn open.

Amy went back inside, but Nate just stood there, his mind refusing to tell his feet to move. He heard Brandon dial a number and tell the person on the other end to handle things at the office for the rest of the afternoon, then he felt a pair of iron-strong arms wrap around him and pull him close.

"Are you okay?"

"I don't know. After all this time, what could he possibly have to say to me?"

Brandon just shook his head and held Nate tighter.

Nate wasn't sure how long they stood there like that, but he was thankful he and Amy had a private parking spot where patients and passersby couldn't see them. Within minutes, the warmth from Brandon's body began to sink into his own, causing Nate's muscles to relax and his head to clear. He was reluctant to end their embrace, but he knew he would have to face Seth sooner or later. He might as well get it over with. He pulled away and took Brandon's hand. "I think I'm ready now."

"Are you sure?"

"No, but I don't have a choice. Will you go in there with me?"

Brandon nodded. "If you want me to be there, then I'm there."

Nate pulled him toward the office. "I do." He stopped before he got to the back door, the one only employees used. "Before we go in, there's something I need to tell you."

Brandon led him over to the picnic table that stood just outside the doorway. He and Nate sat across from each other, Nate holding his hand in a death grip. "You can tell me anything. I think you know that by now."

"I'm learning." Nate took a deep breath. "Remember how I told you my dad got a restraining order forbidding me from contacting either my parents or my brother?" When Brandon nodded, Nate went on. "Well, since Seth was a minor when my dad took out the order, it expired when he turned eighteen. After that, it was up to Seth to take out another one."

Brandon gave his hand a squeeze. "You went to see him, didn't you?"

"On his eighteenth birthday. I found out where he was from some mutual friends. See, I convinced myself that the only reason Seth wouldn't see me was because my dad wouldn't let him. Don't worry, though. My little brother set me straight." Nate managed a weak smile. "Well, maybe straight isn't the right word. Let's just say, he let me know in no uncertain terms exactly what he thought of me." The sympathy he saw on Brandon's face was almost Nate's undoing.

"What happened?"

"He started screaming at me, telling me to get away from him. He said I was dead to him, that I died in his eyes the day I decided to become a fag. He said he only hoped that someone would come along and put me out of my misery before I decided to molest a child or something." When Nate saw the anger that reddened Brandon's face, he rubbed his fingers across the back of Brandon's hand and added, "He was only repeating what my father said the night they all found out I was gay. My dad said it was a good thing I would never have children, because a pervert like me would end up either raping them myself or allowing another pervert to do it. Anyway, the day after I went to see Seth, he filed his own restraining order against me. That was four years ago. I haven't heard from him since."

Brandon circled around to Nate's side of the table and pulled him close. "You don't have to see him, Nate. I'll go in there right now and tell him he has to leave."

"No. I can handle it, as long as you'll stay with me."

Brandon kissed him tenderly. "I'm not going anywhere. Face it, babe — you're stuck with me."

* ~ * ~ * ~ * ~ *

Part of Brandon's training, first as a profiler and then later as sheriff, was never to let his emotions get in the way when dealing with a case. Nate may have started out as a case, but he'd been more than that from almost the minute Brandon laid eyes on him. The thought of anyone hurting Nate made Brandon want to hide him away from the rest of the world and stand guard at the door. It was hard to hate a man he'd never met, but the things Seth Morris had done to Nate made it difficult for Brandon not to despise him.

When they walked into the office, Seth was seated in one of the chairs in front of Nate's desk. Nate teased Brandon about how much he and Keith favored one another, but the resemblance between the Morris brothers was startling: same dark-blond hair, same chocolate eyes. Nate was a couple of inches taller and a bit more muscular, but there was no mistaking the fact that they were brothers.

Seth stood up when they entered. He started toward Nate, but Brandon positioned himself between them. Seth stopped short and looked at his brother. "Nate. It's been a while, huh?"

"Four years. You aren't supposed to be here, Seth. You're violating your own restraining order."

"No, I dropped that about six months ago." He looked up at Brandon's hardened jaw. "Uh, Nate, do you think we could talk? Alone?"

Nate reached for Brandon's hand. "Seth, this is Brandon Nash. Sheriff Brandon Nash. He and I are seeing each other. That means what concerns me, concerns him. He stays."

Seth didn't seem to like having an audience, but at least he was smart enough not to object further.

"There's a small sitting room upstairs. If we're gonna talk, we'll have more privacy up there," Nate said. He turned to Brandon. "Will you take Seth on up while I ask Amy to cover my patients?"

"Sure." Brandon started towards the stairs, leaving Seth to follow.

The upstairs sitting room was little more than a landing with a couch and a couple of armchairs, but at least it was private. Brandon sat down on the overstuffed sofa, Seth settled himself into a chair, and the two waited for Nate in awkward silence.

Finally Seth said, "So, you and my brother, huh?"

Brandon crossed his legs, right ankle over left knee. "Yeah, me and your brother. You got a problem with that?"

Seth leaned forward, sizing Brandon up. "You don't exactly seem like Nate's type."

"Meaning I'm nothing like that Landon guy he was engaged to for five minutes?"

"You're definitely nothing like Rick."

The sarcasm in Seth's voice might have bothered Brandon if he gave a rat's ass what the guy thought. As it was, Brandon was having a hell of a time not picking the little bastard up and throwing him head first from one of the second story windows. "You don't say."

"Rick was cultured. He liked the finer things in life, things like the opera and the symphony. You look like you'd be more at home at a tractor pull than Carnegie Hall."

Brandon leaned back against the cushions. "So what you're really saying is, because I prefer Budweiser to Dom Perignon, I'm not good enough for Nate."

Seth fidgeted in his chair. "That's not what I said. I just don't want to see my brother get hurt."

Brandon leaned forward again, his eyes pinning Seth in place. "Now see, that's where I get a bit confused. Must be brain damage from the exhaust fumes at all those monster truck rallies. What I'm wondering is, what's your definition of hurt? Is hurt having the man you love walk out on you because Mommy and Daddy threaten to cut off the ole checkbook, the way Landon left Nate? Or maybe your definition of hurt is having your eighteen-year-old brother throw you out of his life — again — after filing a restraining order against you and calling you a child-molesting pervert?"

Seth's face turned a deep crimson but his eyes were defiant. "I was just a kid. I made a mistake."

"Took you four years to realize that, did it? Well, while you were finding yourself, making your way, or whatever you 'cultured' boys call it, your brother was suffering — alone. And if you think I'm going to sit here and watch you destroy what little peace he's been able to find for himself, you're sadly mistaken. I'll do whatever it takes to keep Nate from being hurt again, by you or anyone else."

"Are you threatening me, Sheriff?"

"No, sir. That would be uncivilized. I'm simply telling you that if you do anything to harm Nate, you won't like the consequences. Where I come from, that's called promising, not threatening."

Seth might have responded had Nate not chosen that moment to come into the room. He took the seat next to Brandon on the couch, close enough that Brandon could feel his trembling. Brandon put his arm around Nate's shoulders and received a grateful smile for the effort.

Brandon was proud of the strength in Nate's voice when he said, "Seth, what are you doing here?"

Seth moved forward to perch on the edge of his chair. From his viewpoint, Brandon could see that Seth was shaking almost as bad as Nate. If the guy wasn't such a self-righteous prick, Brandon might have felt sorry for him.

"If I told you I was sorry for what happened four years ago, would it make a difference?"

"I don't know, Seth. Sorry if that's not what you want to hear, but that's just how it is."

"Will you give me a chance to explain why I did it?"

Brandon's heart sank when he saw Nate nod at his brother's request. Brandon settled back against the cushions, pulling Nate with him and holding him tight to his side. If Seth was uncomfortable with their closeness, he didn't show it.

"Nate, before we go any further, I need to tell you something: I'm gay. I've been involved with another man for several months now."

"Look, Seth, I don't know what kind of game you're playing, but—"

Seth pulled a picture out of his wallet and handed it to Nate. The photo showed Seth with a good-looking man. They had their arms wrapped around each other. "His name is Philip Patterson. He's a few years older than I am, but Mother said, as long as he treats me well, she's all for it."

The disbelief in Nate's voice was cutting. "You're telling me Mother knows about this, and she's fine with it?"

"She and Dad both do. That's one of the reasons I'm here, Nate. We want you back. All of us."

"I'm twenty-eight-years old, Seth. Even if I believed what you're saying — and I'm not sure I do — don't you think I'm a little long in the tooth to move back home with the folks?"

"That's not what I'm asking. I'm just trying to tell you that Mom and Dad want to be a part of your life again." Seth lowered his head. "And I want my brother back."

"Why now?"

"Some crazy guy bashes you in the head, trashes your house, and you ask me why?"

Brandon switched from concerned boyfriend to sheriff in a one-second rotation. "You mind telling me just how in the hell you know about all that?"

Seth again went to his wallet, this time pulling out a faxed copy of a clipping from *The Reed Daily Courier* about Nate's attack. "Mr. Davis at the paper has a son who manages one of the Mor-co franchises in Chicago. Davis recognized the name and faxed the entire article to Dad. He and Mom are scared to death, Nate."

Nate displayed the first show of anger Brandon had seen since Seth arrived.

"And what, they were so concerned they sent you to do their dirty work?" Nate stood up. "Well, you've done what you came for. I'm not sure who that guy in the picture with you is, but I believe he's your lover like I believe Elvis is downstairs waiting in my reception area. You go back home and assure Mom and Dad that I'm not going to do anything to further disgrace the Morris name. And hey, if this guy who's stalking me does happen to kill me, I'll make sure they list 'none' under the 'relatives' column of my obituary. That way neither you nor our illustrious parents will have to answer any embarrassing questions about the family fag."

Seth didn't as much as blink. "I was raped, Nate."

"I beg your pardon?"

"When I was fifteen. I was raped by a guy I met at a party. It happened a few months before you came out."

Nate sat back down. His voice was thin and tight. "What happened?"

Seth rubbed his hand over his face the same way Nate did when he was nervous. "When I was thirteen, I started having feelings for other guys. Girls did nothing for me, but a picture of Brad Pitt gave me a boner every time. I waited to see if it would go away, but it didn't. A couple of years later, I worked up the courage to come out to one of the guys at school who was already out. He invited me to this college party a friend of his was having. I met a few guys, had a few drinks. That's where I met Andy. He seemed perfect: eighteen, sexy, shy, kinda quiet. He asked me out for the following weekend, and I went. That first night, he didn't try anything heavier than holding my hand. I thought it was because he was such a gentleman. The next time we went out, he corrected that impression for me." Tears were rolling down his face, but Seth continued with the story. "On our second date, he took me to his place, an off campus apartment he shared with a couple of roommates. We started drinking, and then he made his move. He was all over me. Hell, I had never even kissed a guy before, and here was Andy, undoing my zipper. I fought him off, but he was too strong for me." Seth shuddered at the memory and stopped long enough to wipe away the tears and pull himself together. "When he was done, he passed out from all the alcohol and I was able to get away. I ran for a few blocks before I found a pay phone. I called Dad to come and get me and told him the whole story."

Nate was speechless so Brandon said, "Did he take you to the hospital? Please tell me you pressed charges."

A shadow fell over Seth's face. "No. Dad was afraid the whole world would find out I was gay if he did that. He said we would handle it privately because the doctors at the hospital and the police just wouldn't understand. Instead, Dad sent me to a shrink who convinced me I wasn't really gay, that I was just confused. I found out later she belonged to one of those religions that believe gays should be rounded up and shot. At the time, I was vulnerable enough to believe her when she told me all homosexuals were rapists and molesters like Andy."

"So, just a few months later, when Nate told you he was gay—"

"I freaked. In all honesty, I think that's what happened with Dad, too. I convinced myself that Nate was evil, that he was just like Andy. It wasn't until after Nate came to see me on my birthday that I began to wonder if maybe Dad and the therapist were wrong. I mean, I still had feelings for other guys. Not even being raped was enough to kill those. I found a therapist at school who helped me work through it all. It took me a couple of years, but I finally realized that being gay and being raped were two entirely separate things. Hell, straight women get raped and they don't just stop being straight."

Nate stood and walked over to the window. After a tense silence, he turned and said, "If everything you say is true, why did you wait for two years after finishing therapy to contact me?"

Seth walked over to Nate and took his hand. "I was ashamed, Nate. I didn't know how to apologize for the things I'd said and done. I know what happened to me is no excuse for the way I hurt you, and I don't expect you just to welcome me back into your life with open arms. All I'm asking for is a chance to get to know you again." Seth dropped Nate's hand and went back to his seat.

Nate ran his fingers through his hair and went to stand by the couch. Brandon stood and wrapped an arm around Nate's waist. Nate said, "Look, Seth, I'm really sorry for what happened to you. And I'm glad you got help, but I'm not sure what you expect of me. I mean, do you really think I'm gonna believe that Mom and Dad have had some miraculous change of heart about me just because you announced that you're gay, and they claim to accept it? I was there six years ago when they decided a fag wasn't worth having as a son. The very fact that they sent you here to plead their case proves they aren't exactly over-whelmed with concern for my well being."

Seth clasped his hands in his lap. "They're scared, Nate. Just give us a chance. Please." He came to his feet and pulled a card from his wallet, handing it to his brother. "This has my cell number and my e-mail address on it. I have to get back to Atlanta — back to school — but I have a three-day-weekend coming up the week after next. I'd like to bring Phillip up here to meet you, if that's all right." Seeing the stern look on Brandon's face, he said, "We'll stay in a hotel somewhere in Chicago, I promise. I'm not trying to force you into anything, Nate. It's just that...we were really close once. You were my hero, remember?"

"Yeah, as a matter of fact, I do."

Nate sighed, and Brandon could hear the exhaustion in his voice.

"Let me talk it over with Brandon and I'll let you know, okay?"

Seth walked over and pulled Nate into a quick hug. Brandon noticed that Nate didn't resist, but neither did he return the embrace. After a minute, Seth broke away and said, "Hey, where are you staying, anyway? Where can I contact you, beside here at the office?"

Brandon was about to tell Seth, "Don't call us, we'll call you," but Nate got to him first.

"I've got your number. Let me make the first move, all right?"

Seth didn't seem to like it, but he nodded and walked towards the door. As he was leaving, he said, "It was good to see you again, Nate. I've really missed you." Before Nate could reply, he was gone.

Brandon fell back onto the couch and pulled Nate down onto his lap. "How you holding up?"

Nate laid his head on Brandon's shoulder. "When Seth told us about being raped, all I really wanted to do was take him into my arms and cuddle him the way I did when we were kids. I wanted to hurt the bastard who did that to him, and I wanted to blast my father for not prosecuting the son of a bitch. My feelings towards my parents may be mixed, but I've never stopped loving Seth. I've always wanted to have a relationship with him, again. I guess it's the timing that makes me a little suspicious."

Brandon kissed the top of his head. "Me, too. Until we know more about this sudden turn-around in your family, let's not take any chances, okay?"

Nate snuggled closer. "I do know one thing. I couldn't have made it through today if it hadn't been for you. Thanks for seeing me through this, Bran."

Brandon just kissed him again and held him tighter. Having Nate in his arms was all the thanks he needed.

* ~ * ~ * ~ * ~ *

Over the ensuing days, they fell into a pattern. Brandon or a deputy would follow Nate to work in the mornings, then the same routine would be carried out on the way home. Usually Nate's day ended before Brandon's, so he would go home and spend a little time with Sasha before starting supper. His Grandmother Morris had passed her love of cooking to Nate, a task made even more enjoyable by the homey warmth of Brandon's kitchen.

Nate took a large mixing bowl out of the cabinet and began measuring out the ingredients for bread dough. He planned to make several loaves, then freeze what they didn't eat the first couple of days. He'd just added the eggs when Brandon came in, tired and frustrated.

Nate walked over to the refrigerator and handed Brandon a beer, then took his coat and hung it in the mudroom. Brandon muttered his thanks and headed toward the living room. Nate finished mixing the bread ingredients and put the dough aside to rise. By the time he got into the living room, Brandon was more than halfway through his beer, but his mood hadn't improved. Nate walked over to Brandon's chair and sat on his heels in front of him. "Rough day, I take it?"

"I'm beginning to think that's the status quo around here." Brandon took another swig of his beer.

"Wanna talk about it?"

"Not much to talk about."

"Considering you've consumed almost an entire sixteen ounce can of beer in less than five minutes, I find that hard to believe."

Brandon set the nearly empty can on the coffee table and leaned back in his chair. "Remember me telling you that some of the most successful businesses in Reed are owned by openly gay couples?"

"Yes."

"Well, H. and G. Dry-cleaning and Alterations is at the top of that list. Well, it was, anyway. The place burned to the ground this morning."

Nate's stomach began to roll. "Arson?"

"The official report is inconclusive, mostly because all the flammable solvents dry-cleaners use make finding a point of origin difficult. At least, it was inconclusive until I found a letter on my desk claiming responsibility." He picked up the beer and downed the rest of it. "According to the writer of said letter, it is now 'fag season' in Reed, Illinois. The fire this morning is just the beginning."

"So the attack on me really was a gay bashing?"

"Either that, or someone is going to a hell of a lot of trouble to make it look that way. The thing is, Hal Wallace and Glen Payne have both lived in Reed most of their lives, the past twenty spent living together as a couple. I can't understand why someone would suddenly decide to target them after all these years."

"You still think the guy who's after me is doing all this to make it look like a gay bashing, don't you?"

Brandon ran his fingers through his hair and sighed. "I just don't know, Nate. Look at it this way. There's an untold number of gay people right here in Reed who make no secret about their sexual preferences. Most of those folks have lived here for years without incident. Why now? We hadn't had a single recorded case of real gay bashing until that first attack on you."

"Meaning my being here in Reed started this whole thing, so it must be my fault, right?" He rose from his crouch and headed for the stairs.

"Where are you going?"

Nate paused on the top step. "If you're right, and all of this is really about me, the rest of the gays and lesbians in Reed will be safe once I leave." *And you would be safe.*

Brandon got up so fast, he turned his chair over. "No way in hell are you leaving, Nate."

Nate didn't answer. He went to the guest room and opened one of the suitcases he'd bought when he replaced all his clothes. He'd just started packing when Brandon came through the door.

"Maybe you didn't here me the first time. I said you aren't leaving."

Nate didn't look up. "Unless you plan on arresting me, you can't stop me."

Brandon leaned against the doorframe. "You think not?"

Nate crossed to the closet and pulled out a handful of shirts. "I'm not going to stand here and argue with you, Brandon."

Brandon crossed his arms over his chest. "Good. Since we aren't going to argue, put your stuff back in the closet."

"No."

Brandon went to stand in front of Nate. "What now? You're going to run out on your patients, run out on Amy?"

"I'll keep paying my half of the expenses until Amy can find another partner for the practice. She'll understand once she hears about the fire and the letter. As for my patients, I haven't really been here long enough for any of them to become dependent on me."

"Where you gonna go? Back to Atlanta?"

"Maybe."

"Where? To your parents? You think you can be one big, happy family, again?"

The tone in Brandon's voice made Nate wince, but he forced himself to shrug and say, "It beats sitting here waiting for someone to torch another business. And what if this guy doesn't settle for destroying property this time? What if he ups the stakes and kills someone?" *What if he comes after you?*

When Nate moved toward the closet again, Brandon blocked his path. "And what if leaving is exactly what this guy wants you to do? What if the whole purpose of his game is to lure you out and get you alone so he can finish what he started?"

"I'm willing to take that chance."

Nate tried to walk around him, but Brandon wouldn't budge. "Well, good for you, but I'm not willing to gamble with your life just so you can play noble."

Nate looked him in the eye. "You have no say in this."

The anger that flashed across Brandon's face was chilling. "That's funny, because I seem to remember a conversation a few days ago in which we both agreed we were starting something here."

"'Starting' is the operative word, Brandon. Since we've been taking things so slowly, there really isn't that much to end, now is there?"

Brandon snorted. "Yeah, well whose fault is that?"

Nate did his best not to let Brandon see how much his words hurt. "I knew you would throw that in my face sooner or later. Guess it's a good thing I'm leaving now, before you implode from sexual frustration." Brandon was so angry, Nate could almost feel the rage vibrating from his skin.

"You know what? Maybe you're right. Wouldn't want you to be uncomfortable. God forbid anyone should offend your virgin sensibilities." He turned to go downstairs, but not before saying, "Thank God I never fucked you. I don't relish the thought of frostbite on my dick."

Nate listened in stunned silence as Brandon's footsteps echoed down the stairs and the front door slammed shut. He gathered the rest of his clothes and headed for his car, his heart breaking a little with each step. He wanted to go back and tell Brandon the truth, that Brandon was the one he was really scared for. In just two short weeks, Brandon had become everything. His heart skipped a beat every time the man walked into the room, not to mention the way he felt when Brandon kissed him. Nate felt more at home in Brandon's house than he had anywhere else, ever. If the psycho who was after him found out about Nate's feelings for the handsome sheriff, Brandon would become the next logical target. Better to have Brandon hate him than to see the man he loved hurt.

Nate stopped for a second. *The man I love? God help me, but it's true. I'm head-over-heels in love with Brandon Nash.*

Nate pulled out onto the main road with no idea where he was headed. If he was in love with Brandon, was it possible that Brandon felt the same way? And if he did, was Nate hurting him more by walking out on him than by staying and fighting it through, together? Brandon was a pro when it came to his job. If anyone could catch this guy, he could. Nate was so confused. He needed to talk to Amy; she always knew the right thing to do.

Up ahead, Nate saw a curve in the road. If he turned around on the other side, he could go to Amy's house and get a fresh perspective. Then he'd call Brandon and explain his reasoning. Nate only hoped Brandon would be willing to talk to him after the horrible things they'd both said.

He approached the curve doing fifty. When he pressed on the brake to slow the car, nothing happened. He pushed the pedal again, and his foot went all the way to the floor. As the car entered the bend, Nate knew he wasn't going to make it. He closed his eyes and pictured Brandon's face just before his Honda ran off the road and crashed into a tree.

*~ * ~ * ~ * ~ *

Brandon sat behind the desk in his office and thought back to all the things he'd said to Nate. If they gave out awards for "Ass of the Year", Brandon would win by a mile. He knew Nate well enough by now to know why he was really leaving — Nate was trying to protect him. He'd known Nate's reasoning all along, he'd been just frustrated enough to let his anger get the best of him. Now Nate was gone, and Brandon would have a hell of a time finding him. But he would. No way was he going to let Nate get away. Especially not when Nate was taking a chunk of Brandon's heart with him. If anyone would know where Nate was likely to go, it would be Amy. Brandon picked up the phone and had begun to dial the number when Sam came in.

"Boss, we've got a report of an accident off Highway Four. An ambulance is on its way, and I'm headed out there now, but it sounds like a bad one. You want to ride out with me?"

Brandon grabbed his coat. He usually handled the more serious accident scenes himself because of all the red tape involved. He said a silent prayer that no one was hurt and headed out, sitting shotgun in Sam's cruiser. Fire and rescue was already on the scene. Brandon could see flashing lights in the distance. "Any word on who it is?"

Sam shook his head. "Not yet."

Because of the winding road and the rescue vehicles already taking up the shoulder, Sam parked the cruiser several lengths back. Halfway to the scene, they were met by a deputy.

"Boss, I'm so sorry. I didn't know who it was or I'd have called you personally."

Dread settling in his gut, Brandon stared at the young officer. "What are you talking about, Collins?"

"The doctor. I don't know what happened, but he slid off the road and hit a tree. Must have been going—"

Brandon took off at a flat run. He got to the wrecked car just in time to see the medics extricating Nate's prone body from the twisted metal. Nate had a thick gash above his left eye, and his right arm was bent at an unnatural angle. What affected Brandon the most, though, was the pallor of Nate's skin. He looked lifeless, dead. Brandon took one look at the man he'd come to think of as his and did something he'd never done in his life: he fainted in a rush of blacktop and agony.

Chapter Five

Keith sat down beside Brandon in the surgical waiting room of Chicago General and handed him a cup of coffee and an ice pack. "If you'll come down to my office with me, I'll disinfect that for you."

Brandon's fingers brushed the raw flesh of his cheek. "That's what I get for passing out like some rookie at the scene of his first accident." He took a sip of the scalding coffee, barely noticing when it burned his mouth.

"Under the circumstances, I think you can be excused." Keith leaned back as far as the plastic chair would allow. "At least come down to my office and wait. The surgical staff will know to page us down there as soon as they have any news."

Brandon started shaking his head before Keith even finished. "I'm not leaving him, Keith. I'll wait right here until Nate comes out of surgery."

Keith knew better than to argue. "I called Mom. She's gathering up the troops and heading on over."

"Nate hasn't even had a chance to meet the rest of them yet. We were supposed to have dinner at Grandma's next Sunday."

"There'll be other Sundays, Bran."

"For me, maybe, but what about Nate?" He glanced at the closed doors of the operating wing. "It's been over six hours, Keith. Why haven't they told us anything?"

"He has internal bleeders that have to be sealed off, buddy. You know it takes time to do that." Keith was quiet for a minute. "You're in love with him, aren't you?"

Brandon discarded the coffee cup and icepack, put his head in his hands, and nodded. "You know what the worst part is? I've never even told him. I kept telling myself that I couldn't possibly be in love with him after only two weeks. Now I'm sitting here thinking that if he dies, I've got nothing left. Fourteen days and already I can't imagine my life without the guy."

"Love's like that sometimes. I knew within three days of meeting Maria that I wanted to spend the rest of my life with her. Only took me two years to convince her that she felt the same way."

"Yeah, well, if Nate makes it out of this, I'm gonna have some convincing of my own to do. We had a fight right before he left. I said some really terrible things, Keith. He said some stuff, too, but you know me — I always have to have the last word." Brandon choked. "I never thought I might literally have it. What if I don't get the chance to take it all back?"

Keith hauled Brandon to his feet and pulled him against his chest. "Stop talking like that, Bran. Dr. Lincoln's the best surgeon we've got. The chief of staff asked him to operate on Nate as a personal favor to me. The guy's a complete asshole, but if anyone can repair the damage, he can."

A commotion at the other end of the hall caused them to break apart. When Gale had told Keith she was bringing in the troops, she wasn't kidding. All of Brandon's brothers and sisters, except for Les and Randy, who were away at school, crowded into the waiting room, spouses in tow. Brandon's dad came in next, explaining that the grandparents would be there first thing in the morning, but tonight they were keeping the kids so the adults could come to the hospital. That was fine with Brandon. As much as he loved his nieces and nephews, he had about all the distractions he could handle at the moment. As it stood, twelve people, counting him and Keith, were crammed into a private waiting room built to seat eight. Brandon never knew standing room only could feel so good. For the first time since Nate had been brought in, he felt a glimmer of hope. *Amazing what family can do for a man.* He made a mental note to introduce Nate to this crazy mob the minute he was able.

Gale came over and gave Brandon one of those soothing hugs that only mothers know how to give. "How are you holding up, sweetheart?" She touched his scraped cheek. "And what happened to your face?"

"My face is all right. Physically, I'm fine, but they won't tell us anything, Mom. I'm going out of my mind here."

"Patience never was one of your virtues, son. I'm afraid you inherited that from your father. Let me go up to the desk and see what I can find out."

Keith shook his head. "They won't tell you anything."

His father walked up behind them. Dean Nash was a big man, his body strong and fit from the long hours spent building up his construction company. Now semi-retired, Dean kept fit by helping his son Wayne with his own contracting jobs. Dean patted Keith on the arm and put his other hand on the small of Brandon's back. "Never underestimate your mother, boys. She's a force to be reckoned with." He turned Brandon around so he could see his eyes. "You okay, son?"

"No, sir. But if Nate makes it, I will be."

Keith went to watch his mother do her magic, while Brandon's sisters and sisters-in-law left to get snacks and coffee. Wayne stepped outside to smoke, giving them some privacy. Dean led Brandon over to a couple of empty chairs, all but pushing Brandon down into one and taking the other for himself. "Have you called his folks?"

Brandon's face hardened. "No, and I'm not going to. His friend Amy and her husband Mike are coming as soon as Amy finishes up an emergency call, but I have no intention of contacting Nate's parents. As far as I'm concerned, they gave up all rights to know about Nate's welfare when they threw him out six years ago."

"Your mother said Nate's brother came to visit him a few days back. Don't you think he'd want to know?"

"Last time we talked about it, Nate still hadn't made up his mind about whether or not he even wanted to see Seth again. The last thing I'm gonna do is call Seth so he can summon the rest of the family up here to cry crocodile tears at Nate's bedside."

"Speaking of family, you know your mother's adopted that boy, don't you? She thinks Nathan Morris is two steps away from sainthood."

Brandon smiled for the first time since arriving at the accident scene. "Nate says the same thing about her."

"He has good taste, then. I can't wait to meet this young man who has my wife and my son so captivated."

"He's amazing, Dad. He's funny and loving... God, he has the biggest heart. And Sasha's totally in love with him. Hell, he's even taught her to shake. She won't even sit for me, but Nate's got her doing tricks after only two weeks."

"Sounds like Sasha's not the only one in love with him."

"No, she's not. Does it bother you, Daddy?"

Dean was genuinely confused. "Why should it bother me? By all accounts, Nate's a great guy. Why wouldn't I want to see you settled down with a man like that?"

"It's not that, Daddy. I just... Why didn't you hate me when you found out I was gay?"

"You mean, why didn't I throw you out like Nate's parents did?"

"Yeah."

"Son, I can't explain why the Morris's did what they did, but I can tell you how I feel. I believe that God made you the way you are. I also believe that God doesn't make mistakes. How, then, could I hate you because of the way you were created? That would be like hating you because you have blue eyes."

Brandon leaned over and gave his father a hug. "I love you,

Daddy."

"Same here, boy."

Gale re-entered the room with Keith on her heels. "Am I included in this love fest?"

Brandon got up and kissed her cheek. "You know you are."

"Good, because I have news. Nate made it through surgery. Dr. Lincoln is finishing up now. That nice nurse I talked to said the doctor will be out in about five minutes to talk to us."

Keith just shook his head. "How does she do that? I'm one of the doctors on staff and they wouldn't tell me anything."

Dean pulled his wife down onto his lap. "Son, I gave up trying to figure out your mother forty years ago. Just be glad she's on our side."

Brandon heard footsteps and turned to see the surgeon standing in the doorway, still wearing his bloodstained scrubs.

"Who's the next of kin?"

Brandon said, "I am."

Dr. Lincoln gave him a quick once over, not an easy task considering Brandon was a good eight inches taller than the guy and Lincoln had to crane his neck to look him in the face. Still, Lincoln's tone was cocky when he said, "Can you prove that?"

Brandon was running on caffeine and nerves. No way in hell this little prick was going to keep him from seeing Nate. Still, he owed the man for saving Nate's life. He would keep it civil as long as he could. "Do I need to prove it?"

"As a matter of fact, you do."

Brandon could feel the blood rising to his face. "Now look here—"

"No, you look here. I'm sick and tired of you people thinking you can come in and push everybody around. It's bad enough that Mister High and Mighty Neurologist here," Lincoln motioned toward Keith, "called in a favor to have the head of surgery pull me out here in the middle of the night just to operate on his brother's queer boyfriend. I'll be damned if I'm going to let you walk all over hospital policy, too. Now, unless you can show me proof that you're the next of kin—"

"Actually, he isn't the next of kin. Yet," said the man standing in the doorway. "Technically, that would be me. I'm Nate's brother, and I do have proof." Seth reached into his wallet and pulled out a couple of cards. After handing them to Lincoln, he held up the cell phone in his left hand. Either Seth didn't know about the hospital's policy against cellular phones, or he didn't care. "It's for you."

Lincoln gave Seth a startled look, but took the phone. He didn't say much, only listened, every now and then offering a "Yes, sir," or an "I'm sorry." After about a minute, Lincoln hung up and handed Seth back his phone.

Seth said, "I trust you and Dr. Hanson had a good talk."

Lincoln gritted his teeth and nodded, so Seth said, "Good. Now, as next of kin, I want my brother's partner to be extended full privileges, just the same as any husband would have with his spouse. Any decisions that need to be made concerning Nate, Brandon makes them. I assume that won't be a problem?"

"No." Lincoln looked like he was about to throw up. He started to leave, but Seth stopped him.

"Oh, and Dr. Lincoln?"

"What?"

"As of that phone call, you're no longer Nate's doctor. Dr. Hanson is bringing in someone else."

Lincoln was outraged. "I saved his life. If it hadn't been for me, your brother would be dead right now."

"Why do you think I asked Hanson not to fire you when he heard you calling one of your own patients a queer? You better hope my brother makes it, Lincoln. Your career longevity line and Nate's lifeline now have the same expiration date."

Lincoln paled, but left before burying himself any deeper. Keith looked at the younger man in awe. "Who are you, and how the hell did you get Hanson on the phone? His wife can't even get through to him most of the time."

Seth gave a sheepish grin and stuck out his hand. "Seth Morris." Keith shook his hand much like a ten-year-old would shake the glove of his favorite baseball player. "And to answer your question, Dr. Hanson is now the proud owner of a hundred-and-fifty-thousand dollars worth of new equipment, courtesy of Mor-co Incorporated. I called Hanson to make sure Nate was getting the best care possible. It was just dumb luck that I happened to be on the phone with him when Lincoln threw his little tantrum." He turned to Brandon. "I hope you didn't mind me putting everything off on you."

Keith spoke up. "You know, Lincoln never did give us the complete rundown on Nate's condition. I think I'll go see what I can find out."

"I'll go with you, son," Gale said. "Dean, why don't you track down Wayne? He's had enough time to smoke a whole pack by now. When you find him, go get the girls, too."

The room cleared, and Brandon and Seth were left standing there, staring at each other. Finally, Brandon said, "Thanks for what you did, Seth. I owe you."

"You don't owe me anything. I'm the one who owes Nate. I just hope I get the chance to make up for all the dumb-ass things I've done to him."

"Not to seem insensitive or ungrateful or anything, but what are you doing here?"

"Apparently, Nate still had that card I gave him the other day in his wallet. One of the nurses saw it and called me. I know you're probably pissed off — not that I blame you — but I had to come."

"Did you call your parents?"

"No. I knew neither you nor Nate would want that. Look, I know I'm not welcome here, and I promise I'll go just as soon as I know Nate's going to be all right." Seth had tears in his eyes when he looked up at Brandon. "I just had to see him, you know?"

"Yeah, I think I do. Look, can we start over? Nate's going to need both of us. I'd hate to think you and I weren't men enough to put our differences behind us."

Seth gave Brandon a smile so much like Nate's it was all Brandon could do to look at him. Seth only nodded, and Brandon was grateful. If he didn't get in to see Nate soon, he was going to go slowly insane.

Gale and Keith came back with a surgical nurse, who said, "Mr. Nash?"

Brandon stepped forward. "How is he?"

His father and Wayne came in, followed by his sisters and the rest. They all fell into silence the minute the nurse started giving her report.

"Dr. Morris lost quite a bit of blood, but we were able to replace it before any serious tissue damage was done. He had three arterial bleeders in his abdomen and chest, which Dr. Lincoln closed without incident. Most of the injuries were confined to his midsection. The M.R.I. shows no sign of head trauma. Most likely, he passed out from blood loss. The cut on his head was superficial. We cleaned and stitched it, and we also set his broken arm. He's in the recovery room right now, but I'd say, barring infection, he should make a full recovery."

Brandon grabbed the startled nurse around the waist and lifted her off her feet, spinning her around until they were both dizzy. "Thank you. Oh, God, thank you so much." He put her back on her feet and kissed her soundly on the mouth.

She laughed. "Is it true what they're saying? Are you and Dr. Morris really partners?"

Brandon thought back to all the terrible things he'd said and only hoped Nate was still speaking to him. He wasn't about to tell the nurse that. Instead, he said, "Yes, we are."

She shook her head. "I thought so. Well, on behalf of the nursing staff, as far as both you and Dr. Morris are concerned, all I can say is — what a pity for us girls."

* ~ * ~ * ~ * ~ *

Keith led Brandon and Seth down the hallway of the Intensive Care Unit. "Let me go in first and see what kind of restrictions are in place, then I'll come back and get you guys."

After Keith left, Brandon propped himself up against the wall. Seth took the same position on the opposite wall. Brandon said, "I think you should go in first."

"No way. He'll want to see you first. Hell, I'm not even sure he'll want to see me, period."

Brandon took a deep breath. "Look, Seth, there's something you should know."

"Let me guess. You and Nate had a big fight before the accident, and you said something stupid. Now you aren't sure whether or not he'll want to see you."

Brandon put his hands on the back on his neck and leaned against the wall, again. "How did you know?"

"Nate's my brother, remember? Everybody thinks that because he's kinda quiet, he must be laid back and easygoing, too. Maybe he is most of the time, but get him mad, and that boy has a temper like you wouldn't believe. I guess you found that out firsthand, huh?" He thought for a minute before he said, "I know it's none of my business, but can I ask what you two fought about? I mean, if you want to tell me to go fuck myself, I don't blame you."

A few hours earlier, Brandon probably would have told the guy to do exactly that, but now he felt some kind of kinship with Seth. Maybe tragedy really did bring out the best in people. Either that, or Keith had slipped some kind of tranquilizer into his coffee. Regardless, Brandon found himself pouring out the whole story, including the things they'd both said. When he got to the part about telling Nate he was afraid of contracting a first-class case of frostbite, Seth let out a low whistle.

"Damn. And I thought Nate had a temper. You know he was just trying to protect you by leaving, right?"

"Now I do. I'd just made up my mind to find him and drag him back home when I was called to the scene of the accident. I didn't know it was Nate until I got there."

"God, that must have been hell. For what it's worth, I don't think Nate will hold what you said against you. He's a pretty forgiving guy. I mean, look at us. Nate forgave me for turning my back on him the first time, and what did I do? I turned my back on him again. I'm the one who doesn't deserve a second chance. But I'll tell you this: if Nate can find it in his heart to give me another go, you better believe I'm going to take it."

"If it makes you feel any better, I think he will. He's talked about you a lot since you came to his office the other day. Nate even showed me some pictures from when the two of you were kids."

Tears rolled down Seth's cheeks. "Thanks. That means a lot to me."

Keith came back with a big smile on his face. "Nate's stats are looking good. If he keeps improving, he could be moved to a private room by tomorrow. Right now, he's only supposed to have one visitor at a time, five minutes each visit. I pulled a few strings and got them to let you stay longer, Bran, but I'm afraid the one at a time rule stands. That's for Nate's protection. He's still asleep, but he should come around soon."

Seth said, "Look, it's after two in the morning, already. Why don't I catch a cab to my hotel and come back tomorrow?"

Brandon said, "No."

"No, I can't come back tomorrow?"

"No. I mean, yes, you can come back, but I don't want you to stay in a hotel. You can stay at our house, Nate's and mine. Keith can take you." Brandon turned to his brother. "Do you still have your key?"

Keith nodded. "I'll take Seth to your house and send the rest of the family home. I'll come back here after I get everybody settled."

"You don't have to do that," his brother protested weakly.

"I haven't had to kick your ass since you were in the third grade, Brandon. Don't make me do it now." Keith pointed to Nate's door. "Now go in there and see your guy. Just remember, he looks a lot worse than he is."

Brandon pulled Keith into a rib-crushing embrace. "Did I ever tell you that you're my favorite brother?"

"Just remember that come Christmas." Keith looked at Seth. "You ready, kid?"

"Yeah." Seth started past Brandon, then stopped and gave him a quick hug. "Thanks, Brandon. Tell Nate I'll see him tomorrow."

Before he knew it, Brandon was standing in the hall, alone. A nurse came along a few minutes later and helped him into a sterile gown and mask. All that was left was for him to go on inside. The first thing Brandon saw when he walked through the door of Nate's room was the reassuring, wavy line on the heart monitor. The rhythmic beeping should have been enough to convince Brandon that Nate was still alive, but it wasn't. He slumped into the chair beside the bed and carefully laid his head down on Nate's chest. He closed his eyes and listened to Nate's heartbeat, grateful beyond words for each steady thump.

* ~ * ~ * ~ * ~ *

Nate's first thought was, *I need a toothbrush*. His teeth itched and his tongue felt thick and swollen. His second thought was, *who punched me in the stomach*? He couldn't move his right arm, and his left eyebrow stung. Only when he looked down at the I.V. in his left hand did Nate remember the accident. He also remembered that he had something important to tell Brandon, but the pain was making it hard to concentrate. He had to try, though. Nate focused all his energy on his vocal cords and managed to croak out one word.

"Brandon." The instant he said the word, Nate felt two warm hands encompass his left one, carefully so as not to disturb the needle. He struggled to focus his eyes as Brandon's masked face came into view. "Bran, need to—"

"Shh, baby. Let me call the nurse and get you something for the pain, okay? If you raise a fuss and get all upset, they'll throw me out of here."

"'Kay."

Brandon fiddled with the switch at the side of the bed and, a minute later, a nurse came into the room, syringe in hand.

"Well, hello there. It's good to see you awake. Let me just shine a little light into your eyes, and then I'll give you something for the pain." She pulled a penlight out of her pocket and checked Nate's pupils. "Everything looks good." She depressed the contents of the syringe into his I.V. while she talked. "Your partner here has been telling me what beautiful eyes you have, but I had to see for myself. He was right — they do look like big ol' Hershey's kisses." She checked Nate's blood pressure, and after promising to bring some ice chips to moisten his mouth, she left.

A warm fuzziness crept through Nate as the medication started working almost immediately. He turned his heavy head towards Brandon. "Partner?" Nate could just make out the uncertainty in Brandon's eyes through the drug-induced haze.

"If you don't want me anymore after the things I said, I understand, but God, Nate, I love you so much. Please...God, please don't leave me. I'm so sorry."

Nate felt the soft darkness creeping in. He managed to say, "Me too," before sleep swept him away.

* ~ * ~ * ~ * ~ *

Not long after Nate got settled into his private room, Keith stuck his head through the doorway. Dozens of flower arrangements and plants dotted the tables and windowsill.

Nate smiled. "Come on in and have a seat, Keith. You just missed Dr. Lincoln."

Keith took the chair closest to the bed. "I hope he wasn't bothering you, Nate. Lincoln was told in no uncertain terms that he was being replaced as your doctor."

"Dr. Rinehart is my doctor, now. He's already come and gone this morning. Actually, Lincoln came up here to apologize for a certain off-color remark he made last night. Seems that little brother of mine really put the fear into him."

Keith's grin covered his whole face. "Damned right, he did. I wish you could have seen him, Nate. I've wanted to put that look on Lincoln's face ever since he came to work here three years ago. Seth did in five minutes what I've been plotting for thirty-six months."

As Nate eased back against his pillows, struggling to comfortably situate his broken arm, Keith could tell he was still a little groggy from the medication, but he was lucid, at least. Keith said, "Speaking of your brother, I stowed him at Bran's last night. Seth is anxious to see you."

"I'm looking forward to seeing him, too. I think it's past time we worked this thing between us out. It'll be nice having a brother again."

"You've got more than one brother, my friend. You are now an official member of the Nash Clan. Mother has spoken."

"How does Brandon feel about that?"

Nate's voice had dropped so low that Keith had to strain to hear him. "How do you think he feels?"

Nate closed his eyes. "I honestly don't know. I thought I remembered seeing him last night, but I was so out of it, I wasn't sure. When I woke up this morning, he was gone. I haven't seen or heard from him all day."

"And you thought he might have changed his mind about you once he realized you weren't going to die?"

"Yeah. We had a fight right before the accident."

"I know. Brandon told me all about it. He also told me he didn't mean a single thing he said." Keith could see the relief on Nate's face. He didn't want to give Nate more bad news, but he couldn't have Nate thinking that Brandon was deliberately staying away. Keith finally gave in and said, "Nate, the reason Bran hasn't been here has to do with your accident."

"My brake lines were cut, weren't they?"

Keith nodded. "Yeah. You remembered?"

"Just bits and pieces. I remember trying to slow down for a curve and not being able to. I also remember that odd sensation you have when you mash the brake pedal and your foot goes all the way to the floor. My car is only three years old, and I keep it serviced. It didn't take much deduction for me to realize mine was an accident by design. At least now I know why Brandon hasn't been here."

"Brandon went over the edge when the mechanic who examined

your car said the lines were cut. He's been on the phone all morning with the State Police trying to get them to investigate this as a possible hate crime. Even as we speak, he's got undercover patrols roaming the hallways of the hospital. There's an armed deputy outside your door, too."

Nate shook his head. "That doesn't make any sense. Brandon told me time and again that he believes this is a personal attack made to look like a hate crime. Why would he get the State Police involved?"

Keith patted Nate's uninjured arm. "He's going to do whatever it takes to keep you safe, even if it means calling in the Feds."

"He called the F.B.I.?"

"Yep. Bran still has friends from his days with the Bureau. He called in every favor he had, and a few he didn't. He's also having one of those high-tech security systems installed at the house, and upgrading the system at your office."

Nate nodded. "I knew about the upgrade at the office. Amy called me not long before you came in. She's afraid to come by because she's been exposed to mono."

"That was her emergency last night?"

"Yeah. One of her pediatric patients has it. The little girl's temperature spiked, so Amy met the girl and her mother at the office to see what she could do. She finally had to ice the poor little thing down, but it did the trick, thank God. Amy wasn't happy about not being able to come up here, but she's a fanatic about germs. She wouldn't even let Mike come, just in case he'd picked up the virus from her."

"Better safe than sorry, I guess. Anyway, the new security means at least you'll be covered at home and at work. Hell, Brandon's even talking about sending Sasha to be trained as an attack dog."

Nate laughed. "Now *that* I would like to see."

A knock sounded on the open door. Brandon stood there holding an armload of roses and wearing an engaging grin. He said, "I happen to think Sasha has the heart of a German shepherd." He dropped the flowers on a chair and went to stand beside the bed. "How are you feeling?"

"I'm fine now that you're here."

Brandon needed no further encouragement. He bent down and gave a Nate a kiss guaranteed to raise his blood pressure.

Keith just smiled and slipped out.

* ~ * ~ * ~ * ~ *

Nate groaned when Brandon broke the kiss, but at least Brandon didn't move away. He sat on the edge of the bed and took Nate's hand.

"Wow."

Brandon smoothed Nate's hair away from the bandage on his forehead. "Wow, yourself. It's good to see your eyes looking so clear. Last night they were all glassy and unfocused."

"The doctor decreased my level of pain killers a notch or two. So I wasn't dreaming last night? You really were here with me?"

Brandon lifted Nate's hand to his mouth, kissing the sore spot just above the I.V. "I was here. I would have been here when you got up, but I was called out on business."

"I know. You were terrorizing law enforcement the world over trying to find whoever who cut my brakes."

Brandon's jaw went rigid. "And I *will* find that son of a bitch, too, even if I have to call in the National Guard."

"I think calling in the F.B.I. and installing a N.A.S.A. grade security system is enough, don't you? And what's this I hear about you turning Sasha into a pit bull?"

"I think our dog is canine enough to take it."

"*Our* dog?"

Brandon shifted so that he was looking directly into Nate's eyes. "I know you said last night you were leaving me, but I can't let you go, Nate. I convinced myself that you were only leaving to keep me safe. Was I wrong about that?"

"No. I thought I was doing the right thing. The idea of that bastard doing something to you was more than I could take, Bran."

"I'm not gonna let anything happen to either of us, Nate. I haven't waited thirty-two years to find you just to lose you now." He hesitated. "That is, if you still want me."

Nate reached out and stroked Brandon's injured cheek. "Oh, I want you, all right. What happened to your face?"

"I'll tell you about it later." Brandon leaned forward and nuzzled Nate's neck.

Even as bruised and battered as he was, just the heat of Brandon's breath on his sensitive skin was enough to make Nate's pulse race. "If you don't stop that, a nurse is going to come in here and run you out."

Brandon stopped kissing him, but pulled back only enough to see him as they talked. "Nate, last night...I thought you were running out on me because you didn't trust me enough to keep you safe. It never occurred to me that you were trying to protect me. Well, it did, finally, but only after I'd made a complete ass of myself. All those things I said—"

Nate leaned forward enough to press his lips softly against Brandon's. "Shh. I said things I didn't mean, too. It wasn't that I didn't trust you enough, Bran. I was trying to keep you safe. I should have talked to you about it instead of running away. I had just made up my mind to come back and try to make you understand when my brakes failed."

"It took me a few minutes, but I finally realized what you were doing. I had Amy's number half-dialed in a desperate attempt to track you down when Sam came in and told me about an accident on the highway. I didn't know it was your car until we were already on the scene. When I saw them pulling you out of that wreck, I just blacked out. You were so still."

Nate's heart broke when he saw the tears on Brandon's lashes.

"I guess my mind couldn't cope. I saw you lying there, and I thought I'd lost you." Brandon pulled Nate as close as he could without hurting Nate's tender belly and spoke against his ear. "I can't go through that again. As soon as they let me, I'm taking you home, to our house, with our dog. I love you, Nate. I know you wanted to take things slow, but—"

Nate kissed his temple. "I think we're past the slow stage, Bran. I'm ready to take our relationship to any level you want. I love you; I'm ready to show it."

Brandon kissed just below the bandage on Nate's head. He pulled back and lifted Nate's chin with the tip of his finger. "We'll take this at your pace. You don't have to prove anything. But before we take this any further, I want you to understand what I'm talking about here."

"Okay." Brandon took his hand, again, and Nate was shocked to feel him trembling.

When Nate started to speak, Brandon shook his head. "Just let me get this out." He took a deep breath. "Nate, when I said I wanted to take you home, I didn't mean just until this is over. When I called it our house, I meant from now on. I'm talking your name on the deed, me taking out the garbage, us doing the dishes together — the whole family bit."

Nate wasn't following. "I understand. You're asking me to live with you."

"No."

"No, you don't want me to live with you?"

"No. Yes." Brandon raked his hand over his face. "This is hard." He took a deep breath. "I'm not asking you to live with me, Nate. I'm asking you to marry me."

Chapter Six

Before he met Nate, Brandon had always thought gay marriages were for other guys, not him. He didn't care that the state wouldn't recognize them. As far as Brandon was concerned, God made a marriage, not city hall. No, the reason he didn't take most gay marriages seriously was because half the gay couples he knew thought nothing of cheating on each other whenever the urge struck. To be fair, Brandon knew of several monogamous gay relationships, he'd just never thought he'd have one. Even before he knew about Jeff's propensity for sticking his dick in anything with blond hair and twenty thousand dollars worth of dental work, Brandon had never even thought about dragging him in front of the family preacher. With Nate, it was different.

It wasn't just that Brandon knew Nate would never cheat on him. No, he wanted Nate to be a part of him. Hell, Nate *was* a part of him, his other half, the *better* half. Brandon knew it, and he wanted to share that knowledge with the rest of the world. In front of a hundred and fifty of their closest friends and relatives, Brandon wanted to make Nathan Morris his, forever.

Unfortunately for both Brandon and his nerves, the object of all his desires and affections was sitting in the bed staring at him with open-mouthed astonishment. Brandon got up and started pacing. *Dammit, why isn't he answering?* Was Nate just going to sit there in silence until Brandon lost what little composure he'd gotten back after the accident? Injuries or not, there was no way Brandon was going to let him get away with that.

"Look, Nate, I'm not asking you to wear a white dress and carry a bunch of daisies, here." He crossed back to the bed. "I love you. I want to spend the rest of my life with you. You don't have to answer me right now. Take some time, think about it."

"Brandon, I don't need—"

"Nate, I know I'm nothing like Rick, but I do know we're good together."

"How do you know you're nothing like him?"

"Seth was kind enough to point out our differences that first day we met. Seems Rick is into caviar and crystal. According to your brother, I'm more the beer nuts and Heineken type."

"I believe Seth said you would be more at home at a tractor pull than the opera, but I guess the inference is the same."

Brandon sat down on the bed. "You heard all that?"

"One thing you need to know about me is that I'm a notorious eavesdropper. I'm the kid who always knew what he was getting for Christmas. I heard most everything Seth said to you. For the record, he doesn't know what he's talking about. He only saw Rick a handful of times. Seth didn't even know we were anything more than friends until that last night, and you know how well that turned out."

"Why didn't you tell me you heard us?"

Nate gave him that sexy smile again. "I was speechless. No one's ever taken up for me like that before. Well, except for Amy, but she fights like a girl. Anyway, I didn't mention it because I wasn't about to dignify Seth's stupid comparisons by acknowledging them. I was with Rick ten times longer than I've been with you, but I never felt for him anything close to what you make me feel." Nate leaned back against the pillows and patted the bed. "Here, lay down next to me."

"No. I'm too big. There's not enough room."

"There is if you lay real close."

"I might hurt you."

"Never in a million years. Please, Bran. I need you."

That was all it took. The trust in Nate's eyes was humbling. Brandon eased Nate over and into his arms, then scooted down beside him.

Nate snuggled close and laid his head on Brandon's chest, his broken arm resting on his side. "Umm, that's much better."

Brandon kissed the top of his head. "So, if you love me so much, and I'm such a great catch, how come you haven't answered my question yet?"

"I was going to when you freaked out on me."

"Yeah, well, I've never proposed before. Forgive me for being a little anxious." He ran his fingers along Nate's spine, delighting in the shivers he caused. "Now, for the love of God, quit stalling and answer the damn question."

"I'm not stalling. I'm about to begin negotiations."

Brandon smiled. *Only Nathan Morris could turn a marriage proposal into a meeting of the minds. God, I love this man.*

"I assume this is the point where I ask you what your demands are, right?"

"Right. They're pretty simple actually. I want to be married in the church you and your family go to. This marriage is going to be forever, so we might as well do it right. I was raised in the church, but I haven't attended since my parents and I parted ways. Even through all that, though, I never really lost my faith. I think we should begin our new family by going together. Do you think your minister will marry us?"

"Pastor Oakley has a son who's gay, so he's pretty open minded about it. The whole church is, really. I think you'll like it there. It's the First Christian Church of Reed, but we have people from all denominations in the congregation. We'll have to do pre-marriage counseling, though. Church rules."

"I don't mind. It sounds nice actually, especially if it means having our marriage formally blessed. Which brings me to my second point. I've known gay couples who refer to each other as partners. There's nothing wrong with that, but we're partners now. When we say our vows, you'll be my husband. I don't care what the state says, we'll be just as married as any other couple. You'll be my husband, and that's what I'm going to call you."

"The first two demands sound pretty damn nice. Number three isn't where you tell me you want a bachelor party with a male stripper, is it? You know how jealous I get."

"No, but you may not like it." Nate hesitated. "I want my brother to stand up for me."

A few days earlier, Brandon might have fought him on that one. Instead, he said, "As long as you make him wear one of those puffy pink dresses with all the lace, I'm fine with it."

Nate chuckled, then clutched his stomach. "Don't make me laugh. It hurts."

"Let me call the nurse and get you some pain medicine."

"No. I'm not done with you yet. We still have to go over numbers four and five before we seal the deal."

"Okay. Let's hear them."

"Four is one of the most important. I want kids, lots of them, to fill up that big house of yours."

"It's our house, and I'm more than willing. Hell, I'll get you pregnant right now if you want me to."

"You're a sick man, Brandon Nash, and I love you more than life itself. That brings me to number five. I want to get married on a weekday morning."

"Nate, are you sure they slacked off on your medication? You aren't making any sense. What does loving me more than life itself have to do with getting married on a weekday morning?"

Nate tugged at Brandon until Brandon was positioned over him, looking down at his face. Brandon's breath caught in his throat when he saw the love sparkling in Nate's eyes.

Nate's voice was little more than a whisper and shaking with emotion. "Because, the minute we say our vows, I'm going down to city hall and having my last name changed. I want to take your name, Bran."

Brandon gathered him close. He whispered to him, nonsense words of love and commitment. After a few minutes, he pulled Nate into a gentle but promising kiss.

* ~ * ~ * ~ * ~ *

Nate always thought loving families like the Nashs only existed in T.V. reruns. The forest of plants in his room and the string of visitors he'd had since his accident four days ago blew that theory out of the water. From the minute visiting hours started at nine a.m. until they ended twelve hours later, Nate was bombarded by his future in-laws. He had to admit, he was enjoying the attention. Between Gale and Grandma Taylor, he hadn't eaten a single bite of hospital food since he'd been bumped up to solids. They either brought or sent home-cooked meals every six hours. Brandon had started timing his visits to coincide with mealtimes.

Seth was also a fixture at the hospital. Though Nate kept urging him to go back to classes, he had to admit he was enjoying having his brother back in his life. He and Seth had spent long hours since the accident putting their relationship back together. The only thing they disagreed on nowadays was their parents.

"I still think you should call them," Seth had said during a marathon of conversation over the mint chocolate chip ice cream he'd smuggled in.

Nate had to give him credit, though. The minute he'd refused, Seth had dropped it. For the last two days, Seth had been too excited about the pending arrival of his boyfriend, Phillip, to bring it up again. Nate's musings were interrupted when the deputy assigned to watch over him from four p.m. until twelve a.m., an older man named Jim Mason, stuck his dark head in the door.

"The sheriff just radioed in, Doc. He'll be here as soon as he finishes up some paperwork, but he wanted me to give you a heads up. Seems that the female contingent of the Nash family is on the way over."

"Wedding plans?"

Jim smiled. "You got it. Looks like they'd at least give you a chance to recover first."

Nate shook his head. "You don't know Gale. She's so happy that Brandon is finally settling down. I think she wants to make the whole thing a done deal before he changes his mind."

"There's not a chance in hell of that happening, Doc," Jim said.

"Anyone can see how crazy about you he is. Take my advice, though. Elope."

Over the next hour, Nate began to think Jim had the right idea. After looking at catering options and seating charts until his eyes crossed, Nate was ready to crawl out the third floor window. When Brandon came in, Nate sighed with relief.

Brandon walked over and kissed his mother and his grandmother, then greeted his sisters and sisters-in-law. Finally, he went over to Nate and kissed him softly on the lips. "All these females aren't wearing you out, are they?"

"Nate has been a perfect gentleman about the whole thing," Gale said, "but I think you may have a point, Brandon. I mean, it's hardly fair to expect Nate to plan everything in his condition. I'll come by your office tomorrow and you can do it." With that announcement, she kissed Nate's cheek and left, the rest of the crew following behind her.

Nate almost burst out laughing at the forlorn expression on Brandon's face.

Brandon eased down into the bedside chair. "I set myself up for that one, didn't I?"

Nate reached for his hand. "'Fraid so. Looks like you're going to be busy for the next few days."

Brandon nodded. He looked down at Nate's hand. "Hey, you got your IV taken out. Does that mean I can spring you from this place soon?"

"Tomorrow, if everything checks out like it should. Think you can handle me being at home 24/7 until I'm recovered enough to go back to work?"

Brandon leaned close and kissed the pulse point beneath his ear. "I think I can come up with a few things to keep you busy while you heal."

Nate laughed. "I'll just bet you can. Gale told me you've recruited various family members to stay with me while you're at work. That isn't necessary, Bran."

Brandon kissed him again and then leaned back in his chair. "Non-negotiable, Nate. The guards will also come home with us until we catch the bastard that did this."

"Any leads?"

"We found a partial fingerprint on the undercarriage of your car, but it doesn't match anything in our system. I've sent it to some of my buddies in Quantico to see what they can find. In the meantime, I do have news of a different sort."

"Don't keep me in suspense."

"Seth's boyfriend flew in this afternoon."

"Ah, the mysterious Mr. Patterson. What's he like?"

"I don't know yet. Since Seth didn't have time to rent a car when he flew in the night of your accident, he's been pretty much depending on one of us to take him wherever he needed to go. Mom dropped Seth off at the airport, and then he and Phillip rented a car from there. Seth took Phillip to the house to get him settled in. I was at work, but Keith stopped by to drop off some lasagna Maria and the kids had made, and he met the guy. I don't think he was overly impressed. Oh, and get this — they're sleeping in separate bedrooms."

Nate nodded. "I know. Seth told me a little bit about their relationship. I've got to say, even though I've never met the guy, I already know I don't like him very much."

"That sounds serious. I mean, you like everybody. What makes you so sure you won't like Seth's guy?"

Nate made a face. "That's just it. He doesn't act like he's Seth's guy. Right after they started dating, Seth told him about the rape. He wanted Phillip to know before things got serious. Know what the bastard said to him?"

"From the tone of your voice, I'm guessing it was nothing good."

"You're damn right it wasn't. Phillip demanded that Seth get an AIDS test."

"What's the big deal, Nate? You and I have had that discussion, too. We both get tested every six months because of our jobs. We even discussed the fact that we're both clean and, given our sexual histories, won't need to use condoms when the time comes."

Nate shook his head. "This is different, Bran. When Seth told him he'd already been tested and hadn't been with anybody since the rape, Patterson got angry and refused to even kiss him. Seth finally gave in, and the two of them went and got tested together. They were both negative, but the doctor told them to get retested in six months. That's just standard procedure, but Seth said his so-called boyfriend has decreed anything other than light kissing is off limits until the second test comes back. He won't even consider using condoms until Seth proves himself worthy." Nate clenched and unclenched his left fist. "What kind of jerk treats somebody he claims to care about that way?"

"Loosen up your fingers. You've already got one broken arm, you don't want to add broken knuckles to the mix. Did you ask Seth why he puts up with it?"

"I did, but he just gave me some song and dance about how his relationship with Phillip means more than just sex. I know you've been understanding about my reluctance to make love, and I appreciate that, but this thing with Patterson just feels wrong to me. Something isn't right."

Brandon moved to sit on the bed and started kissing away Nate's frown. Between kisses, he said, "I'll keep on eye on Patterson while he's at our house. Now we need to talk about our own sleeping arrangements."

Nate was having trouble following because Brandon was sucking on his earlobe. His voice sounded squeaky to his own ears when he said, "What about them?"

Brandon moved down to bite softly on Nate's collarbone. "If you want to wait until after the wedding to make love, I'll do my best to keep my hands off you, but I don't want you to sleep in the guestroom anymore. I want you in my bed every night, sleeping in my arms."

Nate moaned as Brandon's tongue found the sensitive hollow of his throat. "I don't want to wait, not for any of it. I want you so bad right now I'm about to come just from kissing you."

Brandon looked down at Nate's erection to where it tented the sheet. "So I see. I know the doctor said you couldn't have sex for a couple more weeks, but Keith said it should be okay for you to do other things so long as you didn't strain yourself."

Brandon started kissing his neck again and Nate barely managed to say, "What other things," before Brandon was pulling at the bottom of his hospital gown. He almost had it all the way up to Nate's lap when he stopped and grabbed his radio. Nate was confused until he heard Brandon speak.

"Mason?"

Jim's voice came through instantly. "Yes, Sheriff?"

"Nobody comes through that door unless you radio me about it first."

"What about doctors and nurses?"

"Nobody. Tell them it's a new security measure or something. Hell, I don't care what you tell them, just keep them out of here for the next half hour, at least."

Nate could almost hear Jim smiling.

"Yes, sir. Remember, Sheriff, Doc just had surgery four days ago. Be gentle." He signed off before he heard Brandon's curses.

Brandon set the radio aside and kissed Nate softly. Nate put his arms around Brandon's neck and opened his mouth. With a growl, Brandon pushed Nate back against the pillows and swept his tongue inside. After a minute, Brandon began kissing a trail from the corner of Nate's lips to his neck. When he got to the collar of Nate's hospital gown, he grabbed the hem and pulled the whole thing over Nate's head. Nate groaned and reached for him, but Brandon stopped him. "No. This is just for you."

Brandon's voice dropped to a husky whisper that did nothing to ease Nate's state of arousal. "Let me touch you, Nate. Let me do what

I've dreamed of doing to you since the first time I laid eyes on that hard body of yours."

Nate sighed as Brandon's fingers toyed with one of his sensitive nipples. Though the sheet was still covering him from the waist down, he felt exposed under Brandon's eyes. "This is the first time you've ever seen me without my clothes."

Brandon dipped his head down to flick the teased nipple with the tip of his tongue. The heat in his gaze when he looked up made Nate shiver. "And you're even more beautiful than I imagined, and believe me, I've spent long hours imagining you naked. I can't wait to see what's under that sheet." To emphasize his point, he lowered the fabric.

Brandon first kissed the bruises on Nate's chest and stomach, treating each mark to his tender examination. He even kissed the bandages covering Nate's surgical incision.

Nate was almost mad with anticipation when Brandon finally reached between his legs and cupped him in his hand. "Oh, God, that feels good."

The feathery touch of Brandon's fingers on him was almost more than Nate could take. He'd never considered himself overly sexual, but knowing that it was Brandon touching him, urging his body to give itself over, caused Nate's muscles to tighten and his release to loom. "Bran, if you...I think I'm going to—" Before Nate could finish his sentence, Brandon leaned forward and took the entire length of him into his mouth.

It was too much, and at the same time, not enough. Nate's hips thrust uncontrollably, but Brandon was with him all the way. The gentle suction and soft stroking was more than Nate could stand. He tried to issue a warning, but no sound came out.

Brandon didn't seem to mind. He took in Nate's release, savoring him. Afterwards, Brandon gathered Nate close and held him as the aftershocks rippled his body. Nate recovered and reached for him, but Brandon caught his hand and brought it to his lips. He pressed a kiss into Nate's palm and said, "When you're better."

Nate wasn't sure what to say, but words turned out to be unnecessary. Brandon held him as Nate fell asleep.

* ~ * ~ * ~ * ~ *

Brandon had actually felt a little bit guilty when he'd told Seth to wait until after Nate was discharged before introducing his boyfriend to his brother. It was obvious that Seth loved Nate and was trying to repair the damage done to their relationship, and Brandon had wondered if maybe he was hindering their reconciliation by asking Seth not to bring Philip to the hospital. Seth had taken the request in stride, but Brandon was still worried. Just spending five minutes with that insufferable ass, Patterson, though, convinced Brandon he'd made the right decision. He thought back to how well the morning had started and cursed himself again for having ever gotten out of bed.

Gale and Brandon's baby sister, Megan, had arrived just after seven to get the house in shape for Nate's homecoming. Knowing the extent of Brandon's culinary skills, Megan immediately started breakfast. The smell of bacon and biscuits lured Brandon from his bed, reminding him that he'd survived on refrigerator biscuits and microwave sausage since Nate's accident five days before.

Brandon wrapped his arms around Megan's waist and kissed her cheek. "Have I ever told you what a great sister you are?"

Megan transferred several crisp slices of bacon from the skillet to the paper towel lined platter. "You didn't say that the day I drove your Camaro into Grandpa's drainage ditch. I believe you described me as the 'red-headed menace.' Where is your car, by the way? All I saw outside was the 'Sheriff-mobile'."

Brandon snuck a piece of bacon off the platter, barely avoiding Megan's slapping hand. "Cain is bringing it by in a few minutes. I sent it out to have some detail work done, so I can pick Nate up in style. He's never seen it."

"Nate will love the car, but that man is so wild about you, he wouldn't care if you picked him up in a booger-green Pinto."

Sasha came into the room and whimpered until Brandon grabbed her a piece of bacon, too, earning himself another slap on the hand, this one hitting the mark. "Please don't mention my classic sixty-eight and Pintos in the same sentence. By the way, why aren't you dressed for school?"

Megan looked down at her ratty sweats. "Today's a teacher workday. Besides, I want to be here when Nate gets home. He's a good one, Bran. Better hang on to him."

"I intend to. Oh, before I forget, Mom told me you've got a hot date for the homecoming dance at school. She also said you've been nominated for Homecoming Queen."

Megan blushed to the roots of her fiery hair. "It's no big deal."

Brandon sat down at the table and stroked Sasha's ears. "It is a big deal. Now tell me about this boy."

Megan sighed, but Brandon knew she wasn't really upset with him. Megan had started dating at the age of sixteen, and now, two years later, was the object of many an adolescent Romeo's attentions. Though it was no surprise given her delicate beauty, it was enough to make her father and five older brothers nervous. Megan had accustomed herself to receiving the third degree about her dates.

"His name is Dillon Carver. He's the same age as me, and also a senior. He has no family history of insanity or premature baldness. He doesn't smoke, drink, or do drugs, but he does have a vicious Dr. Pepper habit. I'll let you know how big his penis is after the dance."

Brandon had just taken a big sip of the orange juice Megan left on the table for him, and juice sprayed in a fountain across the breakfast nook. Megan grabbed a rag and was mopping up the table when Gale walked in.

"Did I just hear you say you say something about Dillon's penis?"

Brandon glared at Megan while trying to clean his shirt with a handful of paper napkins. "The brat was terrorizing me, as usual. And here I was, about to offer her the use of my car to make a grand entrance at the homecoming game."

Megan threw down her towel and flew into her brother's arms, almost knocking them both over, chair and all. "You mean it, Bran?"

"Well, we can't have the future Queen of Plunkett High driving up in that old clunker of yours, can we? Just promise me, no more penis jokes."

"Deal. Thanks Bran. You're the best." Megan kissed him and went back to the stove.

"I'm glad you think so, Meggie. Thanks for coming over this morning, both of you. It means a lot to me, and I know it will mean just as much to Nate."

Gale patted his hand and went to the refrigerator. "Anything for my boys." She glanced toward the upstairs with a look of supreme irritation. "It's nice to know *someone* appreciates the effort."

Brandon knew that look. It was the scowl his mother used when dealing with rude grocery clerks and pushy sales people. "I take it you had a run-in with my newest house guest. I got in so late last night, I didn't have a chance to do more than glance at the guy and nod. Keith wasn't exactly taken with him, though. I'm guessing you share his opinion."

Gale reached for the milk, squeezing it so hard the paper carton almost crumpled.

Brandon was thankful she wasn't holding eggs.

She set the milk aside and said, "No, I didn't have a run-in with him. A run-in implies an argument, an exchange of words. Mr. Patterson gave me my orders and dismissed me before I had a chance to argue."

Brandon got up from his chair, disturbing Sasha, who headed back to her bed by the fireplace. "Mom, if that guy insulted you—"

"Calm down, Brandon. He didn't insult me, exactly. Let me just say,

I don't envy Seth the task of trying to please that man."

Megan pulled the browned biscuits from the oven and popped in another pan. "What happened, Mom?"

Gale set a platter of fresh fruit she'd brought from home onto the counter and removed the plastic wrap. "When I heard Brandon's shower kick on, I went upstairs to put fresh sheets on the bed. I'm assuming Nathan will be sleeping in your room now that the two of you are engaged?" When Brandon nodded, she said, "Good. Anyway, as I was coming out of the bedroom with an armload of dirty linens, I met Mr. Patterson in the hallway. He was kind enough to inform me that, while I was at it, I might as well change his bed, too. He asked if you had any 180-thread count, Egyptian cotton sheets. I told him I doubted it seriously."

Brandon shook his head. "Hell, I always thought cotton was cotton. When I need sheets, I usually just buy whatever K-Mart has on sale."

Gale snorted. "Apparently Seth's boyfriend has more discriminating tastes." She looked at Megan, then with a twinkle in her eye said, "He also sent a message to the chef."

Megan turned another pan full of bacon out onto the platter. "If the guy is that picky about his bed sheets, I can't wait to hear what he has to say about his food."

Gale drew herself up to her full five foot two inches. "Yes, well, after smelling the bacon and biscuits cooking, Mr. Patterson advised me that his fragile constitution couldn't handle the greasy fare that we 'rural folk' survive on. When I reminded him that we live only thirty minutes away from one of the biggest cities in the nation, he ignored that and went on to dictate his breakfast menu."

Brandon was getting madder by the second but Megan took it all in stride. "And what does His Highness require to break his fast?"

Gale leaned back against the work island, laughter bubbling up inside her. "A four egg-white omelet, pepper but no salt, two pieces of five grain toast with the crumbs scraped off, and a cup of mint tea steeped for exactly two minutes."

Brandon started for the stairs, but Gale stopped him. "Where are you going?"

"Mom, there is no way in hell I'm going to let that pompous prick come into my home and treat my mother and sister like the hired help."

Gale shook her head. "We can handle this, Brandon. I won't have Nathan's homecoming ruined because of that obnoxious little snot. Let's just make the most of it. Phillip won't be here long, anyway. Seth is going to go back to school soon and, if God is merciful, he'll take Mr. Phillip Patterson the Third with him."

Brandon sat down, even though he was seething inside. Megan set a plate of bacon, eggs, and biscuits in front of him, along with a jar of Grandma Taylor's apple butter. The food, along with a cup of his mother's dark roast coffee, had almost restored Brandon's mood by the time Seth and his boy came downstairs for breakfast. Brandon's new-found tranquility didn't last long.

Patterson was handsome enough, but the minute he opened his mouth, he spoiled the pleasant effect created by his wavy brown hair and green eyes. Not even the tall, fit body and stylish clothes were able to hide the asshole lurking inside. He took a seat at the table and waited for his meal to be served.

Brandon was about to say something, but Megan shook her head. She brought Patterson his meal with an apologetic smile. "Good morning. I fixed your eggs the way you wanted them, but I'm afraid the toast is whole-wheat, not five grain. Oh, and Nate drinks Earl Grey, not mint, so the tea isn't quite what you requested. I steeped it for two minutes, though."

Patterson heaved a long-suffering sigh. "We all do what we can, I suppose."

Gale brought over the platter of fruit and a plate of homemade cinnamon rolls. Seth walked over and kissed her cheek. "Do you know how much I adore a woman who comes bearing cinnamon rolls?"

Gale patted his cheek. "You're as big a flatterer as your brother. You also have the same sweet-tooth." She handed Seth a plate already loaded down with fruit and cinnamon rolls.

Seth sat down and was about to take a bite when Phillip said, "Surely you aren't going to eat that?"

Seth gave him a puzzled frown. "Why not? Gale's cinnamon rolls are the best. She made them for me the first morning I was here."

Brandon gave his mother an exaggerated pout. "Where was I?"

"At the hospital, where you should have been. And don't talk with your mouth full, Brandon."

Seth smirked and took a huge bite of cinnamon roll. Brandon just laughed and was about to take a bite of his biscuit when Patterson looked at him and said, "I can't believe you're eating that. Don't you care about all that fat and cholesterol?" He next looked at Seth, who had a mouth full of cinnamon roll. "And you, Seth, don't you care about how you look? Your ass will spread out to the four points of the compass if you eat like that all the time."

Megan sat down with her own plate as Gale did the same. "I think Seth has a great ass. If he wasn't gay, I'd be all over it."

Brandon laughed so hard he was forced to swallow or risk choking. Gale had her head down, but Brandon could see the shaking of her shoulders.

Patterson wasn't amused. "Where I come from, young ladies don't say such things."

Megan fluttered her lashes in complete innocence. "Really? Where are you from, B.F.E.?"

Patterson looked at her like she was something he'd just scraped off his shoe. "No, Atlanta. What's B.F.E.?"

Megan swallowed the bite of fruit she was chewing before saying, "B.F.E.? Oh, that stands for a little place south of Cairo called Bum Fuck, Egypt. Perhaps you've heard of it?"

Phillip obviously didn't see the humor, but the rest of the breakfast table erupted into laughter. At that same instant, a car pulled into the drive and a horn sounded. Brandon drank down the last of his coffee and kissed his mother goodbye. "Breakfast was great, but that's Cain. I've got to drop him back at the garage and then go pick up my guy." He kissed Megan and said, "Thanks for the food, Meggie. Can you do me one more favor?"

Megan's blue eyes twinkled. "Anything for you, brother dear."

He shrugged into his coat. "See if you can get me some brochures on that place you were talking about, that B.F.E. Nate and I might want to go there on our honeymoon."

* ~ * ~ * ~ * ~ *

Brandon settled Nate against the mountain of pillows and said, "Are you sure you don't need anything?" It was the eighth time he'd asked.

Nate just shook his head and smiled. "I'm fine, but you're making yourself a nervous wreck."

Brandon sat down on the bed beside him. "I know I'm hovering, but I can't seem to help it. It's just so damn good to have you home."

"I agree, but you're going to give yourself an ulcer if you don't lighten up."

"Is that my fiancé speaking, or my physician?"

Nate grabbed Brandon's shirt with his good hand and pulled him close. "One and the same. Let me give you a little prescription for stress relief." Nate kissed him slowly but thoroughly. He was about to do more when a commotion erupted out in the hall.

"I told you, I don't want to discuss this again." It was Phillip's voice.

Seth sounded out of breath. "Look, Phillip, it was just a kiss, for God's sake. You could have stopped me anytime you wanted to. You were as into it as I was."

"We made a deal. None of that kind of stuff until your tests come back. If you can't abide by that, I'll just have to leave."

They could hear Seth pleading in the background, trying to change Phillip's mind. Brandon started to go out there, but Nate pulled him back. "Don't, Bran. The two of them have to work it out on their own."

Brandon shook his head. "Doesn't it bother you to hear him treating your brother that way?"

"Oh, course it does, but Seth is a grown man. He wouldn't appreciate our interference."

Brandon kissed his temple. "Am I destined to spend the rest of my life with you and never win an argument?"

"Of course not. Sometimes I'll let you win." Brandon's caress showed Nate he had no problem with that whatsoever.

They must have fallen asleep together, because Nate woke a few hours later to find Brandon curled on his side, his face peaceful. Nate knew the hours of fear and frustration had finally caught up to him. He smoothed Brandon's hair away from his brow and was about to go back to sleep himself when he felt blue eyes gazing at him. "Hi."

"Hi, yourself. Sorry I fell asleep on you."

Nate smiled. "I fell asleep, too. You must have been exhausted. You haven't slept much these past few nights, have you?"

Brandon shook his head. "I couldn't rest with you there and me here. It's good to have you home." He stretched. "You hungry?"

"Yeah. What time is it?"

Brandon checked his watch. "Just after one. I'm sure Mom has something ready for lunch. I'll be right back."

He started for the door, but it opened before he got to it. Amy stood on the other side, wearing pajama bottoms and an old Braves sweatshirt. She also had on the teddy bear slippers Nate had given her last Christmas. Her nose was swollen and her eyes were puffy. For that reason, she refused to come any further than the door.

"Amy, get in here and sit before you fall down," Nate said.

She shook her head, her hair a wild tangle. "No, Nate. The last thing you need is a case of mono. I've been dying to see you, but I wouldn't make you sick for anything in the world. I had to come, though. It's an emergency."

Nate sat up against the headboard. "Amy, we've talked on the phone at least three times a day since I came out of the I.C.U. What was so important that you had to drag your sick butt out of bed and come all the way over here?"

Amy weaved and swayed until Brandon took pity on her and dragged a chair over to the doorway. She collapsed in gratitude. "Thanks, Brandon."

"You're welcome. Now tell us what's going on."

"Dr. Evans has been handling our calls. You remember him, right?" When Nate nodded, she said, "Well, anyway, a call came into the office, which Cindy forwarded to my house." She took a deep, gulping breath. "Your parents are on their way here, Nate. They know all about the car accident. They're coming in on the four-thirty from Atlanta to Chicago."

Nate went numb. He heard Brandon say, "Fuck," and then start yelling at the top of his lungs for everyone to come upstairs.

Gale and Megan ran up so fast they nearly tripped over Amy, who was still seated in the doorway. Seth and Phillip came up next. Seth was alarmed, but Phillip's expression showed no emotion at all.

Brandon looked so angry that Gale took a step toward him. "Son, what in the world is wrong with you?"

"I'll tell you what's wrong with me. Amy just dragged her sick self over here to inform us that Nate's parents are on their way to Reed because they know all about the accident. Since I made certain Malcolm Davis kept it out of the papers this time, I want to know how in the hell they found out." His eyes fell on Seth.

The younger man took a step back. "Brandon, I swear to you, I didn't tell them. Yes, I told Nate I thought he should give them a call, but I would never go behind his back like that." He looked to his brother. "Nate, please, you've got to believe me."

"Back off, Bran. He's telling the truth."

Brandon moved to stand beside the bed. "Okay, but if Seth didn't call them, how did they find out?"

Gale and Megan just shook their heads, but Phillip stepped forward with that smarmy grin of his. "That's simple. I told them."

Chapter Seven

Seth just stood there staring at him. "Phillip, why would you do something like that? You know how Nate feels about our folks. I remember telling you myself."

Phillip shrugged. "They gave birth to him. They have a right to know. Maybe now your brother will quit being such a spoiled brat about it, and they'll be able to forgive him."

Brandon was across the room in two seconds, his hands around Patterson's throat. He'd been walking a fine line since Nate's near miss, but Brandon had finally reached his limit. "You arrogant little bastard. You're going to get what's coming to you."

"Put him down, Brandon." Nate started to get up, his legs still shaky.

Brandon dropped Phillip and rushed to Nate's side. "You shouldn't be out of bed. Dr. Rinehart said you should have bed rest for another week, at least."

"He's not worth it, Bran. I'll have to face my parents eventually. Might as well be done with it."

Brandon helped Nate back under the covers, doing his best to be gentle despite the rage swirling inside him. "Fine, but I want Patterson out of my house. Now."

Another set of footsteps sounded on the stairs and then Mike came into the room, frowning at his wife. "Amy, what's going on?"

She looked up through watery eyes. "Mike, what are you doing here?"

He crouched down beside her. "I could ask you the same question. I came home early to take care of you, but you were gone. I should have known you'd be here with Nate. What I want to know is, why?"

When Amy was done giving him the abbreviated version, Mike whistled. "Damn, that's tough. I wish we could stay and help, buddy, but Amy needs to be at home, resting."

"Take her home and make sure she gets plenty of fluids, Mike." Nate gave Amy a grateful smile. "Thanks for the heads up, doll."

She blew him a kiss, then spoiled the effect by coughing. She waved, and Mike hustled her out.

Gale reached into her pocket, pulled out her cell phone, and handed it to Megan. "Here, sweetie. You call your sisters, and I'll get on the phone downstairs and call your father and the boys."

"Gale, that isn't necessary, really," Nate protested.

"Nonsense. You need your family around you, and that's what you'll get." She gave Phillip a scathing once over. "I suggest you pack your bags, young man. I believe you've worn out your welcome."

As Phillip left, Seth turned to go, too. Nate said, "Seth, you don't have to leave."

He gave Nate a sad smile. "I care about him, Nate. I know he's kinda hard to take, but he didn't leave me when I told him about the rape, so how can I leave him just because he makes a mistake?"

Brandon couldn't believe what he was hearing. "You think because you were raped, you don't deserve the same love and affection as everybody else?"

Seth stared down at his feet. When he didn't respond, Nate said, "Look, don't leave. You and Phillip can stay here. Please, Seth. You'll be going back to school in a few days anyway."

Nate turned to Brandon with eyes so desperate, Brandon knew he'd lost the battle. "Fine, Patterson can stay. Just keep him away from me."

Seth nodded and left, closing the door behind him.

Brandon hauled Nate into his arms and held him close. "You don't have to do this, Nate. I'll meet your parents at the door with my twelve gauge if I have to."

Nate settled deeper into the blankets. "I'm not afraid of them, Bran."

Brandon pushed a pillow up under Nate's broken arm to better support it. "What if they give you a replay of your little coming out party?"

Nate shrugged as best he could with his arm immobilized. "It won't matter. At the end of the night, I know you're not going to run out on me like Rick did." He opened his eyes and gave Brandon a slow smile. "You're mine, and I intend to tell them that. Seth keeps telling me how much they've changed; I guess now's their chance to prove it."

Brandon kissed his forehead and got up. "I'm going downstairs to talk strategy with General Mom. Try to get some sleep. I've got the painkillers Dr. Rinehart prescribed. Yell if you need one."

"I will. Amy said they're coming in on the four-thirty flight. Do you think you could help me grab a shower before they get here?"

"No showers. I'm not about to take the chance of you slipping and falling on that wet tile. If you're real persuasive, though, I think I could be talked into giving you a bath."

Nate fell asleep smiling.

~~*~*~*

Two hours later, after helping Nate take a quick bath and then leaving him to rest up from the exertion, Brandon sat downstairs with his family, awaiting the new arrivals. He was glad his entire family was there. Even Grandma and Grandpa Taylor were upstairs in one of the spare rooms taking an afternoon nap. Having so many loved ones close by was a great comfort to Brandon. He was sure it would take the lot of them to keep him from killing Nate's father if that man tried to hurt him again.

Brandon's sister, Alicia, handed her one-year-old daughter, Emily, to her husband, Garth, and plopped down on the couch beside Brandon. Alicia had the same fiery red hair as Megan, but her eyes were green like Grandma Nash's instead of blue like Meggie's. She was short, like all the Nash women, but she had a commanding presence that made her one of the top prosecutors in Chicago. "Mom told me that Nate is going to change his name after the wedding. Is he cute or what?"

"After the way his father treated him, can you blame the guy?" This came from Wayne, who was sitting in a recliner with his wife, Stacy, in his lap and their three boys, Will, Garret, and Ben, stretched out on the floor playing a board game.

His sister Maxine shook her head, her black curls bobbing as she talked. "Well, that was before. No way is he going to hurt Nate again. Nate belongs to us now." She looked to her husband Steve for approval, but he was too busy trying to keep their two-year-old twin daughters from riding Sasha to answer.

Brandon's dad came in from the kitchen, Gale by his side. "Just remember, we're going to give the Morrises the benefit of the doubt. People can change, you know."

Gale nodded in agreement, but Brandon thought she looked doubtful.

"I'll be polite simply because they're Nate's parents, but one homophobic comment, and they're out of here," she said.

Sasha lifted her ears to the sound of an engine. Brandon looked out and saw Seth pulling into the drive. "They're here. Mom, will you go upstairs and wake Nate, please?"

"Of course, honey. Should I help him downstairs?"

"No, he's too weak for that. I'll take the Morrises upstairs. You guys can wait down here, if you want. Just come running if you hear the sounds of glass breaking or of flesh hitting flesh." Brandon said it with a smile, but he was only half joking. He heard the opening of the back door and the echoing of voices in the mudroom. He could also hear Seth's voice and what sounded like an argument.

"I'm telling you right now, Nate won't agree to it," Seth said.

A heavily accented voice drawled, "If he's as hurt as you say he is, he has no choice. Nathan needs to be taken care of. There's no one better to do that than his mother and me. Who's going to do if we don't, his lover? No, Nathan is coming home with us, and that's final, even if I have to force him."

Brandon closed his eyes and tried counting to ten, but it didn't work. He was mad enough to go in there and throw that old fart out on his ass. He would have if Dean hadn't reached over and grabbed his arm.

"Steady, son. You can handle this without bloodshed."

The argument in the other room continued. Brandon could see Nate's father coming through the kitchen. The man was almost as tall as Brandon, but the spare tire around his middle made him seem shorter. He had brown eyes, but they were dull, not vibrant like Nate's. His thinning hair was a yellowed white. He was about the same age as Brandon's dad, but where Dean looked younger due to hard work and effort, Calder Morris was definitely showing his age.

Seth was still trying to reason with his father, but Brandon could have told him it was a losing battle.

"Dad, there's no way in hell you're going to take Nate out of this house."

"Really? And just who is going to stop me?"

As Brandon stepped into the kitchen, Seth nudged his father. "I believe you're looking at him, Dad."

Brandon forced his tone to be civil, but his words were harsh. "I'm Brandon Nash, and you aren't taking Nate anywhere he doesn't want to go."

Calder gave Brandon his most intimidating boardroom scowl, but Brandon didn't so much as flinch. "I'm here to see my son."

Brandon leaned against the kitchen doorframe. "From what I just heard, you're here to fetch him, not see him."

"Now see here—"

A slender woman with silvery blond hair and Nate's eyes stepped up next to Calder. "Calder, calm down. This young man didn't say we couldn't see Nathan."

Brandon shook his head. "No, I won't stop you from seeing him, but only because Nate has agreed to it. What I will do is whatever it takes to keep you from upsetting him. Nate nearly died from blood loss not five days ago. He's weak, and if you hurt him, you'll answer to me."

Calder looked ready to argue, but his wife obviously had more sense. "And we would expect no less from the man Nathan has chosen. I'm Leda Morris, and I'd be grateful if you'd take us to Nathan."

Gale came back downstairs. "Nate's awake and ready to see his folks."

Brandon turned to his mother. "Is he all right?"

Gale gave the Morrises an icy stare. "No, but I hope he will be soon."

Brandon didn't say a word. He went toward the stairs, leaving the Morrises to follow.

* ~ * ~ * ~ *.~ *

Nate heard three different footfalls on the stairs and knew his time was up. The first face he saw was Brandon's as he stuck his head in the door and gave Nate a tentative smile.

"You ready for this?"

"No, but I'll do it, anyway."

Brandon nodded and opened the door wider, allowing the Morrises to enter.

His father had more stomach and less hair than the last time Nate had seen him, but his mother was just as youthful and elegant as Nate remembered. Nate propped himself up on his pillows. "Mom, Dad, come on in and have a seat."

Calder stayed where he was, but Leda came forward. "Nathan it's...it's good to see you, son. Your father and I were so worried when we heard about your accident. I must say, I was envisioning much worse."

Calder stepped up to the bed. "For God's sake, Leda, the boy has a cast on his arm, stitches in his head, and bruises on every visible part of his body. How much worse do you want him to look?"

Leda never took her eyes off her son. "He looks wonderful to me," she whispered, and then she reached for him.

Nate had no choice but to raise his left arm as his mother rushed to him.

Leda was a slight woman, but that didn't stop her from hugging the daylights out of Nate. When he grunted, she pulled back. "I'm sorry. I didn't mean to crush your bruises. It's just so good to hold you again, Nathan."

He didn't remember her being so affectionate before. Maybe time had played tricks on his memory. "You too, Mama. You look great." Nate looked around for Brandon and saw him still standing by the door. "Come over here, Bran. Have you guys been properly introduced?"

"If by properly, you mean being met at the door, threatened, and almost refused entrance to see our own son, then I suppose we have," Calder said.

Nate ignored the sarcasm in his father's voice, a habit acquired over long years of practice. "Well, just in case, allow me. Calder and Leda Morris, I'd like you to meet my fiancé, Brandon Nash."

Leda's smile was beauty queen bright. "A wedding? You're going to have a wedding? When?"

Nate felt the tight knot of tension in his stomach start to unravel. "We really haven't had much of a chance to plan, but we're hoping to say our vows in about three months."

Calder moved to stand behind his wife. "There is no way in hell you are going to marry this man in three months, Nathan."

Nate felt all the blood drain from his face. He'd been hopeful, especially after his mother's joyful though reserved reaction, but it was obvious his father hadn't changed. Nate hadn't realized just how much he wanted to reconcile with his folks until that minute. Still, he would hear his father out. If this was the last time Nate was to talk to his dad, he would allow Calder to say his peace.

Brandon was about to say something, but Nate held up his hand. "And why is that, Daddy?"

"Because, you are my eldest son, and there is absolutely no way I'm going to have you married in some last ditch, thrown together ceremony. Your mother and I are going to see this thing done right. It takes at least six months to put together a proper wedding. We have to print the invitations, arrange the music, call the caterers, and so on and so forth." He looked to his wife for help. "Tell him, Leda."

Leda nodded, her smile even more radiant than before. "He's right, Nathan. When your father and I got married, it took eight months just to make all the arrangements, and that was with both our mothers working together."

Nate barely heard her. He was too stunned by what his father had just said. "Did you mean it, Daddy?"

Calder gave the first smile he'd given since arriving. "Of course I meant it. We're going to do this thing right. When your children—" He stopped and looked at Brandon. "I'm assuming the two of you plan to adopt?" When Brandon nodded, Calder continued. "When your children are older, they'll want to know all about their fathers' wedding. You'll want to have some first rate tales to tell them. I don't want my grandchildren to think their parents got married in some tacky, two bit service."

"So, now you want me to have children?" Nate said.

"Of course. Your mother and I aren't getting any younger, son. It's about time you settled down and started a family."

God help him, but Nate wanted to believe his father was telling the truth. One part of him, though — the part that was nearly destroyed six years earlier — refused to accept the turn-around that readily. "Aren't you afraid I'll molest them? Six years ago, you accused me of being some kind of deviant child predator."

Calder shuffled his feet. "We all make mistakes, Nathan. I've come here looking for forgiveness."

Nate looked to Brandon, but Brandon shrugged. "It's your call. I'm behind you, no matter what."

Nate nodded. "I'm willing to try, Dad."

A gleam sprang into Calder's eyes. "That's all I ask, son. That's all I ask."

* ~ * ~ * ~ * ~ *

Brandon went downstairs to find his father surrounded by a throng of grandchildren, all enthralled by one of his many stories. The funny part was, his brothers and sisters, all of whom had heard that same story a hundred times, were just as wrapped up as the kids. His mother saw him and excused herself from the group. They walked into the kitchen away from the others. Brandon pulled out a chair for Gale and then sat down at the table opposite her.

"How did it go with Nate's parents?"

Brandon folded his hands on top of the table and looked his mother in the eye. "It was perfect, Mom. It couldn't have gone any better if the whole thing had been written down on paper."

"In other words, it was too perfect."

"Exactly. Nate's mother seems genuine enough. It's his father I don't trust. I just can't see the guy who wanted to have Nate sterilized for fear he'd reproduce and pimp out his kids suddenly having a change of heart. Calder is up there right now helping Nate plan out our wedding. It just doesn't gel."

Gale played devil's advocate. "People can change, Brandon. Seth did. I have no doubt his feelings for Nate are real."

Since Gale knew all about the circumstances that had led to Seth and Nate's estrangement, Brandon was sure she would understand his next point. "Neither do I, Mom, but Seth had real reasons for feeling as he did. Even if you go on the theory that Calder was so traumatized by Seth's rape that he turned on Nate, it doesn't explain why Calder didn't want the son of a bitch that raped his son prosecuted. Hell, he didn't even take Seth to the hospital, not to mention that shrink he sent the poor kid to who tried to convince him he wasn't gay. No, Calder Morris is a bigot. I would bet my last dollar on it. And you know as well as I do that a bigot doesn't change without some type of heavy intervention."

Gale smiled and patted his folded hands. "Sometimes I forget you have a degree in psychology. For what it's worth, I agree with you. The question is, what are you going to do about it?"

"At the moment, nothing. Nate wants to give his folks another chance, and if I interfere, Nate might end up resenting me for it later on. I love him too damn much to let that happen. If Calder does have an ulterior motive, he'll tip his hand eventually. And when he does, I'll be waiting."

The phone rang before Gale had a chance to comment. Brandon grabbed the kitchen extension. "Nash."

Sam sounded out of breath. "Sorry to bother you, Bran. I know you'd planned to spend the rest of the day with Doc Morris, but this is an emergency. We've had another fire."

Brandon gripped the phone so hard his knuckles turned white. "Who was it this time?"

"Marjorie Newman. Her bookstore is a total loss. That's not the worst part, though. She was inside the building when the fire started. Marjorie always closes right at five, no matter what. At six o'clock, when she still hadn't come home, Eva went looking for her. She got there just in time to see the windows blow out. The medics pulled Marjorie out about thirty minutes ago and had her transported to Chicago General. The Fire Department is on the scene, but I haven't received word on Marjorie's condition."

"I don't suppose the fire marshal has found anything, yet."

"No, and he may not. The last fire was ruled inconclusive as to origin. Marjorie might be able to help us, if she makes it, but right now that's a big if."

Brandon glanced at the clock. It was six forty-five. He knew that the first two hours after a crime was committed were often the most crucial. "Sam, I'm on my way. Don't let the guys from Fire and Rescue contaminate my crime scene any more than necessary. I'm bringing in my own expert on this one, so it may take me a few minutes to get there."

"Hate to burst your bubble, Brandon, but it could take weeks to fly in a trained arson investigator."

"Not when you happen to have one upstairs taking a nap in your guest bedroom."

"Who?"

"Grandpa Taylor."

"Shit, I forgot that he used to be the Reed County Fire Marshal. But he's eighty-four years old. Think he'll feel up to it?"

"We're talking about the same man who just last week won the

Third Annual Arm Wrestling Championship at Shorty's Pub. Hell, he and Grandma still have sex four times a week. No, he'll want to do this, especially if it means catching the guy who's after Nate. I'll be there as soon as I wake him up."

He hung up and turned to his mother. "I have to go, Mom."

"So I heard. What do you want me to tell Nate?"

Brandon kissed her and headed upstairs to fetch his grandfather. "Just tell him I was called in on a case. I'll tell him the rest of it when I know more details. Do me a favor, though. When Keith gets here, have him check Nate over. I'm afraid he's had too much excitement. And keep an eye on Calder for me. I don't trust that guy. Tell the rest of the family to go home whenever they need to, but I'd appreciate it if you and Dad would stay."

"Of course, honey. We're always here for you and Nathan. You know that."

Brandon nodded from the doorway. "I'm glad, Mom. I have a feeling we're going to need all the help we can get before this thing is over with."

* ~ * ~ * ~ * ~ *

Anyone looking at Gene Taylor would see the quintessential little old man. With his unruly shock of white hair and his faded blue eyes, no one would ever guess Gene had the mind of a crack detective. During his thirty years as fire marshal, not a single arson went unsolved. Brandon was counting on those skills to pull this one off.

He spent the ride downtown filling his grandfather in on what little he knew. He also briefed him on the details of the H. and G. Dry Cleaning case. Gene was silent, but Brandon could almost see the old man's mind working.

The ruins of The Book Barn were still smoldering when Brandon whipped his S.U.V. into the parking lot. Luckily, the blaze was contained before the fire spread to the surrounding businesses. Several anxious tenants and shopkeepers stood outside, most awaiting word of Marjorie's condition.

Sam met Brandon and Gene at the curb. His short brown hair was streaked with soot and he had smudges under his gray eyes. Sam's tall, thin body was covered in ash, his uniform ruined. Brandon gave him a disapproving inspection. "What were you doing in there, Sam? That's the firefighters' job. You were supposed to be out here securing the crime scene."

Sam disregarded the criticism with the ease of old friendship. "I know, I know, but I think you're going to be glad I went in when you see what I've found." He steered them through the crowd and into the burnt shell of the building. He pointed to a spot in what used to be the back corner. "I found it when I came in to secure the scene."

Brandon saw a clear speck of yellow lying on the charred ground. He pulled a handkerchief from his pocket and lifted the scrap of paper for closer inspection. Gene looked on, but still didn't comment.

Brandon walked out of the darkened husk back to his S.U.V., Sam and Gene following behind. He opened the car door and held the paper up to the interior light. "Well, I'll be damned. It's a rental car receipt. Name's been burned off, but the tag number's still intact."

Sam nodded. "I've already called the rental car company. They're running a check on it now. I left it where it was after I got the number off of it because I wanted you to see where I found it. Looks to me like the perp dropped the thing when he was starting the fire, but for some reason, it didn't burn. My guess is, whatever accelerant he used caught fire before that receipt had a chance to burn completely. The fire guys took some samples for testing. As soon as we get the name that goes with that slip of paper, we'll have our guy."

Gene spoke his first words since getting out of the S.U.V. "Sounds like you've got it all figured out, son. In fact, the whole thing couldn't have been easier to solve if your arsonist had gift wrapped it and slipped it under your Christmas tree."

Brandon leaned back against the car. "I agree that it's too easy, Grandpa, but I'm going more on a gut feeling. From the look of you, I'd say you've got something a little more concrete."

Gene stared at his grandson a few minutes before speaking. "You think the same guy who's setting these fires is the one who's after Nate, don't you, boy?"

"Yes, sir."

"The way I see it, the guy was smart enough to club Nate on the head, wreck his house and the doctor's office, tamper with his brakes, and set up the H. and G. job to make it look like a hate crime. The perp did all that without getting caught. You think he's suddenly developed a bad case of dumbass?"

"Mr. Gene, are saying this guy got caught on purpose?" Sam said.

Gene directed his comments directly to Brandon. "So far, your perp has targeted only businesses that already contain natural accelerants, like the cleaning fluids at H. and G. and the fiberglass book binding resins here at The Book Barn. No need to risk exposure by bringing in your own stuff if the fuel's already there. Look at that paper you're holding, Brandon. What do you see?"

Bran turned on the high beams and stepped into the light. He studied the paper and said, "The corner where the name should be is the only part of the paper that's burned. There's no soot or tar marking the surface of the receipt, even though the thing was inside a burning building for a good half hour before the fire was brought under control." Reasoning dawned. "The son of a bitch set fire to the corner, then put it out before the incriminating numbers had a chance to burn. I'd be willing to bet he started the fire in the other end of the building after he planted this where he knew we would find it."

Sam scratched his head. "How in the hell did he keep the paper from burning up in the heat?"

Brandon held the paper out for Gene's inspection. "Flame retardant?"

"Yep. I've been out of the loop for a while as far as the latest technology goes, but I'd say it's an aqueous based resin, maybe one of the brominated compounds. It's not that hard to come by. Most building supply companies stock it."

Sam's cell phone rang while Gene was still talking. The expression on his face as he talked to the party on the other end went from anticipation to disbelief. Sam muttered his thanks and closed the phone.

"That was Bingham's Car Rental. They traced the tag and came up with a credit card number. MasterCard just confirmed the identity of the card holder."

Gene said, "Son, I've always liked you, but damned if you don't have a habit of stringing out the drama. Just tell us who the car was rented to."

Sam took a deep breath and said, "Seth Morris."

Chapter Eight

A deputy escorted Seth to the main interrogation room of the Reed County Sheriff's Department. He was still wiping the ink off his fingertips when Brandon came into the room and sat down at the table across from him.

"You mind telling me why I was brought in here like some kind of criminal and fingerprinted? Next you'll be reading me my rights and taking mug shots."

Brandon shook his head. "I don't think that will be necessary. As soon as my expert compares your prints to the partial found on the undercarriage of Nate's car, you'll be cleared and free to go."

"If you're so sure I'm innocent, why in the hell did you bring me in?"

Brandon held up the plastic bag containing the rental car receipt. "Because somebody went to a lot of trouble to implicate you. I want you cleared, with all the forms filled out in triplicate, so I can nail the bastard responsible."

Seth eyed the baggie. "I don't understand how I could be implicated. I didn't rent the car. Phillip did."

Brandon opened the file he'd brought in with him and pulled out Bingham's copy of the receipt. He handed it to Seth. "That's your name on the bottom of that form, and MasterCard says it's your card."

Seth stared at the paper with a blank face. "First, that's not my handwriting. Second, I use American Express for my personal transactions. The only time I use MasterCard is in my business dealings." He reached into his back pocket and pulled out his wallet. He removed his driver's license and gave it to Brandon. "Go ahead. Compare the signatures."

"Look, Seth, I already know you're innocent. You were in Georgia both when Nate was attacked and when he had his accident. Believe me, I already checked. So there's no reason to lie about the credit card."

"Exactly, so why *would* I lie?" He leaned forward. "Look, Brandon, I'll admit that I wasn't crazy about you when we met, but I've developed a respect for you since then. It's obvious how much you and Nate love each other, and since I plan on being a part of my brother's life from now on, it's in my best interests to get along with you. I'm not lying."

"Then why did the credit card company identify you as the client?"

"I'm *one* of the card holders, but not the only one. My father and I both have cards that we use for Mor-co business. I've been working for Dad while finishing up my degree, so I've used the card quite a bit, but only for business expenses. As for the car, Phillip rented it the day he came in. If you'll remember, I took a taxi from the airport to the hospital that first night. The next morning, Keith gave me a ride to your house. I depended on the kindness of various members of your family to get me where I needed to go until Gale dropped me off at the airport yesterday. From there, Phillip rented a car, and we drove back to Reed."

"Why would Phillip sign your name, and what in the hell is he doing with a Mor-co Company credit card?"

"That, I couldn't tell you. I do know that he didn't use my card because I've had it with me ever since I flew in from Atlanta. I used it to purchase all that equipment for the hospital."

Brandon sat in quiet thought before saying, "Seth, I know how you feel about Phillip, but—"

"But if he's involved with what happened to Nate, I want you to fry his ass. No matter how I feel about Phillip, Nate comes first. And whether Phillip's involved or not, I'd like to know what in the hell he's doing with a Mor-co credit card."

"If that's how you feel, I think I know of a way to make him tip his hand. Does anyone know why you were brought in here tonight?"

"No. Sam dropped off your grandfather and told the rest of them that you wanted me to sign Nate's hospital report since I'm listed as his next of kin. If anyone was suspicious, I couldn't tell."

Brandon nodded. "Good. We'll have to take Patterson by surprise. How are your acting skills?"

Seth raised his voice an octave and said, "Just call me Seth Morris, drama queen."

* ~ * ~ * ~ * ~ *

It was after midnight before Brandon slid into bed beside Nate's sleeping body. He gathered Nate close and was almost asleep himself when Nate said, "Where have you been?"

Brandon sighed. He'd hoped to at least avoid this conversation until morning. He turned Nate over so he could look into his eyes. Brandon gave him a brief overview of the case, including the latest news that Marjorie was in guarded condition. He also told Nate about Seth's credit card and his plan to incriminate Philip.

Nate was quiet for so long, Brandon began to worry. "Nate, you know I would never do anything to hurt you or your family, don't you?"

Nate reached up and stroked Brandon's still-raw cheek. "I trust you. I just have a bad feeling, that's all."

Brandon kissed his forehead. "Me too, baby. Me too."

* ~ * ~ * ~ * ~ *

Nate decided to have breakfast in the kitchen with the rest of the family. All of Brandon's siblings had gone home late the night before, except for Keith, who, after checking Nate over and finding his heart rate elevated, decided to stay. Grandma and Grandpa Taylor opted to go home, but Dean and Gale stayed too. Nate had a feeling that as long as his parents occupied one of Brandon's guest rooms, Dean and Gale would be close by.

Nate was seated at the table drinking juice when Brandon came down. Brandon leaned in for a soft kiss before turning to the counter and grabbing the coffee pot.

"You aren't really going to drink that coffee in front of me, are you?" Nate said.

"Since when can't you have coffee?"

Keith came in and took the pot from Brandon. "Since I checked him last night and found out that his heart rate was up. I don't want him to have caffeine in any form for the next few days."

Brandon sat down next to Nate. "Is this something I should be worried about?"

Keith added a generous helping of cream to his coffee. "Not really. I'm sure it's just a reaction to the blood thinners they gave him to reduce the possibility of clotting. I just don't want him over stimulated until they clear out of his system."

"Damn. That puts the nix on what I was going to do to him this afternoon." Keith and Brandon both laughed at Nate's blush.

Phillip came in with Seth. "Where I come from, we keep sex talk out of polite conversation."

Nate started to say something, but Brandon beat him to it. "Considering you and Seth sleep in separate bedrooms, seems like you don't have much to talk about anyway."

Phillip's face turned a mottled shade of red, but he didn't say anything. The sound of a door opening and then closing caught their attention as Gale entered through the mudroom. She reset the alarm and walked into the kitchen.

"Sorry I wasn't here to start breakfast, kids. Your dad got an early call from one of Wayne's job sites, so I asked him to take me by the house so I could pick up my car. I'll have something fixed in just a minute."

"Gale, you don't have to wait on us, you know," Nate said. "Brandon has enough sugary cereal in the cabinet to cause diabetes in an entire third world country."

Brandon stuck out his tongue and blew Nate a raspberry before turning back to Gale. "He is right, though, Mom. We can make do without you going to a lot of trouble."

"Brandon, there isn't a mother alive who doesn't enjoy fussing over her children. You're my boys; it's a mother's right."

Calder walked into the kitchen. "That's funny. I could have sworn Nathan was my son, not yours."

Nate saw the flash of anger in Brandon's eyes and knew he was about to let Calder have it for being rude to Gale. Leda came to the rescue.

"Calder, sit down while I pour you some coffee. Gale, how about I make my Grandmother Winston's buttermilk pancakes? Nathan and Seth just adore them, don't you boys?"

A double reply of "yes, ma'am" took the spotlight away from Calder. Nate said a silent prayer of thanks for his mother's rare interference. He glanced at the clock. Ten minutes until show time. Brandon saw where Nate was looking and squeezed his good hand under the table.

Gale sliced some fruit while Leda mixed pancake batter. She'd just heated the griddle when someone knocked on the back door. Gale wiped her hands on a dishtowel and said, "Sit down, Brandon. I'll get it. It's probably just Megan coming by for lunch money. I forgot to give it to her before I left."

Nate kept his eyes on his heavy cast so no one would see his apprehension. He glanced at Seth and was rewarded with a slight smile.

Gale's voice carried through from the mudroom. "Good morning, Sam. We were just about to have breakfast. Will you join us?"

"Thank you, ma'am, but no. I'm afraid I'm here on official business." Sam walked into the kitchen and moved to stand by Seth's chair, whipping out his handcuffs as he went.

"Stand up, please." When Seth complied, Sam pulled Seth's arms behind his back and snapped the cuffs on his wrists.

Calder jumped up. "Just what the hell do you think you're doing, Deputy?"

Sam ignored him. "Seth Morris, you're under arrest for arson and attempted murder." He pulled Seth toward the door as he continued the Miranda warning.

"Now wait just a damn minute here," Calder said. "You have no proof that Seth has done anything wrong."

"I'm afraid we do, sir. His credit card was used to rent a car three days ago. The receipt for that car was found at the scene of last night's arson."

Seth let out a frightened whimper. "Dad, I'm innocent, I swear it. I didn't even rent a car when I got here."

"Leda, call my lawyer. Don't you worry, son. I'll get you out of this."

Brandon stood up. "No offense, Mr. Morris, but if Seth's credit card was used to rent the car, I'd say the evidence is pretty solid."

"Which credit card was used?" Calder asked Sam.

Sam pretended to think about it. "I believe it was a MasterCard."

"That's the company card. I have one, too."

"Yes, sir, the credit card company told us that, but you weren't in Illinois when the car was rented. Your son was the only one in the state with that particular card at the time it was used."

Nate couldn't help but enjoy the look of fear on Phillip's arrogant face. He must have sensed what was coming.

Calder said, "Seth and I aren't the only ones on the company account. There's one more card, and Phillip has it."

Brandon eased over beside Sam. "I wasn't aware you worked for Mor-co, Patterson."

Phillip's voice lost its smugness. "I don't."

"Well, unless you can tell me what you're doing with a Mor-co credit card, I'm afraid we'll just have to believe you and Calder are lying to protect Seth. Sam, take Seth out to the car. I'm right behind you."

"Wait, dammit." Calder's eyes darted around the room like a scared rabbit's. "Patterson does have a card. I should know; I gave it to him."

~~*~*~*

Brandon took a perverse satisfaction in watching Phillip sweating and pacing through the two-way mirror of the interrogation room. Sam walked up with a package in his hand. "I've got good news and bad news. Which do you want first?"

"Hit me with the worst news first. That way I have something to look forward to later on."

"You've got it, Boss. Patterson's prints don't match the one on Doc Morris's undercarriage. Not only that, but the fire marshal says the fire at The Book Barn was set between five-thirty and six o'clock. There's no way Patterson could have started that fire because—"

"Because he was sitting in my living room at the time. Damn. What's the good news?"

"Well, technically, we've got him on credit card fraud." He held up the package he was carrying. "This is the surveillance tape from Bingham's. It shows Patterson renting the car. The time stamps on the tape and the receipt match."

Brandon nodded. "I doubt Seth will press charges just because Phillip signed his name to a receipt. It might be enough to scare Patterson into telling us the deal between him and Calder, though."

Sam's smile lit the hallway. "I'll be out here watching. I can't wait to see you shake up that cocky bastard."

"I'm looking forward to it. Before we start, though, I want you to bring Seth into the hall so he can see the whole thing. Whatever's going on involves his father. He has a right to hear it first hand."

"Where is Mr. Morris, anyway?"

"Sitting in my office, demanding that Seth be allowed a lawyer. Calder hasn't yet caught on to the fact that it's all a set-up. I might feel sorry for him if he weren't such a pompous jerk."

Sam agreed and went to get Seth. When they returned, Brandon put a hand on the younger man's shoulder. "Are you sure you're up for this?"

"No, but what the hell? It's not like Phillip and I have this great relationship at stake. To tell you the truth, I'm starting to wonder if the guy's even gay."

Brandon wondered the same thing, but he didn't comment. He clapped Seth on the back and stepped into the interrogation room, videotape in hand. Phillip gave him a hunted look that told Brandon he was on the verge of cracking.

"Look, Sheriff, I know my rights. You have to let me call a lawyer. I don't even know what I'm being charged with."

Brandon turned his chair around backwards and straddled it. "That's because you haven't been charged with anything, yet. You're being detained as a material witness."

"Witness? Witness to what?"

"To the transaction that produced the receipt we found at our crime scene."

"You mean the car rental? No, that was all Seth. I wasn't even there."

Brandon walked over to the television in the corner and popped the tape into the built-in VCR. Patterson stared in slack-jawed astonishment at the film of himself behind the counter at Bingham's.

Brandon crossed his arms over his chest. "Funny thing about security cameras. Everybody's got them these days, even car rental places. The time stamps on the tape and the receipt match exactly. That tape proves you're guilty of credit card fraud."

"I didn't steal that card. You heard what Calder said — he gave it to me."

"What I want to know is, why?"

Some of Phillip's smugness returned. "I don't have to tell you anything."

Brandon walked to the door. "You're right. You don't have to tell me a thing. I'll turn the case over to the F.B.I. and let them handle it." Brandon could almost hear Patterson swallowing.

"The F.B.I.?"

Brandon gave him a look of feigned surprise. "Well, sure. I thought a smart guy like you, so up on the law and all, would know that forgery is a federal offense."

"Seth will never press charges against me. He loves me."

"After you were ready to hang him out to dry to save your own skin? I seriously doubt it. Here, let's ask him." Brandon opened the door, and Seth stepped inside. "Seth, you gonna press charges or what?"

Seth's face was a mask of disgust and hurt, but his voice was strong. "Oh, I think so. It isn't every day a guy finds out his boyfriend is willing to send him up the river for a crime he didn't commit."

"All right, then. Let's go get the ball rolling," Brandon said.

Phillip's desperation was sickening. "Wait! I'll tell you whatever it is you want to know if you promise not to prosecute."

Brandon said, "That all depends on what you have to say."

"Please. I'll cooperate. Just...don't arrest me. Please."

Brandon took a seat and waited for Seth to do the same. "We're listening."

"Where should I start?"

"How about telling us why Calder gave you that card?"

"For expenses. I've been using it to take Seth out to dinner, rent hotel rooms, and buy clothes. You name it."

"Why would you need to do that? You told me your parents were well off."

This time Phillip's disdain was for himself. "If by 'well off' you mean able to afford a double-wide trailer instead of a single, then yeah, they are." He lowered his head. "My folks are poor, Seth. Dirt poor."

Seth just shook his head. "But you go to college. If your family is so poor, how can you afford it? Surely my father isn't paying for that, too."

"No. I got a scholarship. It pays for tuition and books, but nothing else."

"Let me guess. It's a drama scholarship, right?" Brandon said.

"Damn, you're good. Yeah, it's a drama scholarship. Have you figured the rest of it out, too?"

"I think so, but I want Seth to hear it from you. And don't even think about lying. The least you owe him is the truth."

Phillip nodded. He addressed his next statements to Seth alone. "I'm an actor, Seth. I've been doing community theater in and around Atlanta, but I've also had a few voice-over parts. Your father contacted my agent and said he wanted somebody to play the part of a rich gay guy to come on to his son. My agent chose me because your father thought I was your type."

"How would he know? He thought I'd gone straight."

"Apparently, that campus shrink you started seeing after you broke away from Calder's therapist has a secretary who was hurting for cash. She sold a copy of your file to your dad. Everything you told that counselor went straight to him. As soon as he found out you were still having feelings for other guys, he decided to step in and do something about it."

"So what, exactly, did he hope to gain by hiring you?"

Seth spoke in a flat voice that worried the hell out of Brandon.

"I was supposed to make you fall for me. Your father provided everything I needed to show you a good time. He wanted me to put it all on the credit card so he could make sure his money was being put to good use. He even told me to sign your name so if you saw the receipts, you would just chalk it up to a business expense. He wanted me to get you hooked. Calder was adamant about no sex, though. I was to give you just enough to keep you interested. It was his idea to use the rape as an excuse to make you have an AIDS test. Your dad said that would buy me six months, at least."

"Maybe I'm just stupid — and obviously I'm not too bright or I wouldn't have fallen for your act — but what exactly did you need time for?"

Brandon saw the first signs of remorse on Phillip's face. "Seth, your dad still thinks this gay thing is a choice. He thinks you'll snap out of it. He wanted me to make you love me, and then turn around and dump you. He wanted me to break your heart."

Seth sank back into his chair. Brandon could only guess at the pain he must be feeling, but he didn't have time to offer comfort now. Too many questions were still unanswered. Brandon trained his cop's eyes on Patterson. "Morris thought if you hurt Seth badly enough, he'd decide to try his luck with girls?" As hard as he tried, Brandon couldn't keep the disbelief out of his voice.

Phillip nodded. "Calder thinks that Seth has chosen to be gay. He thought that if Seth's first gay relationship since the rape ended in disaster, the two bad experiences combined would make Seth give up on guys for good." Phillip looked at Seth's stony face. "As I'm sure you've guessed, Seth, I'm not gay. I took the job because my girlfriend is pregnant. Not that it'll make you feel any better, but I don't believe being gay is a choice. And Seth, if I was gay, I'd consider myself lucky to be with a guy like you."

"How much?"

Phillip was thrown by the question. "I'm not following."

Brandon was relieved to hear some emotion in Seth's voice, even if that emotion was anger.

"How much did my father pay you to dick me around?"

"Fifty thousand. Twenty-five up front, the rest when the job was finished. That doesn't include what I put on the credit card."

"Nice work if you can get it, but where does Nate figure into all this?" Brandon said.

"According to Calder, Nathan is the reason Seth 'turned queer' to begin with. His words, not mine. When Seth started talking about seeing his brother again, Calder panicked. Then the newspaper guy's son faxed them that clipping about the attack outside the doctor's office. Leda wanted to fly up right then, but Calder stalled her by saying he wanted to reconcile with Nathan. Calder convinced her that he was all right with the whole gay issue and wanted time to fix things."

Seth shook his head in amazement. "That's why Dad took it so well when I told him I was sure I was gay. He already knew because he had my psych files. At least Mother wasn't in on it, too."

Phillip nodded. "As far as I can tell, Leda is fine with you being gay."

"What's Calder's plan concerning Nate?" Brandon asked. "To come up here and pretend to accept our relationship? I got that, but to what end?"

Phillip shook his head. "That, I couldn't tell you. Calder gives me just as much information as I need to do my job, but we aren't exactly pals." He leaned back a little. "So, what's the deal here? Are you charging me with fraud, or am I free to go?"

Brandon inclined his head. "That's up to Seth."

"When's your baby due?"

Seth's question caught Phillip off guard. "April. We hope to find out the sex pretty soon."

"You gonna marry that girl?"

"Yeah. That's why I took your father up on his offer. I'm not really a prick, you know. That's just part of the act. Shelby, my girlfriend, and I wanted to get married right before Thanksgiving. We were going to use that money to buy a small house. One without wheels. Not that I deserve a house, after what I've done to you."

Seth was quiet for a few minutes. Then he did something that surprised the hell out of Brandon. He smiled.

"I'll drop the charges on one condition."

"I'm listening. It's not like I have a whole lot of bargaining room."

Seth pulled a checkbook out of his pocket. "This account draws directly from the trust my grandmother left me. My father has no control over this money. It's mine, free and clear. Two hundred thousand of it is yours if you agree to use your phenomenal acting skills to help me turn the tables on my father."

Brandon whistled. "Can you afford that?"

"You really have no idea how much money our grandmother left us, do you? Nate said you didn't want anything to do with it, but I thought you at least knew how much we each started out with."

"No, and I don't want to know. Nate can leave it all to the kids after they come along. Until then, if anything happens to him, it all goes to Amy so she can continue to help patients who can't afford to pay. Even after Nate and I sign over power of attorney to each other, that won't change."

Phillip broke in. "I appreciate the gesture, Seth, but I owe you. I'll do it for free just to thank you for not pressing charges."

Seth shook his head. "No. I'm definitely going to pay you. If you can pull this off, it'll be worth every penny."

* ~ * ~ * ~ * ~ *

Brandon walked into his office and found just what he expected, a furious Calder Morris. *So much the better.*

"You've kept me waiting long enough, Nash. I want to see my son, and I want to see him now."

Seth walked in behind Brandon, his fingers tightly laced with Phillip's. "I'm right here, Dad. I'm all right, but we need to talk. Phillip told me why you hired him."

Calder flushed and started to stammer, but Seth cut him off. "It's okay, Dad. There's no need to make excuses. Phillip and I have talked through all of it, and we've decided it doesn't matter. I love him enough to forgive him. And how can I be mad at you for your interference when your meddling brought us together in the first place?"

Calder looked at their entwined hands much like one would look at a freeway accident. It was as if he knew he shouldn't look, but he couldn't stop himself. "What the hell are you talking about?"

Phillip put his arm around Seth's shoulders. "Let me tell him, sweetheart. Over the past few months, I've come to care deeply for Seth, Mr. Morris. I'm not sure exactly when it became love, but after

Seth was arrested today, I realized how empty my life would be without him. I'm giving you back your money, sir. Seth and I are going to build a life together."

"For God's sake, Patterson, you're straight. Your girlfriend is pregnant."

"We know, Dad," Seth said, "and we regret hurting Shelby, but we both believe that she'll be far more hurt if Phillip marries her when he's in love with me. We hope that she'll share joint custody of the baby with us. You know how much I love children." Seth gave Phillip a lingering look before Phillip gathered him into his arms and stuck his tongue down Seth's throat in a kiss so passionate, Brandon even blushed. Much as he was enjoying Calder's suffering, it was time to move on to phase two.

Like clockwork, Sam came in and cleared his throat, breaking the pair apart. "I'm sorry to interrupt, but Seth needs to be processed out before he can leave."

Seth gave Phillip one more peck on the lips and said, "I'll be right back. Maybe you can fill Dad in on our plans while I'm gone. Dad's been so excited about Nate's wedding, I know he can't wait to start planning ours." He left, but not before giving Phillip's ass a hefty squeeze for good measure.

Brandon sat down behind his desk and motioned for Calder and Phillip to have a seat as well. "Kick back, guys. He'll be finished and free to go any minute now. Phillip, I believe you were about to tell us about your future plans."

"Well, I have one more year of school left before I earn my bachelor's degree. Seth and I thought we might go out to California so I can audition, go to casting calls, that kind of thing. Of course, it all depends on how cooperative Shelby is about custody. Either way, Seth and I hope to be married before Christmas."

Calder didn't have a chance to comment before Seth came back in. "I'm ready to go if you are."

Phillip got up, but Calder said, "You go on ahead, son. I want a word alone with Brandon."

"Okay, Dad. Phillip and I could use a little time alone, anyway. Now that the pretense has been dropped, I don't see any reason why we can't take our relationship to the next level, do you, babe?"

Phillip's grin was that of a man who was two seconds away from scoring. "I thought you'd never ask." They left holding hands.

Calder waited until they were out of sight and then got up and closed the door. "All right, Nash. I'm ready to talk price."

Brandon propped his feet on the desk. "Mr. Morris, I know how excited you are about the wedding, but I have more than enough in savings for Nate and I to have the type of ceremony we want. There's no need for you to chip in."

Calder slammed his hand down. "Dammit, that's not what I'm talking about, and you know it. I want to know how much it'll cost me to get you out of Nathan's life."

"I'm not sure I understand, sir."

"Don't play me, Nash. You're too smart to play the part of a moron. I want you to name a figure."

Brandon nodded. "And if I do?"

"Then you agree to drop Nathan like hot lead. The more you hurt him, the better."

Brandon's stomach turned, but he forced his face not to show it. "If the price is right, I'll do it. But why should I make it more painful than necessary?"

"You want all the cards on the table, huh? Fine, then. I'll tell you. After what Landon did to him, having the first man he's dated since then drop him on his ass ought to turn Nathan off men for life."

"How did you know I was the first man Nate has dated since Landon?"

"The private investigator I've had keeping track of him for the last six years told me."

"So, just like with Seth, you think Nate will stop being gay if he gets his heart broken again."

Calder snorted. "There's a big difference between Nathan and Seth. Seth is strong, just a little confused right now. Nathan has always been weak, spineless. Just look at his choice of professions. Hell, he gives a good portion of money each year to help those worthless indigents who can't even pay their own medical bills. When the little pansy told us he was gay, I wasn't surprised. In fact, I'd known for some time. No way in hell was I going to let him corrupt Seth, though. Not then, and not now."

Brandon had never wanted to hit a man so badly in his life. He knew he had no choice but to tamp it down and finish this, but his knuckles were straining for contact. "You heard about Nate's attack from your investigator, not from one of your store managers."

"That's right. Malcolm Davis's son does work for me, but he didn't say a word about the attack. Not to me, anyway. Davis did tell Seth, but I found out from my investigator first. If you ask me, the only shame is that the guy didn't hit Nathan a little harder."

Visions of Calder Morris clutching a broken nose tempted Brandon's restraint. "If you hate him so much, why hire an investigator to keep track of him?"

Calder shook his head. "You just don't get it, do you? Seth has always adored Nathan, looked up to him. Nathan is the reason Seth wants to be queer in the first place. I knew it was just a matter of time before Seth tried to contact him. When Seth started seeing that campus witch doctor who convinced him it was all right to be a fag, I knew his next logical step was to come up here and beg that lowlife butt-fucker for forgiveness. No, my only hope for Seth is to convince Nathan not to be queer, anymore, either. Once you dump him, we'll take Nathan home with us and pressure him to see the same psychiatrist who helped Seth the first time. Seth will go back to see her if Nathan does, and I'll have a normal family again."

"What about Phillip?"

Calder's smile was nauseating. "Patterson? Hell, he's already proven he can be bought. I'll just have to up the price, that's all."

Brandon nodded. "So, you're the one behind the attack on Nate? You hired someone to trash his place and cut his brake lines?"

"No, all that was just a happy coincidence. Wish I'd thought of it, though." Calder looked almost disappointed. "When Leda and I got that call from Patterson saying Nathan had nearly bled to death, all I could think was, 'Why the hell didn't it take them a little longer to pull him out of that car?' No, I'd gladly do away with the little fairy, but he simply isn't worth risking a murder charge." Calder pulled a cell phone from his pocket. "Now that we're clear on things, tell me how much you want. I'll make a call to my accountant and have the whole thing set up."

"Interesting choice of words, Calder, seeing as how that's exactly what this is, a set-up."

Calder looked up to see his wife standing in the now open office door. "Leda, what in God's name are you talking about?"

"Save it, Calder. Next time you decide to make a grand confession, have sense enough to make certain the intercom isn't on. We heard the whole sordid thing. In fact, Brandon was kind enough to have his deputies make a tape of it for us. I'm sure my divorce attorney will find it most helpful."

"It's entrapment to tape a man without his knowledge. My lawyer will never allow it. I'll sue this whole damn department."

"Obviously, you didn't read the many signs posted throughout the office." Brandon pointed to one on the bulletin boards above the desk. "All communications in this office with the exception of those that fall under attorney/client privilege may be monitored and/or documented." Brandon read it word for word, pleased by Calder's rapidly falling countenance. "As it is, I have enough to book you on assault charges while I work to make a murder charge stick."

"Are you talking about the attempts on Nathan? I told you, I had nothing to do with that."

Brandon stood and circled around to the front of the desk. "Like your word means anything. In my opinion, any man capable of wishing his own son dead is capable of murder. Calder Morris, you're under arrest for the assault and attempted murder of Nathan Morris and Marjorie Newman."

As Brandon read Calder his rights and cuffed him, Calder's denials grew more frantic. "I'm telling you, I had nothing to do with it. That little fag probably tried to fuck the wrong man and got what he deserved. Damned perverts. The whole lot of you is headed straight for Hell."

Leda shook her head in disgust. "No one is more deserving of Hell than a father who can say what you just said about his own son. I've allowed you to beat us down and abuse us for almost thirty years. My only comfort is that Nathan didn't hear the vile things you just said."

"Actually, Mother, I did." Nate stepped away from Sam's desk where he'd been sitting and listening over the intercom. He was wobbly and shaking, but his voice was clear and strong. Brandon rushed to his side and put his arm around Nate's waist. Nate leaned into him, and Brandon was overpowered with worry as he felt the extent of Nate's weakness.

"How the hell did you get down here, Nate? You're supposed to be at home, resting."

Keith came in, his face flushed and his lungs working for breath. "I'll tell you how he got here. When Seth called and told Leda the plan to gaslight Calder, Nate was listening on the upstairs extension. Mom had to do some grocery shopping, so I volunteered to baby-sit your intended. When Sam came by to pick up Leda, Nate tried to convince them to let him ride along. When I put my foot down and said he was too weak to go, he pretended to go along with it. The little fucker waited until I turned my back, snatched the keys to the Camaro, and drove himself down here with one good arm and a head full of painkillers. You ought to arrest his ass for reckless driving."

Nate tried to shake his head, but he was trembling too badly. "I haven't had any pain medicine today. I had a right to know what was going on."

Nate looked at his father with so much burning hatred, Brandon almost let go of him in surprise.

"I knew this old bastard was up to something, but I never thought he'd take it this far."

Sam had Calder by the cuffs and was leading him toward booking, but his predicament did not have any affect on Calder's bigotry. "Call me whatever you want, you little shit. You're the one who's going to pay. All you faggots will."

Leda put her hand over her mouth. She turned to her oldest son. "Oh, Nathan. I am so sorry, son. I had no idea how sick your father really was."

Nate didn't answer. Brandon felt dead weight against his side and was just able to catch Nate as he crumpled to the floor.

Chapter Nine

"For the last time, Brandon, he's okay."

"I still think you should check him again."

Keith slipped the stethoscope back into his pocket. "You think I missed something the first four times I checked him?"

Nate gave them a sleepy look from his nest of pillows. "Lay off, Brandon. I'm fine. Blood thinners give you the shakes sometimes, is all."

"You're not on my happy list right now, Nathan. I wouldn't push it, if I were you." The look that appeared on Nate's face would have made Brandon feel guilty had he not been so mad. The fact that he'd had to carry Nate's prone body out of the station and into the car didn't help Brandon's mood. Nor was he placated when Nate had to be helped back into the house and up the stairs. Brandon even had to undress him, a task he would have enjoyed had he not been so damned worried.

"Don't give me those big brown puppy dog eyes, Nate. You could have been killed driving in that condition, not to mention killing someone else. Keith was right. I should have arrested you for reckless driving."

"Look, Bran, I was upset when I said that." Keith made a face. "Go easy on him. He's had a rough time of it."

"Speaking of people who've had a rough day, how's my mom?"

"She's tired, Nate, but she's a tough lady. She's resting right now."

"What about Seth? Not only did he find out the truth about Phillip, he heard every filthy word Dad said."

"He took Phillip to the airport about an hour ago." Brandon covered Nate with another blanket. "He seems to be holding up well under the circumstances."

"Not to interrupt." Keith spoke from the foot of the bed. "But Jacob and Jessica have a riding lesson at four and I promised Maria I would take them so she could do a little birthday shopping. I've got to run if I'm going to be there on time."

"I still can't believe the twins will be ten years old next week."

"Imagine how I feel. I always wanted to be a father, I just never dreamed they'd come in pairs." Keith smiled at Nate. "If you guys decide to use a surrogate mother instead of straight adoption, make sure not to use Brandon's sperm. Twins run thick in our family."

"I'll remember that, but I think it would be kind of nice to have twins. It would be like a complete family on the first try."

"I'll remind you of that when you're walking the floor at two in the morning with a colicky baby on each shoulder." Keith laughed and then checked his watch. "I'm out of here, guys."

"I'll walk you out." Brandon turned to Nate. "I expect you to be in this bed when I get back."

"Don't worry. I'm not planning on sneaking out for another joy ride anytime soon."

Brandon smiled. "I know. I've hidden my extra set of car keys." He winked and walked with Keith to the door. Once they were out of ear-shot, Brandon said, "Now tell me how he's really doing."

"Brandon, I know you love the guy to the point of insanity, but you're starting to scare me. Physically, he's fine. I'd say he suffered another batch of emotional scars this afternoon, but he's stronger than you're giving him credit for. He survived the break-up with Landon and desertion by his parents all at once. This time, Nate has you to help him deal with it."

"Yeah, but last time he didn't have some psycho trying to off him, either."

"Any word on Calder?"

"Sam called about an hour ago and said Calder's prints don't match the partial, but we're going to hold him as long as we can while we gather evidence. Eva called and said Marjorie's vitals were improving, but she still hasn't regained consciousness. Her doctor did say that she received the blow to the head before the fire started, so I'm hopeful she'll remember something that can help my case when, and if, she comes around."

Keith didn't look hopeful. "I know your degree is clinical, not medical, but you learned more than enough in Shrink One-O-One to know that most head trauma victims have only partial recall. For that reason alone, I wouldn't set my sights on any big revelations from Marjorie. Add that to the fact that she's nearly sixty, and I'd say your chances in that sector are slim to none."

Brandon thanked him again and was on his way back to Nate when he encountered Seth. "How you holding up?"

Seth gave him a crooked smile. "As nutty as it sounds, I think I'm more relieved than anything. The way Phillip kept putting me off, I was starting to think there was something wrong with me. Now I know he was just another flunky on the old man's payroll."

"Do you think Calder's stable of flunkies includes a good combination arsonist and hit man?"

"You want to hear the funny part? Even after everything he's said and done, I still don't think my father is capable of hiring someone to murder his own son. I was in the dispatcher's office listing to every word he said to you. I know the man is a lousy, rotten bigot, but murder just isn't his style."

"As much as I'd like to pin this on your father, I agree with you. For one thing, why risk exposure by planting that receipt? We already know Calder's prints don't match the one on Nate's car. I have a feeling I'm going to have to turn him loose in a few hours." He pursed his lips in disgust. "Makes me sick to even think about having to let that son of a bitch go."

"How's Nate?" Seth asked.

"Keith swears he's all right, but I know this whole thing has been a nightmare for him. Nate was really hoping Calder wanted to reconcile."

"Me, too. I think out of all of us, though, Mother was hit the hardest. She never saw it coming."

"Keith said Leda's resting."

"Yeah. She was sleeping when I last checked. She's worn out. She was on the phone all afternoon trying to find a good divorce attorney with no luck. Hey, didn't you tell me your sister is a lawyer?"

"Alicia's a prosecutor; she doesn't handle civil cases. What about Mike? Doesn't he work for a firm in Chicago?"

"I forgot all about him. I'll tell Mom when she wakes up. Thanks, Brandon. Tell Nate I'll be up to see him later."

Brandon nodded and returned to the bedroom. Nate was sleeping, not that Brandon was surprised. He said a silent prayer of thanks that Nate was safe, also praying that he'd be able to keep him that way.

* ~ * ~ * ~ * ~ *

Calder was released the next morning, though Brandon tried his best to delay it. Nate appreciated the effort, but he could have told Brandon nothing would keep Calder Morris down for long.

Nate was lying in bed going stir crazy when Leda came in with Seth. She gave her eldest son a kiss on the check and settled into the chair beside the bed. Though she looked lovely as always, something was different — Leda seemed happier, freer. Seth stood behind his mother and propped his hands on the back of her chair.

"How are you, Nathan?"

"Fine, Mom. The question is, how are you?"

"Actually, I feel better than I have in a long time. According to

Mike, I have one heck of a divorce settlement coming. Calder will fight it, of course, but Georgia is an equitable distribution state, so I'm entitled to half of everything he owns. And until it's all settled, I have enough money to keep myself comfortable."

"Mom, Seth and I both have more money than we could ever spend. Let us—"

"No. That's the money your grandmother set aside for you in case her son turned out to be a jackass. Insightful woman, your grandmother. I have more than enough, thank you anyway." She paused. "Seth and I are flying back to Georgia tonight. From there, I'll be able to start the proceedings. I'll stay at a friend's house until after the necessary papers are filed, but I'll leave a number where I can be reached. Mike referred me to a good divorce attorney just outside Atlanta. I have an appointment with him in the morning." She took Nate's hand. "Seth's talking about transferring to an Illinois school and changing his major from business to journalism. When this is all over and done, I'm thinking about moving to Reed. That way, I'd be close to both of you."

"Journalism?" Nate looked to his brother. "Since when have you been interested in that?"

Seth shrugged. "I've always wanted to be a writer. The business degree was just to please Dad. He called me this morning when he got out of jail. He still thinks Phillip has gone over to the dark side and that he and I are really trying to make a go of it. He told me that if I 'hitch my faggoty-ass to that two-bit actor' he'll disinherit me, and I can forget about a future with Mor-co Incorporated. I took great pleasure in telling him that I planned to be one of those bleeding heart, liberal word jockeys he's always complaining about."

"Won't this set you back quite a bit as far as graduation goes?" Nate frowned. "I'd hate for you to have to start all over again."

"I won't. The basic requirements are about the same for the first two years. I figure one more year to get in all the extra English courses, and I'll be ready to join the ranks of those actively seeking gainful employment." Seth put his hand on his mother's shoulder. "We'd better get cracking if we're going to make our plane." He leaned over and gave Nate a firm but careful bear hug. "I love you, Nate. I'll be back just as soon as I get everything straightened out."

Nate kissed his brother and mother good-bye, praying that the next time he saw them, the dark cloud hovering over all of them would be lifted. He had a sinking feeling that it wasn't going to happen anytime soon.

* ~ * ~ * ~ * ~ *

Five days after his release from the hospital, Nate was going sys-
tematically insane. He'd spent most of his time in bed, and, except for
his trip to the police station in Brandon's car, he hadn't even ventured
outside. When Brandon got home from the station, Nate was in the
kitchen, waiting for him. "You've got to get me out of here, Bran. I'm
going crazy."

Brandon hung up his coat and kissed Nate gently. "Where's Mom?
Didn't she come today?"

"Yes, but I sent her home about an hour ago. I love Gale with all
my heart, but a man can only eat so much chicken noodle soup and
watch so many soap operas before he climbs a clock tower and starts
taking out bystanders."

Brandon grinned. "Did you have a specific destination in mind?"

Nate nodded, but his throat was too dry to speak. He went to the
refrigerator and poured two tall glasses of iced tea, handed one to Brandon, and took a long drink of his own. When his mouth was moist
enough to function, he said, "Actually, there is someplace I'd like to
go." He cleared his throat. "I want you to take me down to Old Pepper
Road."

"Where did you hear about Pepper Road?"

"Megan came by to keep me company after school today. She told
me about it." When he saw Brandon's eyes darken, Nate hurried to
explain. "She told me that she'd never been down there, but that a lot
of the kids at school ended up there on Friday and Saturday nights. I
figured since this is Thursday, and a school night, we should be all alone
down there."

Brandon set down his glass. "You do know that Pepper Road is
known for one thing, and one thing only, right?"

"Yep. I want you to take me parking, Bran."

* ~ * ~ * ~ * ~ *

Brandon selected a spot underneath an old oak and cut the
Camaro's powerful engine. "I can't believe I let you talk me into this."
Nate looked damn sexy in the soft moonlight filtering through the car
windows.

"Have you ever been parking before?"

"Nope. Becky Bradshaw tried to get me to bring her down here on
prom night, but I begged off. I guess you can imagine why." Nate
smiled, and Brandon felt a tug in his groin.

"I think I can. For the record, I've never been parking, either. I
thought it might take our minds off things for a little while."

Brandon took his hand. "Nate, you know I'd do anything for you, but you're still healing. Two days ago you nearly collapsed. We can't—"

Nate put his finger against Brandon's lips. "The doctor said I couldn't make love until he gave us the go ahead. He didn't say anything about making out. I want us to be like other couples, to do normal dating stuff. Neither of us was 'out' in high school, so now we can go back and do all the things we missed, together."

"We have a perfectly good bed at home to make out in." But even as he said it, Brandon knew he was only offering a token resistance. Already his body was responding to the closeness of his mate. When Nate leaned over and kissed him, Brandon swore he saw sparks.

Nate wrapped his left arm around Brandon's neck and pulled him closer. He snaked his tongue into Brandon's mouth and kissed him breathless. When he was done, Nate moved down and started licking and sucking on Brandon's neck.

Brandon hissed when Nate's hand drifted from his chest to his fly. "Nate, you have to stop."

Nate's lips continued their assault on his ear. "Why?"

"Because you're still not well, and I'm not sure how much control I've got left."

"For what I want to do to you," Nate said between licking and chewing, "the last thing you need is control." He raised his mouth to Brandon's ear and whispered, "I want to suck you, Brandon. I want to feel you in my mouth. I want to taste you."

Brandon almost came in his jeans when Nate's fingers went to work on his button-fly. Nate was working with only one hand because of his cast, but somehow the awkwardness made it that much more arousing.

With excruciating slowness, he eased the top button through the slot and started on the next one, his hand brushing Brandon's hardness through the soft cotton of his boxers. By the time Nate reached the third button, Brandon's underwear was soaked. Nate made quick work of the remaining two and soon had Brandon's clothing pushed down just enough to free his erection.

Nate's touches were light and hesitant at first, but when Brandon covered Nate's hand with his own and showed him how he liked to be touched, Nate quickly found a rhythm that had Brandon panting for breath.

"Baby, I can't hold off much longer."

Nate kissed his jaw. "I want you to come, but not like this." Before Brandon could respond, Nate lowered his head and took the tip of Brandon's hard-on into his mouth. He leaned forward and moved the lower half of his body back across the bucket seat until he was lying across Brandon's lap. He cupped Brandon's sac in his hand and increased the gentle suction, taking more of him into his mouth with each downward movement of his head.

When Nate used his tongue to tease the hole at the tip of his shaft, Brandon felt the orgasm tightening his stomach muscles. "Jesus, Nate, I'm gonna shoot." He thought Nate might back off and finish him with his hand, but he kept up the tender assault. Brandon's fists knotted against the leather of the seat as the first wave of release hit. Nate was with him every step, holding tight as Brandon's hips bucked with the intense pleasure.

When Brandon finally collapsed against the seat, Nate pulled off and rested his head against Brandon's chest, listening to the racing of his heart.

When Brandon spoke, his voice was husky and low. "I love you, Nate."

"I love you, too. I never realized how good it could be to give pleasure to someone else."

Brandon reached for him. "I can make it even better for you."

The blush on Nate's face and the way he backed away from the touch told Brandon he'd missed something. "What's the matter? I only want to give you the same feeling you've just given me."

"That's just it. While I was...while we were... This is so embarrassing. It's just that, when you came, I got so excited, I...I did, too."

Brandon took Nate into his arms. "You came without even touching yourself?"

Nate looked so miserable when he nodded, Brandon kissed him, tasting himself on Nate's lips. "Baby, that's nothing to be embarrassed about. In fact, it makes me hot all over again just thinking about it." He reached under the seat and pulled out the paper towels he kept in the car for spills and clean-ups. He eased Nate back against the seat and unzipped his jeans. With aching tenderness, Brandon cleaned away all evidence of Nate's release. He had Nate take off his shoes and then yanked at his jeans until Nate wriggled out of them — no small task in the tight confines of the car — and then Brandon pulled Nate's boxers off and held them while Nate put his jeans back on.

When Nate reached for his underwear, Brandon shook his head. "Nope. These are mine. I've heard about straight guys keeping their girlfriends' panties as trophies. Well, these are mine. It's not every day a man gets his guy worked up enough to come without ever being touched." Brandon pretended to think about it for a minute. "In fact, I've seen other men hang garters from their rearview mirrors. I wonder how these would look dangling above the dash."

"No way, Brandon. I'm not about to have my underwear on display for all of Reed, Illinois to see." Nate made a one-handed grab for them, but Brandon caught him and pulled him backward across his lap.

"I've got you now, boy. Wonder if I can think of something really nasty to do to you?" He claimed Nate's mouth with renewed passion, and probably would have done more had a bright light not landed right across his eyes.

"What the hell?" Brandon looked up and saw the silhouette of a man against the window, flashlight in hand. He let Nate go back to his own seat, fear and adrenaline racing through his veins. He cursed himself for being stupid enough to come out to this isolated spot without letting anyone know where they were. Brandon rolled down the window and reached under the seat for his pistol, in one fluid motion.

The man behind the flashlight laughed. "If you're gonna shoot me, Boss, don't you think you should at least button your pants first?"

Brandon exhaled in a rush of air. "Dammit, Sam, you scared the shit out of me. I thought you were that nut who's after Nate."

Sam lowered the flashlight, the moonlight bright enough to reveal the grin he was having trouble hiding. "What would you have done if I had been? You'd have been screwed, no pun intended."

Brandon heard Nate trying his best not to laugh. Brandon ignored him and turned his irritation on Sam. "What are you doing down here, anyway?"

"I got a report about some kids parking down on Old Pepper Road and came to check it out. You haven't seen any horny teenagers, have you?"

"Ha-ha. You've investigated, so now you can leave."

Sam shook his head. "I was headed to your place after I finished this call. On my way over here, dispatch radioed in. The F.B.I. came up with a match on that partial from Doc's car." He leaned down so he could see Nate through the open window. "Hey, Doc. How's it hanging?"

Nate dissolved into another fit of laughter, but Brandon had switched into cop mode. "Did dispatch give any details?"

"No, but apparently the guy they've identified is into some heavy shit because the U.S. Attorney's Office is sending a man on the next flight from Washington to go over the case with you."

Brandon felt Nate stiffen beside him and reached for his hand without looking. "Thanks, Sam. I'm going to take Nate home, and then I'll come to the station and see what I can find out."

Sam nodded and said good-bye, leaving Brandon and Nate to rearrange their clothing and head home. As Brandon started the car, Nate said, "Why would the U.S. Attorney be involved?"

Brandon backed the car out and started up the gravel road. "I'd be afraid to speculate. The Attorney General's office could be in on this for any number of reasons, Nate. They have divisions for everything from organized crime to counter terrorism." He stopped at the end of the road and gave Nate a reassuring kiss. "Let's make a deal not to worry about it until we have to, all right?"

Nate agreed, but Brandon could feel the tension in him. He didn't blame Nate for being scared. Brandon had the feeling things had just gone from bad to worse.

* ~ * ~ * ~ * ~ *

Brandon was sitting at his desk the next day when his assistant, Lorna, stuck her head through the door. "Sheriff, the representative from the Attorney General's office is here. I've already checked his credentials and received confirmation. Should I send him in?"

"Please. And, Lorna? Make sure we aren't disturbed. Sam's off today, but if anything major comes in, Dewey can handle it."

"Sure thing, Sheriff." She left and returned a few minutes later with a tall man in a three-piece suit. Brandon estimated him to be between forty-five and fifty, his black hair peppered with gray.

His green eyes were warm when he introduced himself, his crooked smile softening the sharp angles of his face. "Rex Howard, U.S. Attorney's Office."

Brandon shook his hand, noticing Howard's firm grip. "Brandon Nash. Come on in and have a seat." Brandon returned to his desk as Howard seated himself. "I understand you have some information for me. Can I get you some coffee before we start?"

"No thanks. I drank a gallon of it on the flight in. My wife has been after me to slack off, but since I quit smoking two years ago, I figure I need at least one vice. I'm afraid my wife doesn't see it that way. You married, Nash?"

"Engaged. My fiancé's already nagging me about my eating habits, though, so I know how you feel."

"Sounds like you do. Now, I imagine you're ready for me to stop the small talk and tell you the reason I'm here." He picked up his briefcase and indicated the desk. "May I?" When Brandon nodded, Howard put the case on the desk and opened it, taking out a thick file. He put the case back on the floor and handed the folder to Bran. "The F.B.I. took the partial you gave them and entered it into their database. It took some doing, but they finally came up with a name." He pointed to the mugshot at the top of the file. "Meet your perp, Nolan Wilson."

Brandon looked at the picture, searching for any recognizable features. All he saw was a man of about forty with auburn hair and bloodshot hazel eyes. Nothing, from the guy's hawk-like nose to his pointed chin, struck any cords of familiarity for Brandon. "Doesn't look familiar. What can you tell me about him?"

"Nolan Wilson, alias Ned White, is a real hitman's hitman. He's quick, thorough, and discreet. He has an arrest record as long as my forearm, but no convictions. He's been linked with some of the biggest crime families in the business, but he's a freelancer, going with whoever pays the best and never pledging allegiance to any one family."

Brandon nodded. "I understand that the Attorney General is cracking down on organized crime, but if Wilson has no real family affiliation, why the interest?"

"The thing about Wilson that sets him apart from most hitmen is the fact that he doesn't specialize. Wilson prides himself on his versatility. He's been suspected in four arsons, three bombings, and at least fourteen murders. It's rumored that if a client requests a service beyond Wilson's expertise, he'll study and learn until he has the skills to perform the job requested. That's where our office comes in."

"Six months ago, Ross Donavan, owner of the Norwegian Woods restaurant chain, found out that one of his distributors was supplying meat that hadn't been graded by the U.S.D.A. Donavan canceled his contract and found another supplier. Unfortunately, the supplier he stopped doing business with was connected to the Nikoli crime family. Within one week of canceling the contract, the first restaurant burned down. By the time our office became involved five weeks later, Donavan had lost four restaurants. An anonymous tip points to Wilson as the perp. If we can corner him and make a conviction stick, we might be able to convince him to roll on the Nikoli family. We want this guy bad, Nash. He's a heavy hitter with almost limitless resources." Howard leaned back in his chair. "Before we go any further, though, I want to know why a small town sheriff is after a key player like Wilson."

"Let me spell it out for you. I was with the feds long enough to know how the system works. I don't care who prosecutes this guy as long as you get to him before I do. I'm telling you now, Howard, if I get to Wilson first, there may not be enough of him left to prosecute."

Howard didn't seem shocked by the declaration. "Sounds like this is personal."

"You have no idea. To answer your question, though, I suspect Wilson is behind a series of purported gay bashings. I say purported because I believe he's really after one man and is using the 'bashings' as a cover. So far, two local businesses, both owned by gay and lesbian couples, have been torched. The first one was clean, but a woman got caught in the middle of the second. She's still in a coma, by the way, so any information she might have isn't going to be forthcoming anytime soon. As I said before, I think the arsons are just a cover. I believe his real target is a man named Nathan Morris, a doctor here in town. Three weeks ago, Nate was coming out of his office when this piece of shit grabbed him and knocked him over the head. Nate was smart enough to trigger the alarm, but that same night, both his office and his home were ransacked, words like 'queer' and 'fag' painted on the walls and animal blood dumped all over his clothes. I have reason to believe Wilson was going to kill him, then went into a rage when he couldn't find Nate. The first burning happened a few days later, and a note was sent to this office, making it appear to be a hate crime. A little too convenient if you ask me. Two weeks after the assault, the son of a bitch cut the brake lines on Nate's car. I almost lost—" Brandon cleared his throat. "Nate almost bled to death. The day after he came home from the hospital, the second fire happened. No note this time, but the doer planted evidence making it look like Nate's brother was the perp. Seth, the brother, has been cleared, so that leaves us where we are now. Wilson's print was lifted from the undercarriage of Nate's car, but no other physical evidence has been found. So far, Wilson is our only lead."

"I'd say you're right about the gay bashing angle being a screen," Howard said. "Wilson himself is a known bisexual with a heavy preference toward men. It's unlikely he'd suddenly jump on the anti-gay bandwagon. The thing about this that confuses me is why Wilson would target a small-town doctor. Wilson is strictly for hire. He has a slew of personal enemies, as I'm sure you can imagine, but hasn't lifted a finger against any of them. The only time he kills, it's business. And a guy like Wilson doesn't come cheap." He put his fingers to his chin. "You say the last burning was three days ago?"

"Yeah. We're hoping the victim will be able to give us something to go on, but even if she makes a full recovery, it's doubtful she'll remember anything."

Howard sat in silence, but Brandon could almost see the man's mind working.

"The thing about Wilson is, he doesn't leave a job until it's successfully completed. Take the Ross Donavan case, for example. Wilson targeted the four most popular restaurants in the Norwegian Woods chain, nearly crippling Donavan's whole empire. We believe that was the objective all along. If Wilson is behind these attacks, and his intent is to kill Dr. Morris, he won't stop until he either gets caught or finishes the good doctor off."

Brandon's whole body went rigid. "That ain't gonna happen, Howard. The bastard will have to go through me first, and I guarantee you, he doesn't want to do that."

"I believe you, Nash. I know if someone was threatening my wife, I'd be ready to kick ass and take names."

"How'd you know?"

Howard smiled. "That Dr. Morris is your fiancé? It wasn't hard to figure out. I may have a fancy title, but at heart, I'm just a cop. Maybe it was the way you said his name, or the way you tensed when you talked about the attempts on his life. Whatever, it's plain to see you're in love with the guy and willing to do whatever it takes to protect him."

"Do you have a problem with that?"

"With your being willing to do whatever it takes to protect him? Nah. I'd prefer to bring Wilson in alive so we can nail the Nikoli family, but if you have to take him out to save your boy, I'm all for it. The world won't mourn Nolan Wilson, believe me."

Brandon shook his head and smiled. "I meant, do you have a problem with me and Nate?"

"I'm the first to admit that a good looking guy with a big dick does nothing for me, but I have no problem with homosexuals. My oldest son is gay. The guy he's dating has sixteen piercings between his eyebrow and his bellybutton. I shudder to think what he might have below the belt. If I have any negative feelings at all, it's that my son can't find a nice young doctor to settle down with instead of that pincushion he calls a boyfriend."

"I'm definitely blessed to have Nate. Now I've got to catch Wilson and whoever is bankrolling him so we can settle down to a normal life together, whatever normal is."

"I think that's where I come in. Like I said, Wilson never leaves a job until he's finished. I'd like to bring some of my men down here, undercover. When Wilson makes his next move, we'll be ready." Howard stood and fished a card from his pocket. "I'm staying at a hotel in Chicago. It will take me two days, tops, to set this thing up. You can reach me any time on my cell phone. I'll contact you as soon as arrangements are made, unless I hear from you first. Don't worry. I'll make it clear that this is your case. There'll be no pulling rank on this one. A man has a right to defend what's his." He extended his hand.

Brandon shook hands with Howard. "I'll await your call. And I appreciate your help." Howard nodded and left.

Brandon studied Wilson's file until his neck cricked and his eyes crossed, but he couldn't see a connection to Nate. When he couldn't take it anymore, he packed up his stuff and headed home.

When Brandon was single, he didn't particularly care what time he got home. With only Sasha waiting for him, his grandparents' cavernous old house just reminded him of how alone he was. Now, he couldn't wait to leave work each day. As much as Brandon enjoyed his job, nothing compared to the prospect of seeing Nate.

He wasn't surprised to see several cars parked along the driveway.

His mother was still coming every day, despite Nate's insistence that he was able to stay by himself. Brandon's entire family had fallen in love with Nathan Morris, and Brandon could certainly understand why. He saw his mother's car, and Megan's, but he also saw a Saturn Coupe he didn't recognize. Pulling in behind Keith's mini-van, he parked and got out of the S.U.V. to be greeted at the door by an agitated Sasha. It was unusual for Nate to let her out by herself, even though she had several acres to run. She was going around in circles and whining, weird coming from such a happy-go-lucky dog. Brandon stooped down to scratch her ears.

"What's the matter, girl? It's cold out here. Why did Nate let you out by yourself?" The sounds of raised voices coming from inside gave Brandon his answer.

On full alert, he opened the door to the mudroom and slipped in unobserved, the commotion in the kitchen masking the sound of the door opening. Brandon typed in the alarm code and peeked around the corner, just out of sight.

Nate was leaning against the counter, his face flushed and his eyes glittering. Gale stood on one side of him, Megan on the other. Keith was in front of Nate, almost like a shield. Amy was seated in a chair in the middle of the kitchen, begging Mike to calm down. Mike was standing in front of Keith, his finger in Keith's face.

"Who the hell do you think you are? I have a right to talk to Nate about anything I want. Just because your brother is screwing him doesn't mean you can cut him off from his friends."

Gale and Megan gasped, and Amy moaned. "Mike, please don't say things like that. Keith never said we couldn't talk to Nate."

Keith nodded. "That's right, I didn't. What I said was, I'm not going to allow you to come into my brother's house, hurling accusations about him and upsetting Nathan, my mother, and my sister. I also said, if you say one more word against Brandon, I'm going to kick your sorry ass across this kitchen and into the backyard."

Mike looked at Nate. "Are you going to let him threaten me like that?"

"Nope." Nate put his arm on Keith's shoulder. "You can't kick his ass, Keith." Keith looked stunned and angry until Nate continued. "Because if he says anything else about Brandon, that privilege is mine. I kicked your ass once, *Michael*. Don't think because I'm a little run down I can't do it again."

"Dammit, Nate. Do you really think I would drag my sick wife out in the middle of the fall in Illinois unless I thought this was a matter of life and death. You want Brandon Nash, then I say take him. Fuck him raw on a daily basis for all I care. But before you go and do something stupid like marry the guy, think long and hard about what's happened to you since you met him."

"I don't have to think about all that's happened. I live with it every day. Brandon has done nothing but try to protect me since the day we met. He's turned his whole life upside down to keep me safe."

Mike tried to shoulder Keith out of the way, but Keith didn't budge. "Has he really, Nate, or is that just what he wants you to think?" Nate started to respond, but Mike said, "No, dammit, listen to me. We've been friends for too long for you not to let me have my say. Go back to the night you were hit on the head, Nate. Who answered the 911 call?" When Nate remained silent, Mike said, "It wasn't even his turn to take evening calls. I checked."

Gale stepped up beside Keith. "If you're implying that Brandon had something to do with the attack on Nate, then I should remind you that my son didn't even know Nate at the time."

"So he says. But he freely admits that he knew *of* Nate. His old high school friend works for the answering service that takes Nate and Amy's after-hours calls, and his cousin is the billing clerk for the practice. I'm sure both women told Nash all about the handsome, gay doctor. The *rich*, gay doctor."

Megan's face was as red as her hair. "Nate was with Brandon when his apartment and office were trashed. How do you explain that?"

"Nash deals with lowlifes on a daily basis, little girl. You can't work in law enforcement without knowing how to hire some scumbag to do just about any dirty job you want done. Occupational hazard, I guess."

"What you're saying doesn't make any sense, Mike. Why would Brandon want to hurt me?"

"I can give you four million reasons why. He's after your trust fund, Nate."

Chapter Ten

Every muscle in Nate's body tensed. "That's bullshit, Mike. Brandon won't touch my money."

Mike rolled his eyes. "God, you are so naive. He's got to tell you that to gain your trust. How else would he get you in his house, under his thumb? Nash didn't waste any time proposing to you after your accident, now did he?"

"That just proves my point. Why would Brandon engineer that accident and try to kill me? If I'd died that night, he wouldn't have gotten a dime."

"I don't think he meant to kill you. I talked to the mechanic who examined your car. He said your brake lines were frayed, not cut. I believe Nash's intention was to drain enough fluid to scare you, not make you crash. Did you know he restored that Camaro of his from the frame up and did almost all the work himself? A man who knows as much about cars as he does could fray those brake lines in his sleep. Now Nash has come up with this cock-and–bull story about a homicidal maniac who's burning down gay businesses just to get to you. I'm telling you, Nash is behind all of it. He'll gain your trust, and the minute he has your power of attorney, this so-called stalker will close in and you'll meet with an unfortunate accident."

Nate's rage was festering just below the surface, begging to come out. "Get out, Mike. When you're through talking crazy, you and I are going to have a serious discussion about what I will and won't tolerate."

"Crazy? You're calling me crazy?" Mike's laugh was grating, bitter. "That's an ironic statement considering your choice of lovers. Maybe it's time I told you a few things about the man you're sleeping with."

"That's enough, dammit." Keith's lips curled into a snarl. "Nate asked you to leave. Now get out."

"Not until Nate listens to me."

Keith started to say something else, but Nate stopped him. "Fine. Say what you've got to say. I'm sure you aren't going to tell me anything I don't already know."

"Oh, really? How about the fact that three years ago, your boyfriend flipped out over a case he was working on and had to be institutionalized? Did you know Nash had a complete break with reality, that he was loonier than a toon for almost four months? Did you know one of the victims was his lover, and that for a while Nash was the chief suspect in his murder?"

Megan said, "That's a filthy, rotten lie. My brother was sick, not crazy."

"Honey, your brother was fucking nuts."

Nate edged around Keith. "Don't talk to her that way, asshole. The correct term for the condition is post-traumatic stress disorder. The case Brandon was working on involved a killer who mutilated his victims and then delivered the remains back to the families. Brandon was the chief investigator. Yes, he was a suspect for a brief period when it was discovered that he was friends with the victim, Kyle Washburn. He and Kyle were *friends*, not lovers. The reason Brandon 'went nuts', as you so eloquently put it, is because the killer left what little remained of Kyle's body on Brandon's doorstep. Brandon was cleared when the real killer was caught in the act of leaving another body on another doorstep. He spent three months in a private hospital — not an institution — to which he voluntarily checked himself in, I might add. Brandon is fine now, and that's all that matters to me."

Mike's cocky smirk made Nate feel like slugging him. "Who told you all that? Nash? You can't possibly think he'd tell you the truth."

"Brandon didn't tell me anything. Seth had him investigated. When I refused to read the report, Seth read it to me. I'll tell you the same thing I told my brother: I don't care about Brandon's past, except that I'm sorry for what he went through. The only thing I care about is the future, Brandon's and mine. For your information, if and when I die, everything in my trust fund will go to Amy. As far as that goes, Grandmother Morris left just as much to Amy as she did to Seth and me. I didn't accuse you of marrying Amy for her money, did I? I gave you the benefit of the doubt, even though we didn't exactly see eye to eye when you and she first started dating. Why can't you extend the same courtesy to Brandon?"

"Nobody was trying to kill Amy when she and I were dating. You're family to me, Nate. To us. I don't want to see you get hurt by some psycho who's hard pressed for cash."

Gale crossed her arms over her chest. "My son has plenty of money, you little creep. Even if he were flat broke, which he isn't, he has far too much integrity to ever marry for money."

"Sure he does, lady. I don't suppose you have any proof of his financial status, do you?"

Brandon stepped out of the mudroom. "No, she doesn't, Vaughn, but I do." He walked over to one of the kitchen drawers and pulled out a sheaf of papers. "Nate's always after me to store my records somewhere other than the kitchen. Guess you never thought it would come in handy, did you, baby?" He handed the papers to Nate. "Everything you ever wanted to know about the monetary dealings of Brandon Nash is in these papers, Nate. All you have to do is look. I certainly don't have a high dollar trust fund, but I'm comfortable. I've made some good investments, have a couple of CDs. Everything I have is yours, regardless of the amount."

Nate could only guess at how much Brandon had heard. He looked into those deep blue eyes and saw something he never thought he'd see in the ever-confident sheriff. Fear. Brandon Nash was afraid of losing him, afraid Mike's paranoid delusions would come between them.

Nate shook his head and refused the offered documents. "I don't need to see those."

Mike came up and snatched the statements from Brandon's hand. "Maybe Nate doesn't, but I do." He examined the records like a tax auditor. Nate was surprised he didn't ask to see Brandon's pay stubs, too. Finally, Mike looked up and said, "So you've got about two hundred thousand in savings. What does that prove? Just because you've got a little doesn't mean you don't want more."

Brandon didn't say anything, but Nate had reached his limit. "All right, Mike, you've said what you came to say. Now it's time for you to go."

Amy stood up, her face pale and her eyes bleary. "Nate, I'm so sorry about all of this. You know how Mike is when he gets a notion in his head."

Mike whirled on his wife, his eyes narrowed. "Don't defend me. I know what I'm talking about. Why is it whenever there's a line drawn between me and Nate, you always seem to be on his side of the line?"

Amy put her hand on Mike's arm. "You know that's not true, Mike. You're my husband. I married you, not Nate."

"Only because he wouldn't have you. Don't think I don't know how you feel about your so-called best friend. You've been hot for him for years. Hell, I'm surprised you didn't have a sex change just to satisfy good ole Nate. I'm sure he'd have been on you in a second if you'd had a dick and some balls." Mike was in Amy's face, yelling so that the sound bounced around the room.

Nate got in between them, Amy against his back. "Whatever half-baked theory you've got going about me and Amy, I will not have you yelling at her like that. Make of it what you will, but that's the way it's gonna be."

Mike didn't back up so much as a step. "What's with you, Nate? Are you so desperate to get laid that you'll throw away your friends and possibly even your life? Damn, if Nash is that good in bed, maybe I should start taking it up the ass, too. Beats sticking it to a frigid bitch who's pining for a fucking queer night after night."

Brandon tried to stop Nate, but he was too late. Nate made a dive for Mike and sent them both tumbling to the floor, the financial papers flying through the air and littering the linoleum. Nate smashed his left fist into Mike's jaw, obscenely pleased at the feel of bone crunching bone. Mike shifted his weight, throwing Nate off and coming down on top of him. Nate's cast made an ominous thump on the hard floor as it fell uselessly aside. Physically, Nate was stronger, but lingering weakness from the accident gave Mike the advantage. He drew his arm back and was about to hit Nate in the head when Keith and Brandon pulled them apart.

Keith had his arms underneath Mike's armpits, pinning him against his chest. Brandon held a struggling Nate around the waist, trying desperately not to put pressure on the still healing bruises dotting his chest and stomach. Brandon was also doing his best not to get winged by Nate's heavy cast.

"You'll pay for that, Nate. I'll press charges and sue your ass for assault." Mike made a bid for freedom, but Keith held firm.

"Go right ahead. It'll be worth it to have the whole world know that the great Michael Vaughn got his ass kicked by a fag, not once, but twice."

Amy moved to stand between the men and their captors with an air of command. "Nobody's pressing charges, unless there's a law against making an ass out of yourself, which I'd say you've both done rather nicely. Now, when I count to three, Brandon and Keith are going to let you go. If you so much as snarl at each other, I'll make sure Brandon locks you both up." She looked at Brandon. "Okay by you?"

Nate couldn't see Brandon, but he could hear the amusement in his voice. "Yes, ma'am."

"Good. One...two...three." Brandon and Keith let go at the same time. Nate and Mike stared each other down over Amy's head, but neither said anything. Amy gave them both a quick once over, then focused all her attention on Mike. "You and I are going home. You can call me frigid all you want, but I promise you haven't seen anything close to the bitch I can be if you cross me." She turned around and gave Nate a sad smile. "I'm sorry about this, Nate. He may be a perfect bastard sometimes, but he's my bastard and I love him. If it's any consolation, he'll start feeling guilty in a couple of hours and want to make it up to you. My advice is to make it as hard on him as possible." She whirled on her heel and made an exit worthy of a queen. Mike followed without saying another word.

When they were gone, Gale said, "Thank God that's over with. I wasn't sure how much longer we were going to have to listen that nonsense."

Brandon maneuvered Nate to the chair Amy had vacated and said, "Sit down and take off your shirt."

The tone of his voice was so stern, Nate couldn't resist. "Now, honey, I know I'm sexy and damned irresistible to boot, but do you really think we should be doing this in front of your family?"

"You're not funny, Nate. I want Keith to check you out to make sure you haven't done any damage to yourself with that prizefighter routine. If I have to take you back to the hospital to have that arm reset, I'm going to ask the doctor to put you in a full body cast. That's about the only way I can keep you out of trouble." Brandon grabbed the hem of Nate's t-shirt and tugged it over his head, working it over his broken arm.

"You aren't really mad at me, are you?" Nate's voice was muffled through the fabric of his shirt. "I couldn't just stand there and let him insult you and Amy like that. He had it coming."

Brandon laid the t-shirt on the table and stepped back so Keith could begin the examination. "He may have had it coming, but you didn't have to be the one to give it to him. I've spent all afternoon trying to figure out ways to keep you safe. I'm not about to let you undo all that by tearing out your stitches and bleeding to death."

Gale and Megan took chairs at the table and looked on in amusement. Gale said, "I hope Nate didn't hurt himself, but I have to admit, I enjoyed seeing that little punk get what he deserved."

Megan sighed. "I can't believe Seth hired a private investigator."

"I can." Brandon snorted. "He and I didn't exactly get off to the best start." His face softened when he looked at Nate. "I'm just grateful I've got someone who doesn't hold my past against me."

It was Nate's turn to snort. "You were sick, Brandon. Most people wouldn't have fared as well as you did. Kyle was your friend. Losing him that way must have been a nightmare."

"How did you know Kyle and I were just friends? Was that on the report, too."

Nate wanted desperately to erase the uncertainty he saw on Brandon's face. "It wasn't on the report, but I didn't need it to be. You've told me about all of your serious relationships. If you and Kyle had been anything more than friends, you would have told me. I trust you, Bran."

Keith bent down to examine Nate's ribs. "Do you really have four million dollars? 'Cause I've got tell you, Nate, I'd consider spreading my legs to you for that much cash."

Gale was horrified. "Keith Edward! What a horrible thing to say to your own brother's fiancé."

Nate and Brandon shared a smile. "I'm flattered, Keith, but you aren't my type."

Keith paused. "What do you mean I'm not your type? You think I'm not man enough for you?"

Brandon moved to put his hand on Nate's shoulder. "I've seen you naked, Keith. Trust me when I tell you, you definitely aren't."

They all laughed, but Gale broke the mood. "What did you mean when you said you've spent all day trying to find ways to keep Nate safe, Brandon?"

Nate listened as Brandon told them about his meeting with Howard and gave them the details on Wilson. When Brandon was done, Nate said, "Why would a professional hitman be after me? I don't have any ties to organized crime."

Keith pronounced Nate sound and handed him his shirt. While Nate was dressing, Brandon said, "I need you to think long and hard, Nate — who would benefit from your death?"

"You mean financially?"

"I mean for any reason."

"The only person who stands to gain anything financially is Amy, and if she hasn't already killed me after some of the things I did to her growing up, I think it's safe to say she isn't going to."

Keith took a mug down from the cabinet and poured himself a cup of coffee. "What about Mike? Wouldn't he get his fair share if you died? What's Amy's is his and vice versa, right?"

Nate was adamant. "No way. I know the guy can be a pain, but he somewhere deep inside loves me." He laughed. "Way down deep inside. Besides, why go to all the trouble of moving me up here and helping cement the partnership with Amy if he was going to kill me? I made Amy the beneficiary of my trust the day after my parents dumped me. If Mike wanted to off me for my money, he's had years to do it. Why now?"

"Did you really kick his ass once before, Nate?"

"I sure did, Megan."

"What happened?"

Nate sighed. "Basically the same thing that happened tonight. Amy and I have been friends since grade school. All through high school and the first year of college, it was just the two of us. She rarely dated, and I didn't date at all. She met Mike at the end of our sophomore year. They hit it off, but Mike wasn't too crazy about his girlfriend having a guy for a best friend. One night they got into an argument about the amount of time she spent with me, and Mike told her she had to choose between us. She dumped him and called me. When I got to her apartment, she was a mess. I cleaned her up, took out a couple of quarts of mint chocolate chip ice cream, and let her cry on my shoulder. At one point, she crawled into my lap so I could hold her while she cried. That was when Mike walked in and saw her curled up in my arms."

All the Nashs in the kitchen said, "Ouch."

"He was beyond pissed. He started hurling wild accusations like he did tonight. He even said the whole gay thing was just a cover so I could get into Amy's pants. It was when he called her a slut that I knocked out a couple of his teeth." Nate went to the cabinet and grabbed the aspirin. "I'd have knocked out a couple more tonight, if I hadn't been fighting with a handicap." He filled a glass of water from the tap and downed the pills. "Anyway, after that night, Mike and I actually became friends. He and I have a friendship separate from Amy's and mine. Lots of times we have guys' night out with just the two of us. If he wanted me out of the picture, he's had ample opportunity. Why now?"

Brandon nodded. "What you just said makes perfect sense, but we aren't ruling out anybody, no matter how good the logic."

"What about Calder?" Gale made a face. "I know he's your father, sweetie, but I have to tell you, I don't give two hoots in Hell for that old snake."

"He certainly wouldn't put on sackcloth and ashes if I bought it tomorrow, but I just don't believe he's behind all this. See, everything with my father is a matter of honor. His honor was insulted when I decided not to go into the family business. His dignity was impugned when I announced to the world that I was gay. His sense of righteousness took a beating when I refused to crawl back to him and beg forgiveness for being born unworthy of the Morris name. My father would be more likely to challenge me to a duel on the courthouse lawn than to put out a contact on my life."

"I thought you said Mr. Morris was cleared. You let him go."

"There's a big difference between being cleared and being let go for lack of evidence, Megan. Calder is by no means off my list of suspects."

Keith took a healthy swig of coffee. "Not to be a jackass, but shouldn't Seth be on that list? Does it seem strange to anyone else that he showed up at the exact same time that all this started happening, or is it just me?"

"Normally, I would say it's just you, but I'm not taking any chances with Nate's safety." Brandon crossed his arms over his chest. "Nobody's above suspicion as far as I'm concerned."

Nate was shocked. "You suspect Seth? I thought you said you trusted him."

Brandon walked over to the counter where Nate was leaning and bracketed him with his arms, his body pressed tight against Nate's.

Nate could feel the heat through his clothes and did his best not to get hard with his in-laws looking on.

Brandon leaned down until his forehead was touching Nate's and said, "I trust him as far as I'm going to. For what it's worth, I don't think he's the one, but I'll be damned before I get sloppy and make a mistake that might cost me my life."

Nate's voice came out a harsh whisper. "Don't you mean a mistake that might cost my life?"

"No. Your life and my life are the same. There is no me without you."

Gale took Megan by one hand and Keith by the other. "I think it's time for us to leave." She dragged them to the door. "Take care, boys."

Neither responded, too wrapped up in each other to hear the door open and close. Sasha came in as Gale and the others left, but gave up trying to get her masters' attention and lumbered off to bed. Nate wasn't sure how long they stood there just holding each other, but it was Brandon who finally broke the silence.

"You don't know what it did to me, hearing you defend me like that. If I wasn't nuts about you before, I would be now."

"You would never hurt me, Bran." Nate kissed a spot just below his jaw. "Of all the people in my life, you're the one I know I can always count on."

Brandon nuzzled his ear. "I'm glad you feel that way. You don't know how scared I was that you would rip your stitches when you jumped Mike. As it is, you're damn lucky you didn't crack that cast open."

Nate cleared his throat. It was now or never. "I agree with you about the cast, but you're wrong about the stitches."

"The hell I am. You could've torn every last one of the damn things out."

"That's just it. I don't have any stitches. Dr. Rinehart had a cancellation this afternoon and called to see if I wanted to come in. Since I was scheduled to see him tomorrow afternoon, I went ahead and switched times. Rinehart said my cast can come off in about four more weeks, and then he took out all my sutures. See, even the ones in my head are gone."

Brandon bent down for a closer examination. "How come I didn't notice that when I took your shirt off? You had at least ten from the surgical incision alone."

"Eight, to be precise. Dr. Lincoln may be a dick, but he's a damn good surgeon. The incision was so small and neat, I doubt I'll even have a scar. Dr. Rinehart said all my wounds are practically healed. I can go back to work the first of next week, albeit one handed. I guess you didn't notice the stitches were gone because you were too busy threatening to arrest me."

"I have had this prison fantasy lately. Wonder how you'd look in one of those orange jumpsuits?" Brandon smiled.

"I don't know about the prison fantasy, but Dr. Rinehart said I was well enough to indulge in some of your other fantasies."

"You mean—"

"Yes."

"I thought he said we had to wait two weeks. It hasn't been two full weeks yet."

"Consider it time off for good behavior. According to Dr. Rinehart, I'm on the mend and can resume all normal activities."

"Meaning?"

Nate gently bit Brandon's lower lip, tugging with his teeth. "Whatever you want it to mean."

Brandon wasn't sure why he was so nervous. It wasn't like it was his first time, but he wished someone would tell his body that. He ached like a teenager on prom night. "Oh God, baby, you have no idea what I want." Brandon framed Nate's face with his hands. "Are you sure?"

"Yes, Brandon. Please, make love to me."

~~*~*~*

Having been celibate for almost four years, Brandon wasn't exactly prepared. He left Nate to go upstairs and shower while he ran to the store, deciding to go to one of the chain drugstores rather than Simpson's, the one he normally used. Mr. and Mrs. Simpson were old family friends who wouldn't hesitate to tell the entire Nash clan that their son was about to get laid.

Brandon pulled into the parking lot of Savings Central Drugs and got out, scanning for anyone he might know. He knew he was being ridiculous. The entire town already thought he and Nate were sleeping together. Still, he wanted to keep tonight private; some things were just too special to share.

Since condoms weren't necessary, Brandon headed straight for the lubricants. He probably could have made due with the lotion he had at home, but Brandon didn't want just anything coming in contact with Nate's tender skin. Nate might be sore tomorrow, but Brandon wanted to make sure it was a good soreness, if there was such a thing.

Brandon stared at the bottles and tubes in mute wonder. *Who would've thought there were so many different kinds?* He picked up bottle after bottle and tube after tube, trying to read them without being conspicuous. He knew his efforts to blend in had failed when he felt someone come up behind him.

"Can I help you, sir?"

He turned around and came face to face with Dillon, Megan's would-be boyfriend. Brandon started to speak and then realized he was holding a bottle of something called *Slick and Slippery Intimate Moisturizer* in his hand. He put it back, but it was too late.

Shit. Megan told him the kid worked here, but damned if he hadn't forgotten. "Uh, hi Dillon. I think I've got it covered, thanks."

"Hi, Sheriff. I didn't recognize you from the back. Sure I can't help you with anything?"

Brandon took a moment to look at the guy his sister was interested in. Dillon was tall, almost six feet, and probably still growing. His shaggy brown hair was cut in that permanently messy style that kids seemed to like, and his green eyes were flashing with amusement over Brandon's discomfort. Brandon decided to turn the tables.

"No. I can manage on my own, but while you're here, I'd like to talk to you about your intentions toward my baby sister."

He was rewarded by the flush that crept into Dillon's cheeks. "Yeah, uh, sure, Sheriff, but I really need to get back to work. Some other time, man." And before he knew it, Brandon was looking at Dillon's retreating back.

That was too easy. Brandon went back to his shopping, finally deciding on a tube of good, old fashioned KY Jelly. *When in doubt, go with what you know. The only problem now is, which size?* He disregarded the smaller tube. *Maybe I'm being optimistic, but hey, might as well think positive. If I buy the economy size, Nate might freak out, afraid I'm planning on chaining him to the mattress for the next two months. Then again, if I buy the medium size, Nate might take that as hesitancy on my part to begin the sexual side of our relationship. Fuck it.* Brandon picked up the jumbo size and headed to the counter.

The clerk was a sixteen year old skater wanna-be with purple streaks in his hair, but enough sense not to comment on Brandon's purchase. The kid ran the tube over the U.P.C. sensor, but it refused to scan. He tried it over and over with no success. On the fifth try, he gave up.

"Sorry, Sheriff. I'm gonna have to run a price check on this." Before Brandon could stop him, he reached for the loud speaker. "Price check on the large size of KY Jelly. Price check."

All right. It's safe to say things can't get any worse. Almost as soon as that thought crossed Brandon's mind, his father came up behind him carrying a tube of hemorrhoid cream.

"Well, hey there, son. Didn't expect to see you here."

That's an understatement. "Me, either. I thought you always shopped at Simpson's."

"Usually, I do, but your mom sent me after this. She needs it fast, and this place is closer." He held up the tube. "She always says having eight kids has left her with piles the size of kittens."

Too much information. "Yeah, well, I—"

The pharmacist came up. "Carl, did you need a price check?"

"Yes, sir. I need a price for this economy size tube of KY Lubricant."

"I didn't realize they made it that big. Live and learn, I guess." He thumbed through the book he was holding. "The manual has that listed at five dollars and sixty cents, not including tax. Hi, Sheriff. This yours?"

Brandon wildly hoped someone would come in and rob the store. At least everyone wouldn't be staring at him, waiting for his answer. Face flaming, he said, "Yeah. Uh, if you don't mind, I'm kind of in a hurry here." The minute he said it, Brandon knew it was the wrong thing to say.

The pharmacist and his dad exchanged grins. Dean said, "I imagine you are, son, from the looks of it."

Brandon didn't say a word when the pharmacist added, "If you plan on using all that tonight, Sheriff, you might want to pick up some liniment and a bottle of ibuprofen. You and Doc will need it for all those sore muscles."

Carl snickered as he rang up the purchase. Brandon paid and was about to say good-bye to his dad when Carl, in all seriousness, said, "Hey, Sheriff? You might want to pick up some condoms, too. My sex-ed teacher says when you sleep with someone, you're really sleeping with every person that person has slept with. Can't be too careful."

Brandon gritted his teeth. "Thanks, Carl, but that won't be necessary."

The pharmacist and Dean were all but rolling on the floor in near hysteria. Finally Dean settled down enough to say, "Cheer up, son. At least Nate won't ever send you to the store in the middle of the night to buy him a box of tampons."

* ~ * ~ * ~ * ~ *

Nate heard the sounds of the door opening and the alarm being reactivated, and then Brandon came in carrying several bags of Chinese food. He greeted Nate with a smile.

"I thought you might be hungry. I hope Chinese is okay. It always amazes me that Reed has two full service Chinese restaurants, but you have to drive thirty minutes before you reach the nearest hospital." He gave Nate a quick once over. "Have a good bath?"

"Yeah, but I had a hard time wrapping my arm. I'll be glad to get rid of this damn cast. How was your trip to the store?"

"Humiliating, but we'll talk about that later. Why don't you set out the food while I grab a quick shower?"

Nate nodded and got out plates and utensils, including forks. He might be handy with a stethoscope and scalpel, but he was hopeless with a pair of chopsticks. Add to that the fact that he was still learning to use his left hand after twenty-eight years as a right-hander, and there was no way he was even going to attempt it.

Brandon came back while Nate was transferring the food from cartons to platters, saw the forks, and laughed. "I have some chopsticks stashed in the silverware drawer. Didn't you see them?"

"We've had this conversation before, Nash. You know how I feel about eating with twigs. Besides," Nate nodded towards the cast, "I'm temporarily disadvantaged."

"Says the man who doesn't know how to use chopsticks when he's working with his good hand." Brandon grabbed up a plate and started dishing large helpings of everything onto it.

"All the food will mix together like that."

Brandon narrowed his eyes. "It's Chinese food, Nate. It's already all mixed together." He grabbed a pair of chopsticks from the drawer, picked up the plate, and headed for the stairs. "Tuck that bottle of wine from the fridge under your arm and grab a couple of glasses, please."

"What about my fork?"

"Trust me. You won't need it."

~~*~*~*

Holding another bite of ginger chicken up to Nate's mouth, Brandon said, "Sure you don't want any more?"

Nate groaned. "No more. I think I've consumed at least half a chicken as it is."

They were sitting cross-legged on the bed, facing each other, and Brandon looked at Nate's trim body, clad only in a pair of boxers and a t-shirt. "You could use a little fattening up."

"Trying to change me already?" Nate smiled and took a sip of his wine.

"You know better." Brandon set the plate on the bedside table and leaned in for a kiss. "My mother always says, 'Don't mess with perfection.'"

Nate put down his glass. "I wish I was perfect. Maybe then I wouldn't be so damn scared of messing this up."

"You know, if you aren't ready for this, we can—" Nate tackled Brandon and kissed the breath out of him before he could finish his sentence. Brandon chuckled. "Okay, so you're ready."

Nate shivered as Brandon tugged his ear with his teeth. Brandon pulled Nate's shirt over his head and threw it on the floor. Nate inhaled sharply as Brandon's mouth found one of his sensitive nipples.

Brandon kissed his way down to the waistband of Nate's boxers and then kissed his way back up to torture the other nipple. When Brandon took off his own shirt and rubbed bare chest against bare chest, Nate moaned. At last, Brandon lay full-length on top of Nate, the only thing separating them was the thin cotton of the underwear they each wore.

Brandon was careful to balance most of his weight on his forearms in deference to Nate's still-tender abdomen. He glanced down at Nate's firm stomach and well-defined chest. "You are the most beautiful thing I've ever seen." When Brandon returned to sucking on his neck, Nate sighed. The sighs turned to gasps as Brandon increased the suction on his neck.

Nate's voice was a hoarse rasp. "You've already seen me naked. Time to return the favor."

Brandon didn't have to be told twice. He stood and pulled off his boxers, then cast them on top of the pile of shirts. Nate reached for him, but Brandon shook his head. "Your turn."

Nate stood and wriggled out of his shorts, then Brandon pulled Nate tight against him and kissed him with savage ownership. His breathing was ragged, on the edge of control, his erection and Nate's pressed together between them.

Mouth dry and body on fire, Nate lay down on his back in silent consent, spread his legs, and offered himself.

Brandon grabbed the tube from the pharmacy and squeezed some KY onto his fingers. "If I hurt you, tell me and I'll stop."

Nate nodded as Brandon worked the gel with his fingers, warming it. When Brandon's index finger made contact with his virgin flesh, Nate jumped, but he soon relaxed as Brandon began preparing his body for what was to come. He tensed slightly when Brandon's finger gained entry, and Brandon stopped, but Nate shook his head. "Don't stop. It feels good. Different, but good."

Brandon smiled. "If you like that, you'll love this."

He touched a place deep inside, and Nate was sure he'd been zapped with a dozen volts of electricity. Brandon added another finger, increasing the pressure on that same spot. Nate's hips came off the bed and he grunted in pleasure.

Brandon then slicked himself with more of the gel and moved into position between Nate's legs. Nate felt intense pressure but little pain as Brandon pressed the head of his cock inside.

Blue eyes smoky, Brandon looked into Nate's. "Forever, Nate. Say it."

Nate whispered, "Forever," and Brandon slid in all the way to the hilt. The air left Nate's lungs in a rush of pleasurable agony.

Supported by his arms and making no movements, Brandon lay above Nate and inside him. His eyes were closed and his breathing was shallow, but he remained rigidly still, allowing Nate time to adjust.

Nathan reached up and stroked Brandon's face, at the same time tilting his hips. The change in position brought Brandon even deeper inside and caused an exquisite friction against Nate's prostate.

When Nate whimpered, Brandon lost it and started to pump.

Nate met him thrust for thrust until they were both covered with sweat and fighting for breath. Every withdrawing movement caused Nate to tighten and every inward push made Brandon grunt. Nate felt himself nearing the edge as Brandon stepped up the rhythm. Just as Nate's release started, he felt Brandon tense before groaning and filling Nate with his seed.

* ~ * ~ * ~ * ~ *

The great thing about the claw foot tub in the master bathroom was its capacity to hold two people. Brandon sat against the back wall of the tub with Nate between his legs, back against Brandon's stomach. Nate's plastic-wrapped cast was propped against one side of the tub as Bran made lazy soap circles on Nate's body.

"Sore?"

Nate closed his eyes as Brandon's fingers grazed his nipple. "Maybe a little, but not much. I like it. It's like I can still feel you inside me."

Brandon licked a drop of water from Nate's neck. "Good. That way you'll be thinking about me all day tomorrow."

"I do that already." Nate snuggled closer as Brandon's arms came around him.

"Oh, before I forget, Pastor Oakley called. He wants to meet with us after services Sunday to discuss our wedding plans and set up an appointment for premarital counseling. He sounded perfectly comfortable with the idea of two men getting married."

"I told you you'd like our church. I warn you now, though, my whole family goes there, so be prepared for organized chaos."

Nate rinsed off the soap, but didn't move out of Bran's embrace. "I'm beginning to like organized chaos."

As he reached over to let the water out, Brandon said, "So, Rinehart released you to go back to work next week, huh?"

"Yeah, but if you think I shouldn't go, I won't."

Brandon pulled him up and helped him out of the tub, drying Nate first and then himself. "That's a switch. Since when have you become Mr. Agreeable?"

Nate unwrapped his cast. "I won't lie. It irks me to think of my whole life being turned upside down by this creep, but I don't want to do anything stupid that might put my life in danger. I have too much to lose."

Brandon handed Nate a clean pair of boxers and then pulled on his own. "I'm not crazy about the idea of you going back out there until we catch this guy, but I know I can't keep you under lock and key." He pulled Nate into his arms and leered at him. "Of course, I have had a couple of lurid images of you handcuffed to my bedpost."

"For a sheriff, you have a criminal mind. You—" Nate broke off when Brandon pushed him behind his back. "What's wrong?"

Brandon put his finger to his lips and mouthed. "Downstairs." He opened the bathroom door, slipped into the bedroom, and grabbed his pistol from the bedside table. "Someone's in the house. Stay here."

"It could be your mom, or Keith. They both have keys and the alarm code."

Brandon shook his head. "No. They would knock. I'm going to check it out."

"Please, Brandon, call for back-up. Don't—"

Brandon gave Nate a quick peck on the lips. "If I'm not back in five minutes, call Sam." And before Nate could protest, Brandon was gone.

Nate paced back and forth, watching the bedside clock. After a wait of about two and a half minutes, he picked up the phone and had just dialed the number when he heard the first shot.

Chapter Eleven

In the forty seconds it took Nate to get from the bedroom to the kitchen, he died a thousand times, expecting to find Brandon lying dead in a pool of blood. He raced down the stairs and rounded the corner, where he spotted a red trail leading from the kitchen to the mudroom. He snagged the cordless phone from the counter and dialed as he ran.

Nate found Brandon leaning against the doorjamb, clutching his bloody right shoulder. Only when Nate got closer did he see the handle of the knife sticking out of Brandon's flesh. "Brandon, here, sit down."

Brandon grimaced, but made no move to sit. "The son of a bitch got away. I fired off a shot after he stabbed me, but I don't think I hit him."

Nate heard sirens in the distance. "Brandon, please come inside and sit down. I need to call you an ambulance."

"No. No hospitals. You can take care of it. It's not as bad as it looks."

Just the thought of probing Brandon's soft skin made Nate feel sick. "No, Bran. I can't treat you. I'm too close. Besides, there's no way I can stitch you one-handed."

Brandon wobbled on his feet. "Call Keith. He'll help you. I can't go to the hospital knowing that guy could come back at any time."

"He won't. The guards—"

"Yeah? Where the hell were the guards when that bastard broke into our house? And why didn't the alarm go off? I'm surprised Sasha—" Brandon's face paled, a considerable feat since he was already a stark shade of white. "Oh, God, Nate, where's Sasha?"

Nate took Brandon's hand and led him toward the table. "Sit down, Bran. We'll find Sasha, but we've got to take care of you first."

"Nate, we've got to find her. She could be hurt."

"Sheriff?" Sam's voice carried through the kitchen. "Boss, where are you?"

Nate breathed a sigh of relief. Help had arrived. "We're in the kitchen, Sam. Brandon's hurt." The fact that he and Bran were both clad only in boxers never entered Nate's mind.

Sam took one look at the knife handle sticking out of Brandon's arm and turned green. "Jesus Christ. Let me call an ambulance."

"No, Nate and Keith can fix it. I discharged my weapon. I have to fill out a report."

"Screw the report, Boss. You need to get to a hospital."

Nate could tell by the look on Brandon's face he was going to be stubborn. Giving in, Nate picked up the phone and called Keith and Amy.

"There's no need to call Amy."

Nate gave him one of those don't-fuck-with-me looks. "I've let you get away with not going to the hospital, but we're going to do the rest of this my way. We're going to my office, and Amy and Keith can meet us there. Where you're concerned, I need all the help I can get. And at the first sign of trouble out of you, I'm packing your ass into an ambulance and hauling you to Chicago General. Understood?"

Brandon smiled in spite of his pain. "Understood."

As he left to fetch himself some clothes and Brandon some jeans, Nate heard Sam say, "I like him, Boss. We've finally found someone who can handle you."

* ~ * ~ * ~ * ~ *

"Ouch, dammit. Can't you take that thing out without making the hole any wider?"

Amy clucked her tongue sympathetically, but Nate was ruthless. "You're just lucky it hit bone and not an artery."

"Oh, yeah. I feel real damn lucky. I think when you finish dissecting my arm, I'll go out and buy a bundle of lottery tickets."

"You want me to sedate him?" Keith pointed to the supply cabinet on the opposite wall. "I'm sure you've got something in there that will knock him out."

"Sedate me? Nate already deadened my shoulder. Are sedatives really necessary?"

Keith snorted. "For the pain? No. To get you to stop bitching? Absolutely."

Brandon looked to Nate. "Aren't you gonna take up for me?"

"After you left me alone and went charging into the night like the Lone Ranger? You're lucky I even deadened you before starting on this wound."

"Aw, Nate, don't be mad at me. I was trying to protect you. Doesn't that count for anything?"

"Sure. It would have been of great comfort to me at your funeral had that knife landed about eight inches to the left." In spite of his harsh words, Nate grasped Brandon's left hand and held tight. Keith stood on the right side and held the handle of the knife, wearing latex gloves to preserve fingerprint evidence. Amy stood at the ready with gauze and antiseptic.

"Be sure to bag that for analysis when you pull it out. You—" Brandon broke off in a whoosh of breath as Keith pulled the knife from his shoulder.

Blood rushed from the gash, but Amy was prepared. She sponged away the blood and then applied pressure. Despite the numbing medication, Brandon winced, but remained silent under the pain. Nate gripped Brandon's hand that much harder.

When she was satisfied that the bleeding was under control, Amy disinfected the wound and broke open a suture kit. She'd just drawn the needle through Brandon's flesh when the door opened and Rex Howard walked in.

"Heard you had yourself some trouble tonight, Nash."

"You could say that. How'd you hear about it?"

"I gave your deputy my card this afternoon, just in case. Looks like it's a good thing I did. What the hell happened?"

"You must be the agent Brandon met with earlier. I'm Nathan Morris."

Howard stuck out his hand. "Sorry about that. I'm Rex Howard with the U.S. Attorney's Office."

Nate let go of Brandon long enough to give an awkward, left-handed shake. Brandon introduced Keith, who also shook hands with Howard. Amy politely greeted the newcomer, but didn't pause in her stitching.

When the introductions were finished, Brandon recounted the events for the agent. "Nate and I were upstairs when I heard the back door open. I grabbed my revolver and started downstairs, but by the time I got to the living room, the bastard was already in the kitchen. He saw me and took off. I went running after him, and almost had him, too, when he turned around and threw that fucking knife at me. I guess I must have stood there for a second while I absorbed the fact that I had a six-inch steel blade wedged in my arm. Whatever, it gave him an advantage. He was out the door before I recovered enough sense to take off after him. When I got to the door, I could just make out his back in the darkness. I fired a shot, but I'm pretty sure I missed. Nate came down and found me leaning against the door with that thing," he pointed to the knife, "sticking out of me. He called Sam, and here we are."

Howard was quiet for a minute. Finally he said, "None of what you just described fits Wilson's usual M.O. Don't get me wrong. I don't doubt everything happened just the way you said it did, but breaking in and running away just isn't Wilson's style. First of all, if he was casing your house, he would know that Dr. Morris wasn't alone. One thing about Wilson, he only goes after his established target. In all the crimes of which he's suspected, not a single innocent bystander was hurt. Secondly, Wilson isn't the type to run away. If he was brazen enough to break in with both of you home, he'd have been packing something a damn sight more destructive than a knife."

Brandon nodded. "I thought the same thing."

Amy finished the stitching and pulled out a roll of gauze bandaging. She smeared antibiotic ointment on the wound, wrapped and taped it, and said, "I'll want to change the dressing tomorrow, but I think it should heal nicely. It's going to be mighty sore for the next few days, but I'll write you a prescription for the pain, if you want."

"I can take care of all that. Thanks, doll. I owe you." Nate hugged her tight.

She grinned. "I'll add it to your bill. What should we do with the knife?"

"Is Sam still outside?" Brandon shifted to find a more comfortable position. "He said he was going to wait."

"I think so."

"Take it to him and ask him to lock it up in the evidence room when he goes back to the office, would you?"

"Sure thing."

"Hey, Amy?"

She stopped on her way out the door and turned back to Brandon. "Yes?"

"Thanks a lot."

"No problem. You're family."

After she left, Keith said, "What I want to know is, where the hell were the guards? I thought you guys had someone watching the house."

Howard said, "I spoke to Deputy Whit about that very thing. Best we can figure, the guy was smart enough to enter while the guards were changing shifts. The only question now is, how did he know?"

Brandon shrugged. "Good question. I set it up so that a deputy would be guarding Nate twenty-four hours a day. The shifts change every eight hours, unless the deputy needs to take off early, in which case it's up to him to notify me or to trade with somebody. None of my men would just take off without a replacement."

Howard rubbed his brow. "What about bathroom and meal breaks?"

"As necessary."

"So it could have happened then."

"Technically speaking, yes." Brandon scrubbed his good hand over his face. "But Wilson would have to have been watching at just the right moment, and even then it doesn't explain why the alarm didn't go off, or why Sasha didn't bark a warning."

"About the alarm, I couldn't say, but according to Whit, your dog was probably drugged."

Brandon's body tensed but Nate had enough sense to say, "Is she all right?"

"One of the deputies found her lying in your laundry room and took her to the vet. It looks like she'll be fine. The vet's going to take some blood samples and try to figure out what drug she was given."

Keith, who'd been leaning up against the counter in silence up until now, said, "I'm not a cop, but I think I might know how this guy worked out your schedule and your alarm codes."

Brandon hopped off the table and shrugged into the loosely fitting shirt Nate had brought with them. "I'm listening."

"First, a question. Where were you when you set the schedule for the guards?"

Brandon thought for a minute. "At the office."

Nate shook his head. "You may have come up with it at the office, Bran, but I remember you talking about it the day I came home from the hospital. We were in our bedroom, remember?"

"Yeah, I'd forgotten about that." Brandon reached out and squeezed Nate's hand. "Thanks."

Keith made a gagging sound. "If you two are finished 'appreciating' each other, I have another question. Where were you when you worked out the codes with the alarm company?"

"That one I do remember. I came home to take a shower right before they let Nate out of the I.C.U. The man from the security company had already installed the alarm, so we set the code. Then I showered and went to the accident scene to make sure all the evidence had been gathered."

"I remember you giving me and Mom the code the day Nate came home from the hospital," Keith said.

"Yeah, and I gave it to Nate right before Seth left to pick up his parents at the airport. I remember, because I told Nate he'd have the code if he decided to kick their asses out. That way, they couldn't sneak back in, even if they'd swiped a spare key." Brandon's brow furrowed, and then he yelled, "Son of a bitch! The bastard has our place bugged."

"Chalk one up for the big brother." Keith gave a mock bow.

"My men will be here first thing in the morning," Howard said. "I'll have them do a sweep, but it certainly sounds like the most logical conclusion."

"Have them sweep my office, too, just in case," Brandon frowned. "Until Wilson is caught, I'm leaving nothing to chance."

"I'm on it." Howard stopped in the doorway. "Either Wilson has lousy aim, which I highly doubt, or he meant for that knife to lodge in your shoulder. Either way, I'm glad he missed anything important." He smiled at Nate. "It was nice to meet you, Dr. Morris. If you ever get tired of this guy, I'd like to introduce you to my son. You don't happen to have nipple rings or a navel hoop, do you?"

"Back off, Howard. He's spoken for."

Howard sighed. "I had to try, Nash. Just be glad you got to him first."

Brandon looked at Nate and his voice dropped an octave. "Every time I take a breath."

After Howard left, Keith said, "I assume you aren't going to stay at your house tonight."

"Not until Howard sweeps the place. We'll stay at a motel tonight."

"Brandon Nash, you will do no such thing." Gale stood at the door, hands on hips.

"Mom, what are you doing here? We're right in the middle of a police investigation, for Christ's sake." Brandon turned accusing eyes on Keith. "Did you call her?"

"Don't take the Lord's name in vain. And no, he didn't call me, but he should have. Your father heard it on the scanner." Gale crossed the room and put her arms around Nate. "How are you holding up, darling?"

"Hey, I'm the one who's injured here." Brandon pouted. "Where's all your motherly sympathy?"

Gale sniffed. "According to Amy, you wouldn't be hurt if you hadn't decided to rush downstairs like the conquering hero." She took Nate by the hand. "Now, Nathan, we'll go and pack you and Brandon a bag, and you can stay with me and Dad." She led him out of the room, but not before Nate tuned around and stuck his tongue out at Brandon.

"Is it my imagination, or has my fiancé just stolen my mother?"

Keith laughed. "The first big fight Maria and I had after we got married, she ran home to our mother instead of her own." He patted Brandon on the back. "Welcome to the wonderful world of marriage, brother."

Brandon grinned like an idiot. "Yeah. Ain't it great?"

* ~ * ~ * ~ * ~ *

After breakfast the next morning, a quick call to Sam confirmed that Howard's men had arrived, so Brandon and Nate headed home.

After sweeping Brandon's office and finding the station clean, the electronics wizards had headed over to the house. Howard was waiting by the back door when Brandon pulled the Camaro into the drive. "You look none the worse for wear after last night."

Brandon shook his hand. "Then why do I feel like I've been run over by a truck?"

"Aftershock, my friend. Happens to me every time I take a hit off a perp." Howard grinned and patted Nate on the arm. "How's it going, Doc?"

"I'll be better once I know our house isn't bugged."

Howard nodded. "It's a creepy feeling, isn't it? My men are already upstairs, thanks to your deputy. He met us here with a spare key. Speaking of which, the lock doesn't appear to have been jimmied or picked. Since I don't subscribe to all that metaphysical crap about walking through walls, I think the guy must have used a key. Besides yours, how many have you got floating around?"

Brandon began counting on his fingers. "My mother, Keith, and Nate each have one. I keep one at the station — the one that Sam gave to you today — and I keep a spare here at the house."

"Where, exactly?"

"On a rack in the mudroom, just inside the door."

Howard nodded. "Let's have a look, just to make sure it's still there." He started up the back steps, then stopped. "By the way, how's your dog?"

"I called Dr. Payne first thing this morning. He said she's almost back to her old self, but he wants to keep her one more day for observation. He said the drug she was given was some kind of human tranquilizer. Diazepam, he thinks."

"Diazepam?"

"Generic Valium," Nate explained. "I give a low dose of it to patients who are suffering from mild anxiety. Dr. Payne found a couple of undigested tablets when he pumped Sasha's stomach. He isn't sure just how much she was given, so it could be a while before we know if there's been any long term damage done to Sasha's system."

"Keep me posted." Howard made his way into the house, followed by Bran and Nate. "Show me where you keep your keys."

Brandon pointed to the hanging rack directly above the light switch on the left side of the door. The first thing he noticed was the empty peg where his spare key should have been. "Damn. The son of a bitch must have taken it. That definitely narrows down our list of suspects to someone we know."

Howard sighed. "I don't suppose you have a running list of all the people who've been in your house since this mess all started, do you?"

"Almost every member of my immediate family, and Nate's, too, not to mention at least four of my deputies and a few of the folks from my church who came by to check on Nate when he was recovering. At least fifty people, if not more."

"I knew it wouldn't be easy."

Before Howard could say more, someone hollered, "Agent Howard, I think we've found something, sir."

Brandon followed the voice to the bedroom. A young red-haired man Howard introduced as Agent Miles held up a round, putty colored glob. "I found this stuck to the inside doorframe. Whoever planted it was smart enough to make it look like a piece of caulking. In an old house like this, no one would ever notice." He turned it over to reveal a tiny lump of circuitry. "This thing may be small, but the transmitter is powerful enough to carry even a sigh all the way across the room. Anything said within twenty-feet of this little bug would be as plain as if you were whispering in the guy's ear."

Brandon glanced over and saw Nate shivering. He turned to Howard, who must have noticed it, too, because he said, "Have you finished the sweep, Miles."

"Yes, sir. This room and the adjoining bath are clean; I still have the guest bedroom to do."

"Let's get to it, then." Howard ushered Miles out of the room and closed the door behind them.

Brandon pulled Nate over to the bed and cradled him in his arms. He could feel the trembling even through the heavy coats they both still wore. Brandon stripped Nate of his coat and took off his own, then pulled him close again. "It's all too much, isn't it?"

"He's been in our house, Bran. It could be one of our friends, even a relative. Why does someone want me dead badly enough to go to these lengths? I mean, bugging our bedroom? God, that's like something out of a James Bond movie."

Brandon stroked Nate's soft blond hair. "I know, but we're gonna catch this guy." He tilted Nate's chin up to look at him. "I promise you we will, Nate."

"I know. I just wish this would all end. I'm not sure how much more either of us can take."

Brandon continued to hold Nate, rocking him slowly back and forth. He didn't know who was comforting whom. He only knew he needed the soothing balm of having Nate's body against his own. He wasn't sure how long they sat there like that, but a knock on the door broke them apart.

Brandon cleared his throat. "Come in."

Howard stuck his head in the door. "If you guys would come

downstairs, Miles is ready to give his report."

Brandon nodded and led a too-quiet Nate down to the kitchen. They took seats at the table, as did Howard and Miles. The rest of Howard's team busied themselves by packing equipment and loading up the two, non-descript sedans in which they had arrived.

Miles said, "We swept the whole house, including the porches and outbuildings, even the vehicles. We found one each in the kitchen and bedroom. Your S.U.V. was clean, Sheriff, but we did find a couple in your car."

"Why would he put two in my car when he only put one in the kitchen and one in the bedroom?"

"My best guess: to filter out road and engine noise."

"Do you think you can trace the bugs to the manufacturer?" Howard pursed his lips. "Are there any serial numbers on those things that you could trace?"

"Nothing, doing, Chief. These jokers are homemade. A pro like your guy could walk into any Radio Shack and pick up the components to make them. As far as listening devices go, they aren't real sophisticated, but they'll get the job done."

Howard rubbed his forehead. "Everything we know about Wilson says he has the know-how to make these bugs, but I doubt he could have gotten close enough to plant them without that key and the alarm codes. That means whoever planted them has been in contact with Wilson at least once since he arrived here."

Brandon shook his head. "Twice. Someone had to pass that car-rental receipt to Wilson so he could plant it at the second arson site."

"The victim of the second fire, Marjorie Newman. How is she?"

"Still in a coma. I went by the hospital yesterday at lunch. The doctors remain hopeful, but so far, nothing. Keep her in your prayers."

"I'll do that." Howard paused for a minute, thinking. "What about the knife your brother and Dr. Vaughn pulled out of your shoulder? Any luck?"

"I'm sure you won't be surprised when I tell you no prints were recovered, but it isn't the kind of knife you buy at a hardware store, either. I'm pretty sure it's custom made. Sam's been on the phone half the night and most of this morning trying to track down the manufacturer."

Howard nodded. "Good. Maybe he'll come up with something. My men will be following the two of you everywhere you go until we catch Wilson. He's our best hope for tracking down the bastard who hired him. Your home and offices will be under surveillance, and you'll have a tail anytime you go anywhere."

"Fine, but I want to keep my deputies on the job, too. If your men are discreet enough, Wilson might not notice them and make a mistake that will allow us to catch his ass."

"Good idea." Howard stood up and Agent Miles did the same. "So as not to arouse suspicion, my men and I are staying at different places throughout town and in Chicago, but you can reach me anytime on my cell." He was almost to the door when it flew open and Sam rushed inside, panting for breath.

Brandon raised a brow at his deputy. "I take it you have news?"

Sam collapsed into a chair. "I sure do, Boss." He gave Nate a pitying look. "How are you, Doc?"

"I'm okay, Sam. Brandon was the one hurt last night, not me."

"I know, but..." Sam trailed off and looked down at the floor.

Brandon reached for Nate's hand. "Tell us, Sam."

"We traced the knife to a specialty firm in Atlanta. They only take custom orders. The guy I talked to remembered the knife, just like he remembered the name of the guy that bought it."

"Let me finish it for you, Sam." Nate took a deep breath. "The customer's name was Calder Morris."

Chapter Twelve

"I'd still feel better if I was wearing a suit."

"You'd never get it on over that cast. Besides, our church is fairly casual." Brandon smiled at Nate, who was dressed in khaki Dockers and a dark blue pullover. "You look great, as always. You're gonna cause me to have impure thoughts all during the service."

"You're looking pretty sinful yourself in those black jeans and that white button-up shirt."

"Be sure to mention that to my mother, would you? She's always after me to dress up more. She has a fit that I wear jeans with my uniform shirts."

Nate sat down on the bed. "I think it's hot. I won't be telling Gale that, of course."

Noticing the lines of worry on Nate's face, Brandon sat down next to him. "Still thinking about your father?"

"Yeah. I don't guess you've heard anything?"

Brandon smoothed a stray strand of hair off Nate's forehead. "Not since this morning. The Atlanta P.D. went to his house last night after Sam got that callback from the manufacturing company, but Calder was gone. They went to his office, too, but either he got tipped off about the arrest warrant, or he really is on a business trip like his secretary said. The FBI has all his known hangouts covered, as well as the airport. When Calder comes in, we'll be ready for him."

"I can't imagine Calder 'hanging out' anywhere. He's more of a lurker."

Brandon fastened the last button on his sleeve. "I also spoke to your mom this morning. She's really worried about you." Nate's shoulders sagged, and Brandon regretted even mentioning it.

"I know I should call her, but I just don't think I can face her right now. I'm still trying to process it all. As soon as I saw that knife, I knew in the back of my mind that it was my father's. He's practically famous for his knife collection. He's especially fond of the custom made type. What I don't understand is, if my father hired Wilson, why would Wilson throw my father's knife at you? There's no doubt Wilson meant to lodge it in your arm. He had to know you would trace it back to Calder. And why plant that rental receipt?"

"Maybe your father made Wilson mad. Hell, Calder was here for less than twenty-four hours and he managed to piss me off at least six times. There are lots of reasons Wilson could have planted that knife, Nate. We won't have all the answers until we have them both in custody." Brandon stood, pulling Nate with him. "Come on. We aren't going to solve anything by sitting here asking 'what if'. Besides, if we're late for church, my mother's gonna want to know why. And if she asks, I'll tell her we were late because I was screwing you senseless on the carpet here in our room."

Nate gave him a slight smile. "We aren't doing anything even remotely like that."

Brandon rubbed his hand lightly over Nate's crotch. "No, but we will be if you don't get your tight little ass out the door within the next ten seconds."

* ~ * ~ * ~ * ~ *

The First Christian Church of Reed was an architectural wonder. Built in the early nineteen hundreds, from a distance the building looked like a three-story box. Only when he got closer could Nate appreciate the true beauty of the place. A windowed basement made up the first level, but it was the entrance to the main level that made the place so unique. Fifteen hewn-stone steps led the way to the main sanctuary. Brandon guided Nate through the entry hall into the sanctuary proper. The entire room danced with color as the sun shone through eight, twenty-foot, stained glass windows.

They were all amazing, but Nate's favorite was a scene of the crucifixion. The craftsman had captured Jesus in all His glory and sacrifice. Nate was so intent on studying the window, he didn't hear the man who slipped up behind him.

"Breathtaking, isn't it? I've been the pastor here for over fifteen years, and I never get tired of looking at those windows. Sometimes I come here to do my morning prayers just so I can watch the light dance across the pews."

Nate turned and held out his uninjured hand. "Sorry, I guess I zoned out for a minute. I'm Nathan Morris."

"Walter Oakley. I've been meaning to come by for a visit, but autumn seems to be unusually busy for our congregation this year. Between the youth fall fundraiser and the ladies' prayer group, I've hardly had time to drink an entire cup of coffee." He grasped Nate's hand with a warm smile. "I've heard a lot about you from Gale and

Dean, and from Mr. and Mrs. Taylor. I get the feeling they'd be willing to add you to their family tomorrow, if possible."

Walter Oakley was the quintessential small town preacher. He had thick, graying hair, friendly hazel eyes, and little round spectacles. He was wearing robes and carrying a black Bible. Nate grinned. "They're a great family, no doubt about it. I love them all."

"I hope I'm included in that." Brandon slipped up behind Nate and put one arm around his waist. Nate tried to make him let go, but Brandon held firm.

"Brandon, we are in church." Nate said each word slowly and separately, growling through clenched teeth.

Brandon gave him a goofy grin. "Is that where we are? I thought this was Jimmy's Car Wash." He winked at Pastor Oakley. "I think Nate is embarrassed by my shameless public display of affection."

Walter nodded. "Nothing to be embarrassed about, Nathan. God invented sex, you know."

Nate cleared his throat. "I know that, but Bran and I are, well...Bran and I are just different."

"Because you're gay?" When Nate nodded, Oakley chuckled. "I hate to tell you this, son, but God invented gay people, too. In fact, I've been wondering if that's why God put a man's prostate just exactly where He put it, so both partners can enjoy sexual intercourse equally."

Nate wanted to crawl under one of the walnut pews, but Brandon said, "You know, I've never thought about it like that, but I think you're probably right."

Pastor Oakley gave them a devilish smile. "I'd love to take credit for that little bit of wisdom, but it was actually passed on to me by Mrs. Taylor."

"Grandma Abigail?"

"Yes. She's taken a recent interest in anal sex, you know."

Nate wondered if God gave out extra points for dying in church.

* ~ * ~ * ~ * ~ *

Sunday dinner at Grandma Taylor's house was a Nash family tradition. Except for Brandon's brothers who were away at school, the entire family was there, including that damn Dillon, who winked at Brandon when he asked his sister to pass the jelly. The entire family was gathered around the table, engrossed in the upcoming wedding plans. Brandon was unbelievably proud of the way Nate handled all the attention, especially given that he had been basically alone for the past six years.

Gale helped herself to another roll. "So, boys, now we need to set a date so we can finalize all the plans we've already made."

Brandon groaned. The last thing he wanted to do was have another discussion about caterers and musicians. Gale wasn't going to back down, though, so Brandon said, "Actually, we were thinking about getting married right before Christmas. Les and Randy will be home from school, and Seth will have completed his transfer by then. When I talked to her this morning, Leda told me that her divorce action against Calder has already started. Hopefully, she'll have the majority of the legal work wrapped up by then."

Maxine, balancing a toddler on each leg, said, "If you're going to do it during the holidays, why not wait until New Year's Eve? Christmas is so hectic, and New Year's Eve is the perfect time to start a new life."

Megan took a bite of mashed potatoes. "Personally," she said around a mouthful of food, "I think you can't go wrong with Valentine's Day. It's the most romantic holiday there is."

Wayne took a hefty sip of iced tea. "Valentine's Day is a sham invented by the greeting card companies to fill the gap between Christmas and Easter." Stacy slapped him on the back of the head.

Grandpa Gene waved them all away. "It doesn't matter when they tie the knot; it's the honeymoon that counts. Everybody knows that. Abigail and I rented a room near the old depot in Chicago. Stayed holed up in there for a week. Must have knocked the slats out of the bed a half-dozen times."

That did it for Brandon, and he stood up. "I enjoyed the food, but I think it's time to go walk it off." He looked down at Nate. "You coming?"

The look of relief on Nate's face was comical. "Let me get my coat."

The air was cool, but the afternoon sun made up for the drop in temperature. Brandon took Nate through the leaf-strewn yard at the back of the house. "Sorry about that. My family goes hog wild when it comes to special occasions: weddings, birthdays, christenings, you name it. I hope they aren't putting too much pressure on you."

Nate laughed as Brandon pulled him onto a path leading into a stand of trees. "No, they're fine. I feel blessed to be a part of your family. I'll admit, finding out my father hired someone to kill me isn't exactly cause for celebration, but having you and your family has made it easier."

Brandon wasn't entirely convinced of Calder's guilt. The whole thing was coming together too damned easily. Until he had proof to the contrary, however, there wasn't much he could do. Rather than taking issue with Nate's assumption, Brandon decided on a change of subject. "Did you know this place used to be a working dairy farm?"

"I remember you saying your grandfather used to farm, but I

wasn't sure what kind of farm he had."

"He was the main supplier of milk for the entire Reed area for almost thirty years, back when milk was still delivered in bottles on the doorstep. His boys made money for college by running the place while Grandpa was at work down at the firehouse."

"I bet he was a kick-ass fire marshal." Nate stopped beside a red maple and gave Brandon a sexy smile. "Just like his grandson is a kick-ass sheriff."

Brandon's temperature rose several degrees. "Speaking of ass, how would you like to see the barn?"

"The same barn where you took your old boyfriend to make out?"

"Yeah? Does that bother you?"

"That depends. Are you going to do the same thing there that you've done to me for the past two nights in our bedroom?"

Brandon grinned. "Yep."

"Lead the way, farm boy."

* ~ * ~ * ~ * ~ *

Sasha came home that afternoon. She seemed fine, but Brandon and Nate spent almost an hour petting and pampering her, anyway. The vet was still undecided about what ill effects, if any, she might suffer in the future, but she seemed to be back to her old self. That didn't stop Nate from letting her into their bed that night.

Brandon woke up with a wet tongue in his ear. Normally, he enjoyed that, but this tongue was a little too wet to be Nate's. He turned over and swatted Sasha away. "Dammit, Sasha. I should have put you in the screen porch last night like I wanted to."

Nate came out of the bathroom, fully dressed and freshly shaved. "Is Daddy fussing at you, girl?"

Brandon got up without bothering to pull on his boxers and headed toward the bathroom, his morning erection standing tall. "*Daddy* is fussing because he woke up with his dog this morning instead of his future husband." He gave Nate a good morning kiss and looked him over. "Are you sure you want to do this, Nate? I mean, you'll still need another doctor or one of the nurses to help you with the big stuff because of your arm. Why not just wait?"

"You know why. Howard thinks Wilson will make his move while I'm at work."

Brandon moved into the bathroom and started his morning routine. After emptying his bladder and smearing shaving cream all over his thick stubble, he said, "I'll tell you the same thing I told Howard last night when he called and detailed this brilliant plan of his — I'm not crazy about using you as bait. Sooner or later, Wilson will make a mistake, and when he does, we'll nab him." He moved the straight razor across his face in one solid stroke. "It isn't necessary to set yourself up as a target."

Nate leaned against the door. "I'm hardly a target. I have guards following me, 24/7. Miles already swept the office and pronounced it clean of bugs. You've changed all the alarm codes, both here and at work. I haven't replaced my car yet, and you don't want me trying to drive yours with only one arm, so someone will have to drop me off and pick me up. Hell, I couldn't be any safer if I was wrapped in cotton wool."

Brandon rinsed the blade and then took off another strip of beard. "I wish I *could* wrap you in cotton wool." He cleaned the razor again and looked at Nate in the mirror. "I can always apologize to you later for being an overprotective asshole, but one good slip up, and I won't get that chance."

Nate held up his cast. "You don't have to convince me of the danger I'm in, but I don't believe going to the office will up the stakes. Amy and I have four nurses working for us, plus your cousin and the receptionist. I won't be taking any new patients, and if I have to go outside for any reason, I'll notify Howard and his men. Add to that the fact that you've got Dewey and Sam coming by every hour on the hour, and I'll be fine."

Brandon nodded and went back to his shaving. As a profiler, he'd learned that ninety percent of police work was intuition and gut instinct. Right now, his guts were churning.

* ~ * ~ * ~ * ~ *

Nate filed the chart he was holding and turned to Tina, one of his nurses. She was an older lady, almost sixty, and close to retirement. She had a sweet smile and a terrific rapport with the patients. Today, she'd been a godsend.

"Tina, make sure Wendy Ryan knows to start her little boy on those antibiotics after supper tonight. Make sure she understands he has to eat first."

"I will, Dr. Morris." She looked at her watch. "It's almost lunch time. Dr. Vaughn wants you to meet her upstairs."

"Thanks, Tina." Nate took off his lab coat and hung it on a hook in his office. He followed the smell of barbeque up the stairs. "What did you do, Amy, make a B.B.Q. run? How much—" He stopped when he saw Mike sitting on the sofa.

Mike stood up. "If your next question is going to be 'How much do

I owe you?' the answer is — nothing. After the way I acted, I owe you a lot more than lunch."

Nate looked to Amy for help, but she sat quietly in one of the arm-chairs. Finally, Nate said, "Are you talking about the fact that you accused my fiancé of trying to kill me, or are you apologizing for calling your wife a 'frigid bitch' and me a 'fucking faggot'?"

Mike winced. "All of it. Amy told me about the knife, and about your father. We've been friends for a long time, Nate. When you lost Rick and your parents, I was there for you, wasn't I? Are you going to let one stupid mistake destroy an eight year friendship?"

"That depends."

"On what? Just name your price."

"You have to apologize to Brandon."

Mike sagged in relief. "Already done. I called the station this morning and told him I was sorry."

"What did he say?"

Mike lowered his voice to imitate Brandon's velvet baritone. "He said, and I quote, 'I'll accept your apology, Vaughn, but if you ever put your hands on Nate again, I'll cut off your balls and stuff 'em up your ass.'"

"Did you point out that I was the one who jumped you?"

"I started to, but I figured Nash wasn't exactly in the mood to hear it."

Nate laughed. "Yeah, well, I love the guy, but he is kinda blind to my faults."

Amy stood and walked over to Mike. "Love is supposed to be blind." She put her arm around her husband. "God knows I've been visually impaired since I married this guy."

Mike kissed her forehead. "And you know I'm grateful for that." He turned to Nate. "What can I do to make it up to you, besides apologizing to Nash?"

Nate inhaled the aroma of the barbeque. "Is that barbeque from Hailey's?"

"Absolutely."

"Consider yourself forgiven."

* ~ * ~ * ~ * ~ *

Nate leaned back against the overstuffed chair. "I ate too much."

Amy shook her head. "You've gotten too thin. We need to fatten you up."

"You sound just like Brandon."

Amy smiled at him from her position on the couch. "Great minds and all that. I think Mr. Brandon Nash is going to fit into our little family rather nicely." She looked at Mike, who was seated next to her. "Don't you agree, husband-of-mine?"

Mike leaned forward to see Nate better. "Actually, I do. Have you guys signed your power of attorney papers yet?"

"No. We have an appointment next week with a lawyer here in town."

"Well, I want you to cancel it and let me take care of it for you. I can have the papers drawn up tomorrow, and it's the least I can do after the way I've treated you both. I want to do this, Nate. Free of charge, too. Consider it a wedding present. You know the name of my firm, right?"

"Yeah, it's Oswald and Rafferty. I'll talk to Brandon about it tonight."

"Good." Mike gave Amy a quick kiss and then stood. "I've got to get back to the office. I've got two wills ready to send to probate and a real-estate closing at four."

Nate raised an eyebrow. "You drove all the way here just to bring barbeque?"

Mike pulled him into a rough hug. "And to beg for forgiveness. Don't forget that." He patted Nate on the back and started out the door. "I'm glad we worked it out. You are Amy's only friend, after all."

"I heard that, Mike Vaughn." Amy flipped him the finger. "You are so not getting any tonight."

Mike laughed. "Like I said, frigid." His voice dropped to a loud whisper. "Don't worry, though. My dick has a defrost setting." He left before Amy could get to him.

* ~ * ~ * ~ * ~ *

By five o'clock, Nate was beginning to wonder why he'd insisted on coming back to work in the first place. It seemed like everybody in the greater Reed area had come in to the clinic today. More than anything, he wanted to head home and fall into that big ol' bathtub, but the mountain of paperwork on his desk canceled that idea. Amy came in looking as ragged as he felt.

She collapsed into one of Nate's chairs and put her feet up on the desk. "Tell me again why we became doctors?"

"I can't remember. Something about helping people, healing the sick, that kinda stuff."

"Does that include being kicked by four-year-olds when you try to give them their booster shots?" She rubbed a spot just below her knee. "Damn. That's gonna leave a bruise."

"Occupational hazard, my friend. At least you didn't have to explain to a horny waiter why you couldn't give him a one handed prostate exam."

"Ah, yes, the sexy Shane. Did he really try to get you to give him an exam?"

"Afraid so. Seems he hadn't heard about my engagement."

"I take it you set him straight."

Nate grinned. "I figured I'd better or else Brandon would."

"Good call. Listen, thanks for making things so easy on Mike. You could have made him crawl, but you didn't. You're a class act, buddy."

"You love the guy, and I love you. I didn't have any choice. Besides, Mike's my friend. If you can't forgive your friends when they go nuts, what good are you?"

"Like I said, you're a class act." She leaned back and closed her eyes. "Why don't you call Brandon to come and get you and go on home? You're still not one hundred percent yet. I can finish up these charts."

"No way. I'm not leaving until all this is done. Besides, everyone else has gone for the day. I'm not leaving you here by yourself all night."

"Okay, but one of us has to make a quick run for Chinese food. If you can drive one handed, I vote you do it. I have more charts to finish than you do, and that'll give me a head start."

"I can drive. Let me call Howard and tell him the plan." Nate whipped out his cell phone and pressed the button Brandon had programmed into memory. Howard answered on the first ring.

"Howard, here."

"Hi, Rex. It's Nate."

"Oh, hey, Doc. What can I do for you?"

"Amy and I are working late. I'm gonna make a Chinese food run, if you think it's okay."

"I don't see why not. We've got your office covered. What kind of car will you be driving?"

"A red Saturn, last year's model."

"I'll have one of my guys follow you to and from, Doc."

"Thanks, Howard." Nate disconnected and turned back to Amy. "Mu-shu pork and egg drop soup sound okay to you?"

"Yeah, but pick up some crab-meat and cheese wontons, too. Oh," she tossed him her keys, "and don't forget the fortune cookies."

Nate slipped out the back door. There was no moon, and it was already dark, so Nate had to feel his way out to Amy's car. Paradise Gardens was the closest Chinese restaurant to the office. When he got there, he decided to run inside rather than brave the long line of cars at the drive through, thinking it would be quicker. It might have been, if Mrs. Chen hadn't stopped Nate on his way out to ask him about the best treatment for sciatica. By the time the doctor was finished with his curbside consultation, it was almost six o'clock. He loaded the food into the Saturn and headed back toward the office. A couple of times, Nate caught a brief glimpse of a large black sedan in his rearview mirror, but otherwise, Howard's men kept out of sight.

Nate parked in the front lot, rather than the private one he and Amy usually used. The walk was shorter, and he was going to have a hard enough time carrying all the food as it was. He scooped up the first bag, looped the handles of the second one over his cast, and started toward the front of the office. He put his right foot on the first step and felt a slight shift in the wind. The hairs on the back of his neck stood and his skin tingled. He looked around, but saw no one. Dismissing his reaction as nine parts exhaustion and one part paranoia, Nate slid his key into the deadbolt and turned the tumbler. He would later remember hearing no sound as the office exploded in a swirl of fire and timber. His only memory was of being thrown backward by the force of the blast. After that, nothing.

Chapter Thirteen

Gale poured herself another cup of coffee and sat down at the table across from Brandon. "How long has he been like that?"

"Since the funeral."

"He's been in that room by himself for three weeks?"

Gale sounded as outraged as Brandon felt, but outrage was the least of what he was feeling. He also felt helpless. He understood grief. Hell, he'd stood over the mutilated body of one of his closest friends, too. But even knowing that, even understanding it, didn't take away his sense of loss. He wanted his partner back. He missed the early morning smiles and the quiet nights of holding each other. He wanted Nate.

Brandon took a sip of his own coffee. It was cold, but he didn't care. "He came out once after the funeral, when I insisted he go see one of the staff psychiatrists at Chicago General. I thought he might be suffering from post-traumatic stress, like I was after Kyle died, but the shrink says he isn't. According to Dr. Carson, Nate's grieving, and there isn't a damn thing I can do about it. So much for a degree in clinical psychology, huh?" Brandon took another swig of his bitter drink. "You know what the worst part is? He hasn't even cried. Not one tear. Not for Amy, not for himself, and not even when I told him Howard's men had arrested his father at the airport in Atlanta."

"How strong is the case against Calder, do you think?" Gale asked.

"Circumstantial. Calder was here when the rental receipt was planted, and he could have stolen the key and planted those bugs while he and Leda were in our house. Sasha was drugged with a generic form of Valium, which Calder could have gotten from any one of his stores. We haven't found a definite link between him and Wilson, but with Calder's connections, he would have had no problem tracking down and hiring a hit man. His hatred of homosexuals is clearly documented and would explain the arsons and the attempts on Nate. The fact that Calder hired Patterson to break Seth's heart doesn't exactly make him a father-of-the-year candidate, either. A good prosecutor could sell it to a jury."

Gale nodded. "Alicia said the same thing." She studied Brandon's face. "You just aren't convinced, are you?"

"I hope it is Calder, but I've got my doubts. Why would the man have Wilson plant that rental receipt? He had to know it would expose his relationship to Patterson."

"Could Wilson have gotten angry with Calder? Maybe this was his way of getting even."

Brandon walked to the sink and dumped the dregs of his coffee. He folded his arms and leaned back against the counter, ankles crossed. "That's the way the DA will spin it, and it could very well be true. Maybe I'm making too much out of nothing. God knows I'm rattled over everything that's happening with Nate. Maybe my instincts are off."

Gale nodded. "Mike's behavior at the funeral didn't help. I know the man is devastated by the loss of his wife, but that's no excuse for the way he treated Nate. Mike practically accused him of killing Amy."

Brandon clenched his fists. "I should have arrested the little bastard when he made a dive for Nate at the graveside service. I would have if Nate hadn't insisted I leave him alone. As it is, I wish Dad hadn't held me back when I took a swing at the son of a bitch."

Dean came in from the living room and poured himself a cup of coffee. "I wanted to see you deck Mike, believe me. But that wasn't what Nate needed, and you know it."

Brandon did know it, but knowing didn't make it any easier. Lashing out seemed the best way to rid himself of the frustration. "So just what does Nate need, Daddy? He doesn't want me to touch him. He's made that clear enough. He won't talk to his mother, or to Seth. He even insisted they not come to Amy's funeral. He doesn't need food, doesn't need sunlight. The psychiatrist can't tell me what he needs. Nate *won't* tell me what he needs. Maybe you can." Brandon was yelling by the time he finished.

He expected Dean to yell back, maybe even to swat him on the backside like he would have done years ago. He never expected Dean to wrap him in his arms and start rubbing his back. He certainly never expected himself to need it so much.

"I know it hurts, son, but you have to think about how much worse it could have been. At least Nate is still here. In time, he *will* get better. If he'd gotten back to his office just a few minutes sooner, we wouldn't be having this discussion."

Brandon pulled away and went back to the table. He made no move to sit down. Instead, he stood with his hands braced on the back of a chair. "Don't you think I know that? Not a day has gone by since that bomb went off that I haven't gotten down on my knees and thanked God that Nate wasn't in there. I'm sorry that Amy died. I wish things could have been different, but not if it means Nate would have had to take her place. I may be a selfish bastard, but that's the way it is."

Gale shook her head. "You aren't selfish, Brandon; you're human. No one expects you to make a choice like that."

Brandon ran his fingers through his hair. "Nate does. When I brought him back here after the funeral, he kept saying it should have been him instead of Amy. He wanted me to agree with him. We argued, I opened my big mouth, and all hell broke loose."

"Not to pry," Dean's eyes were sympathetic, "but is that what landed you in the guest room?"

Brandon winced. "Partly. I told Nate he was being selfish and Amy wouldn't want him to stop living just because she died."

"That doesn't sound so bad." Gale tilted her head and studied her son.

"It wouldn't have been if I'd stopped at that." Brandon took a deep breath. "I told Nate that he should be grateful to be here. I told him that bitching and moaning because he was still alive was like killing Amy all over again."

Dean swore. "Jesus Christ. I love you, son, but you can be a real dumbass sometimes."

The back door opened, and Brandon heard the electronic melody of the keypad being reprogrammed. Keith came through the mudroom and into the kitchen. He took one look at the serious expression on Brandon's face and said, "What are we talking about?"

"Nothing important. Just the fact that I'm a dumbass." Brandon shook his head.

"Well, hell, I knew that." Keith grinned.

Gale ignored him. "We were talking about the situation with Nate."

"Still no change?"

Brandon turned to his brother. "Not unless you count moving from the bed to the chair as a change."

"How are the cuts on his chest from the impact of the blast?"

"How should I know, Keith? Nate can't stand to be touched."

"I know. Mother told me. That's why I brought someone with me who can help."

Grandma Taylor came out of the mudroom carrying a heavy brown shopping bag. "Was that my cue?"

"Grandma, no offense, but what are you doing here?" The last thing Nate needed right now was another lecture on the joys of butt-sex from an eighty-three-year-old woman. The fact that Grandma was wearing a purple shirt-dress tied in the back with a giant pink bow did not bode well.

Abigail looked up at Brandon with a patient smile. "I know you all

think I'm dotty because I dress funny and say the first thing that comes
to mind. Well, tough. I'm old and I can do what I want to. Right now, I
want to see my new grandson, and I'd like to see you turkeys try and
stop me."

"Grandma—"

Keith interrupted. "Bran, just let her try. What have you got to
loose?"

Brandon thought of all he'd already lost. Three weeks without Nate
and he was in purgatory. He was desperate enough to try anything. He
nodded and led the way upstairs.

Sasha lay outside the door to the master bedroom. She missed Nate
as much as Brandon did. For three weeks, she'd kept an almost constant
vigil. She scratched and whined and begged, but Nate refused to open
the door. He'd shut her out just as he'd shut out the rest of the world.

Shooing Sasha out of the way as he went, Brandon opened the door
without knocking. It was just past lunchtime on Sunday, but the bedroom was dark and stale. Nate had the shades pulled and the curtains
drawn. He was sitting in a chair with his back to the door, staring at the
wall. Brandon could barely see him, but his heart ached at just the sight
of Nate's unruly tuft of blond hair sticking up above the back of the
chair. Brandon wanted to pull Nate out of the chair and hold him until
Nate cried out all the bitterness and pain. Instead, Brandon walked out
of the room and closed the door behind him.

* ~ * ~ * ~ * ~ *

As Abigail made her way over and turned the other chair around
until she was sitting next to him, Nate watched with detachment. She
sat in silence for at least ten minutes. Finally, she said, "Are you planning on remodeling sometime soon? Personally, I think that's a fine
wall. The way you're studying it has me thinking you might be ready to
tear it down with your bare hands."

Nate wanted to say something, anything to make her leave so he
wouldn't have to think. It didn't hurt as bad when he didn't think.
When no excuses came to mind, he kept his mouth shut and his eyes
focused on the wall. He expected Abigail to try and force him to talk,
the way Brandon kept doing, but she didn't. She seemed to be having a
conversation all on her own.

"I've always liked this house. Brandon's other grandmother, Emily,
and I was a friend long before she married Ed Nash. Went to grammar
school together. When Emily told me she and Ed were buying this
house from Ed's father, I made her a quilt for this very room. Nothing
fancy, just a simple Nine-patch made from fabric I bought with my

trading stamps, but she loved that old quilt. Still has it, too. She took it with her when they moved to Florida. I don't really know why. The whole purpose of moving to Florida is so you won't need a quilt in the first place."

From the corner of his eye, Nate could see her looking at him but he gave no response. If he stayed quiet, he could pretend he was alone and he wouldn't have to feel anything. He should have known Abby wasn't finished.

"Every bedroom needs a quilt. I mean a real one, not those stamped monstrosities they sell in discount stores. I'm talking about a quilt that's been cut and sewn by flesh and blood hands, not a machine."

Nate could hear the rustling of a paper sack and the unfolding of cloth.

Abby laid the bundle in his lap and said, "I believe this belongs to you."

Nate stared at the familiar hues of gray and burgundy in disbelief. "This looks just like my quilt, the one my Grandmother Morris made for me."

"No, honey. It doesn't look like your quilt, it *is* your quilt."

Nate's voice was struggling to rise. "That isn't possible. That bastard destroyed my quilt. The same bastard who..." He couldn't say it. If he said it, it would be true.

Abigail ignored the sudden stop. "He almost destroyed it. In fact, he did his level best. I'll give him that. But you see, Nathan, your grandmother knew something that Mr. Wilson didn't." She didn't wait for him to ask, she just kept right on talking. "There are lots of ways to make a quilt. I learned to sew on my mother's old treadle machine. When I was a teenager, electric sewing machines were still considered new and exciting. As they became more popular, strip piecing was all the rage. I know you don't sew, so I'll tell you that strip piecing involves sewing the whole quilt top together by machine and then attaching the backing. It's quicker, and all us girls wanted to try it. My mother laughed when I told her I wanted to strip-piece a quilt, but I did it anyway. It was beautiful, all purples and reds. I can still see all those little squares floating around in the water after it fell apart on the first washing. No, Nathan, your grandmother was smart. She foundation pieced your quilt."

Nate didn't want to ask, but he couldn't stop himself. "What's 'foundation piecing'?"

"Your grandmother sewed each piece by hand to a muslin backing. She didn't scrimp on the fabric, either. No sir, she bought the best fabric money could buy and secured each scrap of fabric with the strongest thread she could find. That nasty Mr. Wilson damaged the top of the quilt — the surface — but he didn't touch the foundation. I was able to repair the surface because the foundation was so strong." She looked at the bandages on Nate's shirtless chest. "Looks like your surface took a beating, too. I'd be willing to bet your foundation is still just as strong as that quilt's, though."

Nate's laugh was bitter, resentful. "Strong? How can you say that? I've spent the last three weeks staring at a wall because my best friend is... If it weren't for me, she would..."

Abigail said, "She would be alive. You're right. If she'd gotten into that car instead of you, Amy would be alive and Brandon would be the one up here staring at the wall. The only difference is, you've got a man down there who would stop breathing if you asked him to. If you'd died, Brandon would have had no one."

"He'd have you and Gale and—"

"No, he wouldn't. Because if you had died, a vital part of Brandon would have died, too. I know that Amy was your friend, and I also know that you blame yourself for her death. She held a piece of you that went into the ground with her. But she didn't own you, not like you own Brandon. Not like he owns you. You can punish yourself by cutting him out of your life, but you'll never cut him out of your heart. You could die tomorrow or eighty years from now, but it wouldn't matter. The two of you have the real thing, Nathan. You gave Brandon a piece of your soul, and he did the same. You can't take back something that was freely given."

Nate got up and paced in front of the shrouded windows, still clutching the quilt in his hands. "You don't understand. It's my fault Amy is dead. If I hadn't left her there by herself, she'd still be alive."

"Maybe, and maybe you would have died with her. But the fact remains that you're alive and she isn't. Do you think if God had given her a choice, Amy would have had you die in her place?"

The very thought was blasphemous. "Of course not. Amy loved me. She would have given her life for me in an instant."

"And so she did. Is this how you choose to repay her — by ruining the life she so generously paid for?"

Nate sank down to his knees on the carpet, the quilt held tightly to his body. "You're right. Amy paid the price for my life. This time. Who has to pay next? Brandon?"

"If giving my life is the cost of loving you, then I've already paid it, Nate. I paid it the first time I touched you. You were mine from that moment on, you just didn't know it. It took some doing, but I finally convinced you. You can't just give me your heart and then take it back. It doesn't work that way, dammit."

Nate looked up to see Brandon standing in the doorway. He looked tired and worn, his glorious eyes rimmed with red from lack of sleep. Nate thought of Amy's hazel eyes, eyes that would never open again, never see. He thought of Mike and all he'd lost. *What would I do if I were in Mike's place?* The thought of standing by Brandon's grave and watching him being lowered into the ground was too much. Nate let loose with an anguished wail and collapsed onto the floor, his entire body wracked with the sobs that had been waiting for release for days.

Abigail slipped out of the room and closed the door behind her. Nate heard Sasha scratching to come in, but he couldn't have gotten up if he'd wanted to. He felt himself being lifted and carried to the bed by the same strong arms he'd been denying himself for days on end. *Well, no more. If Brandon and I are living on borrowed time, I'm going to take what I can get and be damn grateful for it.* The tears kept coming until Nate finally fell asleep.

* ~ * ~ * ~ * ~ *

Brandon felt a slight stirring next to him and opened his eyes to see Nate propped up on his good elbow looking at him.

Nate smiled. "Hi."

"Hi." Brandon wasn't sure how to proceed. Finally, he said, "Are you all right?"

"Not quite, but I will be." Tears filled Nate's brown eyes. "I'll always miss her, you know? For a long time, Amy was all I had."

Brandon reached out and stroked Nate's unshaven cheek. "I know, but you aren't alone anymore, Nate. You have a family now who wants to help you." He lowered his voice. "You have me."

The tears started falling then. "I know that, and it scared the hell out of me. All I could think about was if losing Amy hurt that badly, what would it be like to lose you? Wilson is still out there, even if my father is in custody. What if he comes to finish the job? I was trying to protect myself." Nate reached out his right arm and flexed his fingers awkwardly around Brandon's hand. His cast had been damaged during the blast. When the E.R. doctor who treated him after the explosion took it off, he'd replaced it with a cotton sling.

For the first time, Brandon noticed that Nate wasn't wearing it. "How's your arm?"

"Better. I don't even need the sling." Nate looked down at their joined hands. "It's well enough to do something I've wanted to do since before the car accident."

Brandon raised an eyebrow. "What's that?"

"Hold you with both arms."

Brandon wanted to cry out his relief. He also wanted to jump into Nate's arms and do all the things he'd been denied for so long. Rather than rush him, though, Brandon said, "Why don't we get you cleaned up first? No offense, but you're looking kinda scruffy."

Rubbing his fingers over his scraggly chin, Nate laughed, the sound rusty from disuse. "Yeah, I guess I am. Not exactly a sex object, am I?" If Nate had known what Brandon was thinking of doing to him at that moment, he wouldn't have asked the question.

Brandon got up and offered Nate his hand. "Come on." He led Nate into the bathroom and turned on the taps. While the sink was filling, Brandon took Nate's shaving cream from the medicine cabinet. Instead of reaching for Nate's safety razor, though, Brandon grabbed his own straight razor.

Nate eyed him with suspicion. "There's no way I'm going to shave myself with that. Grandma Taylor may have fixed my quilt, but I doubt she'd be able to patch me up if I shave with that thing. I'd turn my face into hamburger meat."

"I don't want you to try shaving with it. You aren't used to using a straight razor." He swirled a washcloth around in the sink and then moved closer to where Nate was standing. "I'm going to do it for you."

"Brandon—"

"Let me do this for you, Nate. You know I'll be careful. I would never hurt you."

Nate looked up into his eyes. "I know." He eyed the razor again and then sighed. "Where do you want me?"

Brandon positioned him so that Nate was leaning with his back against the sink. "I think this ought to be about right."

"You'll have to reach around me to get to the water."

"I know." Brandon grinned.

Nate rolled his eyes. "I should have known you had ulterior motives."

Brandon smoothed the warm cloth over Nate's heavy stubble. "How does that feel?"

As Brandon's fingers worked the cloth against his skin, Nate closed his eyes. "Good. It feels good."

When he was satisfied that the beard was sufficiently softened, Brandon tossed the cloth onto the counter and reached around Nate to get the shaving cream. He pumped a big glob of cream into his hand and smoothed it all over Nate's face and neck. When he reached for the razor, he expected Nate to flinch, but he didn't. Brandon brought the edge of the blade against Nate's cheek and removed a wide strip of beard with one smooth stroke. When he reached around Nate to rinse it off, Brandon's groin pressed directly into Nate's growing erection.

Brandon grinned. "Someone's decided to wake up, I see."

Nate's eyes became cloudy. "I know. I tried not to get turned on, but with you leaning up against me like that, I couldn't help it."

Brandon took off another strip of Nate's beard. "Why were you trying not to get an erection? It's perfectly natural, under the circumstances." He paused with the razor in mid-stroke as reasoning dawned. "You feel guilty about wanting me when Amy's only been gone a few weeks."

Nate nodded. Brandon wanted to take him into his arms, but he didn't. Nate was grieving, and Brandon was going to have to be careful not to do or say anything to make it worse. Brandon resumed shaving him without saying a word.

Finally Nate said, "Aren't you going to tell me how stupid that is?"

Brandon rinsed the razor and started shaving another swath. "Nope. Amy was your friend. You have the right to mourn her however you see fit."

"Don't you think it's wrong to be thinking about sex when her body is barely even cold?"

"No, I don't. I think sex is an expression of life, a way to show how glad you are to be alive. Every time you and I make love, it's sacred. Nothing can make that wrong or dirty." Brandon started on the other side of Nate's face. "But it isn't what I think that matters. You're the only one who can say what's right for you. I'm willing to wait as long as it takes."

Nate sighed. "My body is raring to go, it's my mind that's holding me back. Grandma Taylor helped me a lot, but I guess there are still some things I have to work through."

Brandon shaved away the last stubble and then grabbed the washcloth from the counter and patted away the remnants of the shaving cream. "You don't have to explain it to me, Nate. You've had a shock and you need time to adjust." He threw the cloth into the hamper beside the sink. "I'm not in this for the sex, although, I gotta tell you, the sex is great." He took Nate's hand. "I'm in this for life, Nate. We'll take care of what you need right now, and let the rest take care of itself." Brandon turned Nate around so that they were both looking in the mirror. "Well, what do you think?"

Nate ran his hand over the smooth surface of his face. "I was starting to forget what I looked like without all that hair." Brown eyes met blue in the mirror. "Thanks."

Brandon kissed a hairless cheek. "Anytime."

* ~ * ~ * ~ * ~ *

A week passed before Nate returned to some semblance of normalcy. Though he was still skittish about sex, he seemed to be healing, both physically and mentally. The cuts on his chest had been minor, requiring bandages but no stitches. His arm was almost as good as new, with only an occasional twinge. His heart was healing too. He'd started sleeping with Brandon again, even though all they did was sleep. The day before, he'd called his mother and Seth, and was relieved that they seemed to be taking Calder's arrest in stride. And he'd actually smiled this morning.

That smile had been on Brandon's mind all day. He was sitting in his office on Friday afternoon, going over the case against Calder, when the intercom buzzer sounded. He pressed the button. "What is it, Lorna?"

"Agent Howard is here to see you, Sheriff."

"Send him on back."

A few minutes later Rex Howard stuck his head in the door. "Hey, Nash, how's it going?"

"Come on in and have a seat. Haven't seen you since the funeral."

Howard sat down and pulled some papers from the inside pocket of his overcoat. "I've been a busy boy since the explosion. It took some doing, but we've finally pieced together what happened. We also have enough evidence to tie Wilson to the bombing, and we think we may have found a connection between Calder and Wilson."

"You know how Wilson managed to disable the alarm, sneak past both of our men, and plant that bomb?" Brandon leaned back in his chair.

"That part I'm unsure of, but we do know that the blast originated upstairs and that Wilson used plastique — probably C4 — with a remote detonator."

"Damn. So he could have planted that bomb at any time."

"Yep. Wilson must have been watching the office. When he saw the red Saturn leaving, he assumed it was Dr. Vaughn and detonated the bomb, thinking Dr. Morris was still inside."

Brandon shuddered "He very well could have been." He forced his mind away from what could have happened. "Tell me about this other evidence."

"Apparently, Wilson used to live in Atlanta. One of his brothers works for Mor-co at the home office in Georgia. Naturally, the brother denies introducing Calder to Wilson, but I doubt a jury will buy it."

"They might. As evidence goes, it's pretty thin. Half of Atlanta has worked for Mor-co at one time or another; it's one of the largest employers in the city. Nate and Amy both worked part time for Mor-co while they were still in high school. And Seth worked there up until about a week ago. I think Mike even worked there while he was in college. A good defense attorney will say that any of them could have met Wilson through his brother. Besides, Calder isn't exactly known for fraternizing with the hired help. His lawyer will be able to shoot that connection right out of the water."

Howard flipped through the sheaf of papers he held and handed one to Brandon. "Maybe so, but this won't be quite so easy to cast doubt on."

Brandon looked down at the paper in his hand. It was a purchase order from Radio Shack for a mass of different electrical components. Brandon was no techno-junkie, but he recognized what he was seeing. "These are the parts used to make the detonator?"

"Yep. And I have another receipt for the parts used to make the bugs we found in your house."

Brandon kept staring at the paper, but he couldn't see the relevance. "I don't get it."

"We have surveillance footage of Wilson buying all that stuff at a store in Chicago. He went to the same place both times. The tie in to Calder comes from Wilson's method of payment."

Brandon caught on. "Don't tell me the son of a bitch was that stupid?"

Howard grinned. "You got it, my friend. The crazy bastard paid for all of it with a Mor-co company credit card. I have the statements from the credit card company to prove it."

"Well I'll be damned. Patterson said that Calder insisted he use the card while he was gas-lighting Seth because he wanted a record of all his expenses, but I never thought Calder would be dumb enough to give a card to his hit-man."

"It gets better. We found receipts for a hotel in Naperville about a two-and-a-half hour drive from here. Wilson signed in under his own name. Needless to say, he'd already checked out by the time we got there. My guess is that he stayed there while he was making his little toys, but moved somewhere closer to Reed when the time came to do the wet work. My men are looking for him now, but we'll keep the surveillance on Doc until he's found."

"I'm glad to hear it. I'm doing the same thing with my own men." Brandon glanced down at his watch. "Not to cut this short, Howard, but I've got to get home. Tonight is the homecoming game at Plunkett High, and my baby sister is up for Homecoming Queen. I told her she could drive my car." Brandon saw Howard cringe.

"Good luck. No way would I let one of my kids drive a classic like your Camaro."

"Megan's a good driver. And I've got one of my deputies following her, just in case. That way, if Wilson sees the car and thinks it's me or Nate, Megan will have protection."

"Uh huh. And if her date tries to take her parking, the deputy will put a stop to it."

Brandon grinned. "That too."

* ~ * ~ * ~ * ~ *

While in high school, Brandon's game of choice had been baseball, but he still enjoyed a good football game. The fact that the Plunkett Panthers were winning and Megan had just been crowned Homecoming Queen made the game that much more interesting.

He and Nate were sitting on the top bleacher with the rest of the Nash family. It was cold, about forty degrees, and Nate's cheeks were rosy from the icy wind. Brandon thought Nate had never looked sexier. He wished his body would stop reminding him that he hadn't made love to Nate in over a month.

After the game, Brandon and Nate kissed and congratulated Megan, then headed for the parking lot. Brandon waited until Nate was buckled in and then started the engine. As they drove away from the stadium, Brandon asked, "Are you hungry? I could stop somewhere and grab something."

Nate shook his head. "That's okay. I think I'd like to head home, if that's all right with you."

"Home it is."

Sasha was waiting at the door when they pulled up. She had her bowl in her mouth. Brandon started to take it, but Nate shook his head. "Why don't you go on up and take a bath? You didn't have a chance to take one before the game." Nate pushed Brandon towards the stairs. "Go on. I'll feed Sasha."

Brandon agreed, wishing he had the balls to ask Nate to join him. He was so damned scared of doing something that might push Nate away. Every night for the past week, he'd lain in bed beside Nate wanting like crazy to touch him and unable to do anything about it. Facing another lonely night was something Brandon was just going to have to live with. He'd promised Nate time, and time was what Nate was going to get.

Brandon turned on the taps and stripped while the tub was filling. He didn't bother to check the bottom of the tub before he got in. The minute he stepped into the water, he noticed it felt different, oily. He also noticed the smell. Cinnamon. He started to let the water out and run a fresh tub, but he was afraid he wouldn't have enough hot water left to fill it back up. Besides, nobody ever died from cinnamon poisoning. Not that he knew of, anyway. With a shrug, Brandon sank down into the hot water and allowed some of his tension to ebb away. He leaned back and closed his eyes. That's when he heard the music.

One thing Brandon liked about Nate was his taste in music. Nate wasn't prejudiced; he liked all kinds of music and had an impressive collection of CDs to show for it. At the moment, Nate was playing a mix he'd downloaded from the internet. Brandon remembered teasing him about the unholy combination of artists on that particular CD, everything from Pearl Jam to Johnny Cash. At the moment, *Closer* by Nine Inch Nails was playing. When the line "I want to fuck you like an animal" played, Brandon started to get suspicious. That's when the lights went out.

Well, not all the lights. The overhead light went off just as the sconces above the sink, which were on a different switch, came on. The sconces bathed the tub in soft light, almost like candles. A few minutes later, the room was flooded with the smell of cedar, which blended with the cinnamon. Brandon got a good whiff of both and started coughing.

Nate was in there in a second. He was also stark naked. "Are you all right? I heard you coughing."

Brandon was having trouble catching his breath as Nate opened the door wide to let some of the smell escape and then ran fresh water in a paper cup and handed it to Brandon. When he was able to speak, Brandon said, "Would you mind explaining to me why it smells like Christmas in here?"

Nate looked concerned. "You don't like cedar and cinnamon? I thought everybody did."

"I didn't say I didn't like it. I'm just not used to taking a bath at Santa's Cottage, that's all."

"Sorry. I guess I used too much."

Brandon's eyes were so watery, he had trouble looking Nate in the face. "Used too much what? And why is the bathtub so damn slippery? I'll be lucky to get out without cracking my head open."

"I'm sorry, Brandon. Let me just put my clothes back on and cut the music off. Then I'll help you out of the tub and clean up this mess."

Nate turned to leave, but Brandon stopped him. "Nate?"

"Yeah?"

"Come here."

When Nate walked over to the edge of the tub, he looked so cute with his lip poked out that Brandon almost started laughing. He opened his arms. "Get in with me?"

Nate didn't have to be asked twice. He climbed into the tub, forgetting about the oil. He slipped and would have hit his head against the side if Brandon hadn't caught him. Brandon settled him in front and looked at him with newly cleared eyes.

Nate's face was burning with embarrassment. "I guess this wasn't one of my better ideas, huh?"

Brandon was doing his best not to laugh. Whatever this was, it meant something to Nate, and Brandon wasn't about to ruin it for him. Instead, he said, "Not that I'm complaining, but would you mind telling me what this is all about?"

"I put cinnamon essential oil in the tub so you would smell it when the tub filled up. Oh, and I got some of those things that fit over light bulbs. You know, those ring things? These are cedar scented, but I guess you already knew that. Anyway, when the light bulbs heat up, the fragrance is released. I wanted the smell to be really strong, so I put three against each bulb, one on top and one on each side. I probably went overboard, huh?"

"Maybe just a little bit. May I ask why you chose cedar and cinnamon?"

Nate's entire body went red. "They're, uh, supposed to be aphrodisiacs."

Brandon wasn't sure he was hearing right. "You turned our bathtub into an oil slick because you were trying to sex me up? Why the hell didn't you just ask me?" Nate's reply was so soft, Brandon could barely hear him. He finally had to ask Nate to repeat himself.

Without looking at him, Nate said, "I've made you do without for over a month. I was afraid you might..."

"You thought I might be out for a little revenge. Thought I might make you wait, just to see you suffer a little bit."

"Yeah," Nate whispered. "I wouldn't blame you if you did. I deserve it."

Brandon tilted Nate's chin until he was looking up at him. "No, you don't. You've been hurting. I would never hold that against you. Never."

Nate nodded. "Rationally, I know that, but I've been so mixed up, Bran. I've wanted you, and then felt guilty about it. Today I realized the only way I was ever going to feel normal again was just to go on with my life the best that I can. I need you, Brandon. Really need you."

The CD changed from *Closer* to *Colorblind* by the Counting Crows. Brandon pulled Nate up and onto his lap. "You don't ever have to say please to me, Nate." Then Brandon pulled Nate even closer and kissed him.

Brandon noticed two things. He could feel himself getting hard against Nate's leg, and Nate's mouth tasted funny. It didn't taste bad. In fact, it tasted good, all sweet and spicy. Brandon pulled back and raised an eyebrow.

Nate grinned. "Clove flavored toothpaste."

"Another aphrodisiac?"

"Yep. Did it work?"

Brandon pulled him tight. "Come here and let me show you."

He kissed Nate with all the pent up hunger of the past thirty days. Every minute he'd spent missing Nate, longing for him, went into that kiss. When he finally had to come up for air, they were both gasping for breath and sporting first class erections.

"Make love to me, Brandon. I'm ready."

"We need to get out of this tub. The lube—"

"Already taken care of." He grinned as Brandon slipped one finger easily inside him. "What do you think I was doing in the bedroom while you were getting into the tub? Besides, if I hadn't taken care of it, the oil in this water would have. By the way, I asked the lady at the herb store and she said this oil was safe for internal and external use. And before you get all mad about me going out by myself, I took Sam with me."

Brandon added another finger. "I'm not mad. And I'm through talking." With that pronouncement, Brandon extracted his fingers and replaced them with the head of his cock. He watched Nate's face for any signs of discomfort. Seeing none, he slid inside, inch-by-inch, until Nate was sitting all the way down on him, completely impaled.

Nate was so hot, so tight. The warm water lapping up against them and the look of rapture on Nate's face were too much. Brandon wanted to take it slow, to savor the feeling of being inside Nate again, but he couldn't. He grabbed Nate's hips and lifted him almost completely off, then lowered him back down. With each stroke and thrust Brandon felt himself moving closer to the edge. He changed the direction of his thrusts and aimed for Nate's prostate. He used one slippery hand to stroke Nate's erection while his other hand guided Nate up and down. When Nate screamed out and shot all over Brandon's stomach, he thrust upwards one more time and filled Nate with his release.

Nate collapsed against Brandon's chest. Brandon wrapped his arms around him and put his lips to Nate's ear. "I love you, Nate. I've missed you so damn much. I thought I was gonna go out of my mind."

"I'm sorry. I never meant to hurt you like that."

"Shh. I wasn't trying to make you feel guilty. Just don't shut me out like that again, okay? Whatever it is, we'll handle it together."

Nate nodded, but didn't say anything. Brandon could tell he was tired. "Come on. Let's get out of this tub. If you fall asleep, I'll have to carry you. As slick as this sucker is, we're liable to slip and break something vital."

Nate stood up and got out first. He managed to make it onto the mat without falling. Brandon got out next. He almost made it. He would have, if he hadn't accidentally put his left foot on the tile instead of the mat. He slid backwards and grabbed for the first thing his hands came in contact with: Nate.

Nate made a desperate attempt to keep them both upright, but it didn't work. Brandon fell into a sitting position on the commode, which fortunately was closed. Nate landed hard on his lap, knocking the breath out of him.

When Brandon was able to breath again, he said, "Are you all right?" Nate was shaking. At first Brandon thought he was hurt, but he soon realized Nate was laughing.

He turned around and gave Brandon an apologetic grin. "I guess next time I decide to provide a little romantic atmosphere, I should warn you first."

Brandon snorted. "I'm just glad you didn't decide to slip me a couple of Viagra. My dick probably would have broken in half when you landed on it just now."

* ~ * ~ * ~ * ~ *

Brandon held back the covers as Nate crawled underneath and leaned in for a kiss. Being in bed with Nate and having no barriers between them again was heaven. Brandon pulled Nate down, rolled on top of him, and started sucking on his neck.

"If you give me a hickey, you'll have to explain it to your mother."

"If she says anything, I'll remind her of all the times she's had to wear a scarf to church to hide some of the hickeys Dad gave her." Brandon resumed nibbling.

Nate jumped as Brandon moved from his neck to his shoulder. "Does this mean I'm forgiven for oiling up the tub?"

Brandon licked his way down Nate's breastbone. "Yes, but I can think of things I'd much rather oil up."

"I suppose if you must, you must." Nate gave a put-upon sigh.

Brandon moved his hands down Nate's stomach to the dark blond hair between his legs. "I'll show you just what I *must* do." Brandon had just reached the good stuff when the phone rang. He fell back onto the bed. "Fuck. What's a guy got to do to get a little lovin' around here?"

Nate nudged him in the ribs. "Quit bitching and answer the phone. It could be important."

Brandon gave up and reached for the receiver. "Nash."

"Nash, it's Howard. If you aren't already, you might want to get dressed."

Brandon sat up. "What is it? Where are you?"

"I'm at a motel just inside of the Chicago city limits. We've found Wilson."

Brandon was already on his way to the closet to grab a fresh pair of jeans. "Have you questioned him yet?"

"Nope."

Not bothering with underwear, Brandon tugged on his jeans. "Why the hell not?"

"Because I left my crystal ball at home. Hate to tell you this, Nash. Wilson's dead."

Chapter Fourteen

Even though Brandon had seen pictures, the image he'd built of Wilson in his mind was of a man with almost super-human abilities, able to blend in anywhere at any time. A chameleon capable of wreaking havoc and destruction of mammoth proportions. He'd inflated Wilson, made him into some type of mythical phantom. Now Brandon saw Wilson for exactly what he was: a corpse. Death, the great equalizer.

The Sunshine Motel didn't exactly live up to its name, but had the room not been crawling with Howard's men, it wouldn't have been half bad. The single bed and double dresser looked new, and the floral wallpaper gave the place a homey touch. The carpet was clean, and the sheets probably had been, too, before Wilson had the bad taste to die on them. A table beside the bed held a bottle of whiskey and an empty glass.

Brandon was standing in the doorway surveying the scene when he felt a hand on his shoulder. He turned around to see Howard standing behind him.

"Thanks for getting here so fast, Nash. How's Doc doing?"

"Anxious."

Howard nodded. "This place has a coffee shop just around the corner. We can talk there while my guys finish up in here."

Brandon followed Howard into the brightly lit café. An attractive young waitress came and took their order, smiling and laughing as if it was an everyday occurrence to have a customer die in one of the rooms. Not that Brandon could find fault with her. Personally, he felt like doing cartwheels over Wilson's dead body. The coffee arrived and he took a bracing sip before saying, "What do you know so far?"

Howard drank down half of the scalding liquid from his own cup in one long swallow. "Wilson had a telephone call that came through the main desk sometime around eleven o'clock. The clerk transferred it to his room, but no one answered. The caller, who identified himself as Wilson's brother, insisted that the clerk go down there and check. The door was unlocked, so the guy went inside. That's when he found the body."

"Any ideas on cause of death?"

"The coroner didn't find any signs of physical trauma, but you know as well as I do that doesn't mean anything. I've put a rush order on the autopsy, so, barring any complications, we'll know within the next couple of days. Right now, we're running a trace on the phone call and doing the whole 'fine tooth comb' routine on the room. So far, we haven't turned up anything useful, but there's always hope." Howard took another swig of coffee. "At least you know Wilson's no longer a threat to the doc."

"It sure seems that way, doesn't it?"

Howard leaned back against the vinyl booth and eyed Brandon with a cop's perception. "What's with you, Nash? I should think you'd be damn happy right about now. I know I am, and it's not even my fiancé that was being threatened."

Brandon ran his fingers through his hair. "Am I happy that Wilson's no longer in a position to hurt Nate or anyone else? Hell, yes. But doesn't it all feel a bit too easy to you?"

"Explain."

Brandon pushed his cup aside. "I'm not sure I *can* explain it, exactly. It's more a feeling than anything." He pulled a hundred dollar bill from his pocket and laid it on the table in front of Howard. "Ben Franklin there says that the autopsy reveals Wilson died of natural causes. I'll give you four more just like him if the coroner doesn't say Wilson died from some kind of heart failure."

Howard whistled. "Five hundred bucks on heart failure, huh? I might take that bet if you didn't seem so damn sure of yourself."

"All I'm sure of is that this whole thing is coming together just a little too neatly. The evidence against Calder, the connections to Wilson, and now the only witness — the hit man — all nice and dead, almost as if on cue. I've been a cop in one form or another for too long not to know that cases don't just come to a pretty little gift-wrapped conclusion."

"Not that I'm disagreeing with you," Howard said, "but you should know that once the autopsy's done, my office is going to call me and my team back to Washington. With Wilson dead, we're officially out of it."

"No offense, Howard, and don't think I haven't been grateful for the help, but I believe I can take it from here." The gleam in Brandon's eyes was savage, feral. "If Calder isn't Wilson's money man, I'll find the bastard who is. And God help him when I do."

* ~ * ~ * ~ * ~ *

When Brandon got home, Nate was sitting at the table. Brandon took in his bloodshot eyes and uncombed hair. "Did you sleep at all?"

"A little bit." He gave Brandon a sheepish grin. "I have trouble sleeping when you aren't with me."

Brandon thought back to all the nightmares he'd had before Nate came along. "Believe me when I tell you, I know how you feel. I'm sorry it took me so long. I stayed to help Howard's men process the scene and question possible witnesses." His lip curled. "Too bad nobody saw anything."

Nate reached across the table and took Brandon's hand. "Is Wilson really dead?"

Brandon stood, drawing Nate up with him, then led Nate into the living room. He sat down on the couch, pulled Nate onto his lap, and wrapped both arms around him. "He's dead. I saw the body myself." With Nate's head resting on his shoulder, Brandon rubbed his hands up and down Nate's back. "How do you feel about this?"

Nate drew in another deep breath and let it out slowly. "I'm not sure. As a doctor, I was taught that all life is sacred. At the same time, I feel like doing flips in the backyard because the bastard who put Marjorie Newman in a coma and killed Amy won't be able to hurt anyone ever again." He caressed Brandon's shoulder and fingered the ridge of scar tissue under Brandon's shirt. "The stitches may be gone, but you'll always have a reminder from that knife Wilson tossed at you. I wanted him dead for that alone."

Brandon un-tucked Nate's shirt so he could massage the small of his back, skin to skin. "I imagine those feelings are normal. Even if they aren't, nobody's gonna fault you for them."

Nate sighed as Brandon worked the tension out of his muscles. "Any idea as to the cause of death?"

"Howard put a rush job on the autopsy. We should know within the next couple of days."

"What about my dad? What will happen to him?"

Brandon tipped Nate back over his arm so he could look into his eyes. "I'm not going to lie to you, Nate. There's enough evidence for a good prosecutor to put Calder away. Are you going to be okay with that?"

Nate's features hardened. "If my father is the one responsible for this, I want the son of a bitch to rot in prison for the rest of his unnatural life."

Brandon drew Nate snugly against his chest. "He's your father, Nate. You don't really know how you're gonna feel once all this sinks in. We don't have to talk about this right now."

Nate shook his head. "Actually, we do. Now that my father is in custody and the investigation of what's left of my office has been concluded, the insurance agent is anxious to settle. He called me yesterday afternoon. Apparently Howard filed his report, and my insurance company wants it all over and done with."

"Why didn't you tell me last night?" Brandon kissed Nate's forehead.

Nate leaned back and gave him a grin. "If you'll remember, I had other plans last night." His expression grew serious. "Then Howard called, and you had to leave. This is really the first chance I've had to discuss it with you."

Brandon studied his face. "Something about this is bothering you, I can tell. What is it?"

"Just a weird feeling I got from talking to the agent on the phone. His name is Ralph Tatum. He seems like a nice enough guy."

"But?"

Nate looped his arms around Brandon's neck. "Tatum was really nervous on the phone. Kept talking about the importance of settling this right away. He's coming out to the house this afternoon."

Brandon raised an eyebrow. "On a Saturday?"

"That's what I thought, too. Tatum said we need to reach an understanding as soon as possible, whatever that means. When I bought the policy, I thought the whole thing was pretty cut and dried. I bought the building, and since my name is on the deed, I bought the insurance. My policy was all inclusive, so what is there to settle?"

"What time is this guy coming?"

"Three."

Brandon glanced down at his watch. "It's just after eight now."

"Why don't you go upstairs and get some rest? You're dead on your feet."

Brandon hated to admit it, but Nate was right. "Promise you'll get me up in a few hours so I can meet this Tatum guy with you?"

Nate smiled and gave him a soft kiss. "I promise. Now get that sexy butt of yours into bed."

Brandon did as directed, thinking all the while about the things he wanted Nate to do to his butt — sexy or otherwise.

~~*~*~*

Ralph Tatum was a jittery thing. Nate guessed him to be about five-four, five-five, tops. He was paper thin and almost bald, with just a touch of bright red peach fuzz on top of his head. Nate surveyed the twitch in his jaw and figured it was probably a permanent affliction.

Nate and Brandon sat on the couch together while Mr. Tatum took one of the easy chairs. He put his briefcase on the coffee table and cleared his throat. "Dr. Morris, perhaps it would be better if we discussed this in private."

Nate shook his head. "Brandon is my fiancé, Mr. Tatum. Whatever you have to say to me concerns him, too. Frankly, I'd like to know why you're giving us the whole cloak and dagger routine. The policy I bought from you is ironclad. Why the big production over a straightforward insurance claim?"

Tatum shifted in his chair. "There is no insurance claim, Dr. Morris. Your policy was canceled five weeks ago."

Nate felt like he'd been slapped. "I beg your pardon?"

"Five weeks ago, you came into our office and canceled your policy. I have the papers right here."

"Why the hell would I do that?"

Tatum shook his head. "The agent who handled the cancellation said you were adamant about severing all ties with our company."

Nate stared at him in disbelief. "What do you mean, severing all ties? Chicago Security has handled all my policies since I moved up here. You paid my claim when my apartment and office were trashed, and again when I wrecked my car. Are you trying to say that I came in and cancelled everything, even after all that?"

"Are you saying you didn't?"

Nate was doing his best not to get angry. "Hell, yes, that's what I'm saying. And if you're gonna deny my claim, you'd better have proof that I did cancel it."

Tatum opened his briefcase and pulled out a termination of service form. He handed it to Nate with shaking fingers.

Nate moved the paper so that Brandon could see it, too. Brandon was the first to speak. "That's Nate's name, but it isn't his signature."

Tatum looked like he was about to cry. "Are you certain?"

Nate stood and began pacing the room. After a minute, he turned back to Tatum, trying hard not to yell. "Don't you think I would remember canceling my own insurance policy?" A sudden thought crossed his mind. "Did you say I canceled everything, even my malpractice insurance?"

"Yes."

Brandon caught on. "So you would have had to issue a refund check, right?"

Tatum nodded and pulled another document out of his briefcase. "Yes. Dr. Morris, or whoever he was, wanted the money right then. The young agent who handled the transaction offered to mail it to him, but the man demanded it be given to him immediately. Since I was out of the office, my secretary wrote the check. She assures me that the young man showed the proper I.D. and had all Dr. Morris's policy information. Here's the photocopy of the cancelled check from the bank." He handed the paper to Nate. Brandon moved to stand behind him and look over his shoulder.

Nate stared down at the endorsement on the check. It was blurred and hard to read, but Nate was sure he could see a difference. He compared it to the signature on the termination agreement. "I'm no expert, but these signatures don't match each other any more than they match mine."

"It's hard to tell," Brandon said, "but the bank that cashed this check should have video surveillance of the transaction. Since the check is time stamped, it shouldn't be too hard to track down."

Tatum was still sitting in the chair, looking up at both of them. "If you can prove that the claim was cancelled under false pretenses, of course, our office will pay for all the damages."

Nate saw the expression on Brandon's face and felt a chill go down his spine. "We'll prove it, Tatum. You can count on it."

* ~ * ~ * ~ * ~ *

Brandon hung up the phone and went back into the living room where Nate and Tatum were sitting. He took his place by Nate on the couch. "I just talked to Clive Rogers, manager of the Carlin Bank and Trust in Chicago, where that check was cashed. Carlin sends all its security tapes to the main office in Cleveland. Rogers is calling now to ask the main office to ship the tapes back here, but it will take until next week sometime to get them back."

Tatum stood and grabbed his briefcase. "Until this matter is settled, there's nothing my office can do."

Brandon stood as well. "Actually, there is."

Nate couldn't help noticing the way Tatum cringed at the tone of Brandon's voice.

"What's that?"

"Tomorrow, I want you to have everyone who was in the office that day assemble at the Reed County Sheriff's Station by twelve o'clock."

Tatum started to stammer. "But...but tomorrow's Sunday. You can't expect my people to come in on a Sunday."

The color rising in Brandon's revealed his anger. "Look, Mr. Tatum. Your office screwed up, so I expect you and your employees to do whatever it takes to rectify this situation. Are we clear?"

Ralph Tatum looked ready to faint. "Yes, we're clear." He was clutching his briefcase to his chest like a shield. "If you'll excuse me, I really should be going."

Nate stood. "I'll walk you out." When Brandon started to follow,

Nate put his hand against his chest. "You stay here and cool down."

When Nate got done with Tatum, he went back inside and found Brandon still fuming. He sat down beside him and took his hand. "Want to tell me why you nearly took Tatum's head off?"

Brandon ran his hand through his hair in a gesture of frustration. "Because the little runt didn't want to co-operate, that's why. Hell, Nate, his office let some guy come in and cash in all your policies, and he acts like it's no big deal."

"I know, but getting mad about it isn't going to change anything. Why do you want them all at the office tomorrow, anyway?"

"I'm going to show them Wilson's picture and see if he was the one who posed as you. It's all we've got to go on right now."

Leaning back against the cushions, Nate closed his eyes. "What about the different signatures on the cancellation agreement and the check?"

"I'll have a handwriting expert look at it, but the signature on the check has been blurred so badly, it's gonna be hard to tell."

Nate sighed. "He really messed up by not killing me in the bombing, didn't he?"

"What do you mean?"

Nate turned his head so that he was staring Brandon in the face. "Wilson and whoever was paying him cashed in my policies a week before the bombing. If I had died in the explosion, no one would ever have known I didn't cancel the insurance myself."

Brandon reached over and smoothed back Nate's hair. "It's almost over, Nate. At least one of the key players is dead, and Howard is pretty sure we've got the other one in custody."

"My father."

"Yep. He's sitting in a Georgia jail without bond, waiting to be extradited to Illinois."

Nate closed his eyes again. "And what if he isn't guilty? What then?"

Brandon pulled Nate into his arms. "Then we'll find the guy who's responsible. You trust me, don't you?"

"Right now, you're the only one I do trust."

* ~ * ~ * ~ * ~ *

Nate sat waiting in Brandon's office while Brandon questioned the employees of the Chicago Security Insurance Company. After about an hour, Brandon came back in from the interrogation room, grinning from ear to ear.

"Both the guy who handled the cancellation and the secretary who wrote the check positively identified Wilson from his picture. You should have seen the look on Tatum's face. He's ready to settle the claim whenever you are, by the way. I think he's afraid you're going to sue his ass."

Nate shook his head. "It was never about the money. You know that."

Brandon perched one hip on the edge of the desk. "I know." He turned his head to the side and studied Nate for a minute. "You look awful cute sitting behind my desk, curled up in my chair like that. Ever thought of going into law enforcement? I'd love to show you how to use a pair of handcuffs."

"You and your bondage fantasies." Nate laughed. "I would like to talk to you about my job, though."

"Go ahead."

"I don't think I want to open up another practice." He gave Brandon a good looking over and said, "How would you feel about me trying to get a staff job at Chicago General?" Brandon started to speak, but Nate cut him off. "Before you answer, you should know that my hours will be erratic, and I'll be on call a lot more. It won't be as bad as it was when I was a resident, but I won't have anything near regular hours."

"You know I want whatever will make you happy," Brandon said. "I assume you'll be working with premature babies again?"

"Yeah. Keith mentioned that Chicago General has an opening for a pediatrician in the N.I.C.U."

Brandon leaned down and cupped Nate's chin with one hand. "Irregular hours don't bother me. God knows you've put up with enough of them from me lately. Whatever you want to do, I'm behind you one hundred percent."

"I think I'm ready to go back into hospital medicine. When I came up here from Atlanta, I wanted a break, and the idea of working with Amy was a dream come true. Private practice won't be the same without her."

"What about the patients you have now?"

"One of the doctors who's been handling my calls mentioned last week that he'd like to start a practice in Reed." Nate smiled. "I think he'll do well here."

"If this is what you want, then I'm all for it." Brandon was about to say more when a knock on the door interrupted him. "Come in."

Rex Howard came through the door. Offered a seat, Howard settled on the other side of the desk. "I'm glad you're both here. No sense in having to tell the story twice."

Brandon eased away from the desk and went to stand behind Nate's chair, his hands on Nate's shoulders in a subtle gesture of comfort. "What's up?"

Howard wasted no time getting to the point. "Autopsy's back." His eyes locked on Brandon's. "Damned if you weren't right, Nash. Massive heart attack. The medical examiner said it looked like the damn thing exploded."

The doctor in Nate rose to the surface. "Did Wilson have a history of heart problems?"

Howard shook his head. "No, but according to the toxicology report, Wilson was speed-balling. Not long before he died, he shot a massive dose of heroin into his veins and then snorted a nose full of cocaine. Wilson also had a healthy amount of diazepam in his bloodstream, probably from the same batch he used on your dog." He snorted. "Being a hit-man probably wears on the nerves."

Brandon gave Howard a puzzled stare. "The only thing found in that room besides a suitcase and Wilson's clothes was a half full bottle of Jack Daniels and an empty glass. I went over the report myself."

"That's true, but the clerk said Wilson went out earlier in the evening. He could have gotten doped up while he was out. Combined with all that whisky, the junk in Wilson's bloodstream was too much for his ticker."

Nate noticed that Brandon didn't disagree, but he still seemed skeptical. Nate turned to Howard. "So what happens now?"

Howard's expression softened a little. "That's one of the reasons I wanted to talk to you, Doc. Did Nash tell you that Wilson had a brother?"

"Yeah. Brandon said the brother called the night Wilson's body was found."

"That's true. They're half-brothers, actually — same mother, different fathers. We got the phone company's records and tracked him down. His name's Patrick Malone. He had a lot to say about his brother." Howard's face took on that sympathetic glaze that Nate was starting to dread. "Malone also had a few things to say about your father, Doc."

Brandon's hands tightened around Nate's shoulders as Nate said, "Let's hear it."

"Malone works for Mor-co. He says he was the one who introduced Calder to Wilson. He claims Calder told him he needed some muscle, but didn't tell him what for. Malone's willing to make a deal in exchange for his testimony against your father."

Nate looked back and forth between Brandon and Howard. "Can he do that? Even after what happened to Amy?"

"That'll be up to the local D.A., but I'd say chances are good that

Malone will get immunity in exchange for his testimony against Calder." Howard grimaced. "I hate making deals with scumbags, but to prosecute Malone as an accessory to murder, the D.A. would have to prove he knew ahead of time what the plan was. That's gonna be damn hard to do since we aren't even certain exactly what the plan was ourselves." He turned his attention to Brandon. "Wilson's death is officially listed as an overdose. I spoke with my boss not an hour ago. We're off the case as of now."

Nate stood as Brandon came around the chair and extended his hand to Howard. "I can't say I'm surprised, but I will say I couldn't have kept Nate safe without your help. I owe you, Howard."

Howard shook his hand. "You're wrong about that, Nash. I was glad to help, but you had it pretty well covered long before I got here." Howard shook Nate's hand. "Sorry about your dad, Doc. I wish things had turned out differently."

Nate reached for Brandon with his left hand. "I'm sorry my father is a worthless bigot. And," his voice cracked, "I'm more sorry than I can ever say about Marjorie and Amy." He switched his gaze from Howard to Brandon. "But there are some things I'll never regret."

Brandon kissed Nate's palm and returned the look, his eyes full of heat. Howard said his goodbyes and slipped out of the room with a smile.

~~*~*~*

Being in love with someone didn't necessarily mean loving everything about them. Brandon accepted that. He knew he and Nate were always going to have their differences. Brandon never said a word about Nate's obsessive neatness, or the fact that he chewed exactly thirty-two times before he swallowed his food. Brandon didn't fuss because Nate was reluctant to top him in bed. He even glossed over the fact that Nate talked baby talk to their dog. But no way in hell was he going to ignore Nate's callous disregard for one of America's greatest inventions.

"It's just a car, Bran."

Brandon clutched his hand over his heart. "Just a car? Just a car, he says. Was the General Lee just a car to the Duke Boys? Was Kit just a car to Michael Knight in Knight Rider? And what about James Bond and all his different spy cars? Or Batman? Where would Batman be without the Bat-mobile?"

Nate started buttoning his shirt. "Walking?"

Brandon shot him a dirty look from his seat on the bed and continued lacing up his boots. "If you're not going to take this seriously, you can find someone else to take you car shopping."

Nate tucked his shirt into his jeans. "Brandon, it's not that big of a deal." When Brandon gave him another withering stare, Nate said, "If I get the urge to fight crime or join an international spy ring, I promise you I'll consult only the top experts before I buy a car. And since I'm already sleeping with the local sheriff, I don't think I'll need a car like the General Lee." He grinned and slipped his belt through the loops. "If I do decide to start bootlegging whiskey, I won't need a special get-away car. I'll just slip you about six inches and ask you to look the other way."

Brandon threw a pillow at Nate's head. "Six inches, my ass. More like eight. And I still say you should put a little more effort into this. Hell, you don't even know what kind of car you want."

Nate sat down beside Brandon to pull on his socks. "I told you: I don't care what make or model it is as long as it gets good mileage. I want something serviceable, like my old Honda."

Brandon made a gagging sound. "If you look up 'serviceable' in the dictionary, it says, 'See boring.' You're twenty-eight years old Nate. You have the rest of your life to drive something dependable. Don't you want to live a little, have some excitement?"

"I think I've had enough excitement in the last two months to last me a lifetime."

"That's not the kind of excitement I'm talking about, and you know it. Look, in a few years, after the kids come along, we'll get you a nice, quiet mini-van. Right now, don't you want something a little bolder?"

Nate narrowed his eyes. "How bold are we talking?"

"As it happens, I know a guy who sells just the kind of cars I'm talking about." Brandon was all but rubbing his hands together with glee.

"I thought we'd just go to some of the dealerships in Chicago."

Brandon shook his head. "We talked about that last night, Nate. Those places are all the same — cookie-cutter operations selling the same old thing. The place I'm talking about has character. No one will ever accuse Cain Lucas of being a conformist."

As soon as Nate sighed, Brandon knew he'd won. He leaned over and kissed Nate's cheek. "I'll pick you up after work this evening and we'll head over there."

"I'm breathless with anticipation."

Brandon ignored him and finished getting ready for work, whistling as he went.

* ~ * ~ * ~ * ~ *

The minute Brandon pulled the Camaro from the paved street onto a gravel road leading into the woods, Nate knew he was in trouble. When Cain Lucas's place came into view, Nate fought down the urge to beg Brandon to turn the car around.

"When you said you were taking me to buy a car, I had a little something different in mind. I never dreamed you were taking me to a junk yard."

Pulling up in front of a hulking cinder block garage, Brandon cut the motor. "I prefer to think of it as an 'automotive rehabilitation center'."

Nate snorted. "Rehabilitation, huh? I hate to have to tell you, Bran, but this is where cars come to die. We're sitting in the only live one here." Brandon took a deep breath and let it out slowly. If Nate hadn't known better, he'd have said that Brandon was going for the "heartfelt sigh" approach.

Then Brandon said, "All right. If you really want to go, we'll go. I understand that it isn't fair of me to inflict my interests on you. After all, a good marriage is about compromise."

Nate knew it was a crock, but when Brandon turned big blue puppy dog eyes on him, Nate was a goner. "Fine. We'll go in, but if I don't see something really impressive in the next five minutes, I'm leaving." Nate reached over and pulled the keys out of the ignition. "With or without you."

Brandon smiled. "Deal. Come on. I called Cain this morning to tell him we were coming. He's expecting us." Brandon led him around to the side door of the garage and knocked twice. A moment later, a raspy voice yelled out, "Come in," and Brandon opened the door.

Nate expected the inside of the garage to be as cluttered as the grounds, but it was surprisingly neat. All four walls were covered with pegboards that held various wrenches, sockets, and tools. Instead of the harsh fluorescent lights used in most garages, this one had four large skylights with further illumination provided by several rows of track lighting. A lift held a battered Silverado about eight feet off the ground, while two more cars waited their turns in the bays nearby. It wasn't until they got closer that Nate noticed a pair of legs sticking out from under one of the cars.

"It's us, Cain." Brandon's voice rang through the garage.

Nate watched as the legs got leverage against the cement floor and wheeled the man attached to them out from under the car he was working on. He wiped his dirty fingers on his coveralls and shook hands, first with Brandon, then with Nate. "How's it going, Sheriff?"

"Fine. Cain Lucas, this is my fiancé, Dr. Nathan Morris. He's looking for a car."

"Sure thing. I think I might have something he'll be interested in.

Just give me a sec to wash up, and I'll show you what I've got."

While Cain walked across the room to wash his hands, Nate took that moment to study him. He was about thirty and had waist-length black hair secured with a leather thong at the nape of his neck. Most women would have killed to have a silky mane like his, but there wasn't anything feminine about Cain Lucas. He was tall, at least six-four, and had broad shoulders which threatened to burst the seams of his coveralls. When he turned around, Nate noted Cain's bronzed skin and dark eyes, willing to bet those eyes didn't miss much. His chiseled features reminded Nate of the pictures he'd seen of American Indians in books and museums.

Cain dried his hands on a clean shop rag and walked back to where Nate and Brandon were waiting. "So, exactly what did you have in mind, Dr. Morris?"

"Something dependable that gets good mileage."

Cain raised his eyebrows at Brandon. "And you brought him here?"

Those were Nate's thoughts exactly, but Brandon wasn't going to go down without a fight. "Nate just thinks he wants some wimpy little foreign job because he hasn't seen your selection yet."

Cain looked skeptical, but he said, "You know where the other garage is. Go on ahead while I lock up here, and I'll meet you up there."

The drive to the second garage was more pleasant than the drive to the first. Whereas the lower part of Cain's property was littered with car and truck remnants, the upper half was beautifully landscaped. Nate could just make out a house in the distance, but Brandon pulled off the main path and headed down another road through a stand of trees. He parked the car in front of another massive garage, this one made of brick instead of cinder block.

Brandon and Nate got out of the Camaro just as Cain pulled up in a beat-up Chevy truck. He went around to the side of the building, motioning for Brandon and Nate to follow.

Cain unlocked the deadbolt and flipped a switch just inside the door. "Come on in. Everything in here is for sale except the Harley. That one's mine."

Nate started inside but stopped just short of the threshold, amazed at the display he was seeing.

Brandon whispered, "This place is something else, isn't it."

It certainly was. Twenty cars, all of them classics and all beautifully restored, were lined up on each side of the garage. A chopped-out Harley Davidson, the only motorcycle in the garage, stood in one corner. Three of the walls were decorated with antique gas and oil signs, and a display of framed car ads from the Thirties and Forties took up the other. A restored, bubble-top gas pump occupied the corner opposite the bike.

Cain pointed to a red fifty-seven Ford Thunderbird heading up the first row. "If you're looking for something dependable, I'd say this one is your best bet. She's as close to all original as you're going to get. I bought her from the original owner. All I did was drop in a new motor and give her a new paint job."

"She's a beauty, but we're a Chevy family," Brandon said.

"We are?" It was the first Nate had heard of it.

Brandon looked offended. "Yes, we are."

Cain grinned. "In that case, I've got a great little fifty-five Chevy, four door I just finished. I changed the transmission from manual to automatic and painted it back to its original finish."

Cain led them down the row to the car he was talking about. Nate had to admit, the car was nice. He might have even considered it, if he hadn't glanced over and seen the car at the end of the row. With something akin to awe, Nate pointed to the striking black beauty. "What's that?"

Cain followed his finger. "Oh, that's a thirty-four Ford, five window coupe that I bought from a guy in Minnesota. But you don't want that car, Doc."

Nate didn't hear him. He walked over to the coupe and caressed one round headlight. "What year did you say she was?"

"She's a thirty-four, but—"

"Did you do all the restorations yourself?"

"Yeah. She was just a rusted out shell when I got her." A trace of pride tinged Cain's voice. "Took me eleven months, but I finally got her done." He saw the way Nate was tracing the car's curves with one fingertip. "Look, Doc, I think you'd probably be happier with something else. I've got a couple of sedans that are worth looking at."

For the first time, Nate heard what Cain was saying. "Why wouldn't I want this car?"

Brandon spoke up. "Because she's a Ford, and because she's too much car for you, that's why."

"What's that supposed to mean?"

Brandon put his hand on Nate's arm. "Nothing bad. Look, Nate, this morning you were talking about buying a Honda or a Nissan. Something quiet that gets good mileage."

"Right. And you said I have the rest of my life to get a boring family car. You told me to live a little, to buy something bolder, something exciting."

Brandon swore under his breath. "I never expected you to go from a four-door hatchback to a custom street rod." He turned to Lucas. "What's she got under the hood, Cain?"

"I took the motor out of a late model Corvette some kid smashed up. The body was a loss, but the engine was barely scratched. She's got fuel injection and Flow Master pipes. The original transmission was a three-speed, but I converted her to four on the floor."

Nate didn't understand a single word Cain had said, but that didn't quash his enthusiasm. "So, that means it's got a powerful engine, right?"

Cain and Brandon both looked at him like he had an extra eyeball in the middle of his forehead. Brandon said, "Look inside her, Nate. She's got a roll cage. This car was made for racing, not driving back and forth to work." He turned to Cain again. "Is that thing even street legal?"

Cain nodded. "Barely, but yeah, she is. Technically, she would be okay for everyday use, but I wouldn't recommend it."

Nate went on the offensive. "Why not?"

"Well, she only gets about nine miles to the gallon. And then there's this." He walked over to the passenger side and opened the door. Nate was surprised to see that it opened towards the front of the car instead of the back. Cain saw his confusion and said, "They're called suicide doors. They stopped making them in the late Thirties, early Forties. If you see them on later model cars, they were done custom, not factory."

Nate watched as Cain closed the door. "Why are they called suicide doors?"

Cain leaned back against the body of the coupe and put one foot on the running board. "Because if the car gets up enough speed, they have a tendency to come open. The natural inclination when your car door comes open is to reach out and grab it to close it again. In the case of suicide doors, that's a big mistake."

Nate had never heard any such thing before, and he was absolutely enthralled. "Why would shutting the door be a mistake?"

"With a regular door, it wouldn't, but suicide doors are different. See, with a regular door, the wind is pushing against the door and whoever's holding it. With suicide doors, the air pressure is misdirected. The minute you grab hold of the door, all that force is on you. If you don't let go, you'll be dragged right out of the car. I've heard of folks being thrown out and crushed beneath the tires. That's why they stopped making suicide doors."

Brandon was nodding right along with Cain, but Nate wasn't satisfied. "There's got to be some way to keep the doors from popping open."

"There is. I put power locks on both doors. As long as the switch is flipped, the doors stay closed. But you have to remember to flip it each and every time or the danger's still there."

Nate turned to Brandon. "See there. Nothing to worry about."

"Look, Nate, that car—" Brandon's pager went off right in the middle of what had promised to be a long-winded lecture. He glanced down at the number. "It's Sam. I left my cell in the car. Let me run out there and call in."

Cain pointed to a door at the other end of garage. "No need, Sheriff. I've got a phone in the office. Just use that."

"Thanks, Cain. I'll be right back. Don't let him talk you into selling him that car while I'm gone." Brandon left before Nate could protest.

When Brandon was gone, Cain said, "You really want this car, don't you?"

Nate didn't hesitate. "Yeah, but I don't really understand why. To me, a car's always been a necessity, something to get you where you needed to go. This is the first one I've ever felt like I just had to have. Do you know what I mean?"

Cain grinned. "Actually, I do. My first car was a sixty-three Chevy Impala with the top chopped and the frame lowered to about three inches off the ground. I remember telling my dad I was gonna die if I didn't get that car."

Nate smiled back at him. "I think I'll live even if I don't get this car, but I do want it. How much are you asking for her?"

"Forty-six thousand, firm."

"You take checks?"

Cain whistled. "Damn. You're serious. You know that the Sheriff is gonna stick it to me if I sell you this car, right? I won't be able to drive through town without getting a ticket from here on out."

Nate shook his head. "Brandon likes to talk tough, but he's really a pussycat."

"Uh-huh. If you say so, Doc."

For the first time, Nate noticed the wedding band on Cain's hand. "How does your wife feel about you restoring cars for a living? I imagine it must be pretty time consuming."

Nate saw the pain in Cain's eyes before he redirected his gaze to his foot, still perched on the running board. "My *husband* thought it was great. He was as big a car nut as the Sheriff." He looked back up at Nate. "I was widowed three years ago, not long before I moved to Reed."

"I'm sorry," Nate said. "I didn't mean to bring up any painful memories."

Cain shrugged. "You didn't." He switched back to business mode. "If you're sure this car is really what you want, I'll start the paperwork. But I want to include a thirty-day trial period. If you drive it for a month and find out it isn't what you want, bring it in and I'll give you your money back. In fact, I won't even cash the check until the thirty days are up."

"That's very generous of you. Most car salesmen aren't so understanding."

"Yeah, well that's dealerships for you. Modern dealerships—"

"You don't have to say it. Brandon gave me a full rundown of his opinion last night and this morning."

Brandon came out of the office, and he wasn't smiling. "Did I just hear my name?"

Nate nodded. "Cain and I were just discussing your shared philosophy on car dealerships." He studied Brandon's face. "What is it?"

"The D.A.'s office called a few minutes ago. After I talked to Sam, I called them back." He reached out and snagged Nate's hand. "About an hour ago, your father had a meeting with his attorney. He's gonna plead guilty, Nate. Calder just confessed to everything."

Chapter Fifteen

Nate spent the better part of an hour on the phone with his mother and Seth. Three-way calling might have its advantages, but as far as Brandon was concerned, the only purpose it had served today was to keep Nate worried and exhausted. By the time he got off the phone, Nate's shoulders were slumping and his eyes were swollen.

When Brandon handed him a shot glass full of whiskey, Nate gave a weary grin and settled down beside him on the couch. "If you're trying to get me all liquored up so you can have your wicked way with me, I should tell you now that I'm pretty much a lost cause."

Brandon nudged Nate's shoulder and laughed when he almost fell over. "No offense, baby, but I like my guys a little more lively than you are at the moment."

Nate rubbed his hand over his face. "You try talking to a hysterical woman for over an hour and see how lively you look."

Brandon couldn't resist. "How is Seth, anyway?" He made a satisfactory grunt and laughed when Nate elbowed him in the ribs. "You know I'm just teasing you. How's your mom taking it?"

"I think we're all in shock, to tell you the truth. Mom actually seems to be handling it better than Seth and I are. We both knew there was a good chance Dad was guilty, but neither one of us ever expected him to confess. I guess we just figured he'd deny it to the end."

"If it makes you feel any better, so did I. I had my doubts about Calder's guilt."

"I know." Nate took a deep breath. "So now what?"

"With Calder pleading guilty, the death penalty is taken off the table. The most he can get is life without parole. That will be up to the judge, but Amy's death combined with the charges for the attack on Marjorie, the arsons, and the attempts on you, means I can't see a judge giving him anything less than life."

Nate didn't say anything for a few minutes. Finally, he said, "I think I'd like to start seeing that psychiatrist again. I think I'm gonna need some help to process all this."

"I think that's a good idea." He reached out and squeezed Nate's knee. "Everybody needs help now and then. I can't imagine anyone going through an ordeal like this without needing a little professional advice."

"How come you went into forensic psychology instead of going on and getting your medical degree?"

Brandon grinned. "Can you really see me sitting down with patients? I don't exactly have a sparkling bedside manner. Besides, two doctors in the family are enough. Between you and Keith, the Nash clan is covered."

Nate leaned back and closed his eyes. "We really are gonna be a family, huh? I mean, I didn't just dream it all, did I?"

Brandon leaned over and kissed first one eyelid and then the other. "Nope. I'm gonna have you in front of the preacher as soon as you give the word." He sat back against the cushions. "Speaking of which, now that this is officially over, what do you say we set a date?"

"Tomorrow."

"Did I mention that you're a part of the family now? That means my mother has a legal right to kill you."

Nate laughed. "Just what I need, another homicidal parent." Brandon grabbed him and started tickling his ribs. Nate writhed and jumped, finally calling out, "Okay, okay. I give."

Brandon stopped tickling but didn't move his hands. "You ready to answer my question, or do I have to get rough with you?"

"Promises, Nash, promises." Brandon's fingers started to move again. Nate put up his hands. "Don't. I'll be serious."

"Glad to hear it."

Nate reached up and stroked Brandon's face. "The day before Thanksgiving."

Brandon turned his head to the side and kissed Nate's hand. "You realize that's in two weeks, right?"

"Yeah, well, it's not like you have to order a dress or anything. Your brothers and mine will be out of school, and most of our family members will have the day off anyway. Besides," Nate smiled, "the courthouse will be open, so I'll be able to file the paperwork for my name change. I already checked."

Brandon studied him for a minute. "You've given this a lot of thought, haven't you?"

"Yeah. At first I wanted to wait. Without Amy being there... Well, you know how I feel. But she wouldn't want us to wait, and I don't either. Now that I'm out of danger, I want us to make it official."

Brandon kissed his brow. "I'm glad you feel that way." He picked up Nate's hand and started sucking on his index finger. "Have you given any thoughts to our honeymoon?"

Nate moaned as Brandon took his finger deeper into his mouth. "You keep doing that, and I won't be able to think about anything." Brandon retreated, but only a little, and Nate said, "How would you feel about a week at a nice little cabin in the Smokey Mountains?"

Brandon took Nate's finger out of his mouth but kept a tight hold on his hand. "It sounds great, but I doubt we could rent one on such short notice."

"Don't have to rent one. When Grandma Morris died, she left me the cabin she and Grandpa owned. I haven't been in a coon's age, but I pay a crew to keep it maintained. All I have to do is call the service and they'll have it cleaned and ready for us."

"A coon's age?" Brandon narrowed his eyes.

Nate thickened his drawl. "Yep. Us country boys depend on them thar critters to keep track of the seasons. Know what I mean?"

Brandon pushed him down on the couch and covered his body with his own. "Jim Varney, you aren't. I do like the whole bumpkin routine, though."

Nate wiggled seductively beneath him. "Oh, really? Why is that?"

"Something about that twang in your voice gets me hot."

Nate's eyes sparkled with excitement. "Show me."

Brandon didn't need to be told twice.

* ~ * ~ * ~ * ~ *

Brandon shook his head in disgust as Nate wrote out a check for forty-six thousand dollars. "I can't believe you're buying that car after our conversation last night."

Nate handed the check to Cain and then turned back to Brandon with a grin. "Which conversation would that be? The one where you promised not to share the garage with me if I bought that 'souped up death wagon,' or the one where you offered to drive me to a dealership and buy me anything I wanted if I'd forget all about buying that 'rebuilt refugee from a Thirties' gangster flick'?"

Cain was scandalized. "You offered to take him to a dealership?"

Brandon shrugged. "Desperate times call for desperate measures." He shifted his eyes from Cain to Nate. "I almost lost you in that first car accident, not to mention what could have happened at your office." He stroked Nate's cheek. "I can't go through that again, Nate. If I have to beg and grovel to keep you safe, I'll do it."

Nate was filled with so much tenderness for the man before him, he forgot all about the fact that they were standing in Cain's garage. He reached for Brandon and heard a loud clearing of the throat.

"I'll just go put this in the office safe and gather up the paperwork." Cain left before Brandon or Nate could protest.

Nate pulled Brandon into his arms. "Look, Bran, we just got our lives back. Do you really think I would do something reckless or stupid to screw all that up?"

Sighing, Brandon rested his forehead against Nate's. "No. I know you better than that. But a guy's got a right to try and protect his family, you know?"

Nate moved his hands from Brandon's waist and slid them into the back pockets of Brandon's jeans, pulling him even closer. "Yeah, I do know, but you gotta trust me."

Brandon gave up. "You win. You know I can't argue with you when you go all logical on me. I won't say anything more about the car" He narrowed his eyes. "But you can't stop me from thinking it."

Nate nodded in agreement, pleased to have won the round. Cain came back a few minutes later with a manila folder in his right hand and something brown and fuzzy in his left. He handed the folder to Nate. "Here's the title and registration. I've still got temporary insurance on her, so all you have to do today is buy the tags and get the registration changed over into your name." He stuck out his hand. "Congratulations, Doctor Morris. You just bought yourself a car."

Nate felt like a sixteen-year-old with his first set of wheels when he shook Cain's hand. "Thanks, Cain." He pointed to the brown fuzzy thing. "What's that?"

Cain held up a raccoon's tail. "If you're gonna drive a car like that, you'll need one of these for the antenna."

Brandon just shook his head.

* ~ * ~ * ~ * ~ *

Nate was in the kitchen, stirring a stockpot of beef stew when Brandon got home. He yelped when Brandon slid his arms around his waist. Nate clicked off the portable CD player and slipped the earphones down around his neck. "Jesus, Bran. Give a guy a heart attack, why don't you?"

Brandon kissed his cheek. "Sorry, babe, but I didn't see the headphones." He turned Nate in his arms so he could watch his face. "What's with that, anyway? We have a perfectly good system in the living room."

Nate ducked his head a little bit. "Yeah, but Sasha's sleeping in there."

Doing his best not to laugh, Brandon failed miserably. "Are you telling me you're in here listening to headphones so you won't disturb our dog?"

Nate stepped lightly on his foot. "Don't laugh at me, Nash. I've had a hard day." Before Brandon could ask, Nate said, "How did your meeting with Clive Rogers from Carlin Bank go?"

Brandon sighed. "As well as could be expected. I saw the tape. Wilson was the one who cashed that check, no doubt about it."

"How did Rogers explain the fact that the signatures on the check and the cancellation agreement looked different?"

"He said the signature on the check was so blurred it was impossible to tell, just like we thought. At least we have concrete proof that Wilson was behind the insurance cancellation. One more piece of the puzzle in place." Brandon pulled Nate closer and cuddled him to his chest. "Wanna tell me about your day now?"

Nate sighed. "I will, but you aren't gonna like it."

Brandon moved back enough to see him clearly. "Might as well tell me and get it over with, then."

"I ran into Mike today."

"Where?"

"At the courthouse, when I went to register my car. He was there probating Amy's will."

Brandon pushed a lock of Nate's hair off his forehead. "Why would I be mad about that? You can't help who you run into."

"That's true," Nate took a deep breath, "but I sort of invited him to dinner."

Brandon did his best to cool his temper. He kept telling himself he wasn't angry. He counted to ten and back four times. He tried deep breathing, and even prayer.

To his credit, Nate didn't even flinch when Brandon yelled, "You did *what*?"

Nate went back to the stove and pretended that Brandon wasn't standing in the middle of the kitchen looking at him like he was insane. "I ran into him, he asked if we could talk, and I invited him to dinner. I figured you'd rather have him here, with you to chaperone, than have me go somewhere with him."

Brandon walked over to the table and dropped into a chair. "I'd rather you tell the bastard to fuck off. He did his best to take your head off at Amy's funeral. Why in the hell would I want that son of a bitch in our house?"

Nate put a lid on the stew pot and came over to the table. He took the seat next to Brandon and reached for his hand. "He was grieving, Bran. The guy lost his wife not three days before he went after me. Don't you think we should cut him some slack?"

"Nate—"

Nate shook his head. "Just listen to me for a minute. How would you feel if someone had been after Amy, and I'd gotten caught in the crossfire? Would you have been Mr. Calm and Cool if I'd been the one laying in that box?"

Brandon shuddered at the thought. "Hell, no, but that doesn't mean I'm going to sit across the table from the guy."

Nate's voice hardened. "Brandon, I'm not asking for your permission here. If this is really my house, too, then I have the right to invite anyone I want to sit at this table. If I don't have that right, then we have a much bigger problem on our hands than Mike."

Brandon pulled back his hand and stood up. "I'm going upstairs to take a shower."

"Bran—"

Brandon shook his head. "Just give me a few minutes, okay?" He went upstairs before Nate could respond.

* ~ * ~ * ~ * ~ *

Nate was setting the table when Brandon came back downstairs, wearing a pair of faded jeans with ripped knees and a black t-shirt that showed every ripple of chest muscle. His hair was still damp, and Nate could see a little trail of water trickling down his neck. Nate had the urge to walk over and lick the moisture away, but he resisted. It was going to be up to Brandon to make the first move. Nate only hoped he didn't have a long wait.

He didn't. Brandon came around the table and took Nate into his arms. "I owe you an apology."

"Uh-huh."

Brandon grinned. "You aren't gonna make this easy, are you?"

"Nope."

Brandon bent Nate back over the dish-free section of the table. He leaned over him and started sucking on his ear. "I was a real jerk about the whole thing."

Nate could feel himself boning up, but he wasn't about to let Brandon off the hook. Not just yet. "Keep going."

"This is as much your house as it is mine," Brandon kissed his neck, "and you have the right to invite anyone you want to come and eat with us."

"And?"

Brandon rested his head on Nate's shoulder. "Do I have to say it?"

"'Fraid so."

Brandon grinned again. "You were right and I was wrong."

Nate reached up and wiped the water from Brandon's brow. "That wasn't so bad, was it?"

"Hell yes, it was. Damned apology gave me heartburn."

Nate kissed Brandon's chest. "There. I kissed it. Did I make it better?"

"If I'd known you were going to start kissing my body parts and making them better, I'd have chosen blue balls over heartburn as my disorder of choice."

"Blue balls, huh?" Nate wrapped his arms around Brandon's neck.

Brandon turned his head and kissed the inside of Nate's wrist, taking the time to trail his tongue along the fine blue vein leading up to his hand. "Yep. Classic case of blue balls. If I don't get some relief, and get it soon, one or both of those suckers is gonna pop right off."

Nate flexed his hips in an attempt at evidence gathering. "I think you're right. Maybe you should see a doctor." He pretended to think about it, and then said, "Wait a minute, *I'm* a doctor." He was about to give Brandon a thorough examination, when Sasha came in from the living room and started barking. Nate looked up to see Mike standing in the kitchen.

"Sorry to interrupt, but the door was open and the alarm wasn't on."

Brandon couldn't have gotten up any faster had his pants been on fire. His eyes went from sparkling blue mischief to icy control in the space of a heartbeat. "Vaughn."

Mike nodded. "Hello, Nash. I take it you didn't know I was coming."

Brandon shook his head. "Oh, I knew you were coming, all right. See, Vaughn, Nate and I don't keep secrets from each other." Ignoring Nate's warning stare, he went on. "No, I knew all about your visit, I just couldn't think of anything to do to stop it. What I'd like to know now is, when the hell are you leaving? I'd like enough advanced notice to be suitably relieved when you make your exit."

Nate started to say something, but Mike interrupted him. "No. He's right, Nate. After the way I treated you at Amy's funeral—" He broke off, but not before tears rose in his eyes. Mike stood in silence for several tense minutes, working to gain control. Finally, he said, "After the way I treated you, I don't blame Nash for not wanting me here."

Nate knew better than to hope for Brandon to do the polite thing and make Mike feel welcome. Instead, he took up the reins. "Supper's almost ready, Mike, if you want to have a seat at the table. Brandon, why don't you take Sasha for a quick walk while the cornbread is finishing up?"

If Brandon wanted to argue, he didn't show it. He seemed as relieved to get away from Mike as Mike was to have him go.

The minute they heard the back door closing, Mike said, "Listen, Nate, I really appreciate you letting me come over tonight, especially after all that's happened."

Nate went back to the stove and took a peek at the bread. Straightening and turning to face Mike in one motion, he said, "Like I told you at the courthouse, Mike, I understood. As Brandon will tell you, I went a little crazy myself after Amy died."

"Yeah, well, you didn't take a swing at one of your best friends, either." Mike sighed. "No offense, but I doubt Nash is gonna want to tell me anything besides 'go to hell'."

Nate went to the refrigerator and removed a stoneware jug of sweetened tea. After pouring three glasses full, he said, "Brandon's just upset. He'll come around eventually." He managed to sound halfway convincing.

Mike shook his head. "*That* I seriously doubt, my friend, but it won't matter. I'm leaving Reed, Nate. I've already turned in my resignation to the firm and put my house on the market. All that's left now is deciding where I want to go and getting the hell out of here." When Nate muttered a protest, Mike just shrugged. "You know it's for the best. It's not like I've lived here long enough to establish a whole lot of ties." He looked down at the scarred oak surface of the table and fingered a knot in the wood. His voice was dull, emotionless. "You and Amy were my only real links to Reed. Now that Amy's gone, and you and I—" He broke off and looked up at Nate. "You and I will always have a bond, but it'll never be like it was. Not with all that's happened. I think you know what I'm talking about."

Nate did know. "Any ideas on what you want to do next?"

Mike sank a little further into the chair. "Not really. The only family I have is my aunt in Atlanta and a handful of cousins. I may just drift for a while, traveling around and trying out new places. It's not like the five-year plan Amy and I came up with when we moved here means anything, anymore. The bomb saw to that." He gave Nate an apologetic smile. "That sounded like I'm still blaming you, didn't it? For what it's worth, I'm not."

"It's a damn good thing you aren't, Vaughn." Brandon stood in the doorway, his narrowed eyes on Mike. "There wasn't a single thing Nate could have done to save Amy, and you know it."

Nate knew that look on Brandon's face, and he also knew there would be a free-for-all if he didn't step in and prevent it. "Brandon, if you'll pour the tea, I'll take the bread out of the oven and we'll be ready to eat."

Brandon grumbled, but he did as Nate asked. Nate rescued the cornbread, and then carried the stew pot to the table. Within five minutes, they were all seated and ready to eat.

To describe the meal as tense would have been an understatement. Aside from the initial saying of grace, the trio ate in complete silence. Nate reflected that dinner at home with his parents had always been like that. His father wanted complete quiet at the table, and that's what he got. But dinner at the Nash house was different. Whether it was just he and Brandon or the whole noisy clan, there was always laughter and conversation. And when he and Brandon were alone, the food was often abandoned for more pleasurable pursuits. Tonight, though, the silence was almost more than Nate could stand. He picked at his food, and watched Brandon glare at Mike over his bowl of stew. Nate was more than a little relieved when the phone rang and broke the silence.

Brandon started to get up, but Nate shook his head. "I'll get it." He was across the room before Bran could argue. Nate picked up the phone and said, "Hello."

"Doc? It's Sam. Is the sheriff around?"

"Sure, Sam. He's right here." Nate held the phone out to Brandon. "It's for you."

Nate went back to his seat and studied Brandon's face as he listened to Sam, noticing as his expression went from intent to elated.

Brandon was practically hopping up and down. "All right, Sam. Keep everyone out of her room until I get there." He paused to listen. "No, Eva and the doctor are fine, but no one else goes in until I have a chance to talk to her." After Sam's response, he said, "All right. See you then."

Brandon hung up the phone and gave Nate a radiant smile. "Sam was calling from the hospital. Marjorie Newman is awake."

* ~ * ~ * ~ * ~ *

Brandon grabbed Nate and swung him around the kitchen. "She's awake, Nate, and according to Sam, there don't seem to be any signs of permanent damage."

Nate caught his breath and gave Brandon a wet kiss right on his lips. Brandon pulled him closer, and Nate barely heard Mike clear his throat. Brandon reluctantly broke away and turned to find Mike standing by the table.

"Excuse me, guys. I forgot I was supposed to call one of my clients about the closing on his condo. It's been rescheduled."

"You're welcome to use the phone in here," Nate said. "Or there's one in the living room if you need some privacy."

Mike pulled his cell phone out of his pocket. "I've got my own phone, but I'll take you up on the privacy. I'll just step outside for a second." He slipped out while Brandon was still staring at Nate.

When he was gone, Brandon said, "You realize what this means, don't you Nate?"

Nate nodded. "With Marjorie awake, and my father pleading guilty, it's really over."

Brandon pulled him close and kissed his temple. "You've got it. This is the last link in the chain. As soon as I take Marjorie's statement, I can sign off on this case and pronounce it closed."

Nate leaned his head against Brandon's chest. "Is that why you didn't want just anyone in her room, to protect the integrity of her statement?"

"Yep. More than likely, she won't remember anything, but just in case she does, I don't want Calder's lawyer to be able to say she was coerced or coached in any way." He gently pushed Nate towards the mudroom. "Get your coat and let's go."

Nate shook his head. "I can't go with you. We've got company, remember."

Brandon snorted. "Yeah, as if I could forget. Look, just tell Mike you have to go to the hospital with me and send him home. He's a big boy; he can take it."

"No, Brandon. This is the first time since the funeral that Mike has reached out to me, and I'm not going to let him down."

Brandon did his best not to lose his temper. "Nate, you aren't responsible for that guy. You don't have to baby-sit him like this."

Nate clenched his jaw. "Brandon, I'm not going to argue with you about this."

Remembering their argument earlier, Brandon sighed. "Fine. I know better than to try and force you. Look, just promise me you'll call if you need me." He reached over to the counter where Nate's cell phone was charging and handed it to him. "Carry this in you pocket until I get back."

"Brandon—"

Brandon pulled him into a hug. "Please Nate. Just this once. For me?"

Nate pulled back and grinned at him. "You're getting pretty good with that pitiful whining thing, you know?"

Brandon grinned right back at him. "Did it work?"

"As if you ever had a doubt." Nate slid the phone into his hip pocket.

Brandon pulled him into a soft, slow kiss. When they were both sufficiently breathless, Brandon said, "I've had a lot of doubts about a lot of things in my life, Nate, but not about you. Never about you."

* ~ * ~ * ~ * ~ *

Brandon had spent a lot of time in hospitals. In addition to the births of his nieces and nephews, there were accident reports, victims' statements, interviews with the coroner, and on and on. Usually, he dreaded taking victims' statements the most, but Brandon was actually looking forward to this one. Marjorie Newman's statement would put an end to the whole sordid mess and mark the beginning of his marriage to Nate. He smiled as he made his way to Marjorie's room.

He greeted Sam, who was dutifully standing guard in the hall, and then knocked on the door, opening it before receiving permission to enter. He'd visited several times since Marjorie's attack, so he was prepared for the balloons, flowers, and cards filling the room, as well as for the sight of Marjorie's partner Eva sitting near the bed. The only surprise in store for Brandon was Marjorie, who was sitting straight up in the bed, her gray hair beginning to grow back from the shaving made necessary by the blow to her head. Her hazel eyes twinkled as Brandon came into the room.

Eva greeted him with a warm hug. Eva was a beautiful woman who looked closer to forty than sixty with her browned skin and petite figure. Unlike Marjorie, Eva's hair hadn't grayed with age. It was jet black and secured in a braid down her back, clear signs of her American Indian heritage. "Brandon, come on in here and have a seat. Isn't it wonderful about Marjorie?"

Brandon stood behind one of the two chairs next to the bed and waited for Eva to take her seat. When she did, he sat down and reached for Marjorie's hand. "Hey there, pretty thing. You look more like a woman who's spent two months at a spa than in a coma."

Marjorie pooh-poohed him with her hand. "Not...nice for you...to lie to...me."

Brandon gave Eva a quizzical look. She smiled and said, "The speech problems are only temporary, according to the doctor. Marjorie's mind is perfectly intact."

Brandon nodded and turned back to Marjorie. "You up to answering some questions, sweetheart?"

She bobbed her head up and down, so Brandon took out his notebook and said, "Most of these are yes or no questions, so just nod or shake your head, and save your voice." When she acknowledged that, he continued. "Okay, doll, first question. Do you remember what happened the night of the fire?"

She nodded.

"Great. Do you remember the man that did this to you?"

Another nod, this one more forceful. Brandon reached for her hand again and gave it a squeeze. "You're doing fine, Marjorie. Now I need to ask you another question. Did the guy who hit you just walk into the store and club you, or was he hiding, waiting for you to leave?"

"Hiding...in bathroom. Went to close...up. Heard a noise...found him inside."

Brandon let go of her hand long enough to reach into his coat pocket and pull out a picture of Wilson. "Last question, Marjorie, and then I'll go away and let you rest. Was this the guy who hit you?"

Marjorie barely looked at the picture before shaking her head. Brandon held the photo up a little higher. "Take another look, Marjorie."

After another shake, this one more emphatic, Brandon looked at Eva, who only shrugged. He turned back to Marjorie. "Are you sure? Remember, you took a pretty vicious knock to the head. Could you be mistaken?"

"No...mistake. Not him."

Brandon folded the picture and put it back in his pocket. He didn't want her to get upset, but he had to keep trying. "Marjorie, do you know who it was?"

Marjorie fought hard to make her mouth work. Finally, she was able to form the two words that held the most interest for Brandon at that moment. "Mike Vaughn."

Chapter Sixteen

Nate picked up his bowl and carried it to the sink. "Are you sure I can't get you some more stew or another piece of cornbread, Mike?"

Mike shook his head. "No thanks, Nate. I don't know where I'd put any more, but everything was great." He lowered his eyes to the table. "Thanks for having me over here tonight. My place isn't the same with-out...well, you know."

"I know. I wish there was something I could say, but I know there isn't. There's nothing I can do, and it kills me."

"There's nothing either of us can do to bring Amy back," Mike said, "but there is something I'd like you to do for me, if you don't mind. A favor, I guess you'd say."

"What's that?"

Mike stood up and walked over to the kitchen windows, staring out at the night sky. He was quiet for a full minute before he turned back to Nate. "Of all the things Amy wanted, nothing was more important to her than knowing that the two people she loved most in this world cared for each other too." He rubbed his hand over his face. "Did Amy ever tell you that she and I were trying to get pregnant? She wanted to name our firstborn son Nathan."

Nate swallowed past the lump in his throat. "No, she didn't tell me, but I'm sure she would have eventually. Amy and I talk about—" He broke off when he realized what he'd said. "We talked about every-thing."

"I know. You guys were always so close. Sometimes I envied that."

"Mike—"

Mike waved him off. "No, Nate. It took me a while, but I really do understand the bond you guys had. I'm just saying I was a little jealous, that's all."

Not sure how to respond, Nate said, "So what was the favor you wanted?"

Mike sighed. "Like I said, nothing was more important to Amy than knowing that the two men she loved the most were on good terms. When you and I got into that fight over Nash, Amy was crushed. She cried all night long. And even though she's gone now, I can't help but think that maybe, in some way, she knows about what happened between us after the funeral. I want Amy to see that you and I have patched up our differences so she can rest in peace. I want you to drive out to the cemetery with me, so we can tell her, together."

Nate was surprised. He had never figured Mike for the type to wax existential. The only thing he'd ever heard Mike say about the hereafter was they'd better have beer and college football in Heaven or he wasn't going. Now he was standing in Nate's kitchen, carrying on about Amy resting in peace by knowing the two of them had patched things up. Nate started to refuse straight away, but decided to try and talk Mike out of it instead. "Mike, the temperature is in the high thirties tonight. Maybe we can go out there tomorrow afternoon, before the sun sets."

Mike's face took on a look of pleading. "I need to do this, Nate. Please? For Amy?"

Nate sighed. Mike had played the one card he couldn't refuse. "Fine. Let me get my coat, and we'll go." He grabbed his coat and his keys. Giving Sasha one final pat, he motioned Mike outside and then locked the place up tight. When they got to the driveway, Mike moved toward his car, but Nate shook his head.

"Let's use my car, Mike. I haven't had much of a chance to drive it yet, and it'll give me a chance to show you what she can do." Nate thought Mike seemed a little agitated, but he wrote it off as a natural reaction to visiting Amy's grave.

Mike was hesitant, looking down at his watch a couple of times before saying, "Fine, let's just go and get this over with."

Nate waited until Mike slid into the passenger seat before taking his own place behind the wheel. He started the car, switched on the power locks, and backed out of the driveway.

* ~ * ~ * ~ * ~ *

Brandon raced out of Marjorie's room and down the stairs to the basement parking area, the acrid taste of fear burning his mouth. He'd tried to call the house twice, getting no answer either time. He started to call Nate's cell, but stopped short of dialing the number. *Who knows what might set Vaughn off? If he has Nate, all bets are off.*

Brandon barked orders into his radio as he went, Sam at his heels. In between yelling into the radio, Brandon told Sam about Marjorie's revelation. As they reached the garage, Sam said, "What now, Boss?"

"I've called every unit I've got, and I've also got the state police on their way to block all the roads leading out of town." Brandon's hands were shaking as he got into the S.U.V. and grabbed his pistol from under the seat. "Follow me out to the house. Jim and Dewey are already on their way. Stay out of sight until I give the signal to move. I don't know what Vaughn's planning, but he knows Marjorie is awake, and he's got to be afraid she's gonna remember something." He punched his keys into the ignition. "We're wasting time. Follow me in your car, and I'll fill you in on the rest over the radio." Sam nodded and ran to his car.

Only minutes had passed since Brandon had heard Marjorie's statement, but it seemed like hours. Brandon pulled out of the underground parking area with barely a glance at the traffic and headed back toward Reed. He switched on the radio. "Sam, you there?"

"Yeah, Bran, go ahead." Sam's voice came through loud and clear despite the breakneck speed at which they were both traveling.

"Vaughn made a phone call just after you called to tell me about Marjorie. My guess is, he's not working alone. If I'm right, he's gonna call in his partner for backup." Before he could say anything else, his cell phone rang. Brandon pressed the talk button and all but yelled, "What?" into the mouthpiece.

The dispatcher said, "I just got a report back from the deputies I sent to your house. No one's there, Sheriff — no sign of either Dr. Morris or Mike Vaughn."

Brandon swore under his breath. *Where the hell are they?*

* ~ * ~ * ~ * ~ *

Just as they reached the cemetery gates, Nate remembered something. "Mike, I forgot to grab the flower arrangement Grandma Taylor made to go over Amy's headstone. Let me just run back to the house and get it."

Mike shook his head. "I don't think that's such a good idea."

"Why not?"

Even in the confines of the darkened car, Nate could see the glint of silver as Mike pulled out the small pistol he'd tucked into his pocket. Mike held it steady as he pointed it directly at Nate. "Flowers are the last thing you need to be worried about right now."

* ~ * ~ * ~ * ~ *

Brandon flexed his foot on the accelerator, a million gruesome endings playing out in his mind. He refused to give credence to the worst case scenario, because his mind simply couldn't wrap itself around the concept that Nate might be dead. He and Nate were supposed to have the next fifty years to worship each other, to grow old together and watch their grandchildren play on the front porch of that big old house. Brandon wasn't about to give voice to the fear that those things might never happen. Sam came back over the radio and did it for him.

"Boss, are you still there?"

"Yeah, Sam, go ahead."

He could hear the hesitation in Sam's voice. "Bran, we have to be prepared just in case Vaughn has already done something to the doc."

Brandon set his jaw. "No. Nate's alive. There's not a doubt in my mind."

"How do you know?"

Brandon gritted his teeth. "Because I would feel it if he weren't." He was about to say more when his cell phone rang. He almost wept with relief when he recognized the number.

* ~ * ~ * ~ * ~ *

The Reed City Cemetery was one of those old fashioned types with the wrought-iron fences and the gnarled trees dotting the landscape. Some of the graves dated back to the early eighteen hundreds, back to the days when Reed was nothing more than a tiny village of settlers. The old cemetery and the new burial plots, one of which was Amy's, were separated by a copse of trees — a small woods, actually — with only an overgrown path in the middle to lead the mourners from one to the other. There was a way to get to the new cemetery without having to go through the woods, but for some reason, Mike directed Nate to go in the hard way. It wasn't until they were well on their way that Nate realized why. Had they gone around to the gate of the newer portion, Nate's car would have been clearly visible from the road, and Brandon's men would know where they were. Mike was taking no chances.

Walking through the woods at night was hard enough for Nate without having a gun pressed into his back. Every time Nate stumbled, Mike would slap him on the back of the head with his free hand. The only consolation Nate had was that Mike wasn't finding it any easier to navigate through the irregular line of trees lining the path. Several times, Mike stumbled, and twice he actually fell. The second time, Nate used Mike's temporary state of confusion to reach into his pocket and grab the cell phone. The noise of the snapping twigs and Mike's struggle to right himself covered up the sound as Nate pressed Brandon's number on the speed dial. He slid the phone into his coat pocket as soon as he heard Brandon pick up.

Mike made it to his feet and pressed the gun into Nate's back again. "Keep going, dammit. I'm ready to get out into the open so I can see where the hell I am."

Nate kept walking. "If you hate the great outdoors so much, why didn't you just kill me back at the house?"

Mike made a clicking sound with his tongue. "Now where would the fun be in that? Because of you, I've lost everything. Killing you outright would be too easy. No, I'm gonna have a little play time with you first. When I do decide to put an end to your miserable existence, I want the last place you see to be the spot where my wife is condemned to rot, all because of you. I'd hoped to have more time, but Marjorie's waking up put a kink in my plans. I'm sure that by now she's identified me as the one who clubbed her. I should have had Wilson finish her off before I killed him."

"You killed Wilson?"

Mike sounded almost proud. "Sure did. The bastard was trying to blackmail me. Threatened to expose me and my partner if I didn't give him half of the money I was being paid." He snorted. "Half. Can you believe that shit? I'm the one who pulled his sorry ass out of a sling. Wilson's brother and I worked together in the stockroom at More-co. Malone was always bragging about what a tough guy Wilson was. So when my partner approached me with the idea of offing you and framing Calder, Wilson was the first guy I thought of. Let me tell you, he was only too glad to help. Seems he'd crossed the head of the Nikoli family on his last job for them and was laying low. Wilson needed the money, and I needed Wilson's know-how. Seemed like the perfect arrangement. It worked out just fine until the guy got all greedy on me."

"So what — you shot him full of so much garbage his heart exploded?" Nate stopped walking and turned, struggling to see Mike in the non-light. He could just make out the shaking of Mike's head.

"You make it sound so sordid, so cheap. I'll have you know I put a lot of thought and effort into our friend Wilson's grand exit. He called me to tell me he needed more money. Seems the cash he got when we canceled your insurance wasn't enough to hold him. He wanted more."

Nate was stunned. "You cashed in my insurance to pay Wilson? Why not just use your own money? Or Amy's, for that matter? And surely your partner has the cash." Nate could barely see Mike's hand as he waved him forward with the gun.

"Keep walking. My partner is going to meet us there." As Nate resumed trudging, Mike said, "In answer to your questions, yes, we did cash in your insurance to pay Wilson, but that was just enough to cover his expenses. If Wilson hadn't tried to screw me over, he'd have gotten a cool two million out of the deal when all was said and done. As far as Amy's money goes, I couldn't touch it. Your grandmother set it up so that only Amy could access the trust. Now that she's gone..." Mike's voice broke. After a minute, he said, "Now that my wife is dead, all her money goes to me, but I couldn't touch it while she was alive. As for my own salary, let's just say I'm using it to recover from a few bad business decisions I've made over the years. When I was approached with the idea of killing you and framing Calder, I jumped at the chance. Your money would have gone to Amy, and my partner's funds would have been freed up so that I'd have made close to ten million just for bumping you off. Of course, you refused to die like you should have, so the deal's off."

Nate could see the clearing in the distance and he knew his time was rapidly running out. "So if the deal's off, why kill me now?" Mike laughed, a sound so bitter Nate winced.

"Do you really have to ask? Hell, I've wanted you dead since the night I saw you and Amy wrapped up in each others arms on her couch." When Nate started to speak, Mike said, "Save it. The only reason nothing ever happened between the two of you is because you prefer a hard cock over anything Amy had to offer. If you'd been straight, or even bisexual, Amy would've thrown me over and gone to you in a heartbeat. You have no idea how hard it is to be in love with a woman who's lusting after a faggot. I can't tell you how many times she compared me to you. Needless to say, I was always found to be lacking when held up to the great Nathan Morris. I thought maybe if I made nice with you, I could come between you guys. You know, do something to break apart the friendship, at least weaken it a little. But you and Amy were too tight. Killing you seemed like the best option. It would've worked if you hadn't hooked up with Nash. From day one, that guy has been like a gnat up my ass. Since Wilson screwed up, I was sure he'd be willing to make it up to me by offing Nash, too, sort of two-for-the-price-of-one. But the cocky little shit wanted more money, and he was willing to blackmail me to get it."

Mike paused as he scanned his surroundings. When he was satisfied as to where they were, he said, "I was pissed as hell, but I figured once he blew up the office and you were dead, I'd have enough money to keep Wilson quiet. I needed him too much to make him mad. I planted the bomb that afternoon when I brought you and Amy lunch. Wilson was watching the office, waiting for Amy's car to pull out. He thought you were still inside and Amy was clear. He waited just to be sure she was gone, then tried to blow the place. But something went wrong with the detonator. The damn thing stalled. When he saw you coming back, he thought Amy had returned, and he went crazy trying to set the damn thing off. When you got out of the car, Wilson realized what had happened, but it was too late."

Mike brushed a tear from his eye. "You're still alive, and the only woman I'll ever love is dead in your place. Wilson went on and on about how sorry he was, but it was too late. The minute Amy died, Wilson signed his own death warrant."

"And you were only too happy to play executioner."

Mike went on as if Nate hadn't spoken. "So I waited until Wilson went out, and I snuck into his room using the extra key he'd so kindly provided for emergencies. I laced that bottle of Jack Daniel's he always kept on hand with several of More-co's best diazepam, slipped out, and then waited until Wilson drank a healthy glass full and passed out. I came back in and shot him up with a lethal dose of heroin and liquid cocaine. I even dusted his nose with cocaine powder to make it look authentic. When his heart stopped, I replaced the whiskey bottle with a clean one, cleared away the evidence, and left. It was just sheer luck that Wilson's brother happened to call and send that clerk down to his room to find the body." Mike pointed to the graves ahead, now in full view. "Keep walking. Just a little bit further." Mike maneuvered Nate forward until he was practically on top of Amy's marker.

Nate shuddered at the site of an open grave not far from where he stood. It dawned on him what Mike was going to do. "What now? You gonna shoot me and then push me into that hole?" Mike smiled, and now that they were out in the open, Nate could clearly see the malice etching Mike's features.

"Like I said, Nate, we're gonna wait a few minutes for my partner, and then we'll go over the game plan." He looked around, taking in the scenery. "Nice place. Amy and I were gonna buy a plot just like this one day, but we thought we'd have years yet to worry about death and dying. If Wilson had knocked you off that first night like he was supposed to, we'd have had those years together. You have no idea how upset I was when I came back from Atlanta and found you not only still alive, but shacked up with Nash. And after I came up with a sick aunt and everything." Mike sighed. "You caused us all a hell of a lot of extra work. We intended to kill you, then make it look like Calder had hired someone to do the job by exposing his scheme with Phillip and his prejudice against gays. Because of you, we were forced to go through the whole gay bashing scenario. We intended to trash your office and apartment, then cut your brakes and blame the whole thing on Calder. Too bad Wilson screwed up and left that fingerprint on the undercarriage of your car. We were forced to re-think our entire strategy. That's when the arsons came into play. You have any idea how hard it is to torch a place without getting caught? Wilson did it right when he burned H. and G. I'll give him that much."

Mike looked at Nate, his hatred shining in the pale light. "Why didn't you just die like you were supposed to? What the hell are you, a cat? You've got more lives than I can count."

Nate scanned the area for something he could use as a weapon, but apart from a few scraggly branches, he saw nothing. He decided his best bet was to keep Mike talking. "Okay, so you hate me. I got that part. But why hurt Marjorie Newman? What did she ever do to you?"

Mike shook his head. "Nate, Nate, Nate. Don't you realize that in every war, there are a few casualties? I hadn't planned on hurting Marjorie. Hell, I've been buying books from her on a weekly basis since Amy and I moved here. But when Calder announced he was coming to Reed to save Seth from his queer brother, it was just too good an opportunity to pass up. Planting that receipt to expose the connection between Calder and Phillip was a must. Since I'm so well acquainted with the layout of the store, I volunteered to do it. When Amy came to tell you about Calder's impending visit, I snatched the receipt out of Philip's room during all the confusion. I took Amy home, tucked her in bed, and went down to the Book Barn. I waited until Marjorie was busy, then snuck into the men's bathroom to hide out until she left. Marjorie always closes right at five, so I thought I was safe. I waited until five-thirty and then came out, expecting the shop to be empty. Instead, I ran right into poor Marjorie. She apparently got delayed by a last-minute customer. She demanded to know what I was doing, lurking in the bathroom like that." Mike shrugged. "The old bat didn't leave me any choice. I conked her over the head with one of those brass bookends she sells and then torched the place. Went up in seconds, thanks to all those book-binding glues." He grinned. "Not bad for a first time pyro, huh?"

Nate wanted to throw up, but he knew he couldn't afford to be sick. Swallowing hard, he started to speak, but a noise coming from the woods stopped him. He could just make out the shadow of someone coming through the trees and knew that Mike's partner had arrived.

~~*~*~*

When the Reed City limits sign came into view, Brandon exhaled a deep breath. He'd been so relieved when he heard Nate's voice on the phone, but the relief had turned to dread when he heard where Vaughn had taken Nate. He'd instructed his men to surround the cemetery, but to stay out of sight until he got there. Brandon wasn't sure just how over the edge Vaughn really was, but he couldn't take any chances. If one of his men spooked Vaughn, he doubtless would shoot Nate without even thinking twice about it. Brandon took little comfort from the fact that Vaughn was waiting for his cohort to arrive, but at least it bought them some time. Just as Brandon turned onto the main highway into Reed, he heard Nate's gasp over the cell and knew that his grace period had ended.

* ~ * ~ * ~ * ~ *

Mike turned his head slightly at the sound coming from the tree line, but he kept the gun trained on Nate. After a minute, Mike turned back to Nate with a smile. "I see our special guest has arrived. Nice night for a family reunion, don't you think?"

Nate watched as the figure stepped into view. The moonlight cast a halo around the blonde hair, turning it silver. The brown eyes were lost in the shadows, but Nate could see a faint glimmer coming from them. He wasn't certain if the twinkle was caused by excitement, madness, or a combination of the two. Nate forced himself to show no emotion as Leda Morris stepped into place beside Mike.

She gave Nate her best pageant smile. "Hello, Nathan. I suppose you're a bit surprised by all this."

Nate wasn't sure what shocked him the most: that his mother was the one who wanted him dead, or that she was standing there talking to him and smiling at him like they were at a tea party instead of at the planned scene of his demise. Nate fought back all the questions, too numb and too stunned to even feel pain. He forced a calm into his voice he didn't feel. "Leda."

Leda shook her head. "Now is that any way to greet your mother — calling me by my first name like some casual acquaintance?"

Nate pushed his shaking hands behind his back. "You'll forgive me for dispensing with the usual formalities, but most mothers don't hire a hit-man to bump off their offspring. Sorry if I'm not exactly certain how to respond to you, but I don't think this particular situation was ever covered by Emily Post."

Leda clicked her tongue against the roof of her mouth. "Still so headstrong, even at the end. You were always such a bright boy, Nathan, the best in your class. A shame, really, that it had to be this way."

Nate saw Mike inch his way closer to Leda, causing her to step even nearer to the edge of the open grave. Nate wasn't sure what was going to happen, but he wasn't about to quit talking now. "Why does it have to be this way? What could I have done that was bad enough to make my own mother want me dead?" Even in the dim light of the moon, Nate could see Leda's brows furrow and her eyes narrow.

"What did you do? God, how can you even ask that? You ruined my life, that's what you did."

Nate could hear her agitation, but he had to keep Leda talking.

"How? How did I ruin your life? I loved you. I'm your son, for God's sake."

"Don't even pretend you don't know." Leda started wringing her hands. "I was a debutante when I first met Calder. I'd just been crowned Miss Georgia." Her eyes took on the sheen of remembrance. "He courted me hot and heavy for months, made me feel like the most precious thing on earth. I thought he was after me, but what he really wanted was a feather in his cap, a sweet little trophy belle to crown his growing empire." She shook her head, harder this time. "I didn't care, you know. I wanted his money and the recognition of being Mrs. Calder Morris. I realized almost from the start that Calder didn't really love me. But he wanted me, and as long as he wanted me, Calder gave me what I wanted. It was the perfect arrangement." She looked at Nate with raw hatred. "Then you came along and ruined everything."

"How? Tell me how a little boy could possibly be responsible for his mother's happiness."

Leda shifted her weight from foot to foot. "Because from the moment my pregnancy became obvious, Calder wouldn't touch me. He found a mistress, started calling me fat, ugly, a cow. He stopped giving me money, stopped taking me to parties. I thought it would get better once you were born, but it only got worse. I thought if I played the good wife, the devoted mother, things would improve, but I was wrong. Oh, our sex life resumed, but it was cold, methodic. By the time Seth was born, I knew our marriage was over. I wanted a divorce, wanted to be rid of all three of you. I hated you boys for turning my husband against me, and I hated Calder for being turned. I was a good actress, though, pretending to be the devoted mother, all the while ruing the moments you and your brother drew breath. I was all set to leave the lot of you behind, but Mother Morris put an end to that."

Nate just stared at her. "What does Grandma have to do with this?"

Leda sneered. "Your grandmother was a sharp old bitch. She knew her son, and she knew more about me than I would have liked. She came to see me a few days after I told Calder I was leaving him. She brought with her a sheaf of papers I'd signed right before Calder and I married. I thought they were just the usual pre-wedding preparations. You know — insurance policies, deeds, that sort of thing. I didn't even look at them, just signed every one."

She sighed. "That was a mistake I've lived to regret a thousand times over. One of the papers was a prenuptial agreement. Like the fool I was, I signed away all my rights to any of Calder's money. Calder never even knew about the existence of the papers. That's just how shrewd your grandmother was. I could leave, but I'd have been penniless. My own family was less than sympathetic. I had nowhere to go, and no choices. Then Mother Morris made me an offer."

Leda stopped bouncing and stepped closer to Nate. "She told me if I stayed and gave you and Seth the mother you both deserved, when Seth graduated from high school and went off to college, she would tear up the pre-nuptial agreement, and I could take Calder for everything he was worth."

Nate just stared at her with amazement. "So you stayed all those years, just pretending to love us?"

Leda shrugged. "Like I said, I'm a great actress. I was all set to stay until the day Seth graduated from school. I had incentive, something to look forward to. Too bad the old crone died when you were eighteen and Seth was only twelve. The paper was never destroyed, and I was stuck." Leda grinned, a sickening parody of a genuine smile. "But I've always been smarter than I was given credit for. I managed to secure a copy of the original paper from your grandmother's lawyer and went to see a lawyer of my own. He told me that, while the agreement was airtight, no judge in the country would withhold a divorce from me — or withhold Calder's money — if he was convicted of a felony, caught committing adultery, or found to be physically abusive. Calder might be the world's biggest bastard, but he would never raise his hand against a lady, so I knew the abuse scenario was out. I thought my best bet was to catch Calder committing adultery, but once again, fate stepped in."

She shook her head and barked a harsh, bitter laugh. "Poor Calder has a tiny little problem. Seems the sorry bastard can't get it up anymore. After all those years of screwing everything in skirts, the one time I need him to stick it where it doesn't belong, and the S.O.B. let me down. Not even Viagra was enough to revive his tired ol' pecker. So typical of him."

Nate saw that Mike had moved during Leda's speech so that the two of them were almost touching.

If Leda noticed, she gave no sign of it. She was too caught up in her own tirade. "When I realized I was going to lose everything if I didn't think of something, I went through all of Calder's records looking for any sign of shady business dealings that might constitute a crime. I'd hoped for some sign of tax evasion or maybe even under-the-table drug sales, but I found nothing. As scandalous as Calder is in his personal life, he's almost angelic in his business dealings. For over ten years I kept watch of his records, scrutinized his every move. When you came out to us, and Calder cut you off, I hoped maybe his anger would move him to get violent with you, maybe even provoke him to do you in. But other than hiring a private detective to follow you and make certain you stayed away from Seth, Calder's way of dealing with your homosexuality became the denial of your very existence. No matter what avenue I took, I couldn't catch Calder breaking so much as a traffic law. I'd almost given up hope when I found out Calder had hired Phillip to break poor Seth's gay little heart." Leda gave a humorless chuckle. "Homophobia might not have endeared Calder to a judge, but it certainly isn't crime enough to invalidate our marriage contract." She shook her head. "No. I knew I would need something stronger."

Try as he might, Nate couldn't keep the sarcasm out of his voice. "So like any good mother, you naturally thought of killing me and framing my father for it."

Mike interrupted before Leda could speak. "Actually, that was my idea. Leda came to see me because she'd guessed a long time ago that there was no love lost between you and me. That private detective Calder hired was very thorough, especially about all the time you and Amy spent together. Leda was smart enough to know I must hate you because of the way Amy felt about you. Even so, she only thought I might be willing to use my legal knowledge to help her get rid of Calder. She never guessed that I would come up with a plan to eliminate two of her biggest headaches with one shot, no pun intended."

Leda pursed her lips. "You may have come up with the plan, but I certainly did my part. I was the one who procured the Mor-co credit card so that dreadful Wilson could use it to buy all those electronic doo-dads he needed. I stole one of Calder's best knives so Wilson could stab Brandon Nash with it." She held up her fingers and began ticking off each item as she went. "I passed the listening devices from Wilson to you so you could plant them. I stole the diazepam from the Mor-co warehouse so you could drug Wilson and the dog, and I even paid Mr. Wilson's trashy brother to lie and say he'd introduced Calder to Wilson to begin with." She stamped her foot like a small child in the throes of a tantrum. "If it weren't for me, Calder never would have confessed to trying to have Nathan killed in the first place."

In all the chaos, Nate had completely forgotten about Calder's confession. He turned to his mother. "Are you saying my father is completely innocent in all this?" When Leda nodded, Nate said, "Then why in the hell would he confess?"

Leda preened like a show pony. "That was my idea, too. As much as Calder hates you, Nathan, he loves Seth that much more. Calder's convinced you turned Seth gay and that one of these days the boy will simply go back to being straight. I think Calder sees Seth as his last hope to pass the Mor-co Empire on to future generations of the Morris clan." She sighed. "Mike helped me fabricate some evidence that made it look as if Seth was trying to kill you and then framed Calder to get revenge when he found out about the ruse with Phillip. I made Calder see that if

Seth went to prison, there would be no hope of him ever coming out and going straight." She giggled like a little girl. "I think Calder has read too many of those prison sex and rape stories. Anyway, I told Calder that if he confessed to the crime, I would find some other poor bastard to pin it on. As soon as I did, Calder was going to recant his confession, and the three of us were going to be one big, happy, heterosexual family. Calder's gotten whatever he wanted for so long now, he actually believed me." She sneered. "The untouchable Mr. Calder Morris is going to be in for the surprise of his life this time."

Leda was so busy congratulating herself on duping Calder, she didn't notice that Mike had stepped away from her so that he was standing several feet behind her. She just kept on smiling at Nate as she gloried in her accomplishments. "After almost thirty years of bullying and abuse, Calder is finally going to get his."

She turned back to Mike, her smile fading a little. "I would like to know, however, why you thought it was necessary to drag me out here in the middle of the night. This was never part of the plan."

The grin that spread across Mike's face chilled Nate to the marrow. Mike said, "I'm glad you asked, Leda. You see, plans have changed."

Nate knew what was coming, and his mind raced as he thought of ways to stall for time. He said, "So, Leda, you've been close by this whole time?"

Leda nodded. "Yes. I had all my calls forwarded to the dreary little Chicago motel room where Mike insisted I until this mess with you was settled." She turned back to Mike. "What's all this about a new plan? I haven't authorized any new plan. I'd say it's too late to make changes at this stage of the game."

Mike's face went from maniacal grin to full-blown snarl in the space of a heartbeat. "Game? You think this is some kind of game, lady? My wife is dead, and that old bat I knocked over the head is probably spilling her guts even as we speak. If I make it away from here without getting caught, I'm still going to be looking over my shoulder for the rest of my life. I figure I'm already implicated in two murders, so what's two more?"

Since Nate had already guessed that Mike brought them out there to kill them both, he wasn't surprised, but the look on Leda's face was priceless, as was the panic in her voice.

"What are you talking about, Michael? We made a deal. We're partners. We—" The report of the gun cut Leda off as the breath rushed out of her lungs and she toppled backward into the open grave.

Nate was too numb to even react as he watched his mother draw her last breath. He knew his time was up and that all the hopes and dreams he'd held for a future with Brandon would die with him in that Godforsaken cemetery. Nate's mind conjured images of Brandon's smile, his scent, his taste, the saltiness of his skin and the strength of his arms. With Brandon's face fixed in his mind, Nate closed his eyes and waited to die.

* ~ * ~ * ~ * ~ *

Brandon raced through the trees, heedless of the thorns biting into his flesh and the branches tearing at his clothes. He couldn't risk parking in front of the gates of the new cemetery for fear that Vaughn would panic and shoot without thinking. His plan was to approach Vaughn calmly and try to cut some kind of deal with him. He knew he'd never get off a shot before Vaughn could squeeze the trigger and hit Nate first. All those plans went to hell when Brandon heard the first gunshot. He was close enough to the new part of the cemetery that he didn't need the aid of the cell phone clipped to his belt to tell him that Leda Morris was dead. He pulled his gun and stepped from the trees just as Vaughn cocked the hammer and prepared to fire his second shot.

* ~ * ~ * ~ * ~ *

Nate's eyes flew open as Brandon's voice cut through the crisp night air. "Drop it, Vaughn. My men have the whole place surrounded."

Mike never took his eyes off Nate. "Give me one good reason why I shouldn't just shoot him and be done with it. If your men have this place covered, I'm never gonna make it out of here alive anyway."

Brandon's voice never wavered, not even with the terror he was feeling. "You put down that gun, Vaughn, and I give you my word you'll still be breathing when all is said and done."

Mike didn't so much as flinch, his finger resting firmly on the trigger. If Brandon shot Mike, Mike's finger would automatically depress, and Nate would be a dead man. "And if I decide to hang on to it instead?"

Brandon's gun hand was rock-steady. "You put so much as one mark on Nate's skin, and you'll die where you stand."

Mike shook his head, the movement excruciatingly slow. "I have a better idea." He lunged at Nate, wrapping his arm around Nate's neck and pressing the gun to his temple. Nate struggled, but desperation gave Mike a strength that was impossible for Nate to overcome. Mike tightened his stranglehold and pressed his face to Nate's ear. He spoke loudly enough so that Brandon would have no trouble hearing.

"This is how we're gonna play it. I want Nate's car brought around to the front gates so he and I don't have to go traipsing back through the woods. We're all gonna stand here nice and calm until it's done. I see one person put so much as a toe out of line, and Dr. Morris here is gonna have a brand new hole in his head. When the car arrives, everyone is gonna stand back and let us pass. Nate's gonna drive, and no one is gonna follow us. If I see anyone behind us, be it a police cruiser or a busload of nuns, it's lights out for my boy Nate, here. Understood?"

Before Brandon had a chance to answer, Nate rasped, "If you're gonna kill me anyway, why the hell should we co-operate?"

Mike kept his eyes on Brandon. "'Cause like all good cops, Nash knows that there's always a chance that you'll get lucky and survive. He's not going to do anything to reduce your chances. Right, Nash?"

Brandon grabbed the radio at his shoulder and spoke into the mouthpiece. "Sam, bring Nate's car around to the front gates of the new cemetery. All other units maintain their original positions. No one moves unless it's on my command."

Nate had heard other hostages say that time seemed to drag in the face of death. Some even claimed that time virtually stood still when one's life was at stake. For Nate, it was different. Time had no meaning as he stood staring at the man he loved for what was most likely the last time. Nate used the silent standoff between Mike and Brandon to memorize Brandon's moonlit face, the inky darkness of his hair, the slight curl of his soft lips. He could see the faint shimmer of tears in Brandon's eyes and the slight trembling in his still-raised gun hand. He had just enough time to mouth the words, "I love you," as the gunning of the V-8 announced the arrival of his car.

Mike frog-marched Nate to the gates, all the while hissing orders into his ear. "Slow and steady, buddy. Almost there. When we get to the car, I want you to get in on the passenger's side and slide over. Just in case you feel like trying any funny business, remember I've got my gun cocked, and I'm more than ready to use it. It's gonna be pressed to your head the whole time."

The walk to the car was agonizing, but they made it without incident. Just as Mike had ordered, Nate opened the passenger door and made a move to slide in. Mike released his arm from around Nate's neck, but he kept the gun pressed firmly to Nate's skull. After a bit of awkward maneuvering, both Nate and Mike were inside.

"Start her up and head east out of town." Nate reached for his seat belt, but Mike shook his head. "You won't be needing that."

Nate did as he was told. The road was completely deserted, just as Nate knew it would be. Brandon must have ordered all the roads from town cleared, willing to take no chances. Nate was thankful for the cell phone still in his pocket. At least Brandon would know what was happening inside the car. Nate was so caught up in wondering what was going to happen next that he didn't realize Mike was still speaking to him.

Mike sighed. "I really thought it would take Nash longer to figure out where we were. If I'd known he was gonna get here so fast, I'd have just killed you back at the house."

Frustration and fear came spilling out of Nate like poison. "So why didn't you? Why put yourself at risk by going through an elaborate execution? Why didn't you just shoot me when you had the chance to make a clean getaway and be done with it?"

Mike tightened his grip on the gun. "Because killing you like that would have been too fucking merciful. I wanted you to know what Leda had done to you, to see your own mother's hatred for you. I wanted you to lose everything the way I've lost everything. It wasn't enough to destroy your body. No, sir. I was after your soul."

Nate knew he was running out of time. Mike would kill him the second he got a chance. Time and again, Brandon had saved his life. This time, Nate could depend on no one but himself. His first thought was to swerve off the road and wreck the car, but as a doctor he'd seen enough auto accidents to know that the outcome was anyone's guess, a crapshoot at best. Even with the roll cage, the Ford could still become his coffin if he was the slightest bit off. It was when he saw the hairpin curve ahead that he remembered Cain Lucas's warning about the doors and their tendency to fly open under pressure. Without a second thought, he slammed his foot down on the accelerator and took the curve at sixty miles an hour. Since Mike had never given him the chance to arm the power locks, Nate prayed the passenger door would fly open the minute he guided the car through the sharpest part of the bend.

Mike was still going on about Nate's impending demise when Nate rammed his foot down on the accelerator. Mike waved the gun around wildly. "What the fuck do you think you're doing, Nate?" He aimed the pistol and would have fired except, at that exact moment, the door came open.

Mike reached for the handle. The instant his fingers fastened around it, the force pulled him forward. He grabbed at Nate with his right hand, but his futile efforts were no match for the strength of the wind and the speed of the car. Mike was hurled outwards just as Nate lost control and ran off the other side of the road.

* ~ * ~ * ~ * ~ *

Brandon heard the crash over his cell and increased his speed. He'd instructed his men to follow at a safe distance with their lights turned off. As soon as he heard that crash, all bets were off. Brandon switched on his lights and sirens and ran the S.U.V. wide open. Just as he approached the curve, his headlights made out the still form of a body sprawled across the pavement. He slammed on the brakes, threw the car into park, and jumped out, his heart in his throat.

The minute he realized the body was Vaughn's, Brandon didn't spare the bastard a second glance. From the corner of his eye, he saw Sam and some of the other deputies running toward the scene, but Brandon kept running toward the wrecked Ford and his only reason for living.

The car wasn't nearly as damaged as Brandon expected, giving him hope that Nate had made it through unharmed. He expected Nate to be trapped behind the wheel, maybe even unconscious. The ambulance was already on its way, so all Brandon could do was bide his time and hope they got there fast. The last thing he expected to find was an empty car.

Brandon's heart dropped to his stomach. *Nate must have been thrown out. Oh God, it's worse than I thought.* He raced around to the front of the car, searching desperately for any sign of Nate. Brandon almost knocked Nate over in the process.

Nate sat in the grass, staring off into the distance. Brandon looked him over, seeing no visible signs of injury or trauma. Brandon knelt down beside him and was about to reach out when Nate spoke.

"You heard everything." It was a statement, not a question.

Brandon nodded, but Nate was still staring off into the distance. Keeping his voice as soothing as possible, Brandon said, "Yes, baby, I heard it all. If you hadn't called me, I never would've found you in time." He forced a smile. "I've always said I hooked myself a smart one."

"Yeah. Well, if I'm so smart, why didn't I realize that my own mother wanted me dead? And why didn't I see that Mike resented me to the point of homicide?" Nate shuddered. "You want to know the worst part?"

Brandon was terrified of the answer. He remembered the three weeks of isolation Nate subjected himself to after Amy's death. He'd go out of his mind if Nate shut him out again. Swallowing, he said, "What's that?"

Nate turned to look at him for the first time, his eyes unnaturally bright in the light of the Ford's still burning headlights. Nate's voice was low, but the detachment was no longer present. "The worst part is, I don't care, Brandon. Let them hate me all the way to Hell, but God help me, I don't give a flying fuck. Leda's dead, Mike too for all I know, and I couldn't care less." He reached out, his hand shaking, the tears falling freely as he caressed Brandon's cheek. "All I care about is that

I'm alive, and I can touch you again. Oh God, I thought I was never gonna get to touch you again."

Brandon gathered him close and rocked him back and forth in the glow of the headlights, stroking his fingers through Nate's dirty hair, savoring the smell of him. Kissing Nate's temple, Brandon closed his eyes and thanked God.

Chapter Seventeen

Brandon complained all the way to the car. "I told you, I don't want a bachelor party."

Keith shook his head. "I don't remember asking whether you wanted one or not. Every guy has to have a bachelor party. Back me up, Wayne."

"I'm not sure, but I think maybe it's a law." Wayne grinned.

Les, home from college for the wedding, opened one of the rear doors on Keith's Stratus. "If I ever talk about getting married, just shoot me." He raked his fingertips through his dark red hair, which glowed orange in the glare of the security lights brightening Brandon's driveway. "I think single's the way to go, but I'm happy for you and Nate."

Randy, the youngest Nash brother, also home for the wedding, grabbed the handle of the opposite door. "I second the well wishes for you and Nate, but unlike Mr. Single-and-Loving-It, here, I hope I do get married." His expression turned grim. "Not that I think I ever will. Gay and bipolar isn't exactly a sought after combination."

Brandon climbed into the passenger seat. "That's bullshit. We've known you were bipolar for years, and it's not like you don't keep it under control with meds. I admit, the gay part was a shock, but since I'm on the verge of marrying the man of my dreams tomorrow, I think you can probably guess that you've got my blessing." He turned around to Randy and cracked a grin. "Everyone says you look just like me with that black hair and those big ol' blue eyes. How could anyone not fall for you?"

Randy ignored that. "Yeah, but you guys are my family. You have to love me."

Wayne squeezed into the back seat with Les and Randy. "We do? Damn. I didn't know that."

Just as Randy popped Wayne on the back of the head, Keith slid behind the wheel. "Don't make me come back there. We're running late enough as it is. Grandpa and Dad were expecting us to be at Shorty's a good half an hour ago."

Brandon glared at Keith. "Hey, it's not my fault the rehearsal ran late. Since Nate started working at Chicago General, his hours have been crazy. He was almost an hour late getting there. And since you're the one who got him the job, it's conceivable that I can blame the whole thing on you."

Keith snorted. "Don't even think about it. Who gets married the first Friday in January, anyway? You could have at least waited until Valentine's Day."

Brandon shook his head. "No way. We had to postpone for two months as it was. I was afraid Nate would shut down again, like he did when Amy died. I thank God that didn't happen."

Wayne stretched out his legs as best he could in the cramped back seat. "I still can't believe Nate went to Leda's funeral. I'd have been hoping the old bitch was rotting in Hell, myself."

"Me, too, but Nate's not like that. I do think he went more for Seth's sake than anything. And there was no way I was gonna let Nate face Calder alone, no matter how much I hated Leda for what she did." He turned around and looked at his brothers as Keith started the car and pulled out of the drive. "In case I never told you guys, I really appreciate the way you rallied around Nate at the funeral. And at Vaughn's arraignment."

Keith shrugged. "Nate's family. We wanted to be there."

"What got to me," Wayne said, "was the way Calder refused to even look at Nate or Seth during the service. Seth was sobbing his heart out and Nate went all to pieces, but that old bastard never even glanced their way."

Les adjusted his seat belt. "At least it looks like Vaughn is going to get his. I'm just sorry it took so long to arraign him. No telling when he'll actually go to trial."

"I can't believe he's pleading not guilty. Who does he think he's gonna fool?" Randy shook his head.

Keith turned the car onto the Reed Highway. "He probably thinks a jury will feel sorry for him because he lost the use of his legs. Being paraplegic is humane compared to what he did to Nate, not to mention to his own wife."

Desperate for a topic that didn't make his stomach turn, Brandon said, "Speaking of Nate, does anybody know where Seth is taking him tonight?"

Randy laughed. "Like we'd tell you if we did."

"I'm just curious." *And if Seth took him to one of those gay strip clubs, I'll skin Seth alive.*

Conversation continued in the teasing vein until Keith maneuvered the Stratus into the parking lot of Shorty's Pub. Brandon noticed the parking lot was unusually empty, even for nine o'clock on a Thursday night.

Brandon saw his dad and Grandpa Taylor leaning against the back-end of his dad's mini-van. Brandon and his brothers climbed out of the car and walked over to where the two elders stood.

Dean looked down at his watch. "You're late. Good thing we rented this place for the whole night."

No wonder the place looks deserted. Brandon grinned. "Sorry, Daddy, but you know the rehearsal got a late start. You were there. And I thought we'd never get away from Mom when the thing ended."

"That woman is a sucker for weddings. By the way, did you and Nate ever settle the argument of who's gonna wait at the altar and who's gonna walk down the aisle?"

"Yep. Nate's a'walking and I'm a'waiting."

Grandpa Taylor's eyes went wide. "How did you talk Nate into that?"

"We flipped for it. I won the coin toss." And just the thought of watching Nate come down that aisle and into his arms was enough to make Brandon's heart beat a little faster.

Dean clapped him on the back. "Well, let's get to it, then. I promised Gale we wouldn't keep you out too late. She's scared to death you'll be all bleary eyed and hung over for the wedding photos." He led them all into Shorty's.

The old pub had been in existence since before Brandon was even born, and little had changed about the place since. Same old neon signs, same vinyl covered chairs and stools. The only difference now was the shiny, silver foil banner hanging above the cigarette-scarred bar which read, "Congrats Brandon and Nate."

Earl, the bartender, came out and shook Brandon's hand. "Congratulations, Sheriff. Shorty says the drinks are on him tonight. What can I get you guys?"

"Bring us all a beer, please, Earl." Dean gave him a wide smile. "And tell Shorty we said thanks."

"Will do, Mr. Nash."

While Earl went to fetch the beer, Dean led them all to a table at the far end of the building. When they were seated and the drinks arrived, Dean held up his glass. "To my boy, Brandon. Not only do I thank the Lord every day for making you my son, but now you're giving me a new son, and I didn't even have to watch Gale puke her guts out for nine months to get him."

Brandon said, "Gee, Daddy, that's very, um...touching."

Dean laughed and a round of toasts and well wishes followed. A few minutes later, the door opened and Sam came in. He gave Brandon a pat on the back and slumped into the chair beside him. "Congrats, Boss. Or I guess I should give you my condolences. After all, your bachelorhood is about to die an agonizing death."

Brandon's smile went from ear to ear. "Yeah. Ain't it great?" He took a swig of his beer. "Hey, who's on duty tonight?"

Sam shook his head. "Oh no, you don't. You officially went on vacation at two o'clock this afternoon. For three weeks, that station is not to see or hear from you."

"Yeah, yeah. I hear you." Not that Brandon minded. Three weeks alone with Nate was the closest thing to Heaven on earth he could think of. He was so intent on what he was going to do for those three weeks, Brandon didn't realize his father was talking to him.

"I think it's time for phase two, men. We're losing him."

"Sorry. I was just—"

Grandpa Taylor finished it for him. "Thinking about Nate. We know. And I'm with Dean. Time for phase two."

Brandon sighed. "I'm afraid to ask, but what's phase two?"

"Phase two," Keith did his best imitation of an evil cackle, "is the entertainment."

Brandon was beyond skeptical about what six straight guys and a twenty-year-old gay virgin considered entertainment for a gay man's bachelor party, but he followed his dad and the rest to the back room, anyway.

The back room was legendary. Since Shorty's was neither a strictly gay nor a strictly straight establishment, the back room — where the stage was — had seen its share of varied entertainments, including everything from best breast contests to the Reed Annual Arm Wrestling Championships. Brandon had the sinking feeling they'd hired a stripper. He appreciated the thought, but there was only one man he wanted to see naked.

Dean escorted him to a chair located directly in front of the stage. But instead of sitting down with Brandon, Dean and the others turned to leave.

"Where are you going?"

"This is a one man show, son." And before Brandon could ask Dean any questions, the lights dimmed, the spotlight came on, the music started, and Brandon was alone. He shrugged and turned his attention back to the stage.

When the curtains parted and a figure dressed in scrubs, a surgical mask, and a cap stepped out onto the stage, Brandon had to fight the urge to flee. It wasn't until the man started dancing that Brandon's urges shifted from flight to desire. He'd have recognized that uncoordinated wiggle anywhere. Nate might work magic as a doctor, but he couldn't dance for beans. Brandon cupped his hands in front of his mouth and hollered, "Take it off, Nate."

The figure stopped dancing and pulled off the mask. He gave Brandon that crooked grin and said, "How did you know it was me?"

Nate looked so darn cute with a stethoscope draped over his neck and that silly smile on his face, Brandon had to force himself not to grab him up and rip his clothes off. Instead, he said, "It wasn't hard for me to figure it out, Nate. No offense, baby, but you have no sense of rhythm."

Nate's eyes took on a wicked gleam. "I don't know about that. You've never complained about my rhythm before." He slid the cap off his head and tossed it onto the stage. "As I recall, last night you thought my rhythm was right in step." He drew the scrub shirt over his head and pitched it down alongside the hat.

Just recently Nate had taken to topping Brandon like a pro. Brandon's body went into overdrive at the memory. He swallowed hard. "You think so, huh?"

"Yep. As I remember it, my rhythm last night was right in keeping with your breathing."

Nate undid the drawstring to his scrub pants and Brandon's mouth went dry. He squeaked out, "My breathing?"

"Yes, sir." Nate twitched his hips. "Don't tell me you've forgotten already? Every time you took a deep breath, I thrust into you. And when you exhaled, I pulled back out and did it again." And with that last remark, Nate grabbed the left leg of his scrub pants and ripped them completely off.

He was wearing a g-string made of gauze and medical tape. It looked so ridiculous, Brandon couldn't believe he got so hard that he actually started aching.

Nate danced to the edge of the stage. "So, Nash, you gonna stuff a dollar in my g-string or what?"

Brandon stood and pulled a twenty out of his pocket.

~~*~*~*

"Are they here, yet?" Brandon tugged at his tie.

"Calm down, Bran. Seth just called, and they're on their way." Keith sank into one of the plush chairs that decorated the church's dressing room. "If you don't start taking it easy, I have Mom's permission to give you a sedative."

"Take it easy? It was bad enough that Mom insisted Nate spend the night at her house last night so we wouldn't see each other before the wedding, but this waiting is killing me. And you're one to talk. You weren't exactly calm and cool on your own wedding day." Brandon pulled on his black tux jacket. "As I recall, you were a nervous wreck."

"There's a difference between being nervous and being a complete mental case."

"I know, but I can't help it." He ran his fingers through his tousled hair. "I've almost lost him so many times, Keith. I can't believe Nate's finally going to belong to me."

Keith came to his feet and patted his brother on the back. "He's belonged to you since the day you met him, Bran. Do you really think a ceremony is going to make him any more yours?"

Before Brandon could answer, Wayne stuck his head in the door. "Time to start seating the guests, Keith."

With one final pat on the back for Brandon, Keith left. A few minutes later, the door opened again and Dean Nash came in, laughing when he saw the shape his son was in.

"Damn, Brandon. And I thought I was a mess on my wedding day." He fished a comb out of his pocket. "Do something about your hair. Looks like you've been running your fingers through it."

Brandon did his best to tame his hair. "Tell me again why I asked you to be my best man?"

Dean moved in front of Brandon and straightened his tie. "Because you've got good sense. Your brothers make decent ushers, by the way. They've gotten most of the guests taken care of. Now we're just waiting on you."

"Does that mean Nate's here?"

"Yep. Got here about ten minutes ago. He's in the other dressing room. We're ready to get to it."

Dean started for the door, but Brandon stayed him with a hand on his arm. "Daddy?"

"Yes, Brandon?"

"Thank you. For everything."

Dean drew him into a bone-crushing hug. "You're welcome, son." He pulled back and chucked Brandon under the chin. "Enough mushy stuff. Nate's waiting."

∼∼*∼*∼*

There were events in Nate's life that he prayed to forget, episodes he sent to the fringes of his memory so he wouldn't go crazy from the pain: the sight of his mother's coffin as it was lowered into the ground, the sobbing of his brother at her funeral, and the icy coldness of his newly-released father as Leda Morris was laid to a twisted sort of rest. Nate also hoped to forget the sight of Mike in a wheelchair, being arraigned on two counts of murder, two counts of attempted murder, and an assortment of arson and conspiracy charges. Nate felt some guilt over the satisfaction he felt knowing that a degree of punishment had been dealt to Mike when the crash had severed his spinal cord, leaving his body paralyzed from the waist down. Nate and his therapist, Dr. Carson, had spent long hours discussing the normalcy of his feelings, and Nate was finally beginning to rebuild the shattered security he'd briefly lost.

As much as Nate had to put behind him, there was so much more to commit to memory, to hold to his heart so he could savor each wonderful episode, over and over: the feel of Brandon's arms as he'd scooped Nate up at the scene of the accident; the warmth he'd felt as the Nash family crowded around him at the hospital that night; the love of his brother as they'd cried out the misery together, both trying to make sense of it all. Those memories would serve Nate well to block out the anguish of the past. *And here I am, in the church, ready to put Nathan Morris to rest and begin life as Nathan Nash, a new man.*

The door to the dressing room creaked open and Seth slipped in. "We're almost ready, Nate. The music has started."

"Gotcha." Nate stood and gave Seth a wicked grin. "You're looking pretty studly in that tux, brother."

Seth laughed. "Imagine Brandon's surprise when he sees I'm not wearing that puffy pink dress he ordered for me."

"Yeah, well, no one ever said Brandon didn't have a sick sense of humor." Nate tugged at his bow tie. "Have you got the ring?"

"Yes and no."

"What do you mean 'yes and no'? Seth, this has to be perfect. I—"

Seth went over to Nate and put his hands on his brother's shoulders. "Calm down, Nate. I know how important this is to you. Do you really think I'd do anything to screw it up?"

Nate took a deep, calming breath. "No, of course not. I just need everything to go right today. I'm a nervous wreck."

"So what else is new?" Seth punched Nate lightly on the arm. "Lucky for you, you have such an understanding brother."

"Yeah, yeah." Nate rolled his eyes. "You still haven't told me what you meant by 'yes and no'."

The expression in Seth's eyes softened. "I do have a ring, but it isn't the one you bought at the jewelry store. I thought maybe you'd like Brandon to have this one instead." Seth pulled a worn velvet bag from his pocket and pressed it into Nate's upturned palm.

Nate's fingers caressed the velvet, his fingertips finding the threadbare spots as if from memory. Nate didn't need to open it to know what was inside, but he found himself loosening the strings and working the bag open, as he'd done so many times before. The gleam of the over-head lights picked up the sparkle from the sole diamond situated at the center of the wide gold band. It was a little bigger than Nate remem-bered, having been sized up to fit Brandon's larger finger, but there was no mistaking whose ring it was. Nate looked up from the treasure in his hand to stare at his brother. "How did you get Grandpa's ring?"

Seth shrugged. "It was no big deal. I remembered Grandma Morris showing it to us when we were kids, and I thought you might like to have it for Brandon. The ring you bought him was great, but I thought maybe this one would mean a little more to you both."

Nate nodded. "You know it does. Grandma Morris bought this ring for Grandpa when the two of them barely had two nickels to rub together, before his business took off. She took in mending work from the neighbors to make enough money to buy it." He smiled. "When she found out I was gay, Grandma told me I could have the ring to pass on to my own husband someday. Then she died, and all her things went to Dad." Nate looked at his brother again. "How did you get it, Seth?"

"I went to see Dad a few days ago, Nate." Nate started to say something, but Seth stopped him. "Before you get all riled up, let me explain. When you told me you were getting married the first weekend in January instead of the day before Thanksgiving like you'd planned, I didn't like it, but I understood. To tell you the truth, I was afraid you would end up feeling guilty about what happened with Mother and postponing it even longer. What with the funeral and Mike's arraign-ment, I understood that you couldn't go ahead with the wedding last year, as planned, but it irked me that you and Brandon had to suffer yet again because of what those people did to you. I wanted this day to be as special for you as possible. I figured the ring might help make it so. I remembered the way you always liked to hold it and try it on when we were kids. So, I went to Dad and told him I wanted it. I told him why, too."

Nate snorted. "Bet that went over well."

"Actually, "Seth grinned, "I think he was more surprised to see me standing on his doorstep than anything else. He and I haven't said word one to each other since that day at the sheriff's office. Dad didn't even look at either one of us at Mother's funeral. I told him what I wanted and why. I told him he owed it to you."

"What did he say to that?"

"Not a word. He left me standing there and went to get the ring. He placed it in my hand and shut the door in my face. That was it. I took the ring and had it sized at the same jewelry store where you bought the new one for Brandon." Seth patted his pocket. "I have the one you ordered, too, just in case you'd rather give that one to Brandon."

Nate grabbed Seth and pulled him into a fierce hug. "You know I don't. Thanks, Seth. I love you."

Seth pulled back and cuffed Nate gently on the cheek. "Right back at you. Now it's time to get you hitched."

* ~ * ~ * ~ * ~ *

If there was one thing Nate hated, it was being the center of attention. He thought sure he'd be self-conscious as he walked down the isle, knowing everyone was staring at him, but as soon as Nate saw Brandon waiting for him at the altar, all the other people in the room ceased to exist.

Pastor Oakley smiled as Nate took his place beside Brandon. He pulled a small prayer book from the folds of his robes. "Brandon, Nathan, please face one another and join hands." He addressed his remarks to the large assemblage as well as to the couple. "We're gathered here today, as the friends and family of Brandon and Nathan, to witness the joining of two lives, two hearts, and two souls. Love is not to be taken lightly, but to be savored, cherished. Life is ripe with uncertainty, but the love of a good partner is an anchor to us during times of chaos and doubt. As we are told in the First Epistle of John, chapter four, verse eighteen: 'There is no fear in love; but perfect love casteth out fear.' Brandon and Nathan stand before you in love and ask you to rejoice with them as they seek the blessings of Almighty God on their union."

The vows came next, and though he tried to store up every word, later on Nate could recall very little of the actual verbiage. What he did remember was Brandon's face as he slid his ring on Nate's finger, and also the look of pure joy in his eyes when Nate reciprocated.

Pastor Oakley closed his prayer book and addressed the congregation. "It is with great pleasure that I declare Brandon and Nathan joined in the sight of God. May all His blessings be upon you."

Nate thought his heart would burst. Then Brandon leaned forward to kiss him, and Nate lost the ability to think at all.

* ~ * ~ * ~ * ~ *

Brandon shivered as Nate licked the icing from his fingers. When it was Nate's turn to feed him, Brandon opened his mouth and allowed Nate to ease a small bite of cake between his lips.

Nate groaned as Brandon flicked his tongue across the pad of the intruding index finger. "Do you think we can make our exit now?"

Brandon laughed. "Don't you want to finish your cake first?" The glow in Nate's eyes caused Brandon's face to flush.

"I'm hungry, but not for cake."

"I think maybe we could get away with cutting out early." Brandon took Nate's hand, and the two of them slipped away from the reception. They'd almost made it to the door when they came face to face with Gale and Grandma Taylor.

The two women exchanged knowing smiles, then Gale said, "Looks like we've got a couple of deserters on our hands, Mom."

Grandma Taylor nodded. "I should certainly hope so. They've only been married for four hours. I'd be worried about this marriage if the desire to be alone together had already waned." She hugged each of them tightly. "I'd better go find Grandpa. Too much champagne gives him gas."

Gale shook her head at her mother's retreating back. "That woman does have a way with words." She turned back to Brandon and Nate. "Okay, you two fugitives. If you're going to leave, we need to do this right. Oh, before I forget, did you get the package from Grandpa and Grandma Nash?"

Brandon nodded, "Yes, ma'am, and the card. I know they were pretty upset about not being able to come up for the ceremony, but Grandma's arthritis was acting up again. We understood."

"I know, sweetie." She patted his cheek and then looked down at her watch. "Give the boys fifteen minutes to finish up with the car, and then we'll announce your departure so everyone can line up and throw birdseed at you."

Brandon sighed. "Whatever you think, Mom. I—" He registered what she'd said. "Car? What car? My car? Oh, God, what are they doing to my Camaro?"

Gale just laughed. "You'll see." Then she sauntered down the hall to gather the well-wishers.

Alone together in the hallway, Brandon pulled Nate into his arms and rested his forehead against Nate's. "They're violating my car."

Nate chuckled. "It's your own fault, you know. You're the one who insisted on driving the Camaro today instead of my sensible new Buick."

"I know, I know. I should have guessed our brothers would do something like this." He kissed Nate's cheek. "Do you miss the Ford?"

"No. After what happened with Mike, I don't think I'd ever be able to enjoy it again. It was nice of Cain to take it back without billing me for the damage."

Brandon's eyes darkened. Just thinking about it was enough to make him feel ill. "It could have been so much worse."

Nate didn't say anything. He simply held Brandon until the worry left his face.

* ~ * ~ * ~ * ~ *

Nate reached over and brushed the birdseed out of Brandon's hair. "Well, that wasn't too bad, now was it?"

"Have you actually looked at my car, Nate?"

Nate snickered. "Well, I thought the 'Just Married' sign stretched across the rear bumper was a nice touch."

"That was the only nice part. Sixteen condoms filled with whipped cream and attached to the car with magnets. The words, 'Brandon's Gonna Score' written on the windows with white shoe polish. And let's not forget the exciting array of old shoes and tin cans tied to the bumper. When we get to the courthouse, I'm going to un-decorate while you file your paperwork. Then we'll swing by our place to change and head to the airport."

Nate was only half listening. He patted his jacket to make certain his papers were still inside. In just a few minutes, Nathan Morris would no longer exist. He'd be Nathan Nash for the rest of his life.

Brandon pulled up to the courthouse and cut the engine. "You sure you want to do this? No doubts?"

"None. Your family is already more like family to me than my own ever was, Seth excluded, of course."

Brandon leaned over and kissed his cheek. "Want me to come in with you? I can un-decorate later."

"Nah. You go ahead and start on the car. I'll be right back."

And he was. For such a life-changing event, the actual paperwork consisted of little more than handing over the documents and getting a receipt. After being promised he would get confirmation in four to six weeks, the transformation was completed.

As he stepped from the dimly lit courthouse back into the bright January sunshine, Nate wondered why he didn't feel sadness, even the tiniest twinge at leaving his old life behind. He thought of all he'd lost in the five months since his ordeal had begun, and, except for his beloved Amy, he grieved none of it. No matter how much Dr. Carson assured him that his lack of feeling over losing his parents was normal under the circumstances, Nate couldn't help wondering if it really was normal. Then he caught sight of the tall man in the tux, bent over the hood of his car with inflated condoms in hand, and it all became clear: he didn't grieve his family because Brandon was all the family he would ever need. The rest of the crazy Nash clan was just an amazing bonus.

Brandon caught his gaze, and Nate started walking toward him. Toward home.

Sara Bell is a thirty-something freelance writer living in upstate Alabama with her sexy, baldheaded husband and two beautiful, exceptionally bright daughters. When not busy chugging away at the keyboard, Sara can be found burning cookies for school bake sales and logging time as the family taxi driver. To learn more about Sara and her work, or to contact her directly, please visit her discussion group at http://groups.yahoo.com/group/the-magicinyourtouch/

Printed in the United States
71718LV00005B/86